Praise

"A grittier *Sex and the City*, but make it Providence... That's the thing I love the most, is just how capable [the widows] were—but also all flawed. They are like real women that you've known, that you've loved, that you've hated... They're boss bitches for sure, but they're not going to stop on the backs of other women to get where they think they can go."
—Alaina Urquhart, #1 *New York Times* bestselling author

"An '80s romp with big hair and even bigger secrets! Grab your popcorn and settle in for this incredibly fun and twisty read."
—Jeneva Rose, *New York Times* bestselling author of *You Shouldn't Have Come Here*

"*Young Rich Widows* is hands down the most original thriller you'll read all year. Laugh-out-loud funny, twisty, and full of surprises."
—Wendy Walker, international bestselling author of *What Remains*

"Compelling, entertaining, and loads of fun! A one-sitting read!"
—Liv Constantine, bestselling author of *The Last Mrs. Parrish*

"Crazy fun!"
—Andrea Bartz, bestselling author of Reese's Book Club pick and instant *New York Times* bestseller *We Were Never Here*

"Funny, heartwarming, and action-packed thriller you don't want to miss."

—Heather Gudenkauf, *New York Times* bestselling author

"Break out your crimpers and leg warmers because *Young Rich Widows* will have you (re)living the '80s in style. A phenomenal female-driven mob thriller that's sure to keep you on your toes and make you laugh out loud. Belle, Fargo, Holahan, and Lillie make one heck of a dream writing team. Brilliantly crafted and highly entertaining!"

—Hannah Mary McKinnon, international bestselling author of *The Revenge List*

"I loved the interactions between the widows, both when they're at each other's throats and when they learn to coexist with—and maybe even care for?—each other."

—Megan Collins, bestselling author of *The Family Plot*

"Almost impossible to stop listening. If you're looking for an audiobook that's fresh, fun, and full of surprises (bonus points for being set in the '80s), this is it."

—Tessa Wegert, author of the Shana Merchant series

DESPERATE DEADLY WIDOWS

A Novel

KIMBERLY BELLE · LAYNE FARGO
CATE HOLAHAN · VANESSA LILLIE

sourcebooks
landmark

Copyright © 2024, 2025 by Kimberly S. Belle Books, Layne Fargo, Cate Holahan, and Vanessa Lillie
Cover and internal design © 2025 by Sourcebooks
Cover design by Lauren Harms
Cover image © SENEZ/Getty Images

Sourcebooks and the colophon are registered trademarks of Sourcebooks.

All rights reserved. No part of this book may be reproduced in any form or by any electronic or mechanical means including information storage and retrieval systems—except in the case of brief quotations embodied in critical articles or reviews—without permission in writing from its publisher, Sourcebooks.

No part of this book may be used or reproduced in any manner for the purpose of training artificial intelligence technologies or systems.

The characters and events portrayed in this book are fictitious or are used fictitiously. Any similarity to real persons, living or dead, is purely coincidental and not intended by the author.

Published by Sourcebooks Landmark, an imprint of Sourcebooks
P.O. Box 4410, Naperville, Illinois 60567-4410
(630) 961-3900
sourcebooks.com

Originally published as *Desperate Deadly Widows* in 2024 in the United States of America by Audible Originals, an imprint of Audible, Inc. This edition issued based on the audiobook edition published in 2024 in the United States of America by Audible Originals, an imprint of Audible, Inc.

Library of Congress Cataloging-in-Publication Data

Names: Belle, Kimberly, author. | Fargo, Layne, author. | Holahan, Cate, author. | Lillie, Vanessa, author.
Title: Desperate deadly widows : a novel / Kimberly Belle, Layne Fargo, Cate Holahan, Vanessa Lillie.
Description: Naperville, Illinois : Sourcebooks Landmark, 2025.
Identifiers: LCCN 2024046158 (print) | LCCN 2024046159 (ebook) | (trade paperback) | (epub)
Subjects: LCSH: Widows--Fiction. | Female friendship--Fiction. | Murder--Investigation--Fiction. | LCGFT: Thrillers (Fiction) | Novels.
Classification: LCC PS3602.E45745 D47 2025 (print) | LCC PS3602.E45745 (ebook) | DDC 813/.6--dc23/eng/20241002
LC record available at https://lccn.loc.gov/2024046158
LC ebook record available at https://lccn.loc.gov/2024046159

Printed and bound in the United States of America.
VP 10 9 8 7 6 5 4 3 2 1

*Dedicated to Eighties Ladies—
busting into boardrooms, breaking glass ceilings,
and getting it done in power suits so the rest of us could follow*

PROLOGUE

Want to know the secret to success? How to get that Ferrari, that Tiffany, those designer silks decorated with 24 carats? Well, it's not hard work, sugar, or setting goals, or managing your time—none of that psychobabble crap peddled in Brian Tracy compact discs. It's money, pure and simple. Cold, hard start-up capital. Cash is king, any which way you can get it: beg, borrow, or steal, that's the only way to the American Dream. Of course for some, you don't even have to lift a finger because you were born with a silver spoon or, better yet, a gold one jammed right into your entitled mouth.

Money not only paves the way for whatever the hell you desire, but that silver spoon? Well, it's something to sell when it's time to buy a ticket out of trouble. 'Cause second chances don't come cheap. It's simple math: the fatter the wallet, the less morals matter. Fortunes are made convincing good people to forget their principles.

And once that fortune's in the bag, baby, people will pay for a peek. Folks will buy into any Ponzi scheme and pie-in-the-sky vision, provided it's being sold aboard a private plane or eighty-foot yacht. Throw on a captain's hat, every man becomes Hugh Hefner.

Money—real money—is possibility. Choices. The power to decide for oneself whether to take the high road, the low road, or pave another way altogether.

And whatever that road is, money ensures other people will get right on it. You lead, they follow. Even when it's simply a direct route for more dollars to end up in *your* bank account.

Money is reinvention. Slip enough bills into the right hands and robber barons become philanthropists. Philanderers become family men and faithful public servants. Money holds the magic to becoming someone else entirely.

But what to do if the family forebears didn't set sail with Columbus, intent on riches at any cost? If they came in cargo vessels with only the clothes on their backs for warmth, starving from famines and poverty, seeking safety from violence?

If they came in chains, heavy with the trauma of losing their freedom? Or had to endure the perpetual loss of everything they'd built their lives upon? If they'd watched the fruits of their labors consumed by others—stolen, not only from them but from their descendants?

What if they didn't set sail at all? What if they were already here? What if they're still here, despite all the odds, and their very presence reminds us what it cost to build the U-S-of-A?

Well, all is not lost. If you don't come from money, there's another secret to success, albeit not as surefire.

Being out of options. Having no other choice.

Nothing's a bigger driver of success than desperation.

And nothing's more dangerous, sugar, than a widow with nothing left to lose.

CAMILLE

PROVIDENCE, RI, 1987

I am getting too old for this shit.
 I stand against the bar at the edge of the strip club and wonder if this is it, then—if I've officially aged out. George Michael blaring in the speakers, a thumping bassline so hard it vibrates deep in my bones. The swirling disco lights above my head, barely breaking through a room that's dark as sin but blinding me with an occasional lightning bolt to the face. All these men, large and small and bald and potbellied and thin, businessmen in fancy suits and mobsters with Popeye arms. Every type of man you can think of, leering at the waitresses and lap dancers and the topless brunette riding the pole.

And so far, not a single one of them has noticed me. God, what a depressing thought.

I suppose it doesn't help that the room is filled with gorgeous women in various states of undress, or that all of them are younger than me by a mile. I take in their smooth stomachs and perky thighs, their tight foreheads without even the slightest hint of a line, and a surge of something bitter burns in my throat. A lady never reveals her age, but I'm no lady and these girls make me feel like a grandma.

"The room's all set up for you. The champagne is chilled and waiting."

I look up to find Meredith leaning against the slick bar. Former stripper, fellow widow, and owner of this fine establishment. The Luna Lounge, Providence's only female-owned strip club. These past few years, she's also become a dear friend, one of the best I've got, and no one is more surprised about it than we are. The kind of drama we survived together will do that, I guess—stitch together a kind of unbreakable bond.

I give her a saccharine smile. "Only the best for Mayor Tom."

The vippiest VIP in the champagne room, by far. He's supposed to arrive any minute now, via a back door that will lead him straight into the private area. A big fish, with an even bigger payday. The two bouncers guarding the door will make sure nobody gets in there but me.

The champagne is expensive, but Meredith will give me the bottle at cost. She knows as well as I do that a lot is riding on tonight, and for all the widows. When two years ago the plane carrying my husband and his law firm partners exploded over the icy Atlantic, so did our cushy lives. All those shopping trips, all the flashy vacations and sparkly tennis bracelets just because… They were suddenly a thing of the past. And in their place? The widows and I were handed the keys to a law firm on the verge of bankruptcy with a four-million-dollar debt to the mob. Let's just say we're lucky to be alive—but the point is, we've been paying our own way ever since.

Meredith plunks both elbows on the bar and leans in. "He requested Luxe tonight, you know. My best dancer, and not just because she earns the most tips. Her lap dances are the stuff of legends."

"Honey, by the time I'm through with Mayor Tom, he'll be asking *me* for a lap dance."

She purses her lips, painted a dark red. "I have no doubt. Though watch out. Word on the floor is that he's a real perv."

Oh, I know. The mayor and I go way back to a previous life, to long before he got elected. Parties. Benefits. Political fundraisers, even though everybody in town knows that Davenforth money bought him that seat. Before my late husband Peter boarded that plane, he and Tom ran in the same circles. They don't call him the Playboy Mayor for nothing.

"I wouldn't need all these schemes if you'd just let me set up a camera. One little shimmy from anyone here and he'd pounce. And I'd have more than what I need to take him down."

Meredith gears up for a protest, but I've heard her arguments before, and dozens of times. I wave her off with a hand. "I know, I know. Your club is fancy now."

Fancy might be a bit of an overstatement, but still. Ever since Meredith took over this place, the club is tight as a drum. No more strippers snorting lines of coke behind the bar, no more shady mobster deals decided in the back rooms. No more shenanigans from anyone, at all, ever; otherwise, they get tossed to the curb and blacklisted. But the Luna Lounge is still a strip club, and half the men in here are married. Hidden cameras would kill Meredith's business.

But it sure would help mine—gathering evidence for the city's wronged wives to prove their husbands are liars and cheats. Rhode Island allows no-fault divorce, meaning all assets are split down the middle—unless I can give the wives ammunition for divorce court. A photograph of her husband with his hands up another woman's skirt, for example, or a tape recording of him explaining all the ways he plans to pleasure his mistress later that night. Anything that provides undeniable proof there were more than just two people in the marriage.

And it turns out I'm good at my job. After all, I know from experience what motivates a man like Mayor Tom to get handsy with a woman who's not his wife. I know how to whip him up with whispered promises in his ear, how to answer his indecent proposals with a smile that will make him forget all about the woman waiting for him at home. I'm not proud of how I gained this knowledge or the people I hurt along the way, but I figure at the very least, sticking it to Providence's most devious philanderers will clean up some of my karma.

"Miss Camille?" I twist around to find one of the bouncers, a sweet man named Mikey, towering above me. "The limo just pulled up."

That's my cue. I slide off my barstool. "Showtime."

Meredith straightens, slapping me hard on the ass. "Go get him, hot stuff."

I make my way across the dimly lit room, and the girls clear a path. They know I'm Meredith's friend, and they spin with their drink trays and grinding dance moves in the other direction. At the edge of the stage, a dark corridor leads me to a plain wooden door marked with two clinking champagne flutes lit up in pink lights. I reach for the handle, right as the DJ fades into a song that I couldn't have planned any better: "Need You Tonight" by INXS.

There is no need for Mayor Tom to *slide over here*, as he's already seated smack in the center of the sole red velvet couch, his big body spread to take up most of it. The King of Providence on his throne.

I stand for a moment in the doorway, letting him drink me in: My hair, perfumed and curled into shiny waves that tumble down my back. My bejeweled heels, as high as any stripper's. These few well-placed strips of fabric that are masquerading as a dress. It wasn't easy hiding a microphone in this skimpy thing, and I pause to let him appreciate the effort I've made, with a smile that says it was all for him.

"Camille Tavani." A slow grin spreads up his face. "Fancy seeing you here."

He pats the couch cushion next to him.

Bingo.

I close the door behind me, snuffing the music from the club. The bass rattles the walls and the lampshades on the sconces, the fringe trilling in time to the beat. I step around the center table where a bottle peeks from a silver ice bucket. I toss my bag to the couch and sit, crossing my legs in a way that gives him a preview of coming attractions.

"I could say the same about you, too, Mr. Mayor, except I happen to know you come here all the time. But don't you worry. The owner is a good friend of mine, and we girls can keep a secret."

"Don't tell me you're a lesbian too."

His voice is deep and imposing and a tad arrogant but crisp as a new hundred-dollar bill, which is a bit of a disappointment since it's a day that ends in *Y*, so the mayor has been drinking for hours. Multiple martinis at happy hour, a bottle of wine with dinner, followed by at least one glass of Kentucky bourbon three fingers deep. Tom Bradley always could hold his liquor.

"Actually, *do* tell me." He smiles, and it's too bad the man is such a snake because he really is handsome. Green eyes and square jaw, a full head of salt-and-pepper hair. "Tell me about you and your lesbian friend's secrets in great detail."

I laugh and slap his arm. "Meredith's bisexual, silly."

"Even better." He leans in, so close I can smell the liquor on his breath. "Because I like to do more than watch."

Yup. This guy is definitely screwing around on my client—his second wife—not that I'm the least bit surprised. It's how he left his first wife, Nancy, by parading around town with a towering blond the tabloids crowned the She-Wolf of Wall Street, a woman he married less than a year later. Divorce by paparazzi and tabloids. Because he's the mayor. Because his first wife is a Davenforth, Providence's very own version of royalty. The gossip wasn't pretty, but it sure was entertaining.

"You may like to watch, Mr. Mayor, but I don't like to share. For the record, there's only one lady allowed in my bed, and that's me."

It's a bit of a risk, saying this to a married man, but by now I've been around enough cheaters to know they don't think of their own infidelity as sharing. In my experience, cheaters try very hard not to think about anything at all, least of all the women they're cheating on, the wives and fiancées waiting for them at home. At this point, the only thing that matters for men like Mayor Tom is the conquest.

"I can work with that." His fingertip brushes over my bare thigh, so featherlight I look down to see if I've imagined it. I think of the recorder humming away in my skirt, and I have to work to make my smile stick because it's not enough. Not yet. Mayor Tom's been in politics long enough to talk his way out of most situations. To catch someone like him, the evidence has to be irrefutable.

I scoot to the edge of the couch, serving Mayor Tom a long slice of bare leg as I pull the bottle from the bucket. I peel off the foil wrapper and take my time popping the cork. For men like Mayor Tom, a little sexy waiting time is akin to foreplay. I fill the glasses and hand him one, tapping mine against his. "Cheers, Mr. Mayor. Now where were we?"

He tosses half the liquid back in one giant gulp. "You were telling me about your bedroom."

"I was?" I pause, the champagne so close to my lips I can feel the bubbles popping on my nose. My mouth waters, but I lower the drink to my lap. "Well, let's see. It's done up in peach and creamy white, with wall-to-wall carpeting and floral paper on the walls."

"I don't give a shit about the decor." Another gulp, a big one. He holds out his empty glass to me like I'm a waitress. "Tell me about the bed."

I exchange my glass for the bottle, refilling his glass to the brim. "It's a king."

"Nice and big."

"Too big for just me."

He swipes the glass from my fingers, bouncing a brow. "A woman like you, I bet you sleep naked. You do, don't you?"

Even though I've known the mayor for years, I'm still a little surprised at his audacity. Leering at me, touching my leg, leaning in way too close. Drinking all the good champagne before I've had the first sip. That second glass went down just as fast as the first.

"That depends," I say, refilling his glass for the third time.

"On?" The word comes out of him like syrup, sticky and slow. Finally. The mayor is drunk, and it's about damn time. With any luck, in an hour I'll be at home in bed. Alone.

My smile turns genuine. "On who's in the bed with me, of course."

But the mayor is no longer looking at me. He's looking straight ahead, his eyes big and bulging. I follow his gaze, but the door is still closed, the room still empty. The only thing that's changed is the music in the club, the DJ fading into the next song again. I look back at the mayor, and his eyes are wide and panicked.

"Oh my God. Sugar, are you okay? What's wrong?"

The mayor's mouth flaps open and closed, open and closed. His lips pull tight against his teeth, contracting like he's trying to speak, but nothing comes out except a sloppy pink bubble. Saliva mixed with…blood? It dribbles down the side of his chin, and that's when I notice it's the same color as the rest of his face. His cheeks have gone purple and shiny.

"Are you… Is this a heart attack?"

No, he's not grabbing at his chest. I stare at his starched shirt, the top button on the vest of his three-piece suit, but the fabric is not moving at all. No air going in or out of his lungs. He's choking, but on what?

I pop off the couch and race to the door, banging on it with a fist. "Help! I need help in here!"

I whirl around at a loud crashing sound: Mayor Tom nose-diving off the couch. He hits the table face-first and goes sprawling. His hands claw the slick surface, searching for a hold, but his arms won't cooperate. They flop around at his sides while his big body convulses, bouncing over the table like he's having an epileptic seizure.

Is that what this is?

Suddenly, his body twists into a tight knot, curling and lifting his entire torso off the table right before tipping to the side. The tray, the glasses, the bottle of champagne—they all go spinning. Golden liquid spurts over my ankles and designer shoes, but that's not the worst of it.

The worst of it is when the mayor lands on the sticky floor, I know without feeling for a pulse that he's dead.

MEREDITH

The relentless kick drum of "Addicted to Love" feels like it's kicking me in the skull.

Under the desk, I tap my bare feet along with the beat, trying to distract myself from my growing headache—and whatever's going down between Camille and Mayor Tom in the champagne room—long enough that I can focus on the accounting ledger in front of me.

When I was a dancer, I often slept through the day and worked all night. Now daylight hours mean even more work. Inventory. Bookkeeping. Interviewing new dancers. Hiring and firing an endless string of bartenders because I can't seem to find one capable of keeping his hands on the cocktail shaker and off my girls.

It's still strange to think of the dancers that way: my girls. My responsibility. But they are, ever since the previous owner—Providence mob boss Sal Ponterelli—went to prison, and I bought the place. I knew being the boss would be hard. Turns out, it's even harder when everyone in your workplace has seen you naked.

It's been over a year, and I still feel like I don't know what the hell I'm doing. The club's in the black financially, thanks in part to the updates I've made to transform the place from a shady strip joint to a classy gentlemen's club: a new drinks menu, a facelift for the dated decor, a higher cover charge to keep out low-rolling clientele. Most months, I've even got enough of a surplus to kick the extra over to Krystle and help keep the lights on at the law firm (not that it ever seems to lower her blood pressure). But my staff, from the dancers to the bartenders to the security guards to the guy who scrubs the toilets, still treat me more like a girlfriend than an authority figure.

My regulars continue to ask for me too, even though I've informed them at least a dozen times that my dancing days are done. Lately, I've stopped telling them anything and started sending Destiny over to deal with them instead. She's the club's newest, least experienced dancer, but she looks like a younger, more innocent version of me. Similar measurements, lush lips, long dark hair—though hers has feathery bangs I definitely could not pull off.

In the dark and a couple of cocktails deep, the guys can't even tell the difference, especially since I taught her some of my signature moves. When she started, Destiny was like a baby fawn, stumbling around the floor in the hand-me-down Lucite platforms I gave her since she couldn't afford her own. Now she's raking in tips night after night, and I can't help feeling like a proud big sister every time I catch a glimpse of her strutting on stage.

A couple more pages of tiny numbers, and my eyes are blurring. I lean back and stretch, my spine cracking even louder than the creaky springs of Sal's old office chair. The damn thing is way too big for me, so I look like a little girl taking meetings at her daddy's desk. The decor is mostly Sal's too: a huge oil painting of a wolf pack done in the style of a Renaissance master, and a chintzy clock with an hour hand shaped like a howling wolf head. Right now its snout points just past the seven. If I know Camille, she's probably got the mayor begging on his knees by now.

I was skeptical, at first, about her running the honey trap operation out of my club. But it's proved lucrative for both of us—and necessary for the law firm, which continues to hemorrhage money. Plus it's brought us even closer together. After her last job—catching a philandering ad exec stepping out on his wife *and* his mistress—Camille took me out for a boozy midnight breakfast at the West Side Diner. We stayed there until dawn, talking and laughing and scheming our next moves, and it was the happiest I'd been in a long while.

Until I met Camille—and Krystle and Justine—I'd never really had female friends. I've had romantic relationships with women (not all of which ended as badly as my last one), but that's a whole other challenge. And my connections with other strippers at the club have always been tinged by competition. We were friendly, sure—but we were there to get paid, and we all knew better than to get in each other's way.

With the widows, it's different. The four of us couldn't be less alike, and we might not always see eye to eye, but after everything we've been through together, I know we're in each other's lives for good.

I've just forced myself to focus back on the ledger when my office door bursts open.

How many times have I told people not to come in here without knocking? If anyone pulled this shit when Sal was in charge, they'd be six feet under.

But it's not one of my employees. It's Camille.

She shuts the door behind her, and I glance back down at my work. "You all done with Mayor Tom? I figured he might give you a little more of a—"

"Meredith."

I finally look—really look—at my friend. Despite her pre-summer tanning-bed base, Camille is deathly pale. Her eyes are wide with shock, and her hands are shaking.

"What's wrong?" I haven't seen Camille like this since the day I met her—when we got the tragic news that brought us together in the first place.

"He's…" Camille swallows. "The mayor, he—"

I stand up. "Show me."

We make our way through the club, to the dark corridor that leads back to the champagne room. Usually if I'm out on the floor, I'm dressed to the nines: big hair, small skirts, high heels. I am the face—and the body—of the Luna Lounge after all. But I didn't even bother to put my shoes back on, and I've got a ratty Blondie concert sweatshirt covering my minidress.

Camille's practically jogging, despite her bejeweled Escada

pumps. I grab her hand, forcing her to slow down. No sense alarming the customers until I see what we're dealing with.

Finally, we reach the door. The neon sign above casts us in its fuchsia glow as Camille takes a deep breath, steeling herself. I don't want to see what's inside that room any more than she wants to show me.

But that's the thing about being the boss: if there's a mess, it's my job to clean it up.

Camille pushes the door open. There, sprawled across the floor beside the lipstick-red sofa, is Mayor Tom Bradley. His strong jawline hangs slack, those sparkling green eyes that graced campaign ads all over the city are now blank and staring. Two shattered glasses and a cracked bottle litter the floor beside the mayor.

No: the body.

I push her inside and slam the door closed again. "What the hell happened, Camille?"

"I don't know!"

"A heart attack? A stroke?" The mayor always looked good for his age, but all those cocktails and rich campaign-donor dinners had to catch up with him sometime.

"We were talking. He drank the champagne, and then—"

"Wait. You didn't drink any?"

Camille shakes her head.

I steady her with both hands. "Walk me through everything. You picked up the champagne, then what?"

"The bottle was there. In the bucket."

"Sealed?"

"Yes. I popped the top myself. I poured him a glass, and he chugged it. Fast. Then another. Then before I knew it he—" She shudders, pressing a manicured hand to her mouth. "You think it was the drink? That I... I could have..."

We both turn to look at the mayor's blotched and twisted face with a trail of bloody spittle. That's no heart attack.

"I swear, Meredith, I had nothing to do with this."

I squeeze her shoulder. "I know you didn't."

Not so long ago, I trusted Camille Tavani about as far as I could throw her—which wasn't far, because the woman absolutely towered over me. Camille could be manipulative, selfish, and cruel, but she wasn't a killer.

That wouldn't make a damn bit of difference to the cops, though. If it's what we think it is—that Camille served a poisoned drink—her fingerprints are on the bottle.

She was the last person to see the mayor alive. And she's dressed like a woman who's up to no good. The police would take one look at her and assume all sorts of scandalous motives.

"Who else saw him come in here?" I ask, staring at the contents of her purse—lipstick, tampons, her new mobile phone—scattered all over the table.

"Only the security guards at the back entrance."

Mikey and Enzo were working the door tonight. Mikey's a teddy bear; if I want him to keep his trap shut, all I have to do is ask nicely. As for Enzo, he's one of Sal's old-school mafia heavies—which means he can be bought, and if I'm lucky, he won't be smart enough to demand too high a price for his silence.

"You're sure, Camille? No one else?"

She nods.

"Okay, then." I put my hands on my hips and survey the scene. "You wait here. I'll put my car around back, and—"

"But I didn't do anything." Camille's Southern drawl's coming out, the way it always does when she's stressed. "I'll explain it to the police, that all I did was—"

"Take thousands of dollars from the mayor of Providence's second wife to seduce him in a private room at a strip club for blackmail material—and whoops, he just happens to drop dead, and you're the only witness?"

"Don't you give me that sass, missy. My business is perfectly legitimate."

"Yeah, well, so is mine. And you know what this could do to it."

A corpse on the premises was bad enough—but the corpse of one of the richest, most powerful men in Providence? It wouldn't just be a scandal. It would be the end of everything I've worked so hard to build.

"But Meredith, we can't move him."

"Sure we can. We're strong, independent women. We can do anything."

I was already working it out in my mind. We'd need something to cover him up with, obviously—a rug or a blanket or maybe we could even squeeze him into one of the laundry bins? And we'd have to put him someplace he wouldn't be found for a couple of days. The city dump? The river? Too bad I didn't pay more attention back when I was dancing; mobsters would brag about all sorts of nefarious deeds while I writhed away on their laps.

"No," Camille says. "We can't."

"Why?"

"Because I already called 9-1-1."

"You *what*?"

I didn't mean to speak so loud. It sounds even louder than it should, though—because the music out in the club has stopped. Camille and I freeze.

There are footsteps, the murmur of voices. "Back here?" a man says. Then a fist pounds on the door. "Providence Police Department. Open up."

There's no lock on the champagne room, for obvious reasons. Not that it would have bought us much time anyway. We're caught now. Best to look as cooperative as possible.

I open the door. The officer standing on the other side is young—and what's more, I recognize him. Though last time he was in this fine establishment, he wasn't in uniform; he was doing Jägermeister shots with Krystle's hard-partying son Rom, both of them ogling my tits in a way they probably thought was slick.

Okay, maybe we can figure a way out of this mess yet. I wish I'd thought to whip off my sweatshirt, though; Camille's cleavage will have to be disarming enough for the both of us.

"Thank goodness you're here, Officer," I say, batting my lashes for good measure.

His eyes dart from the two of us to the man on the floor and then back again. Even in the flashing fuchsia neon, his skin looks greener than the champagne bottle. This must be his first dead body. Wish I could say the same for myself.

Another cop comes up behind him. This one's older, more seasoned—not so easy to fool. If only we'd had more time to get our stories straight. We could have claimed we were both in the room when the mayor keeled over, backed up each other's versions. Or better yet, we could have gotten Camille's stuff out of here, wiped down the champagne bottle, and claimed that we simply found the mayor like this, already dead. Such a tragedy.

The older officer doesn't seem fazed by the body. Until he takes a closer look.

"Jesus, Mary, and Joseph—is that Mayor Tom Bradley? What exactly happened here, ladies?"

Camille and I exchange a glance. The old Camille would have lied to save her own ass without so much as a blink of those pretty blue eyes. But one inconvenient side effect of all her personal growth over the last couple of years? She's developing a moral code.

"He drank the champagne," she says, "and then he started—well, it looked like some kind of seizure, but I don't know for sure."

The policeman looks at me. "That what happened?"

Before I can contribute anything, Camille jumps in again. "She wasn't here. She had nothing to do with this. The mayor and I were…alone."

Moral codes—always way more trouble than they're worth.

The older cop nods to the younger one, who takes Camille by

the arm. "Ma'am, if you wouldn't mind coming with us. We'll need a full statement."

Camille flinches at that *ma'am* but doesn't protest as she's led toward the door. I follow them—stepping on a shard of glass from the broken bottle just inside the threshold. I swallow a curse—and the desire to kick that damn bottle right across the room—before I realize something.

It's the wrong bottle.

I instructed the bartender to set aside one of our finest bottles of Dom Pérignon for Camille's meeting with the mayor. This bottle is smaller, and the glass is a brighter shade of green. I crouch down to examine the label. There's the outline of what looks like a wolf head, in gold, and the name of a city in California. No brand name. We don't stock this kind in the club. I've never seen it before in my life. What the hell is going on here?

I rush after Camille and the baby-faced cop. They're in the public area of the club now. With the overheads on, the place seems much seedier—all the glitter on the black-painted floor mixed in with sticky puddles of spilled alcohol. At least the trail of bloody footprints I'm leaving behind me barely shows. The bartender's whispering something to one of the bouncers, while the DJ and dancers loiter around the edge of the stage.

Most of the girls just look annoyed about this unscheduled interruption of their well-oiled hustle, but Destiny actually appears upset. She's standing alone, looking lost, doe eyes gleaming in the harsh lights—until she sees me. She hurries over, still a little unsteady on the brand-new eight-inch heels she recently upgraded to.

"Meredith? Is everything—"

I put a hand up. I don't have time for this now. Destiny falls silent, chewing on her lip.

I'm still trying to decide whether mentioning the unfamiliar champagne bottle will make Camille look more or less guilty when I hear the *crack* of a palm against someone's face.

The young cop isn't holding on to Camille anymore. He's holding on to his reddened cheek, looking stunned—and furious.

"Try it again, buster, I dare you!" Camille shouts at him. Leave it to her to sound imperious when she just hit a police officer. How did she find a way to make this night *worse*?

I sigh, my headache slam dancing behind my eyes. "What did he do?"

"He grabbed my ass!" Camille says, just as the young cop cries out, "Nothing!"

Given the guy's behavior on his previous social calls with Rom Romero, I'm gonna go ahead and call that bullshit. But unfortunately, it doesn't matter. No matter what he did to deserve that slap, Camille's really done herself in now. They were probably just going to question her, give her the option of coming down to the police station to give a statement. That trip to the station's getting less optional by the second.

The officer reaches for her again, trying to pin her hands behind her back. She shrugs away from him. So that's assaulting an officer *and* resisting arrest.

"Just go with them, Camille," I say. "But don't say *anything* else, okay?"

She nods at me, but the fight's draining out of her. She looks scared—and honestly? She should be. We're both in big trouble.

Everyone in the club watches in awkward silence as the cop handcuffs Camille and perp walks her through the front door. The flashing lights from the parked cruisers glint off her rhinestone-covered heels.

"It's going to be okay!" I call after her. "I'll meet you at the station!"

The older officer fixes me with a stern look. "Young lady, this is an active crime scene. No one else is leaving the premises until we've processed the evidence and completed our interviews. Now, where's the owner?"

I don't have time for this shit either. "You're looking at her."

"You own this club?"

Resisting the urge to roll my eyes might hurt even more than my bleeding foot does.

"Sure do," I tell him. "And I'm not saying another word until I speak to my lawyers."

KRYSTLE

Power suit, check. Good lipstick, check. Big corner office, check. Backstabbing employee to fire, you bet your ass.

"Have a seat." I gesture toward one of two chairs in front of my late husband's large oak desk in the partner suites of the Turks Head building in downtown Providence.

"I'd rather stand, Krystle." Our last senior lawyer, Tucker Armand, closes the door a little too loudly before he spins toward me like he's doing me a favor. He stands before me in all his glory: a pink bow tie, which he'd no doubt call "Nantucket red," dotted with whales; a perfectly matching crisp pocket square; and I know without looking, matching pink-and-whale socks.

New England prep really makes my Italian stomach turn.

"I have every right to leave this law firm." Tucker tosses his long blond floppy hair off his forehead. For the millionth time, he reminds me of one of those fancy dogs—Afghan hounds, I think—with the gorgeous long locks sideswept over a too-long pointy snout and beady dark eyes. No offense to Afghan hounds, but what a waste of good hair. Though *little bitch* does seem right on the money.

I stick out my chest and put my hands on my hips. "You're poaching business, Tucker. I've had three calls from loyal, long-standing clients that you had the nerve to ask to move with you when you start your own law firm. It's one thing to leave; it's another to steal as you're walking out the door."

"Please, they basically are my clients. The only reason anyone stayed after...the *change* is me."

The change? Does he think I'm having hot flashes? Try "my husband was murdered in a fiery plane crash." But I don't want to get into it with him. There's too much other shit to shovel.

"From what I hear, you're promising clients that you'll take their cases immediately."

"So what?" He picks at his thumbnail. "Like you can do anything? It's me—an esteemed member of the Rhode Island Bar—against you, a housewife from the Hill turned secretary running this whole law firm into the ground."

"First of all, there's nothing wrong with being a secretary. They do most of your work as it is." I bite my tongue to keep *you stuck-up twat* from escaping. *Keep it professional, Krystle.* I lean over the desk and have to look up to meet his gaze. "Second, I'm your boss. I run this show."

"Clown show," he murmurs.

That cheap shot hits me harder than it should. I know he's not the only one saying it. Still, I have the upper hand, and I take my time delivering the news. "Listen, Tucker. Your contract says you can't practice law in the same areas for a year after you leave."

"No one gives a shit about little contract clauses in this town. But you wouldn't know being…you."

I snap open the file with a copy of the contract Tucker signed five years ago. I highlighted in pink the sections about non-solicitation. "It's true I'm not always one for details. But I do know being sued for…'tortious interference with a contract,' is not the best start to your new law firm."

"You'd never win," he says.

I stick out my chest. "In court, maybe, but public opinion matters much more in this town. And after what I've been through the past couple of years, I would know that very well."

He snatches the contract from my hand. "I figured you'd be more likely to have me dumped in the river by some wise guy."

"It's not off the table."

His laugh is a sneer. "You also wouldn't know this either, Krystle, but on the first day of law school, students are told look to the left, look to the right, only one of you will be here by the end of the semester. Well, I graduated."

"Must have been a real idiot sandwich."

"Actually, it's that I do absolutely whatever it takes to win."

"You're the only one?"

He saunters up to the desk where I'm leaning and drops the contract. He taps on one section and begins to read. "'Once the employee is terminated *and has left the premises*, he or she will no longer be able to initiate contact with any clients for one year after that date.'"

I bite back the stream of curses. "Don't look so smug. I already called security."

He slowly shakes his head. "You should have made me partner. Whatever happens, you brought this on yourself, Krystle. This was never meant for you. None of it."

The elevator dings, and we both look through the glass toward the security guard, Lou, hobbling out. "See ya, Tucker."

"I'm going to be the one left, Krystle. You don't have what it takes." He grabs the contract and throws it in my face.

I jump out of the way as my office door flies open with a thump. "He's right there!" I shout to Lou, but that Ivy-eating bastard is gone, sprinting down the partner suite hallway. "Get back here, Tucker," I scream as I haul out after him. "This way, Lou!"

In my heels, I'm only slightly faster than Lou, who I'm pretty sure only took this as a postretirement gig to get free coffee and black-and-white TV under his desk.

Tucker doesn't slow down as his long legs take him right to his office, where he jumps inside and slams the door.

Click.

"You gotta be kidding me!" I shriek at the wood door, running over to try the handle. My cool is completely gone. "Tucker! You motherfucker! Open this door right now!"

Lou, the security guard, lets out a whistle. "Now he really ain't letting you in. Mouth like that."

"He doesn't need to worry about my mouth!" I slam my palms onto the door until they're red. "I fired you! That's not your office anymore! Get out or I'll…have Lou bust down the door!"

"Ma, why are you yelling?"

My gaze snaps over to see my eldest son, Rom, our firm's only remaining criminal attorney, sauntering out of his office. "Help me over here, will ya? Tucker's gone rogue!"

I hear a laugh from inside the office and a scrape like he's moving furniture. The damn desk. He's shoved it against the door.

I turn the knob and shove, but nothing budges. "Damn it!"

"Let me try, Ma." Rom tosses his dark hair like he's about to step into a photo shoot. I don't know where he got his looks from, but they've done more harm than good, charming him into trouble. Still, beggars can't be choosers.

I step back from the door. "See if you can pry it open."

"I saw a snow shovel somewhere in the basement," Lou says with his bushy white eyebrows raised as if he's about to laugh.

"When I'm done with Tucker, I'm coming for you."

Rom ignores us, and instead of pushing, he kicks at the door with an unsuccessful thump.

"Holy cripes, son! We don't own that door. Use your shoulder, breaking that will cost a lot less."

Rom gives the *oh mom* look he's been sending my way since he was into Legos. He cop-knocks the door. "Come on, Tucker, this is ridiculous. Come outta there."

We both listen at the door, and it's quiet for a moment—until it isn't.

"Yes, this is Tucker Armand for Charlie Beckett. He's not expecting my call, but it's important. We need to talk about his development on Thayer Street. Yes, I can hold."

I kick the door with the toe of my pump and immediately regret it. That little sock-and-bow-tie-matching weasel, he's poaching my clients under my own damn roof. My gaze scans the empty office. "Rom, I need ya to follow me. And hurry. Lou, find the key, will ya?!"

Rom and Lou both sigh but at least do as I say.

With his arms crossed, Rom looms over me at his father's desk. "What's the plan here?"

I don't like his tone, but I keep it to myself. "I need you to dial these numbers of our biggest clients. When you get them on the line, you hand it to me."

I plop the Rolodex and a phone in front of him, where he remains statue-still.

I try to sweeten my tone. "Start with this number and keep going until you reach an actual person. I'll start dialing on my mobile phone." I heft the large leather bag from my drawer onto the desk. I see the line indicating that Tucker is still on his call. I fluff my hair, then whisper a prayer to the Patron Saint of Paddles because we are *way* up shit creek. "Let's do this, kiddo."

I notice Rom's jaw ticking. His arms are still crossed. "Is that it?"

I'm flipping through the Rolodex until I find the first name. "What? Yeah, you need a lollipop? Start dialing, kid."

"No."

"Excuse me?"

"No, Ma. I'm not just dialing numbers for you. I can speak to our clients. Some of them I work with more than you."

There may literally be steam coming out of my ears. I take five deep breaths. I say my mantras. *Keep it cool, Krystle. You have this under control. Woo-sah.* "How about I give you some of the newer clients?" I'd rather take them all myself, but time is our enemy here, not his inexperience.

As I shove a list his way, he frowns at me, disappointed, his father there in that expression. The times I pushed my husband to do more, be more, or maybe just didn't take the time to understand. Kinda like now, because who the hell has time for that?

"Please, Rom, we need to work together on this."

The disappointment doesn't go anywhere, but his shoulders drop as if I've beaten him. We both dial at the same time, and I close my eyes as the phone begins to ring. I had felt so smug finding that contract language. But I didn't think every word through, and Tucker might be a bit smarter than I gave him credit for. I hear Tucker's words: *This was never meant for you. None of it.*

"Tucker Fucker," I hiss.

"Excuse me?" says a voice on the phone.

"Oh, no, not you. Is Mrs. Swanson there? It's Krystle Romero, from her lawyer's office."

"The line is busy." Rom shakes his head.

"Dial the next one," I whisper, unable to stop myself from giving orders even though he's already hung up and punching in numbers. I return to the call. "It's very important. I must speak with her."

"One moment."

"Krystle?" says Samantha Swanson. "I'm about to head out for dinner. What's wrong?"

"So sorry to bother you, but I need to let you know that we had to let Tucker go."

"Oh, really?"

"I can't legally say why, but I want to assure you that we have a seamless transition plan in place. I don't want to keep you, but rest assured, we'll be going over the details with you first thing Monday, at whatever time is best."

"I liked working with him."

Ugh. "He has many fine qualities. But I promise, you'll like his replacement much more."

"Well, Monday morning is fine. My driver is here. Have a good weekend."

"Wait." My gut says I can't leave her open to a follow-up call from Tucker. "Ms. Swanson, if Tucker calls—I'd never tell you to not talk to him, of course, and I'm not a lawyer—but *if* you take the call, I'd advise you to record the conversation. For your own protection."

"Oh my," she says. "Thank you for reaching out."

"Of course." I take Rom's phone as I hang up mine. He writes the name of the man on the other end—one of my late husband's oldest clients—and it's a matter of seconds before he assures me he's staying.

As I'm cinching that up, Rom leaves another message on an answering machine. Then I point to our largest client, Nancy Davenforth. Rom tries her number and shakes his head that the line is busy.

I dial another client Tucker inherited from Camille's late

husband, Peter, the once head of our property law business. But he doesn't take my call. Rom shakes his head and crosses off another name on his list.

Shit.

It's not like we were rolling in active clients. I tap my fountain pen on the few names left. I dial on the mobile phone and have to leave a message with a property development company. I take another call from Rom's list.

"Oh, Brenda, I'm so glad to reach you. I know it's after hours, but—"

"I already spoke to Tucker," Brenda says. "We know his parents from the club, Krystle. How could we face them if we sided with you?"

"What side? He's stealing the firm's clients, which is illegal."

"Well, *you're* not a lawyer, and that's not what *he's* saying. Look, it's been almost two years. We stood by you as long as we could, but…well, we want to go in Tucker's direction. He's assured us he's keeping the Davenforth account, and you know we're heavily invested in the downtown development. You understand."

"Believe who you want to believe," I say flatly and realize Rom's quit dialing. He's through his list. I slam the phone down a little hard. "Try Nancy Davenforth one more time."

He raises his eyebrows at me and doesn't move.

"Pretty please with next month's rent on top?"

He starts dialing on the office line. "It's ringing!"

I snatch the phone from him and hear a cool voice answering. "Hello?"

I nearly drop the phone because I'm so surprised Nancy herself is answering. "Is this Ms. Davenforth?"

"Yes? Who's this?"

"Krystle Romero, from—"

"I'm glad you called, although I expected to hear from you much sooner."

That bastard. "Listen, I don't know what Tucker told you, but—"

"Tucker? Surely you're calling about the statement we need to put together?"

Statement? About Tucker leaving? That can't be it. "Of course…"

"We'll need to be delicate, but not sentimental. I cared for him, of course, despite everything."

I blink at the phone, surprised Tucker makes her voice go soft. "Um, sure thing."

The mobile phone rings, and Rom grabs it. "Wait, what happened, Meredith? Whoa, okay, Mom's right here." He shoves the phone at me. "You have to take this."

I put Nancy on mute as she goes on about something I still haven't figured out. Rich people problems.

"Krystle?! Are you there?" says Meredith's panicked voice as I take the phone from Rom. At least I know it's not Rom in trouble at her strip club since he's here with me. Not that I know what he was doing earlier today. He's supposed to be sober-ish and cleaning up his act. Now that Tucker is out the door, metaphorically, and Rom is the only lawyer on the letterhead, it leaves our offices looking real lean.

I cradle the office phone on my shoulder and press the big mobile phone to my other ear. I check to be sure Nancy is still on mute before I speak. "Meredith, I'm here. What's up?"

"Camille slapped a cop. We're at the jail and need your help."

More disgruntled soon-to-be-ex-wives' shenanigans. I've never liked Camille's side business, but I do like the money it brings in, so I keep my mouth shut. "I'm in full-on crisis mode. Can't it wait?"

"Well, it's not just the slap. The mayor died tonight and—"

"Krystle?" Nancy's voice cuts through Meredith's. "Do we have a problem?"

I stab the mute button. "Oh, not at all, Ms. Davenforth. No problem at all."

I press mute on Nancy again and get back to Meredith. "What did you say about Mayor Tom?"

She clears her throat. "He died in my club."

"What?" I shriek, and then I realize that's what Nancy was going on about. Not losing Tucker, but her ex-husband, the mayor and father of her son, is dead. Of course she'd want a statement.

"We need you. And…"—Meredith inhales deeply as if in pain—"Rom. At the station. We need a criminal lawyer."

Well, I know she is desperate if she's asking for my son's help. No love lost there.

I press two fingers into my forehead, feeling every wrinkle. There's no good answer.

"I'm on my way," I say to Meredith and make eye contact with my son. "And so is Rom."

We're in some serious trouble if Camille's shady

honeypot-for-hire business traces back to the law firm. What little shred of reputation we have left will be six feet under with poor Mayor Tom.

But we can't ignore the Davenforths. I don't know if it's possible to keep the doors open without their money. Nancy needs a statement, and Nancy gets what Nancy wants.

"You're absolutely right, Ms. Davenforth," I say. "I'll send you our best. Trust me, she's exactly the lawyer you need."

JUSTINE

Rich is not the same as wealthy. Rich folk live on tree-lined streets in good school districts surrounded by like-minded professionals with six-figure salaries and jumbo mortgages—all of them a pink slip, divorce, or spousal death away from an asset fire sale. I know. Before my husband's murder, I'd been another poseur in this faux-affluent set. I possessed all the trappings: The big house. The designer accessories. The debt.

More than a year after Jack's death, I barely remember having disposable income, or its more valuable counterpart, disposable time; what it was like *not* to juggle work, caring for my six-year-old son, and commuting to the classes that I hope, someday, will allow us to move from my in-laws' house. Jack's life insurance couldn't cover both our home and his law firm obligations. Shoring up the business and seeking my own law degree seemed the best route to financial independence.

I can't help but doubt my reasoning as I drive down the narrow road to the Davenforths' estate. An hour ago, I was putting my son to bed and now, thanks to being an almost-lawyer in a firm nearly out of them, Krystle has me working after hours, driving all the way to Newport, crossing two damn bridges to help our most important client draft a statement about her ex-husband's death. Krystle didn't even ask nicely: *Get your skinny ass to Newport and razzle-dazzle like our lives depend on it, because they do.*

I've little idea where I'm going, so it's a good thing this road doesn't have any turns. Bellevue Avenue is more tunnel than street, bordered as it is by wrought-iron fences and six-foot-high walls of boxwoods cut into sharp rectangles with facades smooth as cement. Such garden maintenance costs serious moolah. These people probably spend my entire annual budget on yearly landscaping. Yet Krystle thinks I can impress the Davenforths enough that they'll stay with our firm? Unlikely.

What I lack in confidence, however, I make up for in desperation. That's why I continue driving toward the sea. I hear it ahead of me, its waves thrashing the shore. But I can't see it. The moonless night has transformed the ocean into a black expanse. This road seems to stop at world's edge, at least until my headlights catch the chain blocking off the beach. A sign swings from its center: *Private Property.* The Davenforths must own this entire strip of sand on the water, or at least the sole access point to it. Basically the same thing.

An ornate gate breaks the hedges. I pull my Ford Escort beside a silver call box, reach out the window, and announce myself. "Hello, Justine Kelly from Romero, Tavani, Kelly, and Romero. Here to see Nancy Davenforth."

Someone must be listening because the metal wall retracts. I shift my foot from the brake to the accelerator and continue up the long driveway, rehearsing my opening salvo. *Good evening, Mrs. Davenforth.*

Not *Mrs.*, I remind myself. *Ms.* Period. Nancy never took her ex-husband's surname. With a moniker like Davenforth—a name synonymous with money and privilege—why change it?

Good evening, Ms. Davenforth. I'm so sorry for your loss.

Condolences assume Nancy considers her ex-husband's death a loss, of course. It wouldn't shock me if she didn't see it that way. I remember all too well my own anger after learning that my husband had been unfaithful. For a moment, I'd been happy he was dead.

But only a moment. I think of my son, JJ, and realize I could never have truly hated Jack. When someone gives you a child who you love more than your own life, and that child adores their father, all you can do is wish the bastard the very best. Nancy has a son around my age, who I know by name. Harrison Davenforth Bradley must be devastated.

All thoughts of the Davenforths' emotional states are silenced by the sight of their mansion. It appears at the top of the circular drive, a sprawling manor in the English revival style with multiple gabled roofs topping clusters of windows, each a baby house sprouted from the central structure. As I draw closer, I notice the main home is only one of several buildings on the property. To my left is a three-car garage and behind that is a barn, which I assume hosts horses. People like the Davenforths ride or play polo. I doubt they raise pigs.

I consider parking in front of the main house but keep driving toward the garages. My entry-level Ford, purchased after selling my Mercedes back to the dealer, looks gauche before such a palace. I imagine the Davenforths own a Lincoln Continental or a Cadillac. Probably both, with a driver for each one.

A shadowed spot beckons beyond the garage's last bay door. I stow the car here, hoping Nancy didn't see me pull up. A beat-up used car is unlikely to inspire confidence that my firm can handle Nancy's multimillion-dollar property investments and redevelopment projects. There was a reason Krystle's deceased husband, Romeo, shelled out for limousines and private planes, even when he knew the firm was struggling. Money attracts money.

As I exit the driver's side, I hear a door slam. A voice emerges from the darkness. Deep. Gravelly. "You're here to see Nancy?"

I whirl toward it. A man steps into the glow of an overhead lantern. His size is the first thing I notice. The guy's massive, well over six feet and perhaps halfway to seven. I know because seeing his face requires raising my chin, which is atypical. Though I was often considered too short in my former fashion model career, my five-foot-nine height matches most men. When wearing a bit of heel, like the Ferragamo pumps currently on my feet, I stand eye level with the biggest of boys.

But not this dude. My gaze travels up a broad chest swelling beneath a striped polo to a diamond jaw peppered with a five o'clock shadow that's not so much the current style as evidence of a long night. A bow mouth stretches into a weak smile that fails to flare a Roman nose. This man is beautiful. A fair-haired Rob

Lowe, but less *Tiger Beat* heartthrob. Older. Better. In this light, he reminds me of Jack.

"Hi, uh. Yes." I extend my hand as I stammer. "Justine Kelly from Romero, Tavani, Kelly, and Romero."

He comes forward to shake, giving me a good look at his eyes. They're storm blue. Bloodshot. I register the redness in his cheeks. The tension in his neck. He's been crying.

It dawns on me why right before he formally introduces himself. This is Nancy's son. The one who lost his father earlier this evening.

"Harrison Davenforth." I note the omission of his father's last name. "My mother must be in her study. She always is. I was heading to see her myself. I'll take you with me."

He hesitates before starting toward the primary mansion, giving me another moment to appreciate his handsomeness, his resemblance to my dead husband, and the fact that I should have offered condolences by now. "I'm so sorry for your loss."

Harrison runs a hand through his slicked, side-parted hair. "Oh. Yeah. Thanks. It hasn't fully hit me yet." He gestures with his head to the mansion. "Shall we?"

We walk side by side to the entrance, Harrison matching my stride. When I slow due to my heels slipping on the pebble drive, Harrison shortens his steps. I gather he wants to ask what happened but isn't sure what I know or what he's prepared to hear. A similar uncertainty about him holds my tongue. If he hasn't already been told that his father was with Camille at Meredith's strip club—or that two of my firm's owners were brought in for questioning—then I certainly don't intend to inform him. And, the truth is, I don't know much beyond that. At least, not yet.

I follow Harrison through the front door, entering a foyer befitting a queen's castle rather than a New England beach house. Dark wood paneling, shined to a mirror finish, covers the walls. A chandelier large enough to grace a hotel lobby hangs overhead. It smells of a man's cologne: oak and sandalwood, plus a faint vanilla scent presumably from the cut peonies blooming in an ornate vase. Eau de Davenforth.

A man wearing the kind of butler getup I assumed only existed in movies acknowledges Harrison with a nod. Me, he ignores. Either Harrison brings new women to the house so often that there is no point learning their names, or he disapproves of my intrusion. He moves toward a staircase several feet to the right of the front door. I step in the same direction, thinking he intends to lead us to whatever room contains his boss. But the guy shoots me a look that stops me in my tracks before continuing through a swinging door.

Harrison shrugs. "Kitchen's that way. We interrupted his post-dinner cleanup."

I force a smile. "I'm sorry. I know it's late."

Harrison dismisses the apology with a squint and continues forward, passing multiple closed doors, any of which could lead to Nancy's office.

He stops in a cavernous room worthy of Versailles. A double-height ceiling supports a thousand-plus-crystal chandelier. A half dozen floral accent chairs and two plush mauve couches top an oriental rug that belongs in a museum.

Harrison assumes a seat and then gestures to the armchair across from him. "We can wait here. I'm certain my mother's been told you've arrived."

I gladly take Harrison up on the offer. The home's opulence is overwhelming, and I've been spared the view through the towering leaded glass windows thanks to the darkness beyond. I can process it all better sitting down.

To my right is a marble fireplace capable of consuming my entire bedroom wall, though here it is simply centered along one side of the room. Above it hangs a painted portrait of an older couple. The woman has the brown curls and cornflower blue eyes for which Nancy is known, but it's not her. I've seen enough of Nancy on the local news—donating some new building or land parcel or library—to know the real deal.

"My grandparents." Harrison gestures to the portrait with an open palm as if unveiling his own recently donated pièce de résistance. "Alice and Harrison Davenforth, the First—technically the only. As you may be aware, my last name grew an appendage. Though my mother has tried to change that. Cut it off, like a gangrenous toe or third nipple."

I laugh uncomfortably. Making a joke about an undesirable association with your father—the day the man died—seems a bit soon.

"They say laughter is the best medicine."

We both turn to see Nancy Davenforth emerge from a neighboring room. She shuts the door behind her and then strides toward us, back ramrod straight, a document-topped clipboard tucked into her left hand. I recognize Nancy's strut from catwalk instruction, though I imagine finishing schools teach the same posture.

Harrison chuckles. "Who says? Not doctors."

Nancy smiles at her son. The expression is pinched at the corners, more of a brave face than a genuine show of mirth. "No. I suppose doctors would rather prescribe something." She looks at me with the same stiff upper lip. "Still, a smile can help almost as much as a spoonful of sugar. Wouldn't you agree, Ms. Kelly?"

"I hope so." I stand with a polite smile and extend my hand. "Ms. Davenforth, thank you for meeting with me under the circumstances. I am so very sorry for your loss."

Rather than shake, Nancy grasps my hand and holds it for a moment, accepting my condolences like a friend. "Thank you for coming on such short notice. The first moments of grief are so difficult. I do hope it wasn't too much of an inconvenience." She squeezes Harrison's hand. "It's just us now."

Nancy's warmth makes me flush with guilt for griping about leaving my kid. She's doing her best to comfort her own son while taking care of necessities. I know what that feels like. Harrison stands and kisses his mother's cheek. "My mother's right. Laughter is the best medicine, and black comedy is the family specialty. Our own patented brand of defense."

Nancy smirks. "Is it? Then why did you get that Colt revolver?"

Harrison shrugs. "Target practice."

Nancy cups the side of her son's face in her right palm. She regards him seriously, seeing things in his eyes that only a mother would. "You don't look good, Harry."

"He was my father."

Nancy affectionately pats Harrison's cheek. "Blood is everything." With a sigh, Nancy drops her hand from his face and passes him the clipboard. "This is for you to sign."

Harrison smirks. "It can't wait?"

Nancy gently pushes the document toward his chest. "I know, dear. Regrettably, we must take precautions to ensure our grief can't be exploited. Avoiding confusion is paramount. It must be clear what's yours and what's not."

I pretend to take an interest in the chandelier. Another thing wealthy people do differently? Grieve. Asset portfolios must be properly accounted for, regardless of whether someone is still in shock.

Harrison accepts the clipboard and sits back in his chair, crossing his right leg over his left in a wide figure four. He props the documents on his raised thigh, withdraws a sleek black-and-gold pen, and flips to pages already appended with yellow Post-its. I can't help but notice the loopy B in his John Hancock. Evidently he still uses his father's name for some things.

Nancy ignores me while watching him sign, monitoring that he doesn't miss a page. As soon as he finishes, she relieves him of the clipboard and squeezes his shoulder. "Will you be able to sleep tonight?"

Harrison slumps back in his chair. "Don't see how."

Nancy sits in the armchair beside him. "You must sleep. I've called Dr. Hendricks. He'll bring something to help."

"You've read my mind," Harrison says. "I'd intended to ask. He comes more quickly when you call."

"Of course he does." Nancy suddenly turns her attention to me, looking up to where I still awkwardly stand, eavesdropping, awaiting an invitation to resume my seat. "Back to you, Justine."

My face feels hot as I crumple onto the chair. "Krystle said you'd like to craft a statement."

Nancy sets the clipboard on a coffee table. "Tucker Armand was kind enough to do that. He just left."

The desperation that had kept my foot on the gas pedal turns leaden in my stomach. If the statement's done, I don't know what Nancy wants from me. Perhaps she only let me into her home out of politeness since I'd already driven so far.

"Would you like a cup of tea?" she asks.

I force a smile and begin to stand. "I wouldn't want to trouble you. I can let myself—"

"No trouble at all."

Nancy motions for me to return to my seat and then strides toward a wood-paneled wall. As she jabs her finger into a button, I realize there's an intercom embedded inside. "Tea, please."

Nancy crosses back to the armchair. "All this technology is so unsightly. Unfortunately, bells confuse the dogs. The intercom goes through to the office, the kitchen, and the upstairs simultaneously. So there's no excuse not to hear."

She sits across from me, her legs together and ankles crossed. The picture of a proper lady. Her blue eyes zero in on my brown ones. "So, I understand Tucker is leaving and you don't think I should use his services for the statement or otherwise?"

Her attention invites an explanation. I sit up straighter.

"Technically, he's not allowed to represent clients obtained at the firm."

Nancy's smile tightens. "Rules only work if the courts enforce them."

There's no arguing that point. It's the reason lawyers exist. "We at Romero, Tavani, Kelly, and Romero truly appreciate your business, Ms. Davenforth. We want you to know how hard we intend to work, not only to keep it but to grow it. Our named partner, Romeo Romero Junior, the late Mr. Romero's son, is determined to continue his father's legacy of providing rigorous representation."

Nancy looks over her shoulder, seemingly searching for her butler. He appears carrying an adorned tray. "Oh good," she exclaims.

I halt my sales pitch, waiting to regain Nancy's full attention. The man presents the tea set like it's a crown jewel. And it may as well be. The pot is carved porcelain and gold leaf.

Nancy picks up a cup and gold spoon, which she tinkles against the vessel's sides. "I'm afraid that Romeo Senior is most remembered for defending wise guys."

I can't argue that point either. Krystle's late husband *did* work with mobsters. Divesting from all of that less-than-triple-A-rated business is part of the reason that the firm is now struggling.

"That's not our present or future business. Mr. Romero Junior represents—"

"I know all about Rom Romero." Nancy sips her tea rather than share the sordid rumors. A lady never tells. "I'd like to know more about you, Justine. Krystle said that *you* were just what my family needed. That you would be handling the account if we stayed, not Rom."

I know the main reason Krystle didn't volunteer her son was that he was busy making sure Camille wasn't charged with the mayor's murder. But she's right, it wasn't the only reason.

Harrison leans forward in the chair. "Mother, are you going to make her share her résumé now?"

"Do you have a better distraction until the doctor arrives?" Nancy smiles at me. "Certainly not a prettier one."

Harrison laughs lightly and waves his hand. "Good luck, Justine."

I sip my too-hot tea, stalling to mentally prepare my scant credentials. The scalding liquid pools in my stomach, burning through the insecurities that so easily bubble up within me, pushing me to connect with the braver, more confident Justine that I'd promised myself I'd become.

"I'm a Harvard law student with a specialization in property law and development."

"Tucker didn't go to Harvard," Harrison says.

Nancy nods. "He did go to Yale. Continue."

"As you may know from articles in the *Providence Journal* and the *Boston Globe*, I've been instrumental in our firm winning several class-action lawsuits against the city concerning improper development of environmentally compromised lands. As a result, I am very aware of new regulations concerning what can be built and where, as well as how to push positive projects through city hall and forge consensus in our clients' best interests among all involved parties."

Harrison nods at me as if I've said something *very* right. He makes eye contact with Nancy, and even in his bloodshot gaze, I see he's excited by what I've said.

"You're correct," she says to him as she sets down her tea and stands. "Alright, Justine Kelly, let's give this a shot. My driver's waiting out front. We can talk more in my car."

As I rise, I steal a glance at Harrison. The polite smile on his face recalls his mother's, though his expression appears more tired. His helping me charm Nancy clearly took something out of him.

Nancy touches his face as she did earlier. "Wait here, dear. Dr. Hendricks will be by in a bit. I'll handle everything."

I smile sadly at Harrison. "I hope you feel better." It's the wrong thing to say, but I'm not sure of the right words, and I don't have time to think about them as Nancy is already striding from the room.

"Ms. Davenforth? Where are we going?"

Nancy walks as she talks. "To visit a friend. Police Commissioner Buddy Mann."

"We're heading to the police station?"

Nancy whirls to face me. Her blue eyes suddenly become steely. "Of course. My son's father was murdered. And I know exactly who did it."

CAMILLE

"Camille Tavani?"

I startle awake at the sound of my name and lift my face from my palms, staring into the backside of a working girl, her cheap skirt faded and fraying and hiked high enough to see Satan's grin. The jail cell is packed with people just like her—smelly, surly women of every size and color—jammed in like sardines. Except for the lucky few like me, squashed on a sliver of metal bench between two drunks, the cell is standing room only.

I pop off the bench, and my heart lifts a little. "I'm here. I'm Camille."

"Hurry up. I don't got all night."

I shove my way through the bodies to the front, where a guard stands on the opposite side of the metal bars, holding a clipboard to her generous chest. She shoves a key into the lock and twists. "Consider yourself sprung."

I can't help myself: I squeal with excitement. The bars slide open, and I toss a wave over my shoulder. "Bye, ladies. It's been real."

The guard takes off, and I clomp behind her down a secured hallway in last night's ruined shoes. Gorgeous black suede pumps with five-inch stiletto heels covered in sparkly CZs, or at least they were until that manhandling cop got a hold of me outside the Luna Lounge. One of my heels got caught in a grate while he was dragging me across the lot, but the cop didn't so much as slow. He gave my arm a hard yank, and the heel snapped clean in two. Admittedly, not as much of a tragedy as Mayor Tom dropping dead in the champagne room, but still. These shoes are Escada, and it was all I could do to stop myself from slapping him a second time.

At the barred door at the end of the hall, the guard shoves the clipboard at my chest. "Sign here."

I scribble my name across the bottom of the paper without reading a single word, Justine's voice screeching in my ear the entire time. *Are you* insane? *You were married to a lawyer and sleeping with another. You should know to* always *read the small print.*

But Justine isn't here, and she's never spent a second of her life in a jail cell, so she doesn't know how the experience crawls like spiders under a girl's skin and scares you shitless. The only thing worse than being stuck in a stinky-ass coop for hours is the prospect of being locked behind these bars for years. I can't breathe in here, and all I can think about is escape.

The door buzzes, and I lunge through it before anybody can change their mind.

A short hallway dumps me into a crowded lobby, where I spot

Krystle leaning over the desk, working her charms on the two officers seated behind it. She's in business attire, if you can call it that—heels and a pencil skirt so tight it can barely contain two pillows of billowing flesh.

She glances over when she hears me coming—*click-clomp, click-clomp*—then does a double take. "Good Lord, Camille."

She could be referring to one of so many things. The lipstick I chewed off ages ago or the mascara flaked down my cheeks. The dark smears on my arms and the backs of my thighs from getting frisked against a filthy police car. The hard, crusty splotch on my designer silk dress. Her gaze zeros in on the stain and sticks.

"It's puke," I say. "Not mine."

Krystle wrinkles her nose, but she hands me a sweater. "I got here as soon as I could. It's a long story."

All stories are long when Krystle's telling them.

I shrug on Krystle's sweater, and a surge of affection for her hits me so hard that my eyes go fuzzy with tears. "You don't know what kind of hellhole that place is, and I sincerely hope you never have to find out, but tonight you are my savior, Krystle Romero. Truly. I would've died if I had to stay there for another second."

I try to grab one of her hands in both of mine, but she yanks it away before I can make contact.

"Uh-uh. I know where those fingers have been, missy, and they're probably crawling with *E. coli*. Maybe don't touch anything until you've dunked 'em in a bucket of lye." She shakes her head, holding her hands out of reach. "And you can thank Rom, actually, except that he left five minutes ago. He and the cop you slugged are drinking buddies, and Rom promised to pick up the tab for whatever hell they raise in town tonight in exchange for him dropping the charges. Knowing Rom, they're three drinks in by now."

Begrudgingly, I send up a silent thanks to Krystle's oldest son and sole licensed partner at the firm—that is, until Justine gets her degree and passes the bar. Until she steps into the partner role, we're stuck with Rom. Normally, I'd say the dipshit blind leading the blind, but he did score a big win tonight.

"I owe him one." Or quite possibly ten. It's impossible to hear yourself think in a jail cell, much less get any sleep, but by some miracle of adrenaline dump and emotional exhaustion, I managed to doze off. My gaze sweeps the lobby, searching for a wall clock. "What time is it anyway?"

She checks her Rolex, a gift from her late husband—one of his last. "Almost ten. He—"

"Ten? It's ten o'clock?" The words burn hot in the back of my throat and heat the skin on my neck and chest. If it's ten, that means they left me in there for—"Thirteen hours! Y'all left me to rot in a jail cell for thirteen whole hours?"

"Ten at night, Camille. You've been in there for all of forty-five minutes."

The sharp knot between my shoulder blades releases, and the anger bleeds away, draining down my dirty skin like the exhaustion that sucked me under in the first place—easier to sleep than to contemplate whatever charges the police had in store for me. "Oh."

"Yeah, *oh*."

"It was a really long forty-five minutes," I mumble.

She gives me a look. "I bet it was. Now come on. Meredith's waiting outside."

Krystle takes off across the crowded lobby floor, and even in that pencil skirt, she's a lot faster than she looks. I hobble behind on my destroyed shoes, dodging criminals and cops until, hallelujah and praise the Lord, she shoves open the double doors, and I'm outside.

I pause on the top step, sucking in a big lungful of Providence night air: the distinctive tang of the mills and factories up by the river, mixed with an undercurrent of urban pollution, urine, garbage, and exhaust. Stinky, but in my nose it smells like freedom.

"Did they make you give a statement?" Meredith is leaning against the building to my right, halfway down the dimly lit handicap ramp.

"I'm just peachy, thanks for asking."

She rolls her eyes, but she obliges. "How are you, Camille, and did they make you give a statement?"

I nod, tottering her way. "Apparently, I am a person of interest, which is nowhere near as flattering as it sounds. They told me not to go planning a vacation anytime soon, not until they give me the green light, and it didn't sound like they were anywhere near ready to do that. They basically guaranteed they'll have more questions. A lot more."

Meredith makes a sympathetic face. "Yikes. Sorry."

"A person of interest is bad," Krystle says—the understatement of the century. "This is really, really bad. We are in serious trouble here."

"Tell me about it. I was the one in handcuffs, remember? And not the fun kind."

"I meant for all of us," Krystle says. "For Meredith's club. For the firm. I finally fired that little shit, Tucker, tonight, and now he's trying to poach what's left of our clients. It's not like our reputation was squeaky clean to begin with. This little stunt you pulled has put us all in real jeopardy."

"This stunt *I* pulled?" The words are part shriek, part sputter, bouncing off the smooth facade of the police station, echoing down the busy street. "I'm not the one who poisoned the mayor's champagne. All I did was pour it."

A couple of cops lumbering up the stairs freeze halfway to the double doors, their ears perked at the mention of the mayor. By now everybody in town will know what happened to the man, even if they don't know I'm the one who served his deadly last drink. The cops stare down the ramp, frowning at me like I'm a common criminal as I slink into a shadow.

"Would you pipe down?" Krystle says, her voice a sharp hiss. "You own a quarter of a law firm, for crap's sake. Jeez."

She drags us down the ramp to the edge of the building, then leans her head around the corner to make sure we're alone.

Meredith crosses her arms, taking up position next to Krystle under the lamppost. A golden glow spills down from above, a spotlight on matching frowns. Two widows against one. "She's right. I sure hope you were more tactful when you were making your statement."

"Oh, I was plenty tactful. Because you know what I realized

while I was sitting in the slammer, waiting for one of you to haul your ass down here and spring me? I realized it's a miracle that I'm still breathing. If Mayor Tom hadn't been sucking down the champagne faster than I could pour it, I'd be lying next to him at the morgue right now, blue faced and wearing a toe tag."

That shuts them up right quick. Krystle and Meredith exchange a worried look, and I give them a moment to consider just how close they came to mourning the death of their friend. Me. They look so miserable that I sigh, softening a little.

"Look, we've been friends long enough that I shouldn't have to say this out loud, but I'm going to anyway just so there's no misunderstanding. I had nothing to do with Mayor Tom's death. I didn't put anything in his glass but champagne."

Krystle reaches out to pat my hand, then zeros in on the puke stain and snatches her hands away. "We know that. Of course we do."

If only the detective had been that easy. I told him everything that happened, over and over and in great detail. That the champagne bottle was already in the room when I got there, chilling in an ice bucket. That the mayor drank two-and-a-half glasses, *boom, boom, boom*, one right after the other. That he dropped dead before I knew what was happening. The detective's cynical frown never once smoothed.

"I still don't understand how the bottle got into the club, though," Krystle says. "Meredith says it's a brand she doesn't carry."

She nods to confirm it. "It was a label from California. Expensive looking, but not the kind I stock. I sell Dom, Cristal, the other big brands imported from France. Our customers typically want the real stuff."

"How did the poison get into the bottle? I popped the cork myself. It looked just like regular champagne. Smelled like it too." I shudder at the memory of how my mouth watered at the bubbles bursting against my nose, the smooth feel of the glass against my bottom lip. Thank God Mayor Tom was a selfish bastard; otherwise, I'd be in a refrigerator drawer.

Krystle flaps her hands. "Let's slow down for a minute. Think about this logically. Who brought the bottle into the champagne room? Maybe that server knows something."

"On a typical night at the club, there are dozens of strippers walking around with a bottle at any given time. Surprisingly, nobody's copping to delivering this one." Meredith chews a ruby-red lip with her teeth, her gaze flitting between us.

"Unless the poison was in the glasses," Krystle points out. "Or he could have been poisoned before he even walked through the door."

Meredith shrugs. "It's possible, I guess. We'll see what the autopsy says. Plus, the cops confiscated everything, including what was left in the bottle you served the mayor. Hopefully, the lab will be able to tell us what the poison was and how it got into Mayor Tom's system."

"And with any luck, trace the chemicals back to that bitch who set me up." I say the words and I'm hot all over again, remembering the sound of her breathy voice coming down the line. *Whatever your price is, double it.*

"This town is full of bitches, hun," Krystle says. "You're going to have to be a little more specific."

"Tara Jordan. The mayor's wife. His *second* wife. She's the one who hired me."

Krystle sucks in a breath. "But why?"

"To take down her cheating husband, of course. Why else?"

"No, I mean why would she want the mayor dead? It's one thing to want to divorce him, but murder? She doesn't need his money. She's got plenty of it on her own."

And how. Tara owns Jordan Securities, a top hedge fund on Wall Street, run by and catering to women. Tara's is new money, but she's got buckets and buckets of it, more than she could ever spend in a lifetime. She's never needed a single penny from Tom.

I lift my hands. "For revenge then, I don't know. Though the detective wasn't buying it, either. He said he was interrogating me, not Tara."

Meredith crosses her arms, her oversized sweatshirt sliding down a shoulder. "Camille! What happened to the right to remain silent?"

"You try sitting in a cell that smells like vomit and dirty feet and let's see how you do."

"Not the time, ladies. Zip it, both of you." Krystle turns to me with a sigh. "Start at the beginning. What exactly did you say to the detective?"

"I told him everything I told Meredith earlier tonight, and for the record it's not like I could have pled ignorance. They found the tape recorder I hid in my skirt when they frisked me. They heard the mayor's sexy talk."

Is that what you do for a living? Get men drunk and sleep with them?

The detective's questions haunted me ever since. I couldn't stop thinking about all the things I should have said, points Meredith is always making about the pride of being a stripper, words like *sex positive* and *empowered*. And maybe it was the shock of the mayor's death or of being locked in that room, but my mind went completely blank. I couldn't come up with a single way to defend what I'd been caught doing.

"Could they tell from the tape that you didn't have anything to do with it?" Krystle asks.

"They certainly heard the part where I asked if he was having a heart attack. Me banging on the door and hollering for help. I could win an Oscar faking an orgasm, but not even I can fake that level of panic."

"Then it's good they didn't arrest you. Maybe they believe you?" Krystle's voice falters.

I nod. "Or they're waiting for the autopsy report to tell them if it was some freak allergic reaction or murder."

"Somebody slap me," Krystle mutters and shoves her fingers in her hair and pulls, messing up her already frizzy curls as we follow her toward the curb. "Wake me up from this nightmare."

I press a hand to my chest, needing a lot more from both of them in terms of sympathy. "Excuse me, but I'm pretty sure the nightmare is mine. I'm the person of interest here. I'm the one who spent the night in the slammer. Do you know how hard it is to sleep sitting up?"

Meredith frowns, shaking her head. "Stop with the dramatics; it was forty-five minutes. And the nightmare is *my* strip club swarming with cops, chasing off all my paying customers. Do you know what that does for business?"

"I peed in public, Meredith. In a toilet without a rim. Do not ask me what was in that bowl."

"I thought you were from Georgia. Aren't y'all used to peeing behind bushes?" She sneers the words, leaning in hard on the *y'all*.

"Oh, are we gonna go there? Because I'll remind you that the champagne came out of *your* fridge, not mine. All I did was serve it. Strippers in glass houses shouldn't be throwing around poisoned bottles, you know."

Her spine straightens, and her eyes flash with fury. "By now everybody in Rhode Island knows what you served the mayor. I know how difficult it is to put yourself in somebody else's shoes, princess, but if I get shut down, it's all your fault."

"Speaking of shoes, I'd like to remind you that mine are Escada. *Escada*. These things cost more tips than you can make in a week."

Meredith opens her mouth to respond, but the voice that answers comes from directly behind me: "I'll buy you a new pair."

The three of us whirl around, and there she is, watching us from the back of a limo stretched half a city block. The interior lights reveal a face I'd hoped never to see again. The reason we're standing here, outside the jail.

"Get in," Tara Jordan says, popping open the locks. "We have a few things to discuss."

MEREDITH

"You owe me a lot more than a new pair of shoes, you two-faced snake in the grass!"

Krystle and I try to hold Camille back, but she's too strong, and we're too late. She shakes us off easily and lunges at the limo, almost losing one of her damaged heels on the curb.

Tara doesn't even blink at the onslaught. "I understand you're upset, Ms. Tavani. I would be too, under the circumstances. But I promise you, I had nothing to do with this."

"That dog won't hunt, honey. Now get out of that fancy-ass car and tell me to my face, you conniving—"

"Camille!" I yank on her elbow, digging my nails in this time. That gets her attention. "Cool it for a minute, okay? She just lost her husband."

Although...Tara Jordan seems awfully calm and collected, considering the mayor's body is barely cold yet. When I thought I'd lost the love of my life, I spent days sobbing in bed and draining the liquor cabinet to the last drop. Sure, everyone grieves differently, but Tara doesn't look like she's shed a single tear for the mayor. No bloodshot eyes, no telltale puffiness. She's just as polished and put together as she was in the full-page wedding announcement that ran in the *Providence Journal*.

Camille whirls—as much as she can on her one remaining heel—and limps down the dark sidewalk. Krystle and I follow. So does Tara's limo, matching Camille's lurching pace.

"Why don't you get in the car?" Tara calls. "We can talk privately. Sort this all out."

Camille scoffs and starts hobbling faster. The driver keeps up. Tara leans out the window; well, as far out as she can with the wingspan of those giant shoulder pads.

"I can help clear your name," she says.

Camille slows. The limo does too.

"We can help each other," Tara continues, "Like it or not, we're in this together now."

Camille comes to a complete stop—so sudden, Krystle and I almost run into her back.

"We're in this *together*? *I'm* the one who almost died tonight. Maybe that was the plan. Maybe the second I get in that car, you're gonna finish the job."

"I assure you, I don't mean you any harm, Ms. Tavani. But if it would set your mind at ease…" Tara pops the door open. "Bring your friends. I think the three of you could take me."

Camille hesitates for a second. But then she gets in the car—mumbling something under her breath that I don't quite catch, but the general gist is *I could take you all on my own, bitch, try me.* Krystle and I pile in after her.

Tara's limo is even more ridiculous inside: moody lighting, black leather seats monogrammed with her initials, carpet so plush I feel like I'm going to sink knee-deep into the footwells. The three of us squeeze into the seat opposite Tara, Krystle clambering over Camille's lap to sit on her other side. Smart, in case she gives us reason to restrain her again.

Tara presses a sleek panel beside her, and it springs open, revealing a mini fridge filled with pint-sized bottles of Perrier and individually packaged snacks. "Can I get you anything?"

Camille just glares at her. Totally unfazed, Tara turns to Krystle. "What about you, Mrs. Romero? Something to drink?"

"No. We won't be staying long."

Then Tara turns to me. She's gorgeous, obviously, but that's not what takes my breath away when her eyes meet mine. There's something so fierce about the woman. Every picture I've seen of her, she's smiling like she might take a bite out of the person behind the camera, and her demeanor is even more disarming in person.

The local press has tried to downplay Tara's professional accomplishments in comparison to her new husband's, focusing on her youth and beauty and painting her career as a distraction from her duties as Providence's new First Lady, or whatever you call the mayor's significant other. I might've thought she was just another typical spoiled trophy wife too if I hadn't read a *Cosmo* women-in-business cover story about her last year. Tara could have made her fortune on looks alone, but she chose a much harder path in life, breaking into the boys' club of New York finance, and then busting it wide open by founding her own company where she was the head bitch in charge.

I know way too much about her, considering we've never met. Tara extends her hand across the space between our seats. "I don't believe I've had the pleasure. Tara Jordan."

Her handshake is stronger than any man's I've encountered, but her skin is soft and smells like expensive men's cologne—a little musky, with complex spices simmering underneath. Her outfit is the kind of ensemble I can only dream of pulling off: a power suit in a pink so bright that it practically glows in the dark, and stilettos tipped with metal that shines like a knife blade.

Not exactly mourning clothes. Tara is terrifying—and so stunning, I barely resist the urge to bring her knuckles up to my lips for a kiss, the way cheesy guys at the club do to try and get around the no-touching rules.

"I'm Meredith Everett. Owner of the—"

"Oh yes, of course! You took over that strip club near Smith Hill. The Wolf Den."

I try to hide my surprise. "It's The Luna Lounge now."

"That's right. After the alpha female of the pack. How fitting."

No one's ever gotten that before. People always think it's an astronomy reference.

"I read about you," Tara explains. "In the *Providence Business News* report about the Davenforths' redevelopment plan. But I have to admit, I almost didn't recognize you without…" She trails off, searching for the right word.

"The stripper makeup?" I supply. "That wasn't my idea."

A cornerstone of that damn redevelopment plan is "cleaning up" the city—which is rich-asshole speak for bulldozing businesses like mine and replacing them with more "respectable" establishments.

I showed up to that interview determined to come across as an honest, hardworking female entrepreneur rather than a purveyor of filth. I had all my talking points ready, about the up-and-up success of the club since I'd taken over and how the redevelopment plan would kill beloved local businesses that had been pillars of Providence's community for decades. I even let Justine help me pick out a sensible pantsuit.

Then, without asking, the paper decided to run an image of me they dug up from a club flyer a few years back, where I'm wearing a sleazy sequined dress and about a pound of eye shadow. So much for being taken seriously.

"I figured as much," Tara says. "No matter how successful you get, no matter what business you're in, they'll always try to make you look like a whore."

She smiles again, and I'm forgetting why I'm supposed to be mad at this woman.

Camille reminds me with an elbow to the ribs. "Enough flirting. Tell me why you screwed me over, Tara."

"As I said already, I had nothing to do with what happened tonight. You didn't even tell me when or where you were going to approach my husband."

"You could've found out, though. A resourceful business lady like you."

"But I didn't," Tara insists. "I didn't want to hurt him either."

"So you do think it was murder?" Krystle says as if she's onto something.

"The police have been tight-lipped with any details. But from what I've been able to gather so far, it didn't sound like natural causes to me."

Camille shudders. "There was definitely nothing natural about it."

"You must have been planning to divorce him at least," Krystle points out. "Otherwise why hire Camille?"

"I'm in the business of risk assessment. I wanted to assess my risk."

"Well, you sure don't seem all that broken up about his untimely demise."

"You want me to burst into tears and dab my eyes with a lace handkerchief like some poor little widow in a movie? What good would that do?" Tara leans forward. "I don't have time for grief. Once that autopsy report comes back, they'll want to slam the cuffs on someone."

"And you want to make sure it's not you," Camille shoots back. "How convenient that you set me up so perfectly to be your patsy."

"You'll notice you're not in a cell anymore. You may be a person of interest, but you're not the prime suspect. It's only a matter of time before they come after me. They'll say I'm ruthless, a gold digger, I married him for his money and then killed him for it."

"Did you?" Camille asks.

Tara laughs and crosses her long legs. "If I want more money, there are far easier ways to get it than *marriage*. Besides, when Tom and I married, my net worth was much higher than his."

"Maybe that's why you wanted him dead, then," I say. "You were sick of him spending your hard-earned cash."

"Tom did have expensive taste." Tara taps a nail against her metallic heel. "But overall, he was a good investment. I had no desire to end our marriage—or to end him."

The tabloids portrayed Tara and Mayor Tom's relationship as a tawdry, passionate affair, tempting him away from his true love with beloved daughter of Providence Nancy Davenforth. If it was always just a business arrangement… Well, I'm not sure what that says about Tara's guilt or innocence, but it sure is more interesting.

"I think we all need a drink," Tara says. "What do you say?"

Without waiting for an answer, she slides open another hidden panel and retrieves a bottle of champagne. She's about to pop the bottle when the light catches the label, glinting gold. I lunge forward and grab it out of her hands.

"Hey!" she protests. "What are you—"

"This champagne. This is what the mayor drank tonight."

"What?" Camille tilts the bottle toward her, so she can look at the label.

"I didn't notice it until we were leaving the VIP room. But we don't even stock this kind at the club. Someone switched the bottles."

"Maybe one of those new bartenders of yours made a mistake?" Krystle suggests. "Ordered the wrong kind? It's got a wolf on the label; maybe he thought—"

"It's a coyote."

We all look at Tara. She appears truly unsettled for the first time.

"That varietal is from a new vineyard, out in California. There's a large pack of coyotes on the property, so they incorporated it into their logo."

"How do you know?" I ask.

"Because I was an early investor in the company. No one in all of New England serves the stuff—trust me, they've tried to make inroads in the market, but everyone's too attached to their overpriced French and Italian brands."

Krystle mutters something under her breath; I don't have to speak Italian to know it was nasty. Camille narrows her eyes, and I clamp a hand on her elbow just in case she tries anything.

"I knew it," Camille says. "You set me up. You planted poison champagne and—"

"No, no, wait a second," I say. "That means it *wasn't* her."

Camille glares at me, nostrils flaring. She's pissed, but she's listening.

"Why would Tara leave a calling card like that, if she was the one behind the mayor's death? The champagne bottle points straight to her, *and* it could hurt the company's reputation and impact her investment, which means—"

"Someone's trying to frame me," Tara says.

Camille and Krystle still look dubious, but I'm convinced. Tara Jordan may not be nice, she may not be a good person or a good wife, but she's way too smart to do something so stupid.

"Look," Tara says. "We're all businesswomen here, yes? And all our businesses will be damaged, if not outright destroyed, if we don't find the real culprit—and fast."

"Well, if you need a lawyer," Krystle says, "I regret to inform you we already represent your husband's ex-in-laws. We shouldn't even be talking to you, quite frankly."

"I've got plenty of lawyers. I need someone willing to do what a lawyer can't."

"And what's that?"

"Find out who else might have wanted Tom dead. Using any means necessary."

"You were his wife," Camille says. "If he had enemies, surely you'd know about them."

"I've been busy with my own career. I didn't have time to keep track of all my husband's little squabbles running this… Well, I suppose it is *technically* a city."

"Watch it," Krystle snaps. "Just 'cause the Big Apple's bigger doesn't mean it's better."

Though I grew up here too, I can't bring myself to feel much Providence pride. It is a city, but that's all it is to me—and one I would have been glad to leave behind at any point, if a better opportunity had come along. But things that seem like good opportunities have a way of turning sour on me. Especially when they're offered by beautiful women.

"Recently, he was obsessed with bringing a casino to Providence," Tara says. "Turning it into 'the Vegas of the Northeast.'"

I almost roll my eyes at that. Everyone here's too damn Catholic for the flashy vice of a casino. Rhode Islanders want to sin in the dark on Saturday night and then confess to their priest on Sunday morning. But it's a place to start.

"That's a pretty ambitious project," I say. "Who all was he working with?"

Tara looks at Camille. "That's what I'm hoping you can find out, Ms. Tavani."

"Absolutely not." Camille folds her arms. "You seriously think I'd do business with you again, after what went down tonight?"

Now it's my turn to elbow her. "*You* seriously think it's a good idea to wait around for the cops to figure this out? Our reputations and livelihoods are on the line."

Krystle sticks out her chest. "Meredith's right. By the time the cops are done, even if none of us are behind bars, we might all be out on the street."

"I want you to do what you do best, Camille," Tara says.

Camille glares, arms still folded tight. "And what's that?"

"Investigate. Use your…" Tara gives Camille an appraising once-over. "Special skills."

"Why don't you use *your* special skills, huh? Whatever feminine wiles you used to get Mayor Tom eating out of your—"

"Tom's associates will be suspicious if I'm going around asking too many questions. They think I should be a grieving widow, stuck at home crying her pretty little eyes out. But you're an investigator; you'll simply be doing your job. I'm willing to pay, obviously. How about…" Tara tilts her chin, thinking—though I'm sure she had the figure ready to go before she even pulled up to the station—"the same amount I promised you for the sting operation, as a per-day retainer, every day until the case is solved."

Camille's trying to hide it, but her eyes are full of dollar signs. She's supporting herself now, and she'll need plenty of money to mount a defense if she's slapped with murder charges.

"How much was that, exactly?" Krystle asks.

Tara reaches into her blazer and pulls out a fat wad of hundreds. Now Krystle's eyes are going *cha-ching*. Even if it only takes a few days to crack the case, that'll add up. We could all really use the cash infusion.

Tara's eyes narrow. "We don't have to like each other. We don't have to trust each other. But we want the same thing, so we may as well work together."

Camille and Krystle are silent for a second, and I know exactly what they're thinking, 'cause it's what I'm thinking too: it wasn't so long ago we didn't like or trust one another, and look at us now. Tragedy makes strange sisterhoods.

Finally, Camille sighs. "Fine. You have a deal."

Tara brightens. "Wonderful doing business with you. Consider this a down payment."

She holds out the cash. Camille reaches for it, and I stop her.

One other pertinent detail I remember from that *Cosmo* piece on Tara: her advice to never, under any circumstances, accept a first offer.

"You have a deal," I say, "but considering the dire circumstances, the price just went up."

Tara's brows arch higher. I've impressed her. I enjoy it more than I should.

"Triple the initial fee," I say. "Per day, for a minimum of two weeks."

"That's right," Camille says, playing right along. "Triple, or we're out. Final offer."

"And in cash," Krystle adds.

Tara studies the three of us for what feels like forever. Nerves start to bubble up in my chest. Maybe we pushed too far? In some ways, she needs us more than we need her, but having someone rich and influential like Tara bankroll Camille's off-the-books investigation is by far the best option we've got to get out of this mess. Money opens doors. I'm just hoping it'll be enough to keep the doors of my business from closing forever. I've worked too hard to get to this point.

We all have.

So I don't blink. I don't back down. I fold my arms and stare at Tara, imagining that we're across the table from each other in a boardroom, and I'm not leaving without what I want.

"Take it or leave it," I tell her.

KRYSTLE

I know it's more Meredith's department, but planting a big sloppy kiss across Tara Jordan's perfect lips is definitely crossing my mind.

"Here's the rest." Tara digs out another handful of cash and tries to hide a smirk.

I take the stacks on stacks and jam them in the very empty briefcase I brought to the jail just for show. With Camille rarely ever wearing enough material for a pocket, I am now in possession of enough money to put up a fight for this law firm. Even if Justine fails with Nancy—and that's where I'd put my chips since it's a real lamb-to-wolves situation—we might still survive thanks to Tara, the Patron Saint of Second Wives.

"Should we seal this deal with a glass of champagne?" Tara asks.

Camille gasps. "Are you joking?"

"When the horse bucks you off, sister, you gotta get right back on."

Camille's lips twitch. "Giddyup, I guess."

"I'd prefer she doesn't pour," I say, and then Camille smacks my side. "Because you're filthy from jail. Jesus, I know you'd never poison us. Not now anyway." She smacks me again, which was the point. I don't like seeing Camille scared and broken. We need her spark to survive. I know she's tougher than one hour in the clink. We all are.

Queen Bee Tara is laughing as if we're entertaining her, and hey, if she's paying, we're Moe, Larry, and Curly.

"Tell us more about the mayor's more recent enemies," Meredith says as she takes the flute from Tara and, I swear to God, bats her eyes.

I'm about to groan when a town car pulls up near a lamppost and draws Tara's attention away.

"You have got to be kidding me! What does that shriveled-up hag want?"

We all jump at Tara's voice changing from cool business bitch to she-wolf baring her teeth. It occurs to me that maybe we're the lambs with the wolf instead of Justine.

Our faces nearly pressed to the glass to see into the shadows, we watch the town car driver open the curbside door, and a familiar face bounds out as if I've just conjured her. "Wait, is that Justine?" I whisper and look at Tara. "Whose town car is that?"

She purses her lips as if she can't begin to speak the name. Then, she doesn't have to. Nancy Davenforth steps onto the curb and faces the stairs leading to the police station.

"Justine pulled off a Tucker-block," I murmur, more surprised than I should be that Justine was able to get Nancy on our side. Or at least, not kicked out on our keisters. Still, I can't leave Justine to close this deal. "Ladies, please excuse me."

I hop out and suck in some crisp midnight air. Keeping the briefcase of cash tight in my hands, I hustle toward where they're standing but then deliberately slow my steps.

Be a boss, Krystle. Nancy may hold a lot of cards, but you're still in the game.

"Mrs. Davenforth," I call toward her and smooth my blouse with my free hand. "I'm so glad you met Justine. She's the future of Romero, Tavani, Kelly…"

My speech falters as Nancy's sharp gaze flits down to my clearance shoes and size-too-tight suit before narrowing at my puffy red hair. I feel like I'm back in Catholic school and a nun with a big ruler is inspecting my uniform. And finds it lacking.

Nancy shifts back toward Justine. "Did you need help from your firm to get the job done? Perhaps Tucker is the better choice?"

Her firm. As if my last name's not on the door? "We're the firm for you, Mrs. Davenforth. We can go to the press first thing once we get that statement ready."

Justine touches my arm. "*Ms.* Davenforth and I drafted a strong statement in the car."

"Now that I think of it," Nancy says, "Tucker knows Don—the owner of the *Journal*—from the country club. You can see my dilemma."

Justine nods. "Of course I do. But I worked with Don extensively on our last deal. He has a soft spot for redeveloping Providence. I'd like to think that matters more than his backswing."

Nancy smiles at Justine like she's God's gift, and I guess she is at the moment. I'm about to try to be helpful again when Tara's window rolls down and all the interior lights are on again. As clear as day, we can see her: big hair, bigger shoulder pads, and a skin-peeling glare.

Nancy puts a trembling hand over her mouth and whispers, "How dare she show her face."

Tara raises a champagne flute, tips it toward Nancy with hatred burning in her big blue eyes. "Here's to widows," she calls and downs it. Neither break eye contact as Tara's limo pulls away from the curb. Guess Camille and Meredith caught a ride.

Justine puts a hand on Nancy's arm. "Are you okay?"

"I will be. Once that woman pays for her crimes. She's as slippery as a snake, but I won't let that stop me."

My eyes narrow because my peepers ain't what they used to be. "Does Tara's license plate say…"

"M-A-T-G-R-L…Mat girl?" Justine guesses.

Nancy's voice is a cool monotone. "It's from a song by someone named Madonna. The whore, not the saint."

I shift in my jacket—not Chanel—and step around Justine to be back in Nancy's circle.

"Well, now I'll have 'Material Girl' in my head all day."

"Do you have one in your life?" Nancy stares at me. "Justine assured me that criminals were no longer part of your clientele."

"Our law firm would never take on Tara Jordan as a client,"

I say sincerely as I clutch the briefcase with Tara's money tighter. She's Camille's client, I'm just holding the cash.

Justine gently claps her hands with a peacemaker flutter of her eyes. "Of course not. We're so grateful for your business and, as we've discussed, we are already strategizing next steps to push forward your redevelopment plan."

Nancy half smiles at her, and I'm relieved that she seems to like at least one of us. "But Tucker said he didn't brief you on all the issues."

"Can it be that hard if he was handling it?" I put in.

"I'll be fully up to speed by tomorrow," Justine says quickly. "I understand the issue with the tribe."

"What tribe?" I say, annoyed that I'm being ignored.

"Must we discuss this on the sidewalk like construction workers?" Nancy glances at her watch, a brand I don't recognize, which means it leaves Rolex in the dust. Suddenly the door to the police station bursts open, and I get a blast from the past: a guy with a brown cop-stache wearing full police regalia hurries toward us like his ass is on fire. "I'm so sorry to keep you waiting, Nancy."

"Hey, Buddy!" I say with a wave. I've known him since his sister babysat me on the Hill.

He frowns at me, and there's a light flush on his cheeks. "It's Commissioner Mann, now."

I don't hide my annoyance. It's not like he's the first person to leave the Hill and then act like it's a four-letter word. "I put in a couple of calls to your office tonight."

"I've been quite occupied," he says and turns to Nancy. "I'm terribly sorry to keep you—"

Nancy holds up one thin finger, and he stops in his tracks. Her focus remains on Justine. "I can't thank you enough for your help today. Our family needed a steady hand, and it was you."

Nancy takes the offered arm of the Commissioner. "I might collapse the moment we get inside."

"I doubt that very much, Ms. Davenforth," he says as he escorts her up the stairs like the Queen of Freaking England.

Once they're inside, I nod toward Justine. "You know what the papers said when Mayor Tom left Nancy?"

She shakes her head as she glances back at Nancy's car blowing exhaust in the fire zone.

"That the Prince of Providence just left Snow White for the Evil Queen."

"I don't know about Snow White, but Nancy's willing to hear us out." Justine can't help herself. As she talks, pride puffs her chest like a push-up bra. "I think she liked that I—that we'd—been in the papers for helping Providence's poorest move from landfill properties. She said people see me—I mean, us—as a real champion of the little guy's best interests."

"You think that's what Nancy wants with her redevelopment plans? Build up the little guy? Bring in jobs?"

"You sound cynical, Krystle. There are good people in this world."

When her eyes go all Bambi, I just don't have the heart to play hunter, so I change the subject. "What's this deal with a tribe?"

Justine deflates a smidge. "The Davenforths' redevelopment

plans hinge on a parcel of land that Tucker was unable to secure. It belongs to the Narragansett tribe and is an old burial site. We'd have to build over the graves. But we'd—"

"How much?"

Justine's sculpted brows squeeze together. "Excuse me?"

"How much do we have to bribe the right members of the tribe to make it happen? You did ask Nancy for that number?"

Justine looks only slightly shocked but gets down to it. "Nancy mentioned her checkbook is open—if we need it."

Bambi babe in the woods no more? "Well, well, Justine, is law school teaching how the game is really played?"

She crosses her arms across her chest as her annoyed gaze finds mine. "What the Davenforths want is for the good of *all* of Providence. We can convince the tribe of that. We won't need bribes."

"Keep dreaming, Pollyanna, everything has a price. And no one knows that better than the people rich enough to pay it."

JUSTINE

The houseplant was a bad investment. Krystle isn't waiting in the firm's lobby, despite promises to be first to the meeting she'd called for 8:00 a.m. sharp. So I'm greeted by a browning ficus that might as well be a metaphor for our firm's recent performance. No one has watered this sad little shrub in quite some time. The temps that occupy the front desk must assume a service takes care of it, and the receptionist who knew better quit last Christmas after Krystle doled out coupons in lieu of holiday bonuses. *Fifty percent off custom suits at Luca Gallo's fine menswear. Tell them Krissy sent ya!*

    I remind myself to pour a glass of Providence's finest into the planter after our crisis conference. On the cab ride Krystle and I split last night, she'd phoned Camille and Meredith with her shoe-sized mobile and demanded we regroup to work out how to turn recent lemons into limoncello. I hear Camille's voice as I round the welcome desk. The Southern accent that becomes more pronounced whenever she's excited or upset, or both, echoes through the firm's main floor, calling me to the corner office that once belonged to her husband. She's not actually beckoning me personally so much as speaking at a normal volume to someone else.

"Oh, she's totally the type to bite the hand that feeds her. But so am I."

A blurred figure moves behind a frosted glass window. Long dark hair announces that it's Meredith before I hear her. "What choice do you have? Sit back while the cops take their sweet time?"

The fact that I can listen in on their conversation from down the hall speaks volumes. Silence in a law firm, even on a Saturday, is a death knell. As my late husband often said, "Courts might be closed on weekends, but cases stay open." At a healthy firm, associates are in at all hours—phoning clients, penning briefs, and praying the named partners take note of their hustle.

"Far as I'm concerned, she's paying us to clear all our names."

I enter as Camille finishes saying her piece. She slumps into her late husband's Eames chair, stretching out her legs, each long limb ensconced in a white pant leg leading to a sleeveless top. She rests her hands—in white lace fingerless gloves—delicately on the chair arms. June in New England is like the starting whistle to showing skin, and hers is scrubbed clean, which is a surprise. A sexy red lip and smoky eye is Camille's signature. The few hours in jail have transformed her into a born-again virgin.

"Who's paying?"

My question isn't exactly a greeting, but I know Camille and Meredith appreciate me jumping right in. After everything we've been through together, pleasantries aren't required.

Meredith acknowledges me with a weak smile before responding. "Tara Jordan."

It takes a moment to process the name since I can't wrap my head around why we'd accept a dime from the late mayor's wife—the woman our most important client believes murdered her ex-husband.

Krystle did *not* mention any of these details in the cab. It was all Nancy, Nancy, Nancy and how we need to keep sweet-talking her.

Camille must register my confusion because she starts explaining: "At the police station, Tara offered stacks of cash for me to investigate who had reason to want the mayor dead. Apparently, he made some enemies trying to bring a casino to Providence. He was partnering with some big shot in Atlantic City who I'll be interrogating ASAP."

I snort. "She's using you to come up with alternative suspects for when she's slapped with murder charges."

Meredith's exposed shoulders rise in her belted black dress with neon-striped leggings underneath. "I don't think she had anything to do with the mayor's death. If Tara were going to murder her husband, she'd be way smarter about it. She certainly wouldn't hire someone who'd leave a trail straight to her."

Camille leans back in her chair as if Meredith has settled something. "The woman wouldn't pay me to dig into things if she knew I'd only turn up more evidence against her."

Despite myself, I tilt my head as if Camille just grew two of them. That jail must have stunk so bad that it overwhelmed her bloodhound sense for bullcrap. "The money is clearly a bribe, Camille. She wants to keep us quiet about her hiring you to catch her husband cheating. She knows it will send the police right to her door."

My condescension isn't lost on Camille. She stands to stare down her nose at me. Camille's got an inch on me in flats, and she'd never wear flats. "You don't think I considered that? I had a *long* night in there. Hours and hours."

Meredith's pupils roll back into her head, but Camille's too focused on me to catch it. "I'm the last person on God's green earth who wants to work with Tara Jordan again. But talking to her convinced me. You don't lead a trading desk by making obvious moves. She wouldn't have hired me and then poisoned him. She knows how that would look."

I turn to Meredith, assuming the eye roll means she must have some serious doubts about the mayor's new widow. "It looks like motive and opportunity. Motive: she wanted a divorce, and Mayor Tom wasn't making it easy. Opportunity: she knew he'd be at your club and that Camille would be sashaying in with spiked bubbly."

Meredith rubs her temple. "Camille didn't give her details about the sting. And even if Tara guessed she'd pick the club, I wasn't giving out the champagne room's schedule."

Camille crosses her arms over her chest. I realize she's undone the top buttons. Figures it would take more than a few hours behind bars to turn Camille into a conservative dresser. "Tara explained everything. She wanted dirt on the mayor for future leverage. She didn't want him dead."

Frustration makes me raise my hands to heaven. "You know that because…what? She said so? Tara Jordan's a liar. We're talking about a woman who snuck around with the mayor while he was married—to a woman, I might add, who is the scion of one of Rhode Island's most prominent families and *our client*."

Camille's eyes narrow at me. "People can't help who they fall in love with. An affair doesn't make you an awful person."

I suddenly understand why Camille is fighting so hard to investigate on Tara's behalf and, possibly, save the woman's reputation. Having been the other woman in my marriage, Camille sympathizes with the home-wrecking second wife.

The back of my neck grows hot beneath my helmet of curls. Camille is my friend and business partner—now—but our current relationship doesn't completely numb the sting of what she once was to me. "Tara can't be blindly trusted. Lying is like anything else. With practice, it comes easily."

Camille's face flushes. Before she can respond, Meredith takes a step closer. Her new position isn't quite in between Camille and me, but it's close enough that she can insert herself if either one of us tries to throw a backhand. It wouldn't be the first time. "Everyone lies about sex, Justine." Meredith shrugs again, working out that shoulder. "It doesn't make you a murderer. And you don't realize how much money we're talking about."

I fold my arms over my own breasts, imitating Camille. "It doesn't matter how much. After everything that happened, we agreed the firm was done representing criminals. It's too dangerous. It's not what we want to be, right?"

Camille and Meredith exchange a look that I can't fully decipher. If I had to venture a guess, they're debating who should deliver the bad news. Morals are easy to maintain with money. Adhering to ideals is far more difficult when fighting for dollars.

Footsteps sound down the hall, fast as a Clydesdale. No doubt Krystle is racing to get to the meeting she called and is now late for. I turn toward the door, a smile creeping onto my face. Surely Krystle will settle this in my favor. She knows the Davenforth business will shore up both the firm's finances and our overall standing. Krystle's well aware that reputation is everything. Since taking over her late husband's controlling interest, she's been working hard to ditch her "mobbed-up broad from the Hill" image.

The sight of Krystle slaps the smirk off my face. She's grinning like she's won the lottery, and she's brought champagne. She skips in on white kitten heels, dressed like she's about to hightail it to Miami, a bottle of bubbly in one hand and a box from LaSalle Bakery in the other.

"Who wants cannoli!" Krystle sets the pastries on the table and then peels back the lid, revealing enough ricotta and cream to ice a cake. Instead of launching into "Happy Birthday," however, she turns into 1930s Ginger Rogers and starts crooning the *Gold Diggers'* anthem, tweaking the chorus to match our situation. "We got some money. We got some money."

Krystle dances over to plant a kiss on Camille's scrubbed-clean cheek and then playfully slaps Meredith's thigh. Something about my expression keeps her from doing the same to me. She trails off on the line "We got enough of what it takes…"

"We have to give it back, Krystle."

Krystle's red curls shake, a volcano shooting off flames. "Like hell."

I sit on the edge of the desk, coming down to Krystle's level. "You asked me to get Nancy on board. She's giving us a chance to work on her big redevelopment project, which will bring a ton of business to the city and new clients for us."

Krystle pats my shoulder. "Sweetie, both these trains can run on different tracks. You focus on Nancy."

I eye Krystle, wondering if she drank a bottle before she got here. "We're talking years of work for the firm, Krystle. Nancy intends to turn Providence into the Paris of the Northeast. She—"

Meredith's laughing interrupts my explanation. "Did you just call Providence Paris?"

"It's Nancy's vision," I explain. "One that will bring good jobs to this community."

"Someone drank the Kool-Aid," Camille murmurs.

I shoot her a look but return to Krystle. "Do you seriously think Nancy will let us be her lawyers in this huge deal if we're representing the murderer of her son's father?"

The mirth leaves Krystle's eyes. "First of all, *alleged*, sweetie. You want to be a lawyer, you better learn that word. Second of all, we're not *representing* Tara, per se. Camille's investigative services have been retained."

I stand. If Krystle wants to talk down to me, she can do it while looking up. "Nancy Davenforth doesn't mince words."

"Nancy doesn't need to hear anything about it," Krystle snaps.

I gesture to all of my co-owners. "You're being shortsighted. In a year, Tara will probably be in prison. Don't we have enough of those clients?"

It's a low blow since I know Krystle's boyfriend, Sal—our last mobbed-up client—is serving a five-year sentence. But, as far as I'm concerned, she hit me there first with the belittling comment about what I still needed to learn. Krystle might consider herself an honorary lawyer who started this firm, but being married to an attorney and putting another through school isn't the same as pulling all-nighters in the Harvard law library memorizing Supreme Court precedents. At the end of the day, only one of us will be able to stand up in court.

Krystle sneers at me. "We can't afford to turn our nose up at anyone, Justine. Tara's money is just as green as blue-blood Nancy's. But don't worry. You don't have to deal with her. Camille and Meredith will be Tara's Cagney and Lacey. They'll get some answers before the autopsy report starts pointing fingers—"

Meredith holds up a hand like a stop sign. "I have to get back to my club. No dancing, no dollars. Some of these girls have families to support. They all have rent. I'm the boss. I can't leave them after something like this."

Krystle nods, sympathizing with her fellow business owner. "Fine. Camille can handle Tara, while Justine and I work to keep the Davenforths with the firm."

"But—"

The pop of a champagne cork silences me. Meredith has opened Krystle's bubbly, effectively ending the argument.

"Sounds fair to me." She drinks directly from the bottle, as Krystle hasn't brought flutes, and then passes it to her partner in crime.

Camille shrugs. "Back in the saddle—as long as it's French."

After sipping, she holds the bottle out to me. It's a peace offering, but not one I'm willing to accept. "I have to get back to my kid." I turn to Krystle. "The Narragansett tribe's attorney is expecting us at one Nancy said."

Krystle steals the champagne from Camille and takes a swig. "Piece of cake. Nancy authorized us to throw more money at that problem."

I want to scream, but instead I lower my voice. "It might not be about money. We have to convince them that Nancy's plan really is best for the tribe. And it is."

Krystle winks at me as she sets down the bottle. "Honey, like I told you before, it's always about money."

CAMILLE

Atlantic City is the very last place I want to be. Gambling mecca of the East Coast, a flashy town built on the delusion that coughing up yet another dollar you don't have will end in a one-in-a-million jackpot. That of all the people on the planet, *you'll* be the lucky one to land that elusive win, a grand-prize payout that'll swoop in and solve all your money problems. Like that vile Tara said, there are easier ways to get more money. Ones with far better odds too.

I catch sight of an empty spot at the far end of the boardwalk and gun the engine, swinging my Spyder in fast enough to squeal the bald tires. I don't plan on being here long, but still. The casino valets and parking decks cost the moon, and with Tara's money going into what feels like a bottomless hole at the law firm, I'm running a little short on cash.

The Silver Slipper Hotel & Casino is a vast complex of flashing signs and gaudy buildings jutting up from a broad slice of boardwalk, pressed between the Playboy Casino and an active construction site with two giant bobbing cranes. They're not the only ones here, not by a long shot, so many they've become part of the skyline. Atlantic City is booming, and it's nowhere near done.

Inside, the casino is a madhouse, a jumble of noise and lights and people dropping quarter after quarter into slot machines like a bunch of demented robots. I move through them quickly, heading toward a quieter room filled with betting tables, blackjack and dice and roulette. The stakes are bigger here, judging by the suits and flashy pinky rings, but the really big spenders are hidden in a back room somewhere. I wander through the crowd, watching them sip cocktails and toss fifty-dollar chips across the felt like it isn't two o'clock on a Thursday afternoon.

I stop a harried waitress in tiny shorts and a tuxedo jacket on her trek across the floor.

She looks me up and down. "Can I get you something to drink?"

"No, thanks. But you can tell me where to find Mr. Santoro."

I've got her attention now. Mr. Santoro is her boss, the owner of this place, and she gives me another begrudging once-over. My sky-high heels and gold lamé leopard-print suit are not typical casino attire, I know, but this isn't just any typical meeting.

"Does Mr. Santoro know you're coming?"

I match her snarky tone with one of my own. "Yes, sugar. He knows."

"Then follow me."

The waitress leads me deeper into the building, past the

sweating blackjack gamblers and the girls blowing on dice at the craps table and stopping finally at a row of bouncers. Big men in matching dark suits, standing shoulder to shoulder in front of a bank of elevators. I don't miss the weapons at their hips or the buds in each of their ears, and I revise my earlier assessment.

These are not bouncers. They're bodyguards.

The waitress stops before the middle one, hooks a thumb my way. "This lady…"

"Camille Tavani." I look him in the eye, sweetening the introduction with a smile. "I have a meeting with—"

The bodyguard nods. "Mr. Santoro is expecting you."

He steps aside to let me in the waiting elevator, then punches a button for the top floor and backs out. The doors slide closed, and I'm alone.

No, not alone. I clock three cameras, two in the corners of the ceiling and another by the buttons on the wall, and those are just the ones I can see. A lot of security for a casino boss, which means whoever those suckers downstairs are making rich, it sure as shit isn't themselves.

At the top floor, the doors ding open, and I step into a giant space of gleaming marble and glass and sparkling Atlantic views. I take it all in, but there's so much gilded and polished and tufted and frosted that I barely know where to look. It's a living room, I think, but one that looks like it belongs in a five-star hotel lobby, with a dozen shag rugs and deep velvet couches arranged around low tables topped with flower arrangements. I'm staring at a giant palm tree, its fronds high enough to hug the twenty-foot ceiling, when a man's voice comes from the opposite side of the room.

"Ms. Tavani, welcome."

I find him in a leather armchair by the window, his face hidden behind this morning's *Providence Journal*.

He lowers one corner of the newspaper, and his eyes land on mine. "You wouldn't believe what this rag has to say about you."

I cringe, because I read that article, and it wasn't exactly flattering. Even worse, if I don't find some other potential suspects to take off the heat of the spotlight, that damn article will be the last thing people remember of me. "Don't believe everything you read, Mr. Santoro. I have a college degree, I have never in my life even thought about working as an escort, and I definitely didn't poison anybody's champagne." I move closer, crossing a rug as thick as Mississippi mud.

"Please. Call me Marco." He drops the paper onto a side table, pushes to standing, and extends a hand. His skin is warm and firm and one hundred percent male. The rest of him too. The chiseled jaw and the towering height and the way he smells like leather and spice, the dark hair slicked back off a wide forehead, the broad shoulders under a perfectly tailored pinstripe suit. The ringless fingers and inviting smile. The lips that are just the right amount of soft and scratchy when he presses them to the back of my hand.

"*Molto piacere*, Ms. Tavani. You are as enchanting in person as everyone says."

He smiles and straightens, and I stand there and wait for it to hit—that tingly feeling low in my belly, the ticklish little tug for this man. He's the kind of handsome that normally makes my knees go wobbly, the kind of man who sucks up all the air in the room, which makes him exactly my type. I brace for it, but nothing happens.

I frown and snatch back my hand. "Everyone but the *Providence Journal*. And it's Camille."

Marco's expression turns solemn. "I know this is terribly overdue, but I want you to know how very sorry I was to hear about Peter. He and I always talked about doing a deal together one day. He sure loved the tables."

He loved them, but only when he had plenty of money to throw around. That's how I knew when things got tight, because so did his hold on his cash. "Thank you. And please accept my condolences, as well. I know you and the mayor go way back."

It was actually Tara who told me this when she pointed me in Marco's direction, but it took calls from a couple of names in my late husband's Rolodex to get this meeting. Marco and the mayor went to the same college, pledged the same class in a fraternity, and were groomsmen in each other's first weddings. Rumor is their friendship imploded soon after—something about a business partnership that went south. Guess they patched things up.

At the mention of the mayor, Marco's brow crinkles. "Yes, Tom's death was a real shock. A tragedy, and not just for the people who loved him. I spoke with his son, Harrison, last night, and he was absolutely gutted."

I can imagine. "And his wife? Did you talk to her?"

"Which one?"

I shrug. "Either. Both."

"Nancy said all the right things. She expressed shock, swore she'd use every tool in her considerable arsenal to make sure the police get to the bottom of Tom's death, but mostly she seemed worried about Harrison losing his father in such an awful way. Say what you will about that woman's ability to hold on to a husband, but she's always been a hands-on mom. And Tara…" He lifts his hands, shrugs. "Between you and me, I've never understood those two. Put your mistress up in a condo, sure. Buy her jewelry and cars and take her on trips to exotic locations. But for God's sake, don't marry the woman."

Even now, more than a year after my affair with Justine's husband, Marco's words are like a crawdad claw pinching down on my heart. Not that I'm still in love with Jack—not even a little bit. But once upon a time, I was *that* woman too, the one sitting at home while her lover played house with his wife and child, dreaming of the day he would come clean and trade them in for me. Which made me just as much of a sucker as all those people downstairs, didn't it? The ones betting endless rolls of quarters and chips on a jackpot that'll never happen. All of us, chasing some kind of fantasy.

"It's not like he was trying to avoid having some bastard kid running around," Marco continues, tugging me out of the depressing thought. "He had an heir. And as I understand it, having Harrison was some kind of a miracle."

"Miracle how?"

"Twenty years married to Nancy. One kid. People always blame the wife, but Tom never said anything about getting a side piece pregnant. And that was the kind of thing he'd have bragged to me about. Like Nancy, he saw his kids as a legacy. Anyway, what can I get you to drink?"

I give him a practiced smile. "I'll have whatever you're having. Thanks, sugar."

He gestures for me to follow him to a fully stocked bar on the left side of the room, a masterpiece of curved and polished wood lined with a dozen plush barstools. He helps me onto one, his gaze lingering on my legs when I cross them and settle in. He catches me watching, and he doesn't bother hiding his wolfish expression. Honestly, it's no wonder this guy was friends with the mayor.

"Extra dirty martini, coming up." He moves to the other side of the bar, where he pulls a metal shaker from the freezer, spinning it around a finger like a professional. "I hope I didn't give you the wrong impression of Tara. She and Tom were no longer in the honeymoon stage, but she's too smart of a businesswoman to poison him in public. She's already been ripped apart by the press for stealing Tom from a Davenforth. She's not looking for another scandal."

"But a mayor of any city will have plenty of enemies, people he's stepped on during his climb to the top. You've known Tom for so long, you must know who those people could be."

"True, but the letters I saw all had to do with the casino. They—"

I stop him with a palm to the bar. "Hang on, sugar. What letters?"

"Tom was receiving death threats. Lots of them. All

anonymous, of course, but almost every single one of them referred to the casino."

My ears perk at the last word. Bingo—now we're getting somewhere. I frown, feigning ignorance. "But Providence doesn't have a casino."

He fills the shaker as he talks. Vodka. Vermouth. Brine from a jar of fat olives.

"Not yet, it doesn't. But Tom saw what's happening here in Atlantic City. He saw how in less than a decade this town has been completely transformed, how the casinos bring in more than just gamblers. They bring in boxing matches and concerts and pageants. Did you know revenue here is about to surpass the Las Vegas Strip? Think what that could do for a city like Providence. Massachusetts has legal betting. Connecticut has legal betting. Why not Rhode Island?"

"And let me guess. Mayor Tom was lobbying to change the regulations."

"Yes, but only for the traditional casinos like mine, ones built on United States soil. Nothing against the Indians, but we only need their remaining parcel of land for our building, not the tribal status to get around the U.S. gambling laws. I know some states are doing it that way, but we don't want to cut the tribes into this deal. Tom said he had an in with the Narragansett attorney. He said getting their burial ground signed over to us free and clear was almost a done deal."

I raise my eyebrows. "Almost? Doesn't that only work for horseshoes and hand grenades?"

He grins as he jams the top on the container and shakes it

above a shoulder, and the ice makes an ungodly racket—fine by me, as it gives me time to process his words.

So Mayor Tom was lobbying to change state gambling regulations, but only for people like himself and Marco: White. Moneyed. A move like that wouldn't make just one enemy. It would make a whole tribe of them.

"Did you tell the police about the threats?" I ask as Marco pours two chilled martini glasses to the brim.

"Of course. I also told the cops to look into that tract of land downtown. There's a lot of money riding on it, even more if it becomes the site of the state's first casino. I told them if they were smart, they'd start there."

"Still. That's some favor, clearing the way for a casino in Providence. Mayor Tom must have been a really good friend to help you out like that."

"If that's what you think, then you didn't know Tom at all. I hate to speak ill of the dead, but he wasn't the kind of person to do anyone a favor unless it included himself. He'd scratch my back, but only if I scratched his first."

"In other words, for a stake in Rhode Island's first casino."

He drops in a toothpick stacked with olives and slides a glass my way. "Bingo."

We clink glasses, and I take a sip that lights me up from inside. I wish I'd eaten more than just a handful of carrots for lunch. The booze will hit me hard on an empty stomach, and I need to keep my wits about me. I settle the glass back onto the bar and nibble on an olive instead.

"These letters the mayor was receiving," I say, swirling the toothpick through cloudy liquid. "The threats. Were they for or against the casino?"

He frowns, thinking. "Both, as I recall, though the really colorful ones were spewing death and destruction if a casino came to town. They called him all sorts of names. Most I can't say in the presence of a lady, and some I even had to look up. 'Recreant prick,' who says that? I learned recreant means—"

"Cowardly."

Marco points a long finger over the bar. "Exactly. Which Mayor Tom wasn't. If his death proves anything, it's that he was the opposite. He brushed the threats off as the price of doing business, but he was too cocky. He should have been paying better attention." He shakes his head, as if shaking it off. "Anyway, I'd sure like to talk about something a little more pleasant."

"Such as?"

Marco puts down his drink—which as far as I can tell is for looks only. So far he hasn't taken the first sip. "Such as where I should take you for dinner. Or I could have the chef come upstairs if you'd like a little more privacy."

In case I had any doubts as to his meaning, his gaze dips to my cleavage and lingers.

Here it comes, I think. The swell of attraction for this man, one with looks and power and a palace high on the Atlantic City strip, funded by a casino taking in more money than one person could ever spend in a lifetime. I wait for it, but…nothing. Not even a tumbleweed.

Suddenly the only thing I can think about is hightailing it back to Providence. To report back to Krystle and Meredith and Justine. To tell them about the casino, the threats, Mayor Tom versus the Indians—no doubt the same tribe Justine and Krystle had talked about meeting. This information Marco just fed me feels important, like it could clear my name. If nothing else, I guess I like him a little better for that.

"Sorry, sugar, I'm going to have to take a rain check." I slide off the stool and take off for the elevator, my high heels clicking on the marble. "You've been a doll. Thanks for the drink. We'll set something up soon, but for now, I've gotta run."

A whole tribe of suspects. Surely one of them can take some of the heat off me.

MEREDITH

Despite my strong stance against the Davenforths' pretentious city development plan, even I can admit my club looks a little seedy in the harsh light of day. Good thing our customers only come out after dark.

As I pull into the owner's space in the empty parking lot, the summer sun shows off every strip of peeling paint I've been meaning to have fixed on the club's facade. I had a new sign installed when I changed the club's name—a sexy female silhouette posing in a pink neon crescent moon—but even that looks sad in the daytime. Like Las Vegas with the lights out.

Or an exhausted woman without her face on, which is exactly what I am at the moment. I bought the largest black coffee they could legally sell me in the Dunkin' drive-through, and it's barely making a dent. I'm still ready to drop, only now I'm boiling hot too, the coffee joining forces with this weirdly hot June weather to make me sweat through my clothes the second I lock my Buick behind me and step onto the sunbaked blacktop.

I desperately need a shower and a nap, and I wouldn't say no to both at the same time. But I've got business to take care of. The club's already lost one entire night of income. I've got enough money squirreled away to last me a rainy day or two, but most of my dancers don't, and even the most regular of our regulars won't stay loyal for long. I need to get the cash flowing again as soon as possible, or there won't be a club left for the Davenforths to close down.

Every newsstand in the city is already screaming with tawdry headlines about Camille: "Widow Turns Widowmaker," "Strip Club Siren Strikes Down Providence's Favorite Son," "Camille the Cold-Hearted Champagne Killer." At least they don't have a sultry mug shot to print yet, though even in the blurry candids captured outside the police station, Camille can't help looking like a leggy blond femme fatale. Sex sells, and so does tragedy.

Right now it's mostly sleazy tabloid speculation. But as soon as the autopsy confirms the awful truth, there's no telling what will happen. We're in those terrible few seconds before the crash—tires squealing, everyone holding their breath to see who makes it out alive.

Women like Camille and me, we look guilty no matter what we do, and I know it's going to be up to us to clear our own names, with the cops *and* in the court of public opinion. So first things first: I'm going to go into my office, make a list of absolutely everyone who was working last night, and then start questioning them one by one until I get answers. Time to make like Tara Jordan and remind them that I'm the boss, not their friend, and I'm not going to stop until I—

"Meredith?"

I startle, sloshing some hot coffee onto my hand. But it's only Destiny. She's standing by the staff entrance, smoking.

"Shit." I lick the coffee off my knuckles; getting through today is gonna require every last drop. "You scared me."

Destiny might look even more exhausted than I do. Her big brown eyes are bloodshot, and her teased bangs have wilted. She's dressed way down too, in cutoff jean shorts and a Yale University T-shirt she must have stolen from her on-again, off-again asshole boyfriend.

"You're here early," I say. "Everything okay?"

She's probably fighting with the boyfriend again. I don't know the guy—though I assume they met at the club—but from the dressing room girl talk I've overheard, he sounds like a real piece of work. Not to mention a total cliché: yet another entitled Ivy League jerk who gets off on slumming it with a stripper. On her days off, he plies her with extravagant gifts and five-star dinners and sunset cruises on the harbor, and then gets mad when it's time for her to go back to work. If I had a dollar for every dude who got his boxers in a twist over his girlfriend getting naked in front of other men for a living, I could take a real nice early retirement.

That's the main reason why, even though I am (unfortunately) attracted to men, I rarely date them. They can be so sensitive. And the more they insist they'll take care of you, the more you need to look out for your own damn self.

I'm gearing up to give Destiny my classic big-sister,

he's-not-worth-it speech, when she asks, "Is it true, about the mayor? Was he really...*murdered*?"

Destiny whispers the word even though the only other living soul in sight is a homeless man sleeping with his scruffy dog in front of the shuttered corner store.

"Looks that way," I say.

Grinding her cigarette butt into the blacktop with the toe of her Keds, she pulls a pack of Virginia Slims from her purse to light another, but her hands are shaking so hard she can't get her Zippo to spark. I take pity and flick the lighter on for her. She inhales, shoulders dropping as the nicotine hits. I give serious thought to asking to bum a smoke, even though I quit years ago.

"The police are investigating," I tell her. "So I'm sure they'll—"

"You saw him?" She takes another nervous drag. "You saw... the body?"

I nod. She seems really spooked. So am I, but I can't show it. I'm the boss, and a big part of being the boss is staying calm under pressure, whether said pressure comes from concerned employees or unruly customers or actual still-warm corpses.

"Listen, if you need a few days off, I'm sure—"

"No!" Destiny's eyes widen to cartoon-princess proportions. "I can't afford any time off, I really need the money."

She's been bringing in big stacks of cash lately—but spending it just as fast, if the Gucci bag on her arm is any indication. Unless it was a gift from her guy. I could tell her to go to him for the money, but I don't want to make her more dependent on him. I've seen where that leads.

"If you want to stick to the stage and the floor for a little while, that's fine. The other girls can handle the VIP customers."

"Really? Thank you, Meredith; you're the best!"

Her more seasoned coworkers will probably be all too happy not to have to compete with the new girl for private dances. Unless everyone has decided the champagne room poses an unacceptable risk until the mayor's murder case is closed. I don't even want to think about how much money I'll lose then.

"Of course," I say. "But Destiny—I promise—no one's going to hurt you. I know what happened last night was scary, but it was clearly targeted at Mayor Tom."

There she goes again, shaking like it's twenty below out here instead of pushing a hundred. Her cigarette's burning down to her press-ons. I bet she skipped breakfast again, even though I'm always telling her—and the other girls—stripping is cardio, so you've *got* to eat before your shift.

"Hey." I squeeze her arm. "Everything's going to be okay, I promise. Why don't we go inside? I've got Hot Pockets and a couple of Capri-Suns in my office."

My master key turns like normal, but the door won't open. I rattle it a few times—maybe the sweltering heat is messing with the lock?—then yank with all my strength. It's like something's clamped on it, keeping it closed from the inside.

Another car pulls up right behind us. Misty, one of the club's longest-running dancers, pokes her Aqua Netted head out of the driver's side door. "Hey, Meredith!"

"One sec! My key's not working," I call back to her.

"Did you go around front yet?"

I shake my head. I'd come through the alley in the back, like always.

Misty bites her glossy lower lip. "You should go around front."

Cursing a blue streak under my breath, I hurry around the building. A cluster of the other dancers scheduled to work tonight—Luxe, Anita, Debbie, Tawnya—are gathered around the door. As soon as they see me, they explode with questions.

"What's going on, Meredith?"

"Did you know about this?"

"This is 'cause of the mayor, isn't it?"

"What are we gonna do?"

It's not until I get closer that I see the chain on the door—a huge, heavy one with a padlock. And a notice stuck above it, declaring in big bold letters that the Luna Lounge is closed until further notice, pending a police investigation.

Destiny catches up right as I rip the notice down.

"Can they do that?" she asks.

I crumple the paper in my fist. "They can do whatever they want."

KRYSTLE

"Is this mud or poo-poo?" Justine asks as she drops against my Chrysler LeBaron and shows me the bottom of her preppy dress shoe. She's got a whole Rodeo Drive thing going on with the big hat and white dress with big black buttons. "It's poo-poo, isn't it?" she whines.

On cue, a dog barks in the distance. "That's probably your answer." I start to give her shit for saying *poo-poo*, but it's probably a mom-with-a-young-kid thing. "Now suck it up so we can get this over with. South County gives me the creeps."

The wind rustles the pine trees surrounding this cabin on a pond. I've heard of people in Providence getting second houses out this way, but all I can think of is Michael Myers in a mask popping out of the bushes with a chainsaw.

The breeze catches a small sign swaying on the porch: **AIDEN WYATT, ATTORNEY-AT-LAW.** While this location may be bad for Justine's outfit, it's good for our objective.

This Aiden guy is working out of his house. Talk about shooting fish in a barrel. It reminds me of when my late husband, Romeo, put his first shingle up in a triple decker on the Hill. We lived on the third floor, his office was on the second, and we rented both from a barber with his shop on the first floor. I remember when our very first client came in, and I was off to make coffee in our apartment for him. I stared out the window facing downtown Providence and could see One Turks Head Place—that U-shaped office building where big law firms rented whole floors. The place where we now have our offices.

Even on day one, I knew I wanted our law firm to make it big enough to move there. To a real office. To have the downtown view and long, fancy lunches with cloth napkins.

If someone had walked in and offered Romeo and me the kind of money Nancy can pony up, we'd have said "how high" to any offer that meant we could jump outta the Hill and onto Easy Street.

I let out a long angry breath at the thought that even in Turks Head, we're nowhere near Easy Street. Some days it feels like all that work only means working on a different side of the highway, farther from the good cannolis and with much higher rent. More money, more problems, as they say. Still, what does this guy know? It looks like he's practicing law out of his bathroom.

"Okay, I think I got most of it off." Justine is a little flushed as she adjusts her wide hat, which is crooked because she's been scraping her shoe on a big rock.

An insect buzzes past me, and I nearly jump out of my girdle. I try to navigate the mud and rocks and hurry toward the porch before these bees or whatever try to feed me to their queen. Not that I'm that sweet.

"Wait for me, Krystle!"

I don't. I hurry up the porch steps as something else buzzes near my ear and disappears. "Oh god, is it in my hair?"

Justine joins me on the porch, wide-eyed. "What are you doing?"

I shake my head and jump up and down while screeching. I swear to god I feel something crawling on my scalp. "Do you see anything in my hair?"

"No! Hold still!" Justine shakes my hair roughly.

The door to the house opens slightly as I let out another scream. Then it abruptly shuts.

"We saw you!" I yell at the flash of a tall guy who retreated from our crisis.

Justine keeps shaking my hair, then yelps, "Ouch! Shoot!"

I flip my hair back over so I can see, and she's rubbing her finger. "I got stung!"

"There it is!" I yell as that wasp comes back for more. I snatch the hat off Justine's head and attack. "Come here, you Waspy Wahoo!"

"Easy on the hat, Krystle!"

"I'm saving our lives here!" I smack the wasp, who comes right back at me. "Got him!"

Justine snatches her hat back in a dramatic huff. She gets it centered on her somehow still-perfect hair and knocks on the door. "Excuse me. Hello! Mr. Wyatt? It's Justine Kelly from Romero,

Tavani, Kelly, and Romero. We're representing the Davenforth redevelopment. Nancy said you were expecting us."

She sucks on her fingertip as we wait for a response. The digit is double the size of its neighbors.

"Oh, screw this." Justine bangs on the door like a cop. "Mr. Wyatt? I need some ice. An insect stung me in your yard, and I believe we're supposed to be meeting. Hello?"

It's silent inside as if the guy thinks we didn't see him open the door the first time while we were screaming on his porch. "Should we knock on the back door? Or windows?" I call loudly as a threat.

The door slowly opens, and there's a real tall guy looking down at us. He's got a collared shirt with a turquoise-and-silver bolo tie like cowboys wear. Or Indians, I guess, since he's the Narragansett tribal lawyer.

He clears his throat. "I assumed you'd realize there's no meeting and leave."

"Well, you know what they say about when you assume. *Ass*"—I pause to point at him—"You." Then back my way. "Me."

Justine sighs beside me. "Mr. Wyatt, we're from Romero, Tavani, Kelly, and Romero. We need to speak with you for only a few moments. But first, do you have some ice?"

He sighs and a few strands of dark hair slide into his eyes. He runs his fingers through them, and he's actually got a sun-kissed surfer vibe going—not that I know any surfers—but his skin is olive and his black hair is longish, but not braided, which I'd pictured based on the TV ad of the crying Indian wanting us to "Keep

America beautiful." Which I am all for, by the way. I love Smokey Bear and all that tree-hugging hippy shit.

"You're stung?" he asks, and holds out his hand. "May I see?"

Justine does as she's told, and I lean in for a look myself. The side of her bare wedding-ring finger is red and swelling by the second.

She glances at me. "It's getting worse."

I know she's nervous about being sick since she's her young son's only parent. Even little colds set off her anxiety. "We can get you to a doctor and come back," I say, trying to keep my voice neutral. I don't want to screw up this meeting, but I also don't want to be responsible for putting Justine in more danger. She could be allergic. It's not like she's the outdoorsy type who'd know.

"Let's get the swelling down." With that, Aiden leaves us standing on the porch. He retraces her steps until he comes to where she stepped in the big ol' pile of doo-doo.

"You crushed a yellow jacket's nest," he says as if we give a rat's ass.

"It's really throbbing," Justine whispers as we watch him bend down and pick up a handful of mud.

He heads back toward us, and I worry he's going to just launch it our way for trespassing or destroying wasp property. Instead, he passes us and goes inside.

We wait a beat in confused silence and then there's water running. The rattle of a dish. A drawer closes with a sigh. He returns with a towel over his shoulder, two small bowls, and a few sprigs of green.

"Sit down, please," he says to Justine, and I help her over to a rocking chair. He takes the stool next to it. "You can go straight to ice, but I think plantain and mud is more effective with swelling."

"Mud?" She goes wide-eyed to where she'd scraped her shoe earlier. "From?"

"The…earth?" His scowl deepens, and I realize that he's only been frowning at us to varying degrees this entire time. Friendly Native, indeed.

"But there's animal excrement. And bacteria."

"I was careful." Aiden continues to stand there as he waits for her to decide.

I put a hand on her shoulder for support. "Try the mud, Justine. Pretend we're at a spa and it's a mask, and you're paying someone for the privilege." I laugh, and no one joins me.

She wrinkles her nose, but nods nobly, as if she's Joan of Arc off to the bonfire.

There's a hint of a smile in Aiden's eyes as he first applies a wet swipe of the plant, then smears the mud onto her finger. He wraps it lightly with a bandage. "When you get home, just wash it well and apply ice. Most of the swelling should be gone by then. If not, you may want to see a doctor."

Justine nods once. "Thank you."

"If you need the name of an insect guy, I know the best one. He doesn't travel out here usually, but if you tell him Krystle sent ya, then—"

"No." Aiden stands and wipes his hands on his towel before flinging it over his shoulder. "I prefer not to drink poison or poison the land if I can help it. Especially to kill something that lived here before me by thousands of years."

I frown at his tone as if he's saying something that's going way over my head. "Look, if you are having business people out here, then consider—"

"Of course," Justine interrupts, giving me a look. "In fact, we are here to speak to you about a project that will preserve much of the land. And share it with others."

Justine has her Good Cop Lollipop shtick going, so I just nod as if she's making perfect sense.

"Should we go into your office?" Justine asks as she stands.

He slides his hands into his pockets. "Not if you're about to pitch me Nancy Davenforth's plan to build an office park and courtyard over the graves of my ancestors."

Justine's mouth makes a perfect O, but then she recovers. "I absolutely respect the dead. But isn't it the memories that matter? My husband passed recently, but I have the memories and the stories I tell about him to our son. He lives on through me."

Aiden opens his mouth, then shuts it. "I am sorry for your loss, Ms. Kelly. But you're missing the point."

Justine's back goes ramrod straight, ready to deliver the sales pitch that she'd needlessly rehearsed the whole drive over, as if this whole negotiation would hinge on anything other than dollars and cents. "Mr. Wyatt, you're talking about a couple of acres of land in a multimillion-dollar development spanning the entire city. The Davenforths' plans will revitalize all of Providence, attracting new business investment and tourism dollars. Think of all the jobs.

With your involvement, we could guarantee members of your tribe get to bid on contracts and create ways to honor the legacy of the Narragansett in public spaces. This could be an opportunity."

As her big speech finishes, there's real disdain in this man's eyes. Maybe some pity too, as if we aren't seeing the big picture. Like he's standing on his rickety porch with his outhouse law office in the bumfuck boonies of South County feeling sorry for us.

"Ms. Kelly, I will tell you the same thing I told Tucker Armand—no."

As he turns to leave us on the porch, I shoot Justine a look that says *I told you so*. She shrugs as if I have permission to do what we should have done from the very beginning. "Look, Aiden, tell me one thing."

He opens the door and pauses but doesn't turn around.

"What's the number?"

"Number?" he says, playing dumb, as if this all wasn't a dog and pony to get to the almighty dollar.

"We have authorization to grease some wheels. Just give us a number, and we can run it up the flagpole. It's payday, baby. The Jeffersons may have been canceled, but you can still move on up to the East Side."

"A number." Aiden turns toward us. "That's easy: 776,960."

"Oh?" I glance at Justine, realizing I never got clarity on how much Nancy approved. But that seems like a lot of dough for a graveyard. "Is there some wiggle room there?"

"Sure." Aiden smiles but there's no warmth. "One point six billion."

I cough and sputter. "Are you nuts?"

"The first number is how much land was stolen from the Narragansett and other tribes in Rhode Island, based on your colonial acre system."

I blink at him, unsure what he means. *Who stole what now?*

"And one point six billion?" Justine asks, holding her bandaged hand.

"That's how many acres were stolen from all Native people in North America."

I almost laugh though I'm seeing red. "Look, I get it that there's some issues here. But does this high-and-mighty attitude extend to whatever the casinos are offering you?"

A vein throbs at his temple as his mouth twitches. I really am excellent at pissing people off. But he deserves it, giving me the whole I'm-above-money speech. Everyone has a price.

Justine shoots me some side-eye before turning her attention back to Aiden. "We're not trying to imply you'd take a bribe but only that you would want the tribe to extract the most value from the land. The tribe deserves compensation. Obviously, the Davenforths can't atone for all of colonialism. But Nancy has a vision that could put tribe members in a better position for the future. One that brings real jobs and careers. Not just cash-grabbing casinos."

"There's ways to honor the past," I interject. "On the Hill, we have this great statue of Christopher Columbus. We have a parade every year that brings money to business and educates kids. It could be a celebration for your people."

Aiden's jaw drops, then there's a flicker of real anger. Is making people mad a superpower? "That's not a good example since Columbus is the reason the land was stolen. Not to mention he viciously murdered women and children."

"Really?" I say, positive he has to be mistaken. I keep myself from reciting the *In 1492 Columbus Sailed the Ocean Blue* school rhyme.

Justine rises from her chair and steps closer to him. "As a minority, I understand your hesitation to trust the government or the rich. But I've worked on land deals that created housing for people. Brought jobs. Cleaned up the earth and kept people from getting sick from pollution. I know progress can get out of hand, but with the right people, it can change lives for good."

"Your experience sounds like an exception, Ms. Kelly, not the rule."

"I'm not naive, Mr. Wyatt. Some powerful people treat land deals like monopoly cards. It's a game to them, and they only care about winning. But if we play it, we can benefit too."

"This is a game?" He looks us both up and down like we're the shit on Justine's shoe.

"Everything is a game, even justice," I huff. "There's winners and losers, and we're trying to get you on the right side of this."

"I don't play games. Not with my ancestors. Not with the land. Not with anything I hold of value. Especially not for the benefit of a privileged lady like Nancy Davenforth, who has a lot to do with those stolen acres."

Justine grimaces. "Nancy is not her ancestors. She would never—"

"You do not need to tell me what the Davenforths would and wouldn't do. In fact, there's nothing you can tell me that will make any difference at all. Ever. The land is ours and will remain that way—a fact recognized by both tribal laws and federal ones. So, as I said to all the others, try anything, and I'll see you in court."

JUSTINE

A midair plane explosion leaves little to bury. Jet fuel burns at over fifteen hundred degrees Fahrenheit. Add that to ignited magnesium exploding from a bomb tucked under a fuselage, and the fire's temperature rises to over three thousand. That's hot enough to melt every metal. To incinerate bone, hair, and gold wedding rings.

As there was nothing of my late husband to inter, he lacks a proper grave. Life is better this way. I've no need to bring my son to a headstone or pretend his father's presence is stronger atop a particular patch of soil. We return to dust, and dust is not sanctified. It's cobwebs and dirt. Air pollution.

Aiden Wyatt thinks human remains are sacred, but he's wrong. Life is what's sacred. And land is for the living.

I tell myself all of this as I approach the Davenforths' double front door, mentally repeating the last part to drown out Aiden Wyatt's arguments about tribal inheritance. Living in a vibrant city with healthy business centers and beautiful public spaces benefits all Providence's people—including its oft-mistreated minority groups, two of which I'm a member of given my Jewish mom and Black father.

The Davenforths' butler opens the door. Again, he's dressed like a Jane Austen character, his dour black suit appropriate for either a dinner or funeral service.

"Justine Kelly? Master Harrison is waiting for you."

The man's statement bristles for a few reasons. First off, I've come to see Nancy, not Harrison. Secondly, *Master*? I get that the honorific is part of the whole European gentry thing to which the Davenforths so clearly aspire. On American soil, however, *Master* has a very different connotation.

"Nancy should be expecting me."

The butler points over my shoulder to a structure behind the garages. "I was told to direct you to Master Harrison. He's in the carriage house."

I consider inquiring about Nancy's whereabouts, but a mental flash of Harrison's face takes the fight out of me. Would it be so bad showing off my big idea to the family's handsome scion?

Not. At. All.

A cobblestone path leads to the indicated barn. I follow it halfway around before the view stops me. An emerald grass sea leads to an endless sapphire expanse. The sun glints atop cresting waves, adding facets to the jeweled view. Not a single sailboat spills into the scene. The horizon remains untouched. Endless. It's as if the Davenforths' domain extends for eternity.

A throat clears to my left. "Hi."

I turn toward the source. The motion coupled with the breeze whips my hair into my face. Through the curly curtain, I see Harrison, dressed in khakis and a bright blue polo that highlights his electric eyes. They're just as blue when he hasn't been crying. God, they look like Jack's.

He extends his hand. "Pleasure seeing you again, Justine."

My name forces his lips into a smile, or maybe it's the sight of me. I can't help but hope for the latter as I tuck my hair behind my ear and place my right hand in his soft palm, thankful that it's not the hand with hives all over it. Though the mud at Aiden's place brought down the swelling from that wasp sting, the vigorous washing that followed reinflamed the area.

"My mother asked me to ascertain how things went with Aiden." Harrison starts down the path. "She expects not well."

I'm not sure whether I should grimace or chuckle. The smirk on Harrison's face invites either response. "Aiden is very passionate about the land remaining vacant."

Harrison sucks air through his teeth. "No amount of money, right?"

I shake my head. "No amount."

"Same old Aiden." Harrison smiles, as if he almost admires the guy for his stubbornness.

"Do you know him well?"

"That parcel is a lynchpin in our development plans. We've been trying to get him to come around for quite some time—to no avail." Harrison stops in front of the carriage house door and extends a hand, again. "Well, at least you tried."

The abrupt goodbye shake makes me feel like a *Price Is Right* contestant shunted back to the cheap seats before getting to play Plinko. Give a girl a chance.

I stand straighter, assuming my full height. "As long as Aiden represents the tribe, he won't *sell* it to you. But there is another way."

Harrison's hand drops to his side. "I'd love to hear it."

A stronger breeze frees the hair pinned behind my ears, driving the whole windblown mess back at me. Harrison brushes away the strands with his fingertips. The warmth of his palm against my cheek sends blood rushing to my head. I'm giddy. How long has it been since I've felt an intimate touch like this?

How much I've missed it.

The wind subsides. Harrison's hand leaves my face to open the carriage house door. "Let's talk inside."

If horses ever lived here, they've long been evicted. Rich wood paneling melts into wide plank floors. Plateglass windows dominate one wall, allowing the sea to seep inside.

We pass through a sitting area with an open staircase. A glance overhead reveals a loftlike second story. I can just make out the bed. Unmade.

Harrison leads me past a dining room and kitchen to what I can only assume is his office. There's an L-shaped desk topped with the latest IBM personal computer. A rolling desk chair is pushed in beside it.

Harrison doesn't offer me a seat, however. Instead, we walk to the next cabin in the carriage house's train-car-style layout. This new space features multiple bookcases and a drafting table tilted to display a large blueprint, which I vaguely recognize as a map of Providence.

Curiosity pulls me toward it. "Are these the plans?"

Harrison grunts behind me. I turn to see him holding a cantilever chair. He sets it beside its match. "Those are them. The designs to turn Providence, Rhode Island, into Paris, France, complete with its own Seine running through it."

He isn't kidding. Lines divide the city map into numbered sections, though these digits don't correspond to Providence's existing fifteen wards. Instead, there are twenty neighborhoods. The French capital has the same number of arrondissements—if I remember correctly. My memories of Paris's fashion shows have faded. But I think the subway map stuck.

Instinctively, I scan the plans for where I live and other places I know. My in-laws' house in College Hill is labeled "five," corresponding with Paris's Latin Quarter, home of the Sorbonne. I expect downtown Providence to be six, as it's next door, but it's stamped with an eight, matching the business district in Paris. Washington Park, where our firm stopped a mall from being erected on the site of a cancer-causing, chemical-laden landfill, is tagged nineteen.

The number twenty marks the burial ground. It's a prime parcel abutting one of the river's picturesque tributaries. I think of Paris's left bank and imagine groomed parks and walkways passing stately office buildings overlooking the water; shops and restaurants on their ground floors to employ the city's struggling.

I glance at Harrison. "It'll be beautiful."

He runs a hand over his thick blond hair and then approaches. "It would be. A grand design masterminded by my mother. She worked on it forever with her architects. How we could leverage our family's holdings to reimagine Providence as the Northeast's own City of Light."

As Harrison stands next to me, I get a whiff of his cologne, a clean, citrusy scent that I immediately recognize as Obsession for Men. The commercial featured a blonde stroking the chiseled lines of a man's face while a narrator talked about forbidden apples. I'm tempted to move closer, to allow my jacket sleeve to brush the bare skin of his extended forearm.

He points to a parcel behind the burial ground. "That one was my father's. Now mine, I suppose. If the Narragansetts would only come on board, we'd be able to combine the parcels to construct a glass-and-steel convention center overlooking the water with a five-thousand seat theater inside. It'd be something to see. A jewel of downtown."

Harrison retreats to the chair he'd brought over, leaving the other for me. He sits and leans back, testing the furniture's ability to balance. "Pushing this Parisian vision through is something of a tryout my dear mother designed especially for me. A chance to demonstrate my worth to the firm."

Harrison's admission casts him in an even more flattering light. He may be wealthier than me in my wildest dreams, but he has as much riding on this project's success as I do. We're both being challenged to prove our value. Harrison must show he's more than the golden boy that his mother trots out for charity photo ops. And I need to earn the Davenforths' business to secure my own inheritance—the partnership interest in my late husband's failing firm.

I take the seat beside him, sitting on the edge with my legs firmly together and my ankles crossed. It's how Nancy sat. A commanding, elegant pose that demands Harrison take seriously the two words I'm about to say: "Eminent domain."

Harrison frowns, unconvinced.

I sit up straighter. "The government can demand the sale of land, at current market price, for projects that benefit the public."

Harrison shakes his head. "We've thought of that—pushing our pals in government to force a sale. But my family's *friendship*, valuable as it may be, isn't worth torpedoing a political future."

The confidence I'd felt moments before fizzles like abandoned champagne. Of course the Davenforths had explored this option. Had I really believed that I—a mere law student—could come up with a strategy unknown to their throngs of qualified real estate attorneys?

Harrison must notice my dejection because he doles out a sympathetic smile. "It would be a good strategy—for someone with a different name. As Aiden no doubt mentioned, the Davenforths have a regrettable history of acquiring land through…questionable means. Aiden is all too eager to resurrect my family's every ancient transgression in the press, painting our whole clan as robber barons. He'd brand our every political ally a perpetrator of genocide. And legislators can't risk their entire minority vote plus the support of every white resident who wants to believe they'd have broken bread at the first Thanksgiving."

A glance at Harrison's alabaster complexion, chiseled jaw, and Ivy League haircut is all it takes to convince me he's right. If privilege had a picture in the dictionary, it would surely be Harrison's yearbook photo. I imagine him sitting across from Aiden on a local news show, struggling to appear empathetic as Aiden recounts the mass murder and forced relocation of Native American tribes. As attractive as I find Harrison, even my own sympathies would naturally lie with the other side.

I move to the plans again and trace my finger along the lines of the new arrondissements. I picture the revitalized waterfront lined with sculpted trees—their tops razored flat like those abutting Parisian sidewalks. I imagine the shops and restaurants packed with tourists drawn by the convention center.

"It's such a shame. The city could use all those jobs and tourism dollars." I look back to Harrison. "If only history weren't so ugly."

Harrison's pitying smile suddenly morphs into another look entirely. He seems to view me with renewed interest, like I'm a painting whose appeal he's finally realized. He reaches toward my curls as if he intends to test one's springiness, and then drops his hand. "You could do it."

"What?"

"You, Justine. I mean, you're so smart and beautiful."

The compliments ring so loudly that I almost don't hear him say the rest. "And with your track record of saving the city's less privileged from health-damaging projects. If you spoke to the city's lawmakers, agreed to go out with them and address the need for a new Providence—talked about the jobs it would bring and the other benefits—"

"Like preventing sediment in the river by shoring up the banks," I chime in.

"Yeah. All that." Harrison takes both my hands in his. "You could convince legislators. You could show them the political benefits of forcing a buyout with taxpayer dollars and then leasing the land to us."

The warmth of Harrison's hands almost makes me miss the part about taxpayers footing the bill—almost. "Well, to really sell it, the Davenforths should reimburse the taxpayers with a donation of some kind. Money for social programs. Additional compensation for the tribe." Harrison releases my hands. The withdrawal feels like punishment for pushing back against his plans.

He taps his finger against his bottom lip. My late husband did the same thing when he was thinking. "We had planned a park and walkways, and my mother is working on some other ways to compromise with Aiden."

I raise my eyebrows. Compromise didn't seem to be in Aiden's vocabulary.

Harrison laughs, reading my thoughts. "Well, if not with him, maybe the other tribal members." He stands and considers my face with a smile. "You're brilliant, Justine. I see why my mother's been so impressed by you. If anyone can convince the powers that be that repurposing the tribe's land is best for the future of the city and all Providence's residents, it's you, Justine Kelly."

I've been through too much to get emotional from a stranger's praise. Yet I feel a burning behind my eyes. A bubbling in my stomach. I'm Sally Field holding her Oscar. *And I can't deny the fact that you like me. Right now, you like me.*

Which is more than I can say for Krystle. There are good reasons not to have Camille working for the woman who might have set her up, yet Krystle thinks I don't understand legal nuance. I tilt my chin slightly to look Harrison in the eye. "Does that mean you're staying with the firm of Romero, Tavani, Kelly, and Romero?"

Harrison chuckles and averts his gaze. Not a yes. But not a no either. "My mother decides such things. I think we'd certainly be interested in paying you to be the face of this argument."

It's not exactly the guarantee I'd hoped for, but I'll take it. I extend my hand. "I'd be honored."

Again, he places his hand in mine. Instead of shaking, however, he simply holds it and looks at me. It seems he's reading all the inappropriate thoughts I've had about him since the moment we met. The ones about his eyes, the set of his jaw. How much he looks like Jack on a good day with a pricier haircut and more impressive pedigree. He has a law degree too. I've always had a thing for lawyers.

Harrison brushes the back of my hand with his thumb. "My mother is throwing a party to drum up support for the plan. Saturday. Here at the house. I'd appreciate you joining me."

I mentally review my schedule. My social calendar is empty, but taking care of my son is written in permanent marker every evening. "I have a kindergartener. During the day, my in-laws watch him."

As soon as I say it, I regret it. The spark disappears in Harrison's eyes, snuffed out by the implication that I'm married. I desperately try to fan the flames. "My late husband's parents. He died. In that crash."

The spark returns, brighter than before, as if my words were a blast of fresh oxygen.

"Bring him. I love kids. I've always wanted to be a father myself." Harrison's expression becomes wistful. "Show my old man that balancing business success and family was possible."

The heaviness of the sigh that follows reminds me of how recently Harrison's father died and Camille's involvement. For the millionth time, I regret ever turning a blind eye to her side hustle. Some things shouldn't mix with legitimate business—much like my energetic kid.

"That's very kind of you, but I'm not sure my son would be able to behave himself around so many adults."

Harrison's smile returns, this time with a naughty glint. "Understood. I never liked behaving myself at these affairs either. If you could manage, though, this would be a great opportunity to make your case to Providence's power players. The governor will be there, and surely our local officials."

The mention of power players alleviates my mom guilt. This isn't a social call, it's work. "Sounds like a perfect opportunity to push these plans forward."

A flush sneaks into Harrison's cheeks. "Yes. Right. But to clarify"—his smile turns sheepish—"I'm not asking you as my lawyer. I'm asking you to be my date."

CAMILLE

I roll to a stop under a weeping willow and peer through the windshield at Aiden Wyatt's house. Weathered shingle siding, a pair of stacked-stone chimneys, and Barbers Pond sparkling through a thick line of trees. I take in the neat stack of firewood to the right of sliding French doors, the raw linen curtains hanging in front of spotless paned windows, and for a second I wonder if I got the address wrong. After everything I heard from Krystle about Aiden, I was expecting something a lot less…charming.

I kill the engine and climb out, shutting the door with a hip. The bang is loud in the wooded hush and so are my shoes, crunching in the gravel as I teeter on my high heels to the door. A simple sign on the porch tells me I'm in the right place: Aiden Wyatt, Attorney-at-Law.

According to Marco, this man is the "in" Mayor Tom had with the Narragansett tribe, but that connection had never actually gotten Marco's or the investors' grubby hands on the parcel of land for the casino deal. According to Krystle and Justine, Aiden isn't on the side of the Davenforth "Paris Plan" either. Which could mean this guy has got a plan all his own for this very valuable strip of land.

The truth is I don't really much care, because I'm here motive hunting. All I need is a name, for Aiden to tell me who in his tribe might have been angry enough to send threatening letters to the mayor for cutting the tribe out of the deal. Angry enough, maybe, to kill him.

The door is unlocked but inside the office is empty—not a surprise for a Saturday morning. What *is* a surprise, however, is me showing up here unannounced. After Krystle barreled through yesterday, hurling enough insults to get her kicked to the curb, I figured an ambush was my best strategy.

I step around a pristine receptionist's desk and aim my face down a dim hall. "Hello? Aiden? Mr. Wyatt?"

Silence.

I turn back, thinking through my next move. This office I'm standing in was once upon a time a detached garage. Maybe Aiden is the type of lawyer that prefers to read his Saturday briefs while stretched out on the couch or swinging in a hammock by the lake.

I'm stepping back onto the porch when I hear it—the sound of a dog barking, followed by a low and muffled voice that can only belong to a male. There's a splash, and I follow in its direction.

A stepping-stone path leads me around to the back side of the house. In stilettos and my best silk dress, thanks to a June warm enough to make a Southern gal proud, I'm not exactly dressed for trekking through the woods. But something about the fern fronds tickling at my calves and the sunlight streaming through the trees is soothing. My Georgia roots, I guess, tugging at long-buried memories.

The trail opens up onto a flagstone terrace dotted with overflowing flowerpots, and beyond, a stretch of sparkling water that is more lake than pond. The morning sunshine lights it up, blinding me and silhouetting the man at the end of a long dock.

A *handsome* man. Tall. Broad shouldered. Strong jaw. Shaggy hair that even from here I can tell is finger combed at best. So handsome I don't even mind my heels sinking in the mud.

I step up on the wooden dock with a clomp, and he glances over his shoulder, then looks again. I strike a pose and let him drink up the effort I've made—heels, hair, skintight red dress. Not exactly a getup for lakeside lounging, but I was expecting this to be an office meeting, and besides, I always dress to impress, especially when I hear the person I'm trying to impress is not the impressionable type.

"Better not stand there." He turns back without so much as a smile.

Before I can ask why, a big brown dog lurches out of the water and onto the shore, careening around and almost knocking me over in its race up the dock. A soaking-wet whirlwind of flapping ears and churning paws, tearing up the dock with a steady stream of happy barks. At the very last second, Aiden rears back with an arm and chucks a tennis ball in an arc so high it would make a baseball coach proud. The dog veers sharply to the right, flinging itself into a perfect belly dive.

Splat.

Aiden laughs, waiting until the dog comes up for air to say, "Can I help you?"

"I certainly hope so. My name's Camille Tavani. I'd like to—"

"I know who you are. I read the papers."

I give him my best poker face, even though his words ping me in ways that aren't particularly pleasant because of *the papers*. If one more person mentions those hit pieces under the guise of "journalism," I'm going to lose my ever-loving mind.

Before I can come up with a suitable answer, he turns back to the dog paddling furiously across the lake. Fifty feet away, a yellow dot bobs in the water. "Anyway, the answer's no. The burial ground is not for sale."

"I'm not here to talk money. Unlike Krystle and Justine, I don't represent the Davenforths."

Even Krystle knew not to keep beating that dead horse. *Nothing will charm that man out of his land. Not even your manhunter magic.*

In my ears, it sounded like a challenge, but as much as I wouldn't mind charming the tush off this handsome man, his land isn't the reason I'm here. After Marco Santoro enlightened me as to Mayor Tom's push to keep the Narragansetts out of the casino business, I'm much more interested in sussing out who in the tribe might have seen the millions being essentially stolen away and wanted Mayor Tom as dead as that deal.

Still. If only Aiden would look at me like he does that dog, swimming back with a slimy yellow ball clutched between its teeth. While we're at it, why doesn't he? I curled my hair. I put on my tightest dress. Is he really *immune* to my charms? It's a horrifying thought.

I move closer on my tippy toes, careful my heels don't get stuck between the slats. I've already lost one pair of designer shoes, and I'm not looking for a repeat performance. "I'm sure by now you've heard what happened to Mayor Tom and that I was the last person to see him alive."

He glances over. "I hope you didn't drive all the way to South County for legal advice, because I'm not a criminal attorney. Not unless it concerns tribal affairs."

"The thing is, sugar, it might. A man like Mayor Tom stepped on plenty of toes. He made a lot of enemies on his rise to the top."

Aiden frowns, his gaze whipping away from the water to mine. "So you think his killer is someone from the tribe."

Not a question but a statement, though not necessarily an offended one. Just tired, maybe, or resigned. This isn't the first time someone has made accusations against the tribe, and my gut tells me to tread carefully, or he'll shut this meeting down.

"I didn't say his killer was someone from the tribe, only that the mayor was involved in something that got him killed, and everything I've learned in the days since his death points to the redevelopment project downtown. And since according to the Providence Police Department I'm a person of interest, that makes me mighty interested in who else might have wanted him dead."

"So you're here for names." He shakes his head. "Sorry, but I can't help you."

"Can't, or won't?"

He shrugs, a noncommittal gesture, though honestly, I don't blame him. The people I'm asking him to point fingers at could be friends, family. No way he's going to give up any of his people—not to a stranger, and certainly not to a white one. Aiden isn't going to budge on this matter, and as frustrating as that is, I can't help but admire this guy's loyalty.

A sudden wave of water splashes over the dock, the dog hurling the ball at his toes. It chuffs one enthusiastic bark, then takes off, paddling for shore.

It's the perfect opportunity for me to switch gears. "Did you know Mayor Tom was looking to bring casinos to Providence? And not just any casino. A casino that would have belonged to him and a friend of his in Atlantic City. The mayor wanted to keep the tribe out of the casino business. He said he had an 'in' with you so that he could keep all the business for him and his bigoted buddies."

Aiden lifts one of his big shoulders, a response that's a lot more untroubled than I would be in his shoes…not that he's wearing any. My gaze dips to his bare feet, neat and well-proportioned, the skin toasted brown. You can tell a lot about a man by the state of his feet, and these are the kind of pretty that's a shame to shove into shoes.

He bends to pick up the ball, shaking off some of the excess water. "Like every Providence mayor, Mayor Tom ignored the Narragansett people unless we were of some use. I was not his 'in,' and we were not working together. Our interests were not aligned."

"Not aligned? They were a hell of a lot more than *not aligned*. Mayor Tom wanted to screw you and your tribe out of not just your land but also business that could help your people. Shouldn't you be pissed, or at the very least, insulted? You seem awfully calm."

And while we're at it, why? What is Aiden hiding? Does he know who the enemies were in the tribe? Does he suspect someone?

The dock shudders under my soles, the dog galloping toward us. Aiden pitches the ball, and the wood under my feet settles, right before water splashes up the back of my legs.

"I'm not trying to give you a history lesson, Ms. Tavani, but a white man showing up on a Native doorstep with a promise to work together is a tale that goes back as far as your colleague Krystle's beloved Columbus. And it always ends the same."

Krystle had mentioned the numbers Aiden tossed around about how much land his tribe had lost. "So you just let it go? Water off a duck's or dog's back, so to speak?"

He almost grins before he continues, "If I got worked up by every white man trying to take what's rightfully my tribe's, I would have burned out ages ago. It's much healthier for everybody all around if I focus my energy on being strategic."

"As admirable as that is, what about the casino?"

"What about it?" He slides his palms into his jeans pockets and watches me from a few feet away, and I try to picture him in a suit, offering up evidence and arguing briefs in a courtroom. He seems so at ease out here, in his faded jeans and bare feet, that I can't.

"Doesn't your tribe want the money a casino would bring in? Plenty do, and that piece of land downtown would be the perfect spot for one."

"That may be so, but my ancestors are buried there, our fathers and mothers and brothers and sisters. We remember on that land. We honor those who came before us and who made our existence possible."

"And a casino would ruin that."

"Not only would a casino disturb the graves, it would destroy the entire parcel of land. We're trying to maintain the ecological balance of plants and animals that have lived there for centuries. Not that the powers that be have made it easy. Checkerboarding, fractionated ownership, termination of our tribal rights and dignities—all tricks to erase the indigeneity from our land and strip us of our sovereignty." He shakes his head. "My tribe is meant to protect that land, in more ways than one. We don't plan to give it up, and new federal laws make clear it's ours to do with as we see fit."

Aiden is speaking for the whole tribe here, but I'm having a hard time believing everyone there feels the same. Despite all his pretty words, the tribe still lives in the modern world, where cash is king. The lure of the kind of money a casino would bring in is too great. There's got to be someone there who would put dollar signs over the tribe. Someone who would kill Mayor Tom—and maybe even Aiden—to make sure they get their hands on that jackpot.

"Are you sure about that? Because y'all hold the literal keys to that burial ground. You hold all the power, which means you can name your price. Think about the biggest number you can imagine, and then triple it. That's how much that land would have been worth to people like Mayor Tom and whoever else might want to slap a building on it. They need your land, and they'll pay your tribe mightily to get it."

"Now you sound just like your friend."

No wonder Krystle lost her cool with this man, because he's impossible to rile up, and his morals can't be bought. Not with money and definitely not with this slinky red dress. So far his gaze hasn't dipped to my cleavage, not even once. Not that I'm keeping track.

"Sweetheart, no offense, but I couldn't care less what you do with that land. The only thing I'm concerned with right now is saving my hide and figuring out who would have killed to keep a white man's casino off it."

The ball lands on his feet in another wave of lake water, but he ignores it. "Then you should know that a casino is the least of our worries. People wanting that land is nothing new. They have for generations. Currently it's for a casino. Before that, it was a factory. In fact, *that's* why I became an attorney, so I could fight the Mayor Toms of the world and keep them off our land. *Legally*. Which with all due respect is what you should be thinking about right now. Our land will be fine, but what's your legal strategy?"

"Me. My legal strategy is *me*, making a list of suspects, people who had motive to murder Mayor Tom and to use me as a pawn. A list I'm hoping will be a mile long, so I can hand it off to the detectives once the autopsy report proves what everyone is already saying. That's why I'm standing here right now, talking to you, so I can keep my ass out of jail."

"What about your law firm?"

"What about it?"

"What is Rom Romero's role in your defense?"

Krystle's dipshit son—her words, not mine. The thought of him sitting next to me in a courtroom, shuffling papers and shaking in his boots, makes me want to throw up. Rom's the last person on the planet I would choose to defend me for jaywalking, much less murder, and yet he's the only criminal defense attorney we've got. It's times like these that I really miss having an attorney husband.

"Clearly you know Rom, so you also know that the best thing I can do is nip this thing in the bud before it ever goes to trial. So can we get back to Mayor Tom and the casino? Because you see how it looks, right? Mayor Tom was after land you seem pretty intent on keeping."

"As far as issues of interest within the tribe, this one barely registered. I'm not saying that there aren't those among us who do want to see a Narragansett casino. But we don't want to see it built on the graves of our ancestors. That, I can promise you."

"Okay, but did you know Mayor Tom had been receiving threats? All sorts of angry letters, all of them having to do with the casino."

"Not surprising. He barreled over plenty of people in his rise to become mayor, including people who were supposed to be family."

The Davenforths. Aiden's referring to the Davenforths.

I'm about to pitch my next question when suddenly, the dock tilts—or maybe that's the dog, slamming into me from behind. My arms pinwheel and I topple sideways, reaching for the first thing I see: Aiden's shirt. I grab it in both fists and hold on tight, and I'm about to go over when he catches me by the waist, pulling me back with two warm hands.

"Holy crap," I say once the world stops spinning. "That was a close one."

"Sorry about my dog. Kiona is well trained until she sees a ball. Then all bets are off."

He's even more handsome up close. Dark eyes with thick lashes, strong nose and jaw, hair long and wild. I've always thought I liked my men groomed, but I'm starting to reconsider.

"Watch this," he says, his hands leaving my waist but his gaze holding steady on mine. "Kiona, sit."

Kiona doesn't sit, but she does stop prancing around my legs. She plants her four paws into the dock and gives a mighty shake from head to the tip of her tail, spraying us both with lake water. I laugh in spite of the spots now speckling my dress, the sound echoing out over Barbers Pond. Kiona plucks the ball from between our feet and takes off with it, trotting up the dock to a spot in the sun.

"Okay, fine," I say, pulling my hair over a shoulder to shake off the water. "You've made your point. But you brought up the Davenforths, so you probably know they're working on a plan to turn Providence into the Paris of the Northeast, and—"

"Paris of the Northeast." His tone doesn't change at the words, but something about him goes sharp around the edges. Maybe it's the new lines fanning out from his eyes or the way his muscles go hard under the soft cotton of his shirt. "Only Nancy could come up with something so pretentious."

Interesting. Aiden doesn't seem to like Nancy very much, which as far as I'm concerned is a point in this man's Pro column. I've been acquainted with Nancy for years, and maybe it's jealousy talking, but I've never quite bought into the devotion people in this town have for the Davenforths. Aiden tilts his head, studying me. "Have you talked to any of them? The Davenforths, I mean."

I shake my head. "Should I?"

"If I were your attorney, that's where I'd tell you to start. We all know the way he embarrassed Nancy."

I think back to the headlines splashed across every front page when they were going through their divorce, each one worse than the last. Money and revenge are both great motivators, but why now? Why wait all this time to knock him off? There's got to be more to it than that.

Like that plot of land downtown and one very stubborn man.

"I hear you, hun. But she wants your land too, and a woman as smart as Nancy will have built in concessions to appease the Narragansett tribe."

"Appease how? By erecting a building on top of my ancestors? By disrupting their graves and moving them to a spot miles away so they can make way for their version of the Seine?"

"I don't know. I haven't seen the plans."

"That's because the unveiling isn't until tonight, some big event at her estate. She'll have tented the whole backyard for her victory party. That's what she's calling it, a victory party, even though she's going to need our land to win. And I think I've already made my position clear."

My ears perk at the word *party*. I wonder if Krystle was invited to this fancy gathering, if she knows what time it starts. "Word is that Nancy has been working on this plan for ages and that her plans include your burial ground too. You're not going to win a war with the Toms and the Nancys of the world simply by being stubborn."

If he takes offense at that last word, he doesn't show it. His eyes don't go the least bit squinty when they sink into mine. "Which is why I became a lawyer, so I could win on legalities. I'm telling you now. That burial ground is our line in the sand."

I grin and pat him on the chest. "Good luck with that, sugar. You and Kiona have yourself a good weekend." I turn and head back up the dock, tossing a wave over my shoulder.

I'm halfway to Providence before my mobile phone finds a signal, then I punch in Meredith's number. "Hey hun, wanna crash a swanky shindig?"

MEREDITH

Partying with the Davenforths is not my idea of a fun Saturday night. But with the club closed, the best way I can spend my time is helping Camille try to figure out what really happened to the mayor—or at least more suspects that we can point the finger at. A party packed full of every power player in Providence seems like as promising a next step as any.

The mansion's windows are lit up, glowing like glaring eyes against the golden-hour sky as we pull into the driveway. The Davenforths are so damn rich, even their *house* looks judgmental.

As I wait for my turn at the valet stand, I scan the line of people streaming into the house for familiar faces. Krystle invited herself tonight too—and dragged her son Rom along as well, supposedly to seize this golden opportunity to talk business with the Davenforths, but I think it's more to keep an eye on him. Though Rom's kicked his coke habit and generally cleaned up his act, he's still got a tendency to get himself in trouble, and we can't afford any more of that right now. He's the only living lawyer left on the firm's letterhead after all.

We couldn't get a hold of Justine—probably some emergency with her kid or law school or both. I miss her, especially when I get a good look at the well-heeled crowd and realize how much I could have used her fashion advice. I'm wearing my nicest dress—a black strapless Vicky Tiel I got on deep discount at Filene's—but it's showing way too much cleavage for this crowd. Most of the women are in buttoned-up summer suits with skirts that hit a tasteful inch or two above the knee, their hair styled in impeccable updos to show off their inherited jewels and surgically enhanced jawlines.

When I get out of the car and toss my keys to the valet—who can barely conceal his disdain for my dusty late-'70s LeSabre—I'm relieved to find Camille, Krystle, and Rom loitering by the flowerbeds. Camille's wearing a sleek cocktail dress that's a little flashy but still appropriate, while Krystle's in a cream skirt and blazer set that might be the right label but isn't quite the right size for her generous curves. Rom's sporting a tailored navy-blue suit, plus a fresh shave and pomade in his hair; if the guy didn't annoy me so much, I might admit that he's not hideous when he bothers to make an effort.

"You're late," Krystle says.

"It's a party," I point out.

"Not that kind of party." Krystle adjusts her jacket so there's just a little bit of cleavage visible between the wide lapels. Glad I won't be the only one scandalizing Providence's elite with my assets tonight. "Follow my lead. Places like this, you just gotta walk with purpose and they'll let you right in."

She throws her padded shoulders back and strides confidently toward the front entrance: towering double doors that look more like they belong on a medieval castle than a family home. Camille, Rom, and I follow, smiling benignly as Krystle gives the clipboard-holding security guard a snooty nod like the silver-haired couple ahead of us did.

No dice. The guard's arm shoots out so fast he almost clotheslines Krystle.

"Your name please, ma'am?"

"Krystle Romero." She draws herself up to her full height—which is still way shorter than this brick house of a guy. "These are my colleagues Camille Tavani, Meredith Everett, and Romeo Romero, Junior. We're with Nancy's law firm."

"Ms. Davenforth contracts with many law firms." The man gives the clipboard a cursory glance. "Unfortunately you're not on the list for tonight's event, so I'll have to ask you to—"

"Oh, come on. The more the merrier, right?" Krystle takes a crisp fifty out of her bra. "What about if my friend Ulysses comes too, huh?"

Krystle waves the bill under the guard's unamused face. That might work on the heavies at my club, but I have to assume Nancy Davenforth's muscle isn't budging for less than a fat wad of Benjamins.

Another coterie of well-heeled partygoers comes up the steps, and we get pushed off to the side. Krystle keeps giving the guard the stink eye, and he does an excellent job of acting like she's invisible.

"What now?" I ask.

Krystle nudges Camille. "You go talk to him. Give him an eyeful, and—"

"Are you serious?" Camille says.

"You want to get in, don't you?"

"Of course I do! I'm the one who's going to jail if we don't get some answers."

"Well, then stop standing around with that look on your face and use what the good Lord or the good surgeon gave ya."

"You can't throw my tits at every problem, Krystle."

Camille and Krystle have been edgy all day, ever since Camille came back from seeing that lawyer for the Narragansett tribe, after he'd given Krystle and Justine such a hard time on their visit. Or at least, that's their version.

I've never seen Camille talk about a man that way before—she claimed their meeting was strictly business, but her face told another story. Every time his name came up, Camille said the same thing: that he's smarter than everybody was giving him credit for and not to underestimate him. Aiden Wyatt must really be something if he's got Camille, of all people, impressed by something other than his looks or the size of his wallet.

While Krystle and Camille are sniping at each other—and Rom's fiddling with his silk tie like he wishes he could use it to put himself out of his misery—I notice Tara Jordan sashaying up the driveway. She must have had her driver drop her off, rather than availing herself of the valet. She's not dressed to blend in with the rest of the guests either. Her matching blazer and minidress are a lime green so bright it practically glows in the waning light, and she's wearing fuck-me stilettos that somehow don't slow her down on the gravel path.

I wave to her, but she doesn't notice. She's not coming toward the front door after all. Instead, she casts a look around, then darts around the side of the house.

Intrigued, I start to follow. Krystle stops me. "Where do you think you're going?"

I ignore her, calling out, "Tara!"

Tara stops and turns to face us with a big smile, as though she wasn't just caught trying to sneak into the home of her archnemesis.

"Meredith! Ms. Tavani, Ms. Romero. And you must be the young Mr. Romero." She shakes Rom's hand, and he winces at the strength of her grip. "How lovely to see you here. I didn't realize you were invited."

"We're not." I peer at the shadowy foliage behind her. "Guessing you're not either."

Tara keeps smiling, unbothered as always. "I wouldn't have gotten far in life if I stayed out of every place that didn't want me there. Come on."

She slips between the trees, and the four of us follow, Rom bringing up the rear. Tara's neon clothes are like a beacon, guiding our way. She moves fast, weaving around tree trunks like a race car driver until we reach what looks like a dead end: a high stone wall covered in ivy. Krystle's panting behind me, and Camille grumbles under her breath about the leaves in her blown-out hair and ruining another pair of designer shoes.

Tara sticks her hand through the greenery, and there's a *click*. The wall swings open, revealing a barrel-shaped room stocked to the rafters with wine bottles.

"After you, ladies," Tara says. "And gentleman."

Clearly she's done this before—which seems strange. Mayor Tom was still living on Nancy's estate when he started fooling around with Tara, but according to the papers, he and Tara had a love nest in New York City. They made a big deal of the fact that Tara barely set foot in Providence before the wedding. They must have gotten it wrong, though, 'cause Tara's clearly familiar with the Davenforth property.

She leads us through another doorway, and we spill out into the Davenforths' massive backyard. The land sits right on the water—the most expensive real estate in Newport, where everything's already pricey as all hell—and has a panoramic view of the setting sun as it dips toward the sparkling ocean waves.

In the center of the lawn, there's a massive tent that probably cost more than my apartment and boasts more square footage too. The party guests are all packed inside, leaving the yard empty except for uniformed waitstaff busy cleaning up the remains of the hors d'oeuvres and lighting the torches scattered around the grass. Instead of standard tiki torches, the lights are all custom, made to look like those iconic Art Nouveau metro signs I've seen in pictures of Paris.

I tap one with my fingernail, and it clangs. Real metal. "They're really committed to this whole French theme, huh?"

"Ridiculous, isn't it? I mean, Paris, honestly? Money can't buy vision." Tara flicks one of the torches so hard it lists to the side. "Matches the steel rod up Nancy's ass though."

"Come on," Krystle says. "We're missing the big speech."

The staff doesn't give us a second glance; I suppose that's what they're paid for, to be discreet. The tent is standing room only and so full we have to split up and scatter to different entrances in order to fit inside. Rom doesn't even attempt it, instead making a beeline for the open-air bar on the other side of the lawn. Can't say I blame him.

Krystle and Camille squeeze their way in, but I hesitate. Tara stops, waiting for me.

"What's wrong?" she asks.

I yank my dress up an inch, but it doesn't do much good. If only I'd brought a tasteful cardigan. If only I *owned* a tasteful cardigan. "I just feel…a little underdressed."

"Don't tell me you're intimidated by these people."

Of course I am. The Davenforths are like royalty in this state: even if you hate their guts, you still feel compelled to kowtow to their power.

"Here." Tara shrugs off her blazer and holds it out.

"Oh, you don't have to—"

"I insist."

I slip my arms through the sleeves. The lining is cool silk, so smooth it feels like luxurious lotion spreading over my skin.

Now Tara's the one showing a scandalous amount of cleavage. I had no idea she was hiding all that under her signature suiting; maybe it's just the cut of the dress?

Shit. I'm staring. I need to get it together. I'm around gorgeous women every day. I see more perfect breasts in a single night than most men could dream of in their lifetimes. But it's not just that Tara's beautiful. There's something about the way she holds herself that's truly mesmerizing.

Now, wearing her jacket, I feel a little spark of it too. My spine straightens, my shoulders go back. I feel ready for anything. Even the Davenforths.

We head into the tent. I've totally lost track of Camille and Krystle, but Tara stays right by my side, so close my shoulder pads jab into her bare arm.

In the center of the crowd—right under an honest-to-god crystal chandelier—Nancy Davenforth stands on a dais, flanked by full-color renderings of what the city will look like after it's been transformed into their Parisian dream. Her son Harrison stands beside her, looking even more handsome than usual in the soft light. Justine seems fond of the guy, but I never trust a man who's prettier than I am. Plus he apparently lives in a carriage house around the side of Nancy's mansion, which is the spoiled-rich-boy version of living in your parents' basement.

"We've been working closely with local business owners and the Narragansett tribal leaders to ensure that the new Providence is a beautiful safe haven for all residents," Nancy says, and the crowd responds with polite applause, rings clinking against champagne flutes.

"Now, the moment you've all been waiting for." Nancy nods to Harrison, who steps off the stage. "It is my honor to present to you: the new Providence! Voilà!"

Harrison yanks a white cloth away with stage-magician flourish, but I can't see what he's revealed. The crowd oohs and aahs, pressing closer to get a better look. Tara starts pushing through the throng, and I slip into her wake. There are a few yelps and dirty looks as she steps on toes and throws elbows, but no one tries to stop us.

Finally, we reach the front—and the sprawling architectural model that's got everyone so entranced. The Davenforths' "New Providence" is all clean white marble and manicured gardens, and the model is rendered in such fine detail, there are even tiny people walking the pristine streets. It looks more like another planet than the city I grew up in. I might consider it beautiful, if it weren't about to ruin my life. No way Nancy's "Paris" includes a red-light district.

"If you'll indulge me for one more moment," Nancy says. "I'd like us all to raise our glasses to someone without whom this wouldn't have been possible." Harrison passes her a champagne flute, and she holds it aloft. "To Tom. My first love. The father of my darling son."

I glance at Tara. It must bother her to hear her husband's ex talk about him this way, but you'd never know it from her placid expression.

"Now, it's no secret Tom and I didn't always see eye to eye—when we were married or during his mayorship." On that line, Nancy gets a chuckle from the crowd. "But I'm so pleased to say that, in what we now know were the final days of his tragically short life, he gave his full approval and blessing to this redevelopment plan."

The crowd lightly applauds, but there are gasps too—so I'm

not the only one surprised by Nancy's statement. Tara never said anything about Mayor Tom supporting the redevelopment. In fact, she made it sound like he was against it and all in on the rival casino plan. But if this is news to her, Tara doesn't show it. Her face stays high-stakes-poker-table blank as Nancy continues with her toast.

"I'm heartbroken, as I'm sure you all are, that he won't be able to see the final result, but he'll always be a part of Providence. To that end, we've revised the plans to include a memorial statue in his honor. Though he's gone, his legacy will live on forever. To Tom!"

The crowd echoes her, lifting their glasses before bursting into another round of applause. Nancy steps down from the dais—and smiles right at Tara, who flushes red and sticks out her chest as if to remind Nancy why Tom left.

Tara's glare is harsh enough to strip the finish off my faux gold earrings. "She's so full of shit," Tara hisses. The way she says it reveals pain under her posturing. It makes me believe Nancy that Mayor Tom did switch teams. It makes me wonder if Tara knew about the betrayal.

I analyze Nancy too; her smile looks genuine enough to me, but as a former stripper I know a thing or two about playing nice with people you can't stand. "At least she's not siccing security on you," I say to Tara.

"I wish she'd try. But we mustn't have a *scene*."

Nancy maintains her good hostess smile and turns away to chat up the governor and his wife.

"Why do you think Tom left her?" Tara doesn't bother to whisper; she doesn't give a damn who overhears. "He was tired of all this fake manners shit, always having to keep up appearances. He wanted something real."

"And what you two had was real?" A rude thing to say maybe, but during our conversation in the limo Tara gave the impression her relationship with the mayor was businesslike at best. Maybe that explains why she didn't know where he stood on the redevelopment.

Now, though, a strange, sad look passes over Tara's face. "Real enough."

I give Tara a moment and focus back on Nancy's vision. Everything seems so different in the reconfigured cityscape, it takes me a few moments to find the intersection where my club sits now. When I finally locate it, my jaw drops.

"What the fuck is this?"

The society matron next to me gasps like I've slapped her across the face. She's only reacting to my swearing, not to the absolute travesty in front of us.

I knew they wanted to tear down the club. But instead of a new storefront or public park, they've plopped the mayor's memorial on the site. The statue is an obelisk, the words *In Loving Memory of Mayor Thomas Bradley, 1926–1987* engraved across the base.

I've worked my ass off to make the club successful—and now these entitled pieces of shit want to tear it down and build a memorial to some *man*. An unfortunately phallic memorial at that. If I weren't so pissed off, I might find it funny.

"Well, at least they got the size right," Tara says, wiggling her pinky to get her point across.

All these wealthy assholes are here celebrating the imminent destruction of my hard-won livelihood. How *dare* they. I want to jump up on the table and tromp through the miniature city like Godzilla on a rampage.

"Hey." Tara turns to face me, totally ignoring the people behind us waiting their turn to look. "It's only a model. You've built something real, and you're gonna give them a hell of a fight if they try to take it away."

"They've already shut down the club," I say. "What can I do? I'm only—"

Tara holds up a finger. "You stop that right now. You know what you are, Meredith?"

I know what the people in here would call me. A stripper. A hussy. White trash.

"You're better than them. You're better than every one of these entitled fuckers. You *worked* for what you have. You didn't get it from your daddy or your husband. These people, they have to act superior because without all those airs they put on, they've got nothing else. They're just as hollow as this stupid thing."

She pokes at one of the buildings. Her fingernail leaves a dent in the facade. It might look like marble, but it's just plaster, painted to look like stone.

"Case in point: You see that guy?" Tara nods toward a man with his back turned in our direction. Even without the bow tie or the smug expression to tip me off, I recognize Tucker immediately. How can the back of someone's *head* be so punchable?

I have to remind myself not to use Krystle's more colorful nickname for the firm's former lawyer. He used to bring clients to my club all the time, and he was beyond condescending to me and the girls. I swallowed it since the firm needed him, but now? I'm truly looking forward to having him bounced out on his flat ass if he ever comes in again.

"Tucker Armand? Yeah, we're acquainted."

"My sincere condolences," Tara says. "But I meant the man he's talking to."

"Leatherface?" Tucker's conversation partner is a middle-aged man with a tan so deep his skin looks like beef jerky. This is why I'm always advising my girls to stick to bronzer.

Tara snickers. "Yes. Otherwise known as Doctor Hendricks. Half of these snobs can only stomach their miserable existences because of the shit he sells them."

My eyes widen. "He's a drug dealer?"

"They don't call it that when you have an Ivy League MD and a prescription pad. But yes, the good doctor is good for parties—if you can afford him, that is. *I* heard—"

She stops short. I follow her gaze. Harrison Davenforth Bradley has just joined the good doctor's circle. Harrison slides his arm around the shoulders of a tall, slender woman—his date, I assume. She's in all white, including long satin gloves.

It isn't until she tilts her face up to smile at Harrison that I realize it's Justine. Krystle's had her working with Harrison, but this doesn't look like a business meeting. Not at all.

Good for her, honestly. Justine deserves a little happiness. Of course, he seems like a flavor-of-the-week kind of guy, so if Harrison hurts her, I know two other women who will be more than happy to help me hunt his ass down.

"Excuse me," Tara says. "I'll be right back."

She takes off, leaving me alone with the model. My gaze goes right back to that wretched little obelisk. The crowd around me has thinned a bit, so no one's paying attention as I lean down and tap my finger against the memorial sculpture. And then *push* until the base starts to crack.

Tara's right: the Davenforths may be rich and powerful, but I'm a fighter. Let them make their plans, let them play with their fake dollhouse city.

We'll see who's still standing in the end.

KRYSTLE

The still-attached price tag on my Chanel suit is really itching my ass. I'm standing shoulder to shoulder with Newport elite, so I resist the urge to scratch. I'm also terrified the tag will rip off, and I won't be able to return it to the secondhand store I bought it from with credit I don't have.

I glance around at what I can barely believe is considered a tent, it's so fancy. The billowing white fabric with twinkling lights is held up by carved wooden posts in a warm, polished-cherry finish. There are even freaking chandeliers dripping in fresh flowers like they had money to burn.

Who could ever feel comfortable in a place like this? I almost itch my rump after all but put my hand on my hip instead. I stand alone and scan the crowd for Nancy. The problem with being on my own is I'm not flapping my gums. This lets my mind take the wheel, and soon I'm mentally replaying my foot-meet-mouth scene with Aiden. In my anger, I'd even done a little digging on Columbus, and damn if that smug lawyer wasn't right. Columbus wasn't so much sailing the ocean blue as stealing land and murdering anyone Indian who got in his way. Women, children, old people, whatever.

So in addition to feeling stupid for bringing Columbus up, I'm also mad that I never learned that in school. That I'd walked past the statue of him on the Hill a thousand times, enjoyed his annual parade, all the while thinking he'd arrived and made peace with tribes and one happy Thanksgiving feast later, me and my Italian ancestors are here eating cannoli.

Colonizers. That's the word Justine said to Aiden that I also had to look up. As I stare out at the big tent with everyone fawning over Nancy's downtown design, I think of the definition, which is basically sending people to a place that belongs to someone else to take it over and control it by any means necessary. Justine got where Aiden was coming from right away, but as usual, her smarts left me in the dust.

I grab a glass of champagne as that thought leads me to the next one: I need to apologize to Justine. I was not my best self, and honestly, it's hard for me to be lately.

I don't say it, but the truth is I feel mad all the time.

Mad that after twenty years of work, I'm just as broke as day one in that apartment on the Hill.

Mad that I'm wearing a freaking girdle.

Mad that I feel like I have to wear a freaking girdle.

Mad that every time we claw an inch forward, we're drop-kicked a mile back.

Mad that Rom doesn't have a dad to guide him in this business.

Mad that I miss my husband, especially at events like these

or meetings like with Aiden or Nancy, when a little of his charm would go a long way.

Mad that grief still gets to me.

Mad that after all my years of nagging, now that I'm the one who's boss of the firm, I'm not good enough to keep it afloat.

Mad I can't pay Justine enough to even cover her law school books.

Mad that Camille has to hustle herself into dangerous situations to keep the lights on.

Mad that Meredith feels obligated to send money she doesn't have to us each month like a bad bet.

Mad that rich people like every damn person in this fancy-as-hell tent don't have a clue what it's like for the rest of us.

Argh!

I scream internally and take a slug of essentially stolen champagne. I gotta take a chill pill, as my son says. What good does my anger do on the lawn of a Newport mansion?

Instead, I plaster a smile on my face and search for Nancy. I have to believe she wouldn't leave our firm out in the cold. Sure, we haven't secured the Narragansett agreement yet, but Justine had a great plan. She always does.

We'd talked through ideas earlier, and while I don't know my ass from my elbow when it comes to that kind of law, I do know how to encourage Justine and toughen her up so she finds her backbone. When she went to Nancy's mansion, I was sure we'd be on the right side of the Davenforths. I feel mad for Justine too, if Nancy slammed the door in her face.

With Justine going to law school, I know she and Rom will be able to lead this firm into the future. Once she's graduated, it's all upside for Romero, Kelly—

"Can you imagine using mud for a wasp sting? But it worked like a charm."

My attention is snapped away at the sound of Justine's voice. Well, not her normal voice, something louder and like she's onstage or on top of a piano.

I steamroll through the stick-thin crowd of ladies ignoring the buffet table to the group of men in power suits smoking cigars. I see Harrison first. He's casually leaning against a wooden tent post surrounded by guys in suits. The one next to him has got that raccoon-eyed George Hamilton tan. Then I recognize Judge Gatta from the Hill, but he's been on the East Side so long, I doubt he'd know the difference between a crumpet and a cannoli. Next to him is the governor and even the state speaker of the house. And *Tucker*.

As I creep closer, Harrison introduces Justine to a new face in the after-dinner circle, a state senator who's also from the Hill. They are all staring at Justine, who apparently *did* get invited to this party but *didn't* bother to tell any of us.

"You let that man put mud on your finger?" Tucker says with a sneer.

"Well, that's the difference between us. The client comes first, even if I have to get a little dirty." Justine pauses to tap her finger against her chin. "I don't think Aiden Wyatt opened the door when you came knocking. Did you even get out of the car, or were you too worried about those loafers?"

The table of men erupt in laughter, and I can't even enjoy Tucker's embarrassment because I realize she's not scoring one for my team. She didn't bring me as her plus-one. She didn't even tell me about this shindig.

She waves toward Harrison. "Of course, *we* understand why the land is important to the tribe. But we can't help if they won't listen to reason."

Harrison gestures toward the senator who just joined. "Since the Hill's illustrious representative wasn't with us at dinner, want to share your brilliant legal strategy to deal with the Narragansett?"

Harrison beams at Justine and her cheeks flush, but she shoots a glance at Tucker. "Not while the competition is listening."

Harrison smirks. "Sorry, man. Business. I think I hear your mom calling."

Tucker scowls and stomps off, and while it should be a victory that Justine and I toast together, she doesn't even look my way. Instead, I see her raise a white-gloved hand as if she's Audrey freaking Hepburn. "Well, now that we're among friends, two words: eminent domain."

Harrison pats her shoulder. "With someone of Justine's background explaining how this is for the benefit of *everyone* in Providence, how can we lose?"

The governor slaps the senator on the back. "You could use this strategy on the Hill to finally close those bakeries and build something that actually grows a tax base."

A hand goes over my mouth. Did he just imply that these men

in power know more about what the Hill needs than the actual people who have lived there for generations?

Harrison continues, "I'm telling you, Justine Kelly is as brilliant as she is beautiful. Judge Gatta, you'd better start sweet-talking Harvard to get her to clerk for you this summer. Of course, I know you don't pay as well as our family would, so good luck to you."

As everyone laughs, including Justine, the elegant woman in white, all I can see is red.

My throat goes dry. Tears start to sting, and I suck a big ugly breath into my lungs.

Damn it, Krystle, you're mad. *You don't cry. Not for traitors like Tucker or...Justine.*

People like Harrison and Nancy make me feel like a bull in a china shop, so I'll olé right over Justine's social-climbing, skinny ass.

"So your summer associate plans have changed?" I step into their privileged circle and watch Justine's eyes go wide.

"Krystle! I didn't expect to see you here." She hurries toward me as if that'll shut me up.

"Oh, I couldn't be invited?"

"Were you?" Harrison asks, like some white knight. "Nancy didn't mention it."

"Let's go over to the bar and get a drink." Justine puts a hand on my arm, and I yank it away.

"Are you trying to handle me, Justine? Last I checked, *you* work for *me*. Not him. Has that changed in the past twenty-four hours?"

"Krystle, this is not the time or place."

"Really, I've got all the time in the world. Please, continue explaining the legal theory that we came up with in my car."

She presses a hand to her chest and flutters it across her big white lapel. "I came up with eminent domain in the law library and outlined it for you in your car." She lowers her voice to a near whisper. "I'm here working on keeping the Davenforth business, as we discussed. A scene won't help."

"I create scenes? Is that how you're justifying jumping ship? Or jumping onto a yacht? Was this your plan all along? Get in good with the Newport crowd?" I raise an eyebrow toward Harrison, who still has his hand on her. "Get in *real good* it seems."

Justine's jaw drops, and she takes a step back as if I've really hit a nerve.

"Oh my God! You are boinking our client?!" I hear the shriek in my voice, but I can't stop. All this time she's been Miss Prim and Proper and here she is getting golden goosed. "How could you forget who was there for you when you were just a housewife too scared to leave the house?"

There's hurt in her brown eyes. Before I can feel bad, she takes another step back toward Harrison's circle. "I'm out of the house now *and* on the guest list. Perhaps you should go home, Krystle."

I'm watching her whirl around toward the judge, so I don't notice Harrison until his hot breath is in my ear. "Take her advice, or get thrown out with the trash."

JUSTINE

Leave it to the Cannoli Queen to ruin a classy affair.

Here I am doing my best Princess Di in pearls, white gloves, and a double-breasted suit-dress, convincing Providence's political royalty to support our legal strategy—not to mention rendering Tucker a dull court jester in comparison. In other words, here I am doing my *job*. And here comes our matriarch, fiery curls whipping flushed cheeks, tongue burning with insults and vicious accusations, dead set on torching my hard work.

And why?

Why barge over, uninvited, to a group of potential business contacts whom she knows disdain her reputation as a mob lawyer's wife? Why play Ms. High and Mighty, daring to look down at me from the top of Providence's very own hill.

Why wreck this for me? For the firm?

Because I don't factor for Krystle, clearly. The woman's all ego and id stuffed into last season's Chanel wrapper. When her pride's wounded, she couldn't care less about others or how she presents to them. She's this runaway freight train. Furious speed and force without any consideration of the best route forward. And I'm sick of this ride.

I stop nodding at whatever remark the judge in front of me is making to glance over my shoulder. Party guests steer clear as Krystle barrels into the crowd. Some of them look from her to me, ears ringing with whatever sharp words they couldn't help but overhear. My first Rhode Island society party, and I'm at the center of a scene. How mortifying.

A pressure at the base of my back returns my attention to the reason I came. Harrison leans toward my ear, speaking at a volume louder than a whisper, but quiet enough *not* to draw undue attention. Krystle should take note.

"She seems like…a lot."

I face him, grateful that he's siding with me rather than seeing me differently thanks to my association with the party crasher. "Krystle's late husband was a founding partner, so she considers herself the boss. I guess, technically, she has more equity in the firm than I do. She signs the checks. But none of that means much."

Harrison shoots Krystle a scathing glance. "It's difficult to picture *you* working for *her*."

Without thinking, my head bobs in agreement. Our husbands dying in that plane crash might have made us friends, but it clearly didn't make us true business partners in Krystle's mind. Or equals. Despite everything I've done to earn Krystle's respect and prove that I'm more than a housewife, she made it more than clear that she still sees me as a sad, insecure, overwhelmed single mom, desperate for direction.

"Can't be rabbi in the temple you grew up in."

Harrison's expression alerts me to the fact that I've muttered the aphorism aloud. I force a laugh. "Something my mom used to say. It's difficult to change a person's perception of you after they've gotten to know an earlier version in development."

Harrison gestures with his head to our former table. "Well, you made quite a first impression on all our friends over there."

I trace his gaze to where I'd been so surprisingly in my element minutes earlier. The governor had hung on my every word.

"I'm not kidding about what I said to the judge. After you graduate, you'll have a waiting list of clients. A half-Black, half-Jewish female attorney out of Harvard."

The mention of my ethnic background drops the smile from my face. "That's not the only reason why. People appreciate my work history. What the firm and I did—"

"Of course, you're brilliant." He grins at me. "It doesn't matter. I suspect my mother will snap you up first."

As his words register, I scan for Krystle, hoping she's in earshot. Harrison is all but confirming that the Davenforth business will remain with our firm. We've won! Or, I've won on our behalf. See Krystle? See what I was doing all along?

"So, you'll stay with Romero, Tavani, Kelly, and Romero?"

Harrison smirks. "Those are a lot of names, and my mother doesn't like to share. Most of the professionals who work for our family, only work for our family."

Harrison places his hand between my shoulder blades. "So the question is, will *Kelly* remain with a couple of Romeros and a Tavani?"

I open my mouth to answer and realize that I don't have one. Minutes earlier, before Krystle essentially accused me—in front of a judge, no less—of abandoning our firm and sleeping my way into my first solo account, I would never have considered leaving. The firm isn't simply a business. It's what I have left of my husband. His legacy. And, after everything I and the other widows have been through together, my family.

Though Krystle isn't treating me like family.

Then again, maybe she is. She's treating me like Rom. And I'm nothing like Rom.

Harrison's gentle pressure on my back urges me forward. "Consider it while we walk."

He leads me through the well-dressed crowd, beneath curved cedar planks supporting the temporary tent's sailcloth ceiling. The size of the beams calls for a more static structure. Though I suppose the Davenforths can afford to spend permanent prices on passing fancies. A luxury of wealth—the ability to waste.

For a moment, I let myself imagine that I also enjoy such extravagance. I picture myself a princess of Davenforth castle, filthy with disposable time and income, enjoying the life Jack had promised would be waiting for me in Providence, provided I gave up my Manhattan modeling career.

But he cheated on me and died. Now I'm working seven days a week, going to school, barely seeing my son, and living in my in-laws' attic.

As we exit the tent, I glance over my shoulder at the Davenforths' mansion. Their attic is for *the help*. I imagine enjoying a quiet dinner with Harrison—not cooked by me. The Davenforths' stuffy butler calling me "madame" as he informs me of our waiting guests. JJ attending private school, being educated with Providence's elite, and learning to move seamlessly in the upper echelons. He'd never have to hustle.

And I would be a part of all of this. Part of a family with a name that automatically confers respect. Part of a real legacy, shored up by generations. My son would be part of it.

I glance up at my handsome companion and accept that it's all a daydream. With his parentage and looks, Harrison has women fawning all over him. Today it happens to be me.

The thought makes me separate from Harrison's grasp and head toward the cliffs at the edge of the property. Beyond them, rolled out like a burnished carpet, is the ocean. The setting sun has transmuted the sea into molten gold. It crashes against the cliffs, sending sparks above the rock wall at the property's edge. Mother Nature herself lights the fireworks here.

When I reach the rocks, I stop to breathe, pulling saltwater air deep into my lungs, tasting its tang sweetened with flowers. It works like a balm over my Krystle-inflamed nerves. The sea is medicine for the soul. Too bad only the country's most affluent can afford to live by it.

"Beautiful."

Though I hear Harrison's voice, I don't turn toward him. Don't look at what I can't have. Instead, I contemplate the view, savoring a moments' peace, the brief reminder that I'm connected to something greater than the doubts and desires driving my actions.

Harrison wraps his arms around my waist, enveloping me in his warm body. His heartbeat quickens. I feel it in the rise and swell of his chest.

"I don't mean the view," he says, nuzzling my hair. "I mean you."

A sense of déjà vu overwhelms me. I remember this feeling. Being wanted. Being valued.

God, in spite of everything, I miss Jack.

But Jack is gone.

I rotate in Harrison's arms and gaze at his handsome face, staring into the eyes that remind me of the one I'd loved, lost, hated, and now, often, long for. "Thank you for having me."

And then he does it. Harrison presses his lips against mine. My own mouth opens. I taste the caramel notes of the bourbon he imbibed earlier. Feel the hardness of his body against my own. For a moment, I forget that this man is one of our fair city's most eligible bachelors, or that a who's who of Providence watches from Chiavari chairs. I think of nothing except the sensation of kissing someone. My skin tingles as if doused in champagne. Blood swells my cheeks and chest. This is what it's like to feel worthy.

"Surprise PDAs are your style."

I pull away, embarrassed to be called out by one of the party guests. My shame vanishes, however, once I see who's offering her unsolicited opinion.

Tara Jordan folds her arms beneath her chest, unnecessarily pushing up the large breasts all too visible in her look-at-me, neon-lime dress. Like someone installed a Times Square billboard on a private beach.

She smirks at Harrison and me like a high school babysitter after catching her tiny charges playing house. Harrison glares at her. "How did you get in here, Tara?"

She chuckles. "My usual way."

Harrison steps in front of me, blocking her narrowed stare. "You shouldn't have been allowed in. My mother spoke to Police Commissioner Mann. He told her you hired that woman to seduce my father. And then he ended up dead."

I wince at the mention of "that woman" and what he's implying: Camille and the assumption she's killed the mayor has been in the papers, along with her association with our firm. Both Nancy and Harrison have surely seen the articles. No wonder the Davenforths only want to work with me.

But they don't know Camille like I do.

I touch Harrison's arm. "That woman, Camille Tavani, is a private investigator who works with our family law division. She catches cheating spouses for leverage in divorce proceedings. But she's not a murderer. There's no way that she would have knowingly given your father anything illegal or poisonous." I step beside Harrison to fix Tara with my own disdainful gaze. "She was set up."

Tara's face darkens. "Not by me, as Harrison is well aware."

For a moment, Harrison says nothing. He then wraps an arm around my waist. "From where I'm standing, Tara, you look guilty. You wanted to make sure that whatever money Tom received from divorcing my mother went into your pockets, regardless of any prenuptial agreement."

Tara's jaw drops. But she recovers a second later, her lips stretching into their prior devil-may-care smirk. "That wasn't why we married, and you know that, stepson."

Harrison's lips purse at the title. Tara might have legally been his stepmother, but she could never have served as any kind of parental figure. She has three years on Harrison at most.

"I don't have any idea why you married him, Tara. But I have several theories concerning your motive for murder. Money is only one that I'll be sharing with the police."

The expression on Tara's face remains cool, but I notice her hand trembling. She steps toward Harrison, close enough to stare him down. A smile curls a corner of her mouth. "I'm pregnant."

Harrison's hand drops from my waist. "What?"

Tara places a hand on her belly and moves it in a circular motion, massaging the life that I'm not positive is actually there. Her stomach appears too flat to be hiding a baby, though that doesn't necessarily mean anything other than that the pregnancy is still in its early stages. I didn't pop with my son until well into my sixth month.

"Do you really think the police will suspect me of killing my husband when I'm with child?" She gives Harrison a pitying smile, sapped of genuine sympathy. "As busy as I am, surely I'd want parental help. We all know how important fathers are to their sons."

Harrison's eyes narrow at his stepmother. "Why are you only telling me this now?"

She shrugs. "I hadn't decided what to do."

"Now you have?"

Harrison's voice sounds scratchy, as if his throat is closing to keep his emotions in check. I imagine he wants to cry or scream. A child will tie him to his conniving stepmother forever, even if she ends up in prison. Especially if she ends up in prison. An adult sibling is surely next in the line of succession if the parents can't fulfill their duties due to death and incarceration.

Tara grins at Harrison, the Cheshire cat aware of the answer to a seemingly nonsense riddle. "I absolutely have." She turns on her heel and starts toward the house, calling over her shoulder. "Congratulations, Harrison. You're going to be a big brother."

CAMILLE

"I've been here for over an hour, and I still haven't found anyone who knows anything about the casino," I say to Meredith, standing next to me in the tent. She studies the Paris of Providence model while I scan the room as the party in the tent rages all around us.

And by "rages," I mean pasty-faced folks in seersucker suits and gauzy dresses nursing wine spritzers while a lady in a floppy hat plays a harp in the corner.

"Or at least, not anyone willing to admit it," Meredith says without looking up. She stares at the model with a scowl. "As far as the casino's concerned, we're behind enemy lines, remember? I mean, look at this thing."

I lean in, trying to get my bearings. "Where's your club?"

She waves off my question with a hand. "Exactly where it's always been. If that old bat thinks she's tearing it down for this bullshit, she's in for one hell of a fight."

I don't doubt it. I've seen firsthand the blood, sweat, and tears

Meredith has poured into the Luna Lounge. She'll chain herself to the doors before she lets Nancy remove the first brick.

I follow the river north, searching for the familiar westward bend, but Nancy's model makes it hard. "Is she moving the river? Can you even do that? Where's the burial ground?"

"Somewhere in the middle of all that." Meredith stabs a finger at a huge complex of neat squares and rectangles—multiple city blocks filled with offices, governmental buildings, and green space.

I lean forward and read the letters slashed across the biggest building. "'The Netop Complex.' What's a Netop?"

The voice comes from just behind us. "It's a friend."

Meredith and I whirl around, and it's the vile Tucker Armand in that silly bow tie. Today's version is covered with little Eiffel Towers that would look phallic if they weren't embroidered on baby-pink silk.

"It's what the natives said to Roger Williams way back when he arrived," Tucker says. "According to old legend, they said, '*What cheer, netop.*' Greetings, friend. Nancy is honoring the tribe by naming the complex Netop."

Meredith takes him in with squinty eyes. "That's some honor. Kind of like the way she honored my club with a statue that looks like a dick."

Tucker makes a face. "See? This is exactly why Nancy will never work with your firm long term. You people have zero class, which means you'll never fit in this world."

Next to me, Meredith sucks in a breath, but she holds her tongue. I saw her talking to Tara earlier, saw the way Meredith stood a few inches taller after she'd slipped on Tara's jacket. Meredith feels out of place in this snotty crowd, and if she asked my opinion, I'd tell her she's not wrong. As far as I can tell, she's the only one here besides me and Krystle without a stick up her butt.

"What kind of world is that?" I ask. "The kind of world that would bulldoze other people's businesses and a sacred Native burial ground in order to turn a profit? Because where I come from, that's called stealing."

"There it is, the crux of the problem. Where you come from. If you'd been born into this world like I was, you'd see that this isn't just about the Davenforths making a profit. This is about family. Legacy. Something for the entire world to remember them by until the end of time."

"Seems like the word *legacy* is just an excuse to cover up sins. Isn't legacy the only reason you're standing here? Because of nepotism? The old boy network looking after their own. And remind me, how did you get into law school again?"

Tucker went to Yale, but only because his family name is plastered across one of the dorms: *Armand Hall*. His grandfather bought the spot after Tucker almost flunked out of high school. It's part of why Peter hired him, because he thought Tucker's connections would bring in business.

Judging from the purple spots that bloom on Tucker's cheeks, it's a sensitive subject. He cocks a brow, and his gaze dips to my cleavage. "At least what I was born with is not about to land me in jail for murder, Camille. To answer your question,

I got into Yale just like everybody else there, thanks to brains and hard work."

Meredith rolls her eyes. "Sure, you did."

"Here's a little secret I shared with your illustrious boss before most of your clients came running to my new firm," he says, puffing his bony chest. "I do whatever it takes. I'm the one who got Tom on board with Nancy's plan. My connections helped, but I'm the one who changed his mind."

I nearly laugh. "You and Nancy might have your talking points straight, but no way do I buy that Mayor Tom would leave all that money on the table because of one conversation with you, Tucker."

He glares his beady eyes at me, and I can see the insult coming. "That was a nice little write-up of you in the paper. Great mug shot too. I sure hope stripes are your color."

I open my mouth to tell Tucker to go to hell, but the voice comes from behind me.

"Given all the people here who deserve to be behind bars, I'm not sure Camille is the one to focus on."

I whirl around and there he is. Aiden, coming to my defense. Mussed hair pulled back into a neat ponytail. Feet stuffed into leather shoes. Big body draped in a suit. A *good* suit.

"I was only comparing the relative value of assets." Tucker adjusts his bow tie as if Aiden's comment knocked it askew. "Surely you know the value of pedigree, Aiden."

"Camille," he says. "We meet again."

"You clean up nice."

The smile he gives me as a response does something to me.

Maybe it's the glass of chardonnay I drank on an empty stomach, but suddenly I'm remembering the feel of his hands on my waist, pulling me back upright, holding me steady after his dog almost bumped me into the pond. I'm returning his smile when it dawns on me what Tucker just said.

My gaze flips between him and Tucker. "Hang on, the Narragansett pedigree?"

Tucker laughs and slaps Aiden hard on the back. "If anyone has profited by being part of the Davenforth clan, it's this man. If it weren't for his sweet Aunt Nancy, Aiden would still be living in a teepee."

His aunt. Nancy Davenforth is Aiden's *aunt*?

Meredith snorts, nudging me with an elbow. "Suddenly, this party got a whole lot more interesting."

I ignore her, my gaze whipping to Aiden, my mind whirring. I think back to our conversation on the dock, his animosity toward all the Davenforths but especially Nancy. Aiden's expression is carefully wiped clean, but his hands are fists, his shoulders hard as steel under the soft silk of his suit. I don't know this man all that well, but I know one thing: he hates this Tucker fucker as much as I do. That teepee comment was a real low blow.

"God, Tucker," I say, shooting him a scathing glare. "You're a real asshole, has anybody ever told you that?"

"Strangely enough, yes."

"Your own father, most likely," Meredith says, and her words do the trick. They drop that ugly grin right off his cheeks.

I flick my fingers in his general direction. "Now shoo. I've got nothing else to say to you that doesn't include more cussing."

He rolls his eyes but wanders off, and the three of us stand in silence, watching him sidle up to a state senator holding court with a half dozen potential donors, interrupting him like they're old buddies. I swear. That's the most annoying thing about Tucker Armand (and there are a *lot* of annoying things)—that he's just so goddamn entitled.

I watch them schmooze and give myself a minute to collect my thoughts about Aiden, though I do wonder if any of those glad-handers were in on Mayor Tom's casino plans. I spot Marco and wonder what brought him here, especially when he approaches Tara with a smile that says this isn't the first time they've met.

"I recognize that guy," Meredith says, her gaze tracking Tara. "He used to come into the club with Mayor Tom. Big spender and bigger talker. I think he's from Vegas or—"

"Atlantic City," I murmur. "That's Marco, the casino developer."

"I was surprised he didn't try his pitch again when he saw me tonight," Aiden says, then turns to Meredith and holds out a hand. "I don't believe we've met. Aiden Wyatt."

"Here I thought I knew every man in this town. Meredith Everett. Nice to meet you." She turns to me with a knowing look. "I'm pretty sure you can take it from here. Don't do anything I wouldn't do."

She gives us a wave and saunters off.

"You didn't have to defend me back there," he says as soon as she's gone. "I'm perfectly capable of defending myself."

"I'm sure you are, but, honey, I'm from the south. We squash our bugs, not give them a chance to sink their teeth into our skin for a second time. Kind of like I'm about to do with you."

"I'm a bug?"

"No. According to what I just heard, you're a Davenforth."

"You're angry about that fact?"

I nod, then shake my head. "No. I'm angry that you hid it from me. All that talking we did about the Davenforths, you didn't think to mention that you were one of them? It makes me wonder what else you're hiding."

Like maybe plans to use that land as leverage, for example, to hold out for more money or an invitation back into the Davenforth clan. Like maybe all this talk of protecting the tribe's history is a ploy, an attempt to plant his hooks into his family—and with it, their wealth. Like maybe use it to distract me from his own motives for getting Tom out of the way.

But it's hard for me to think of Aiden as that sneaky, especially after seeing where he lives. His bare feet planted on the wooden dock. The way the lake and nature suit him. His dedication to keeping that land pure and untouched, it fits.

"My lineage is not a secret," he says, sweeping a relaxed arm to indicate the crowd gathered on the lawn outside the tent, the sparkling Atlantic as a backdrop. "Ask anyone here, and I'm sure they'd be happy to give you an earful. I've been the subject of Davenforth family gossip since long before I was born. The bastard brown son. None of those people out there ever let me forget."

Something tugs in my chest at the thought of him playing on that big lawn outside, fending off the taunts from the Tuckers of the world, pretending not to hear the millions of daily insults from adults who were supposed to love him but didn't, and just because they thought his blood wasn't pure. Being Narragansett and Davenforth. It can't have made for an easy childhood.

Or adulthood, either, now that I think about it. In fact, I don't know how being here, on this pretentious estate with all these pretentious people, doesn't make him put his fist through the tent walls.

"How do you stand it? Being surrounded by all these Davenforths, I mean, knowing they think those things. Putting on that suit so you'll look like you're one of them. As nice as your suit is, I think I like you better in bare feet and wild hair."

"I'll take that as a compliment."

"It's meant as one. I understand it now, why you're so hard to rile up. Because you've spent your entire life around people like Tucker, learning how to let their repulsive comments roll off your back. I'm sorry if earlier it seemed like I was judging you too."

He goes quiet for a long moment, and for someone who's normally so hard to read, he doesn't hide the way my words affect him. First surprise at the sentiment coming from someone who's essentially a stranger, then gratitude in the form of a warm smile. "Camille Tavani, you are not who I thought you were."

I didn't expect my skin to go so tingly at his words or the way they summon up a bright smile in return. Most men see me exactly as I present myself. Hair. Boobs. Tight dress with just a tad more cleavage than is socially acceptable. That this man sees past all my pretty armor feels like a gift somehow, though I'm not about to tell him that.

I laugh it off with a hand through the air. "My family tree has a lot fewer branches than yours, that's for sure. Now answer the question, counselor. How do you stand being around this den of thieves?"

"My father is James Buchanon Wyatt, Nancy's first cousin. The coddled youngest child who was always getting into trouble so his parents could bail him out. They say negative attention is still attention, and he was good at making sure all the attention landed on him. The Davenforths' beloved wild child, and *everybody* loved him. Until he went and got an Indian woman pregnant."

A waiter breezes by with a tray of white wine, and I stop him with a hand to his sleeve.

"Hang on, sugar. I'm gonna need a drink for this one." I pluck two full glasses from the tray and hand Aiden one. "Now please don't tell me your mother was the maid."

He lifts his glass in a silent cheers. "Close. She worked in the kitchen at the camp where all the Davenforth kids spent their summers, which makes me the biggest cliché in the world. The illicit love child of a Davenforth heir and a Narragansett dishwasher. The Davenforths will deny to the very end that they were ever in love. My mother tells a different story."

"Which is?"

"That until I came along, that summer was one of the happiest of her life. That James loved her as much as she loved him, at least for a while. But money is a great motivator, and his parents knew that all too well. The second they threatened to cut him off, he came running home with his tail between his legs. For the first few years, he pretended like my mom and I didn't exist."

"That's awful."

"Mostly for my mother. He broke her heart: first by leaving us and then for a second time when I was five and he hauled me away from her family and brought me here. They wanted me to become one of them, a Davenforth. I wasn't allowed to speak of her or traditions she'd taught me. I couldn't bring anything with me. They even cut my hair. Took away any traces of my Narragansett identity. They let me see my mom and her family out in South County twice a year."

"But how? She's your mother."

"And they are Davenforths. Nobody ever says no to a Davenforth. Except me. The second I turned eighteen, I was out of here. I started spending every spare second back with her and her family. My mother tells everyone we've made up for lost time, but that's only because it hurts her too much to think about how many years we lost."

I shake my head, my skin going hot. "I say this with all due respect, sugar, but your family's even more messed up than mine is. I hate those bastards for you."

Aiden shrugs, taking a sip from his glass. "Believe me. I've spent plenty of dark moments where you are, marinating in my own hatred and resentment. Harrison was good to me for a while. When we were kids, he actually liked to go with me to see my mom and my Narragansett family. He was an only child and lonely for a brother his parents couldn't seem to produce, and then he went off to college and kind of lost his way."

"You never lost your way?"

"I wouldn't say that, but I decided that my best defense was to use my brain. To learn the rules of the games the people in power play with real lives. It's why I went to law school, so I could learn to be strategic."

"So that's why you're here, then—strategy?"

"As attorney for the Narragansett tribe, it's my job to know who's coming for our burial ground." He tips his head to Nancy's Paris of the Northeast model.

"Looks like the casino's off the table, at least. Though I can't imagine a Netop Complex on top of your burial ground would be much of a consolation prize."

"That name is an insult, and Nancy knows it. But Tom switching alliances was a surprise. Makes me wonder what else I've missed, if there are any new players gunning for the land surrounding ours."

"How do you find that out?"

"By pulling the property records at city hall to see if anything's changed. The parcel behind the burial ground was a big part of Tom's plans. He owned it, but he needed ours to build the casino. So now the question is, did he or Nancy file any new application to rezone that land before he died? And who owns it now? Did he sell it to Nancy before he died, or is it still part of his estate?"

Meaning Tara would inherit it. Unless those two had a prenup, which I'm guessing they did, in which case it would most likely go to Harrison. Maybe that's why Nancy is so sure of this Paris business, because she's gotten her claws on that parcel.

"So what about you?" Aiden says, tugging me out of my

thoughts. "Did you make any progress? Add any more names to your murder suspect list?"

"Aiden Wyatt, are you making fun of me?"

"Camille Tavani, I wouldn't dare. I'm genuinely curious. And admittedly, more than a little concerned. It's been three days since the mayor's murder. That's three days for the police to be building a case against you once they confirm the mayor was murdered."

My heart revs at his words, because Aiden's right, and of course I've thought of this. As the only person of interest that's made the papers, I've thought of little else. While I'm running around town, sneaking into parties and running up against walls, the police are building a case. Three days and I'm no closer to finding the mayor's killer than I was when he dropped dead in the champagne room. Even worse, I'm running out of time.

"I'm sorry," he says. "I didn't mean to scare you. I just want you to be prepared in case…"

Whatever he says next gets lost in a loud buzzing in my ears because there, standing in the doorway on the other side of what's left of the well-heeled crowd, are two policemen. The buzzing builds, rolling quickly into a steady roar. I see their dark uniforms, their stern expressions searching the tent, and my heart gives a hard kick.

"Oh, no. Oh, shit."

One of them says something to Nancy, who listens with wide eyes. She nods once, then turns to point my way. I latch on to Aiden's sleeve.

This is it. They're coming to arrest me for the mayor's murder.

"Oh, no. No, no, no, no, no, no, no."

The thin crowd parts to let the cops through, and there's not enough air. The tent shrinks down to a teeny tiny nub. My heart beats hard enough that I'm surprised I don't pass out, and what happened to all the air?

The cops march straight at us.

Aiden moves to his left, stepping right in front of me, blocking me with his body. "Don't say a word to them unless it's to demand a lawyer. I'll follow you to the station."

His voice is low and controlled and comforting, and I grab on to the back of his jacket, bracing for another round in the slammer, this time maybe for good. My last seconds of freedom. At least I'm being comforted by this man.

Then Aiden's back goes straight. He twists his big body around. Frowns in confusion as the cops breeze right on by.

The relief is like a blast of icy air, turning my bones to slush. My knees buckle, and I have to work to keep myself upright. Those handcuffs weren't for me. They're not—

"Hey!" Meredith's voice, loud and pissy in the hushed tent. "Get your dirty hands off me."

I turn just in time to see fear flash across Meredith's face. The chinking of the handcuffs as one of the cops slaps them on can't drown out those terrible but familiar words.

"You're under arrest."

MEREDITH

I thought the Davenforths' party was a terrible way to spend a Saturday night, but I should have known: it can always get worse.

When the cops perp-walked me past every influential person in Providence and shoved me in the back of the cruiser, it didn't feel real. The whole way downtown—no sirens; they weren't in a hurry—I was floating outside my body, as if I was watching myself on TV. A very special episode of *Hill Street Blues*, starring me, whether I liked it or not.

Now that I've been waiting in an interrogation room for well over an hour, wrists aching and cold from the cuffs chaining me to the table, it's starting to feel extremely fucking real. Plenty of the women I know from the club have been arrested at some point, but this is my first time. And it's not just some trumped-up narcotics or solicitation charge.

This is murder.

My only hope is Rom Romero. Supposedly, he rushed straight

from the Davenforth house to the station after I was arrested, but the cops haven't let me speak to him yet. If only I was still in contact with my ex-girlfriend Frankie... We were a terrible match, a total rebound after my disastrous relationship before that, but dating an FBI agent with connections in the Providence PD sure would come in handy right about now.

Thankfully they haven't stripped me of my street clothes and put me in a prison uniform yet; orange is *so* not my color. Lime green really isn't either, but having Tara's blazer on makes me feel stronger in this moment. Maybe there really is something to this power-dressing thing. The fabric smells like her signature scent too, and I keep taking big whiffs to distract me from the aromas of burnt coffee and sweat hanging in the air of this sad little room.

When the door swings open, though, I nearly jump out of my seat. Rom walks in, and I've never been so happy to see that idiot. The young cop who arrested me—Rom's drinking buddy—is there too, and they're followed by two detectives in plain clothes, a man and a woman.

Officer Frat Boy takes up a guard post by the door. Not sure why that's necessary, since I'm tied down like we're in the world's worst bondage scene, but okay. The detectives go to the opposite side of the table. The woman sits, and the man stands behind her, staring at me. I realize I've seen him at the club too. He's handsy, which is bad, and a terrible tipper, which is worse.

"Are you all right?" Rom asks in a low voice—though there's no hiding our conversation in this claustrophobic, echoing space.

"Oh, sure. Best night of my life."

"I'll do the talking, okay?"

"You always do."

He grips my arm, wrinkling Tara's blazer. "I'm serious, Meredith. Keep your mouth shut unless I tell you otherwise."

I can smell the whiskey on his breath from the Davenforths' open bar, but his eyes are clear—and deadly earnest. I nod and press my lips together. I have the right to remain silent, and I'm gonna take it.

"Thanks for your patience, Ms. Everett," the man says. "I'm Detective Crary, and this is my colleague Detective Reynolds."

I thought the woman might be more sympathetic to my plight, but she's staring at me like I'm about to give the love of her life a full-contact lap dance. So much for sisterhood.

"What were you doing at the Davenforth home this evening?" Reynolds asks.

"Ms. Everett is part owner of my law firm," Rom says. "We represent some of the Davenforth family's business interests."

Detective Crary looks at me with feigned shock, and I sincerely wish he'd go back to ogling me. "You own a law firm? I thought you were an...exotic dancer."

"Ms. Everett is also the sole proprietor of the Luna Lounge," Rom says. "As you already know."

Obviously. They're just trying to rile me. I start to fold my arms—then realize I can't because of the damn cuffs, so I settle for leaning back in my chair with an expression as hard as the uncomfortable metal seat.

"Were you invited to tonight's event?" Reynolds asks. "We

obtained a copy of the guest list from the Davenforths' security, and neither of you were on it."

Rom clams up on that one too. Party crashing isn't a crime—I don't think so, anyway—but it doesn't exactly make us look like upstanding citizens.

"You were seen talking with Tara Jordan," Crary says. "Are the two of you friends?"

I look at Rom. He gives me a small nod.

"I'm acquainted with her. But I barely know her. I wouldn't say we're friends."

"Isn't that her jacket you're wearing?" Reynolds asks.

"It is."

Reynolds eyes the oversized neon lapels. "I don't know about you, but I don't lend my clothing to women I 'barely know.'"

As if anyone would *want* to borrow her clothing. Detective Reynolds is wearing a boxy sport coat and an ill-fitting blouse that gaps when she moves, so I can see her faded beige bra between the buttonholes. If she's going to judge me, I'm going to judge her right back.

"What about Camille Tavani?" she asks. "You two are close friends, right?"

I wish Camille were here—well, not literally, 'cause if they'd arrested us both, the situation would be that much more dire. But she'd be able to insult this woman to her face and still have it come off sugary sweet—a Southern superpower that doesn't come naturally to us New Englanders.

"Yes, Camille and I are friends." Such good friends, that in the effort to clear her name I've somehow become Suspect Number One myself.

"We understand you were helping her run her little operation."

Out of the corner of my eye, I see Rom shake his head. Yeah genius, I know not to answer that one.

After a few seconds of stonewalling, Reynolds moves on. She reaches into her pocket and takes out an item, then places it on the table between us.

"Do you recognize this?"

Shit. Shit, shit, shit.

Rom leans in, squinting at the object.

"We found it in your purse," Crary says.

It's the memorial to Mayor Tom from the Davenforths' redevelopment model. I knew I shouldn't have taken it, but after talking to Tara I was feeling brave—and furious. The tiny statue snapped off so easily. It fit right in my purse. For the rest of the party, I kept sticking my hand into my bag and pressing the point of the obelisk into the pad of my thumb, feeling like such a badass for stealing from the Davenforths right under their fancy party tent's roof.

Now I just feel stupid. The way Rom's looking at me isn't helping. If Rom Romero is extremely disappointed in you, you know you've really screwed up.

"My client has no comment," he says. "I fail to see what this has to do with the very serious allegations you've leveled against her."

"It does demonstrate a certain…animosity toward the deceased," Reynolds says. "But you're right, Mr. Romero: it doesn't prove anything. This, on the other hand…"

She retrieves something else from the pocket of her sport coat and sets it on the table. A plastic baggie, full of pale-blue pills.

"Have you seen these before, Ms. Everett?"

"No," I say, and I'm being totally honest. I've seen my fair share of drugs working in strip clubs and dancing at mobbed-up private parties, but these particular pills are new to me.

"That's interesting," Reynolds says. "Because we found them in your desk."

I try not to react, but I can't keep my eyes from widening. In my *desk*? Unlike my predecessor, I don't keep my office door locked and guarded, so any number of people could have had access. I do keep the filing cabinet that contains all the club's financial records secured, but there's nothing worth hiding in my desk drawers—just stashes of essentials like tissues and hair pins and tampons I keep on hand for any of the girls who might need them.

"You were at the club when Mayor Tom died, yes?" Crary asks.

"Ms. Everett is at the club every night. As I said, she runs the place." The drugs must have Rom worried too, but you wouldn't be able to tell from the smug confidence in his voice.

Reynolds holds up the baggie. The pills have a strange shimmer to them, even under the interrogation room's fluorescents. Definitely not something you can get at your average pharmacy. Some sort of designer drug, maybe?

"Our lab analyzed these pills," Reynolds says. "We also analyzed the champagne Mayor Tom was served at the Luna Lounge. They both contained a high concentration of the same toxic substance that was also found in his bloodstream."

So what she's saying is, the murder weapon was found in my desk.

My hands start shaking so hard, I have to press my palms flat on the table to keep the cuffs from rattling. I'm being framed, all right. But by who? And how hard will these detectives laugh in my face if I try to float that idea?

Better to keep my mouth shut. This is a negotiation, and in a negotiation, whoever talks the most has the least power. The more these cops tell us, the more ammo Rom will have for my defense. At least that's what I'm telling myself so I don't break down sobbing.

"I'll cut to the chase, Ms. Everett," Reynolds says. "You were seen delivering a champagne bottle to the VIP room just before Mr. Bradley and Ms. Tavani arrived."

"What?" I blurt out. "That's impossible."

Rom cringes at my outburst. Both of the detectives smile. They got me to break my silence, and I know I should shut the hell up again, but this is bullshit. I didn't touch that bottle.

"We have an eyewitness who says otherwise," Reynolds says.

"Well, whoever they are, they're lying. I was in my office the whole time."

"Alone?" Crary actually tries to sound sympathetic, like he hopes I'll have an answer that will clear my name.

But I don't. When Camille left to meet with the mayor, I went into my office, and I didn't see or speak to anyone again until she ran in to tell me about his collapse. The only one who can verify my story is Camille, and they're not going to take her any more seriously than they're taking me.

"Could I have a moment with my client?" Rom asks.

Reynolds smirks. This is a show of weakness from our side of the table too. But I'm grateful for Rom's interruption. It's so strange not to want to smack him in the face.

"Five minutes," she says. The two detectives leave, and the young officer follows them, so Rom and I are entirely alone. A scenario that would have made my skin crawl not so long ago.

"We have attorney-client privilege, Meredith. So I won't share anything you tell me, not even with my mother. But I need to know: Did you deliver that bottle?"

I shake my head emphatically. "No. I swear I didn't. My office isn't ever locked. Anyone could have put the pills in my desk, and I've never seen ones like that before in my life. What do you think they are?"

"Painkillers," Rom says, with a little too much confidence. "People used to call 'em 'baby blues.' But they were taken off the market years ago."

"Why?"

"A bunch of overdoses, if I'm remembering right. They're not harmful in the recommended dosage, but it's way too easy to take too much."

So the cops think I'm a murderer and that I did the deed with deadly black-market drugs. Great. In my line of work, it's easy enough to score blow or weed or quaaludes if you want them, but pills like that? I wouldn't even know where to start.

"You think they're bluffing about the eyewitness?" I ask.

"It's possible. They'll have to tell the truth at the bail hearing, though, so it'd be shortsighted. Do you have any idea who the witness could be?"

"If they were back in the VIP area and sober enough to remember what they saw, it wasn't a customer. Probably someone who works at the club."

Whoever it is, they're either mistaken or lying outright. It's heartbreaking—not to mention infuriating—to think someone I work with could screw me over like that.

"Any notable disagreements at work lately?" Rom asks. "Disgruntled employees, or—"

"No. Not that I know of. I just keep thinking: Who stood to gain from both taking out the mayor *and* shutting down my club? I would have said the Davenforths, but—"

"The *Davenforths*?" Rom's eyebrows shoot up toward his slicked-back hairline.

For all I know, the cops have hidden cameras pointed at us, or they're watching through that creepy one-way glass. What do I have to lose at this point?

"They want my club closed as part of their property grab, and thanks to this whole mess, the police shut it down for them."

"Seems like an awful lot of trouble to go to just to get rid of one small business."

"The mayor also wanted to circumvent their hoity-toity Paris plans and build a casino instead. At least, at one point he did. In Nancy's big speech tonight, she claimed he'd come around to her side with the redevelopment scheme."

"Why would she want him dead if they were working together?" Rom asks.

"I don't know. But if we could prove th—"

"Pointing fingers at the most powerful family in the state—not to mention our firm's most important client—is only going to make you look crazy as well as guilty."

I glare at him and rattle the cuffs. "You're lucky I'm tied to this table, Junior. Even a jackass like you should know better than to call a woman crazy."

"That's not what I meant, and you know it. I'm trying to help you here. Your bail hearing is set for first thing Monday morning, which means whatever evidence the state has, they feel really good about it."

"What do you think my chances are?" I hate the vulnerable waver in my voice when I ask him this.

The old Rom Romero would have taken the opportunity to needle me.

Now he turns and takes my hand with something approaching real sincerity. "I'm going to do everything I can. I promise you that."

There must be a broader picture I'm not seeing yet. If anyone can figure it out, it's Camille. Hopefully I'm not already a convicted murderess by the time she does.

The door opens. Rom drops my hand, all business again.

"I think we have all we need for now," Detective Reynolds says. "I'm sure we'll be speaking again soon, Ms. Everett."

"Not without me, you won't," Rom says.

Reynolds gives him a brittle smile. "Of course not. Though you'll have to travel a bit farther next time."

I look at Rom. He's taken aback too. "I thought Ms. Everett would be held here, at least until her bail is set."

"She's being charged with a capital crime. We'll be transferring her to county. Tonight."

Tara's tailored blazer feels too tight now, as my panicked pulse thumps against the silky lining. With an apologetic glance at Rom—not at me—the young cop starts to uncuff me from the table, pulling my hands behind my back again.

"Don't say *anything*, Meredith," Rom tells me. "Not a word. You understand?"

I nod, lips pressed together. I'm shaking so hard it takes several tries to get me restrained again. The county prison is where they take the real criminals. The dangerous people. The cold-blooded murderers.

I don't belong there. I didn't do anything. But if no one believes me, it won't matter. I'm going down just the same, and all I can hope is that I don't take my friends down with me.

KRYSTLE

Hauling a briefcase full of cash seems to be my lot in life. Not that those stacks stay with me for long. I grip the handle tight like my—or Meredith's—life depends on it because it just might. *If* by the skin of Saint Jude's teeth my son Rom is able to convince the judge to grant her bail, we'll need every dime. Getting someone accused of murdering the mayor of Providence out on bail ain't going to come cheap.

The district courthouse is only a block away from our office. The big white stone building is showy, with enough statues and pillars to look like they stole it from Rome. My stomach flip-flops as I picture Rom inside, standing in front of the judge, arguing bail for his first capital case.

A mother shouldn't doubt her son, but this mother has seen this son screw up enough to last ten lifetimes. Drugs, booze, women, totaled cars—he's got a zest for life; I'll say that for his teenage years. Still, he did finish law school. He has stepped up to keep the law firm going as best he can.

He was as shocked as anyone seeing Meredith hauled away. Like Clark Freaking Kent into the phone booth, he sprung into action, following her to the police station for her interrogation and then rushing off to get ready for the hearing. I haven't seen him or anyone since Newport. He told me to get together every dime I could for Meredith's bail, and it's taken every last second to do that.

As I'm muscling my way up those marble steps through the throng of reporters and curious spectators, a woman with big earrings, bigger hair, and a straining, sparkling tube-top dress grabs my arm.

"Excuse me, ma'am. Are you going inside? Do you know where they're holding Meredith Everett?"

I frown at her, guessing she's one of the strippers from the Luna Lounge. "They only let lawyers see her before the hearing."

She sticks out her chest. "Well, her lawyer, Rom Romero, told me to find him."

For what? A lap dance?

I'm proud of myself that I don't say it to her face, though maybe she can read it on mine. She turns on her skyscraper heels and stomps toward the courthouse entrance.

"Hey, missy! Wait right there!"

A security guard who seems to recognize her points her down a hallway toward the conference rooms where lawyers meet with clients. I hustle after her and finally catch up as she's being waved through one of those oak doors by a cop the color of a tomato. Is there any man in this damn building this stripper doesn't know?

The officer is still flustered as I sneak past him. She sashays in there like she owns the place and drops her huge purse on the long conference table. Rom stands at one side of the table reviewing some papers, and Meredith is at the other end, slumped over in a chair, blinking as if in a fog.

"Hey Mere, baby, you okay? I brought ya a Pop-Tart if you didn't have breakfast." The woman reaches into her purse and pulls out the square package.

"I don't have an appetite," Meredith says. "Wait, it's strawberry?"

"Your favorite."

"Thanks."

Meredith opens it with trembling fingers and takes a bite. I pull a bottle of water out of my purse and set it in front of her. She gives me a little nod of appreciation, then I return to Rom at the other end of the room.

"You smell like smoke and booze."

Rom grins. "Hazards of the job, Ma. How much you get?"

"One hundred thousand, and not a penny more."

A shadow crosses his face, but it's gone quickly.

"Can I fix your tie?"

"Sure. You okay? You look out of sorts."

I can't help it; I have to vent as I start to adjust the knot. "Meredith has had enough shit rain down on her to last a dozen lifetimes. All I know is she's too smart to do something as stupid as murder the mayor of freaking Providence in her own club. She sure as hell doesn't mess with drugs. She's the kind of girl who cares for what she has, and she'd never jeopardize something she's worked her tight ass off to build."

"Ow, Ma, you're choking me. I really can do this myself."

"I hate this tie," I murmur as I loop the shiny purple monstrosity to give him a little more breathing room.

"You hated it on Dad too."

I hide my grin, remembering how Romeo loved to wear that tie to piss me off. Then he won a big slip-and-fall case with it on, and suddenly it was his lucky tie, so I couldn't argue.

My anger returns quickly, and I get back to double-checking that he's up for this. "Did you hear from Camille?"

"She's on her way. I told you. I got all this handled."

I step away from him now that his tie looks right. I pick a few pieces of lint off his suit jacket. "You can practice your arguments on me if you want."

Just like your dad did. I can't say that one; it'd hurt too much.

"I got this, Ma. Really." Rom blows out a long breath and runs his finger along his chicken scratches on the legal pad resting on the table. Did I never notice he's got his father's handwriting?

The stripper who was hovering over Meredith heads toward us. "Hey Rom, who do I give these letters to?" She pulls several crumbled sheets of paper out of her pocket. "Here's my list and the girls over at Big Daddy's who used to be with Meredith." She drops her voice as if she's ashamed of what she's saying. "We hated to go to another club, but bills don't stop for tears. We all really hope she comes back. Ain't no boss ever treated us so good."

"Thanks, Misty." Rom sounds so serious as he nods toward

me. "Can you file those with the others in the folder on the table, Mom?"

"*This* is your ma?!" Misty throws her hands in the air as if we're long-lost friends and gives me a squeeze. "Thank you for raising such a nice son, Mrs. Romero. He's going to get Meredith out of this crap. Imagine her having anything to do with drugs. Hey, there's Luxe!"

Another woman in a similarly tight and short dress hurries inside, waving another stack of papers.

"Here's all the girls, waitresses, and bartenders from the Hot Fox."

"Those are for the file too," Rom says to me.

I take Luxe's stack and read the first one. There's a list like she was headed to the grocery store:

1. Always treated me nice.
2. Paid my water bill four different times.
3. Paid a sitter for my kid so I could make the custody hearing.
4. Loaned me money when my car broke down.
5. Taught me to how to 365 twist on the pole and my tips tripled.
6. Always made sure I had something to eat before work and after.

I flip through the next letter—this one from Debbie—who has a similar list of how Meredith helped her make ends meet and even had a handsy customer thrown into a snowbank on Christmas.

I sort them alphabetically, and I'm glad to have something to do while my cheeks heat with shame. Yes, Rom was up all night. Yes, he was hitting every strip club in town. But not for the usual reasons that I'd assumed. He'd gone from my darling dipshit son to a legit justice-seeking lawyer. I was so mad about the past, his past, that I missed this bright future.

I dab my eyes and focus on the chaos. Now that Luxe has arrived, she and Misty descend on Meredith.

"Oh, honey, are you okay?"

"You need some lipstick!"

"Did they feed you?"

"I know you're not a hugger, but group hug, boss!"

Rom stands back and is grinning ear to ear as Meredith is swarmed. Giant purses are flopped onto the conference table and makeup dumped along with Aqua Net spray and combs. She only fights them for a second before it's a full makeover.

"Don't let those bastards think they got to you for a second," says Luxe as she applies thick foundation to Meredith's pale face.

Her shoulders relax slightly, and there's emotion in her scared eyes. "No blue eye shadow, Luxe."

"No doy, boss. We're going business bitch all the way."

After they're done, I cross over to Meredith and lean my caboose against the table. The makeover team heads toward Rom to give him their two cents.

I put a hand on Meredith's shoulder. "We're all set on bail."

"You found my cash okay?"

I'd gone to her condo last night after Rom left her in ACI, a.k.a. the big-ass prison where real bad guys go in Cranston. He'd called me and shared what she told him about cash she had stashed all over her place. Under mattresses, in the ceiling, hidden in vents and bra drawers. "It was all there, right down to the penny. With what's left from Tara, we should be good."

Meredith shows a second of relief, but it's gone like a puff of powder in a compact. "I've been accused of all kinds of things in my life. I was always able to stand up for myself. This is different. I've never felt so…helpless."

I get in her face. "You listen to me. No one is tougher than you. No one. We are fighting this together, and we will win. We get you bail and get you out. Then we figure out who framed you and killed the mayor. We can do this, and we will."

She holds her head up a little higher, looking mad, which is good. Mad we can work with; sad and defeated is a whole other story.

There's a rustle in the hallway and the door flies open. "I'm here!" Camille shouts as she rushes inside and slams the door with her ass. She shoves the dress she's carrying into my hands. "This is the best I could do."

I inspect the neckline and it's low, but not shockingly, or maybe being surrounded by strippers freshly off duty has warped my sense of decorum. I take the bag with undergarments and tasteful pumps. "It'll work."

Camille's blond hair is wilder than usual, or ever, and it's clear she's been working day and night to help too. "I got as many letters as I could." She pulls a stack out of her purse and hands them to Rom. Then she throws her arms around Meredith with a quiet sob.

"Hey, it's okay," Meredith says softly. "It's not your fault. Someone is trying to screw us over."

"I've been so worried about my own tail, it didn't even occur to me they could possibly be looking at someone else. How was last night? And the night before? Was it awful? It was, wasn't it?"

"It wasn't great, but hey, look at me now."

Meredith winks, and you know, she does look pretty great. It's not just the makeup. My guess is it's the natural glow from having a room full of people who have your back. Which reminds me: Where the hell is Justine?

"Have you heard from Little Miss Newport?" I ask Camille.

She shakes her head. "I saw her leave the party with that Harrison guy."

"Figures," I say and don't confess that I feel a little bad about how I'd left it with her. Honestly, I was hoping to at least get her side of things when I saw her today. It's hard to believe she'd really leave us behind for a rich guy in a mansion. No, it's more than that. I lost my ever-loving mind in front of anyone who's anyone at that party because Justine leaving our firm would prove Tucker right. I have turned this firm into a clown show. Or at the very least, a three-ring circus. Seeing Justine standing there polished and poised, well, maybe she wouldn't be wrong if she left.

Camille squeezes my shoulder. "Hey, come on. I'm sure she has a good reason for missing today."

"Oh, I'm sure she has reasons enough." I puff out my chest and do what I do best. Get mad. "I'm going to call her after we get Meredith outta here and give her an earful."

Rom claps his hands. "Okay, ladies, thank you for your help, but we need a few minutes with our client before the hearing starts."

Misty and Luxe grab their purses and give quick hugs to everyone as they leave in a cloud of hairspray and perfume. Camille and I keep close to Meredith as Rom wheels a chair in front of her.

"When we go in there, the attorney general will present enough of their case to try to prove what's called Tier 1 to Judge Gatta."

"He was at the party when she was arrested," I say, remembering him in the circle of men fawning over Justine.

Rom nods, not seeming worried. "It's a good draw for us. He has ties to the Hill and hopefully understands the importance of community."

"What do you mean? Why does *community* matter?" Meredith asks.

"That's part of my Tier 2 strategy, which we will need if the judge rules the attorney general has met Tier 1. Especially if there's really a witness to testify they saw you with the champagne bottle."

She slams her hand on the table. "I told you, that's a lie."

"We'll prove that in court if we go to trial. For today, we need to prove you're not a flight risk so the bail is set and we get you out of jail."

She nods once tightly, but her voice is shaky. "What if we don't meet Tier 2? Are there more chances to make bail?"

He shakes his head, but his gaze is confident. I'm scared

for Meredith and also feeling proud of my son. "We are getting you out."

"Damn tootin'!" Camille yells.

I give Meredith a firm pat. "Don't let the bastards see you sweat."

Meredith stands up with her shoulders back. "Then let's get this shit done so we can find out who should really be in cuffs."

We hug Meredith and exit with Rom so she can get dressed. Knowing Meredith, she wants a moment alone to get herself together before facing a full court.

As the three of us stand there in silence, I don't ask him if he needs anything. Instead I just say what's been bubbling up from deep in my heart. "Your father would be so proud of you."

He grins. "I know, Ma."

I plant a big red-lipped kiss right on his cheek. "See you in there, son!"

"Good luck, Rom." Camille wipes under her eyes and shakes her hair as if she's realizing that she's not her usual glam goddess self. Still, we hurry down the hallway to the main entrance, which is crowded with spectators and reporters gathered outside the courtroom. We elbow through as reporters snap our pictures and shout questions.

"Were you speaking to the Widowmaker?!"

"Did she confess?"

I pull Camille through the crowd. "I can't believe that's what the papers are calling her."

The courtroom is packed and buzzing. We drop into seats

reserved for family, and I realize Luxe, Misty, about a dozen of their girlfriends, and a couple of beefy guys are right behind us. Camille waves at several people—folks she'd know, with her business—and turns back toward me.

A bailiff who gets a few waves from the row behind us makes his way to the front of the room. "All rise for the Honorable Judge Gatta."

We do as we're told, and the judge looks different in black robes versus his fancy Newport suit. As much as Rom thinks this guy knows about community, I can't help but think of what he said in that circle at the party. The advice he was giving about running small businesses out of the Hill for *progress*, whatever the hell that meant.

Well, *we* know what that means. Businesses that come into existing communities and make a few people rich while ruining everything around it. What was Justine's word? *Colonialism*.

I think of my visit—if you can call it that—with Aiden. How he'd tried to explain that some things are about more than progress but instead what matters to a community, including the roots, which let everything grow.

The judge motions in his black robe. "Be seated. I want to remind those here that this is my courtroom. I understand this is a capital case and there's a lot on the line, but I will maintain decorum."

Judge Gatta looks right in our direction, including the ladies and gents of the Luna Lounge.

"Now, I've reviewed the evidence presented by the state in my chambers, and I am ruling that Tier 1 conditions have not been met for Ms. Everett to make bail."

I grab Camille's arm as her big blues go wide. Of course, Rom had warned us this might happen, but it's still a shock that one of the two outs we have for bail is gone.

Then the stripper chorus starts.

"Hey! That's not fair!"

"You can't do that!"

"That's bullshit, Judge!"

"Give her a chance to speak for herself!"

Judge Gatta slams his gavel. "Order in my courtroom! I will have order!"

Everyone quiets down though there's still plenty of murmuring and whispered curses behind us.

"The state has already submitted their arguments for Tier 2, but does Ms. Everett's counsel have more to add?"

Rom stands up and my stomach does a flip-flop. My mind goes to the first day of kindergarten. To his grin when he held his high school diploma. To him walking the stage at Roger Williams Law School graduation. He's gone so far since each of those days—surprised me even—and it's only today that I let him know I'm proud.

Scratch that. I said his father would be proud. I didn't even tell him I was.

"Your honor, it goes without saying this case is incredibly serious. Not only to the family of Mayor Tom, but the city and even state. Community impact isn't only felt by those who loved the mayor. In fact, the woman accused of his murder is also a business owner and supports pockets of Providence often ignored by those in power."

"You tell 'em!"

The judge bangs his gavel, and the courtroom goes silent.

Rom continues, "The state's case hangs on one eyewitness who claims Ms. Everett delivered the champagne. Can we hear his or her testimony before we set bail?"

The AG rises. "The witness submitted their statement, which includes an employment record and schedule proving they were working that night. However, the individual is not in the courtroom today."

My gaze whips around to where the employees of the Luna Lounge are sitting and whispering.

"Who's not here?"

"Who would lie in court?"

"Who was working that night that didn't come today?"

Meredith turns backward in her chair with a deep frown as she scans the crowd. She'd know every single person who was there that night, no question. Her face falls as I begin to hear whispers.

"Destiny isn't here."

"She wouldn't, would she?"

"She's been having money trouble, right?"

"Maybe it's because of that boyfriend?"

The judge again slams his gavel. "Does Ms. Everett's counsel have anything else to say before I rule on Tier 2 and adjourn?"

"Yes, Your Honor. I'm submitting fifty-four signed statements collected over the weekend. They all include details of how Meredith Everett has helped her community. From paying bills to getting employees into treatment programs, she has demonstrated her commitment to people in our community who are often ignored or, worse, taken advantage of."

The bailiff takes the accordion folder to the judge, who begins to review the letters. The judge looks up with a frown, though his gaze has softened. "Running a business might mean she could go somewhere and start over?"

"She has an unused passport in a safe at the Luna Lounge that will be surrendered. All of her money will be held for use in bail if it's granted. She has no family out of state. She is not a flight risk."

The judge looks at Meredith. "So we should automatically set bail for every person who's alone?"

There are gasps in the courtroom, including from me. How dare the judge say that? But Rom stays cool. "If I may, Your Honor, the two rows behind Ms. Everett are typically reserved for family, and though she has none in a legal sense, she has this found family. This is not something she takes lightly—nor does she take lightly running a successful business. Her whole life is here."

Judge Gatta returns to scanning the letters and then glances in Meredith's direction. "I acknowledge she has built a life here. In cases this serious, many others with fewer resources and less support than her have fled."

"With all due respect, Your Honor, a woman who has what it takes to run a successful business that caters to powerful men—some of whom are in this very courtroom—is not running away from a fight. I ask that you give her the opportunity to build her case outside of prison because there is absolutely nothing Ms. Everett wants more than to prove her innocence."

Judge Gatta drops the stack of letters. "I've heard enough. Will the defendant please rise?"

JUSTINE

"Well, Meredith got bail, no thanks to you. What happened? You get lost?"

The rhetorical nature of Krystle's question is clear, even though I'm spared her expression over the phone. She knows I was quite capable of finding my way to the Sixth District courthouse and Meredith's hearing. But how many nonlawyers does it take to secure bail for a murder rap? The punchline is zero. Neither I, nor Camille, nor even Krystle with all her owed favors from the Hill diaspora could have argued Meredith's case. Meredith needed Rom. And, now that she's free until her trial, she needs Camille's investigation to deliver alternative suspects and a high-powered defense attorney to convince the jury one of those people killed the mayor.

That means we need money.

"JJ was in a state when I got home. He had a nightmare that something bad happened to me. I needed to calm him down.

Sleep in his bed. Then my mother-in-law made a point of going out Sunday so I could—and I quote—'parent my kid for once.' I woke this morning to Nancy's call. I'm headed to Newport now."

As I explain, I stretch the coiled cord of the kitchen phone straight so I can reach my shoes—a five-year-old pair of Ferragamo flats. When she'd phoned, Nancy had commented on the lovely weather and suggested we take the meeting "in the garden." Heels become golf tees on grass. I don't want to scrape crud off my shoe a second time this week, especially not on Nancy's stone pavers.

"Of course you are."

I don't know what's worse, the condescension in Krystle's voice or what she's implying.

I ignore it, nabbing a shoe by its signature bow and slipping it on. "Nancy wants me to take her through the eminent domain arguments and then deliver a brief Monday morning to her pals in the state legislature."

Static fills my receiver from Krystle's fuming. "You know, Justine, it's when times get tough that you realize who your friends are."

The comment irritates me more than my stung finger. Tough times are all that Krystle, Camille, Meredith, and I have been through. And I've been there through all of them.

"Question my loyalty all you want, Krystle. But the truth is, the Davenforths are the only reason we still have a firm. We need their money. Show me the other clients we can bill fifty hours a week, let alone count on for repeat business."

"Save your justifications, Justine." Though Krystle's words

are angry, I detect a note of something else in her tone. Sadness? Disappointment?

Whatever the emotion, I can't investigate now. Nancy is waiting. I grab the other shoe. "Of course Meredith made bail. She didn't have any prior arrests, she grew up here, and she owns a business. The only question is how did we pay it? I'm sure we used every dime of Tara's blood money, as well as whatever Meredith has in her savings. What was it? Eighty grand? More? Ten percent of a million?"

"Meredith needs *us*," Krystle snaps. "Yes, we had to drain Meredith's savings and the firm's emergency fund for the down payment. And then some."

That last part likely translates to the larger figure. Rather than try to nail down an exact amount, I grab my other shoe. "Right. So we're completely tapped out. That means *we* need the Davenforths. We'll need cash to hire a serious criminal lawyer."

Krystle scoffs. "My Rom—"

"Did the best he could, I'm sure. But you and I both know he's not up for this kind of fight. A federal courtroom is high stress. We can't stake Meredith's freedom on Rom's sobriety."

I brace myself for a furious mama bear defense punctuated with Italian phrases that I'll be thankful I can't translate. I'm met with dead air. Truth hurts, but it's hard to argue against.

The speaker vibrates with Krystle's sigh. "Well, Rom's who we have. At least he understands the importance of having your ass in the seat when it counts. If there's one thing I can say about my son, it's that he loved his father, and he loves this firm. He understands family. He's been making strides. You should have seen him today with—"

An opening door interrupts Krystle's full-throated defense of the son whom, until recently, she'd not-so-lovingly referred to as *that dipshit* when he wasn't in earshot and sometimes even when he was. JJ rushes in from the yard followed by the woman perpetually mistaken as his biological parent. With her blond hair and blue eyes, Sharon has always looked more like "her baby Jack" than me, and the resemblance has only intensified since we moved in. My mother-in-law has a penchant for dressing JJ in gingham shirts that match whatever she's wearing.

"I have to run."

I hang up before she can say anything more. After the way Krystle treated me at the party, she's not entitled to additional explanation. Besides, someone else is far more worthy of my time.

I crouch to my son's level. "Hey bud. Come here." I open my arms wide. Ever since Jack died, I make sure to hug JJ and tell him I love him before walking out the door. None of us are guaranteed a return trip home.

JJ starts toward me, but Sharon envelops him in her arms, pulling him back to her torso. Her eyes narrow at the pussy-bow blouse and knee-length skirt I've chosen. "Jack Junior, your mother is clearly going out. You'll stay with me."

I straighten back to standing position. "Nancy Davenforth wants a debrief on that case I told you about."

Sharon bestows an approving nod. "The Davenforths are a good family to become involved with. They run much of Providence behind the scenes, and Nancy always looks so lovely at her events. But I'm sure you know all that. *Clearly* you've done your research."

The pride in the first part of Sharon's speech vanishes by the end. I assume she spotted the shots in the local paper's society pages: "Harrison Davenforth with Mystery Woman."

I crouch back toward JJ and open my arms again, leaving them wide until the temptation to run into them becomes too great. JJ squirms, loosening Sharon's grip. A blink later, he's broken free and barreling into me.

"Guess what, Mom? I found a turtle in the backyard. Grandma said I had to leave him there because he's dirty."

I pull JJ to my chest. "Well, it's his home. He might have a family there."

JJ cocks his head. "Maybe he's a daddy turtle, and his kid has spots on his back too."

I smile, even though I hate reinforcing the idea that parents and children all look alike. "Maybe."

JJ grabs my hand. "He eats grass and leaves. I gave him one. Come see."

I kiss his forehead. "That's so exciting. Later, okay?"

His big eyes fill with disappointment. "He might not be around later."

I ruffle his blondish curls and dip down to his level. "Mommy has to work, honey. I was just telling Auntie Krystle." I feel a bitterness in my throat calling Krystle by my son's usual name for her. "If the backyard is the little guy's home, then I'll see him later. I'll help you find him again, okay?"

I squeeze his tiny body and smell his hair, committing the vanilla scent of his shampoo to memory before planting a kiss right next to his pouty mouth. "I love you."

Rather than repeat the words, he retreats to Sharon. I swallow the tightness in my throat and stand to look my mother-in-law in the eye. "The meeting is in Newport. It's scheduled for two, and Nancy is a punctual person. I'm sure it won't be too long. I'll be back this evening."

Her smile screws tighter. "You won't have to defend that woman who killed the mayor?"

I wince, realizing my mother-in-law's disapproval is about more than my dating for the first time in years. She must have already read the newspaper.

"She didn't do it, Sharon. She only owns the club where it happened."

If my mother-in-law believes me, she gives no indication. Sharon turns to go, leading my son back out into the yard.

I let my words follow them. "I love you. I'll be back soon."

I almost don't hear JJ's mumbled response, as he's already stepping out into the yard. But the words blow back at me along with a breeze from the outside. "No, you won't."

The back door shuts, leaving me in silence.

Traffic will turn me into a liar. Instead of the usual forty-five minutes, this warmer-than-usual June means the drive out to Newport takes nearly an hour. Judging from the volume of cars heading toward the beach, I'm certain that the return trip will take even longer as we all exit the island back to the mainland. Even if my meeting with Nancy lasts an hour, it's doubtful that I'll make it back before dinner, let alone anytime *soon*.

After I finally arrive and park, the Davenforths' butler gives me a disapproving once-over before informing me that Nancy has been waiting. It may only be that he's an officious jerk, but I fear I've unwittingly confirmed some stereotype he's held about Black people and tardiness. The back of my neck grows hot. "There was a lot of traffic. Guess the weather is bringing everyone out to the beach."

The butler shows no sympathy. "Good weather typically does." He passes by me and closes the door behind him, urging me to follow by the brusqueness of his gate. "Madame is in the rose garden."

We march across a pebble path leading to a wall of boxwoods. I inwardly congratulate myself on my smart footwear as I keep pace with the butler's stride. He stops before an arched cutout in the center of the twelve-foot hedge. "Through there."

I peer inside the opening and into the darkness beyond. It's not so black as to be blinding, but it's certainly dimmer than the bright, blue sky above the wall. My mind flits to the movie *Labyrinth*, which I took JJ to see in theaters last summer thinking PG meant it was appropriate. We left because he found David Bowie too scary, but not before the part where the little girl got lost navigating the hedge maze. As I remember, the maze wasn't much fun for the child in *The Shining*, either.

"Will you lead the way?"

My request falls on deaf ears as the butler has already turned back to the house. Chasing after him would make me later than I already am. I brace myself and step forward.

Light filters through the leaves, creating a kaleidoscope of flickering shapes on the ground. JJ would find this magical. Yet all I can focus on is where Nancy is and whether she'll be put out by my running fifteen minutes behind. What she might think of *me*.

I hurry through the hedge tunnel and round the first turn. A moment later, I'm in a wide courtyard and relieved that the maze was less of a labyrinth and more of a hallway. The scent of roses weighs down the air. Buds are everywhere, climbing up trellises and cascading from an arched cylinder.

"That one up there."

Though I hear Nancy, I don't see her. Her voice rings out from behind a rose curtain. "No, Henry. The big bloom there, to the right."

I round the rose tunnel to one of its open ends, worried that I've missed our meeting entirely. "I'm sorry I'm late."

Nancy is focused on a gardener perched on a ladder. She's wearing one of her padded-shoulder suits. The gardener is unmistakable in olive-toned overalls with dirt on the knees. Nancy must find all her workers at central casting.

"Ms. Davenforth. I apologize for the fifteen minutes. There was more traffic than I expected."

Nancy turns toward me, dismissing my excuse with a white-gloved hand. "Not your fault. The city's design creates needless jams. Our plan will fix that. Widen the roads. Add more bridges and highway lanes."

"Are you still available to discuss the eminent domain argument?"

Nancy bestows one of her signature closed-lipped smiles. "Harrison filled me in this morning, actually. Those points all sound sensible. You can move forward with the brief."

I struggle to maintain my faux grin. Surely she couldn't think so little of my time that she had me drive all the way out here for a verbal go-ahead that could have been delivered over the phone.

Nancy must notice the strain on my face because she walks over and pats me on the shoulder. "I also want to understand what happened at the party. The police. Your firm's fellow co-owner." Nancy places a hand above her breast. "I understand the whole fiasco must have put you in an awkward position, one that I'd never want to exacerbate, of course. I figured you could be more candid here."

I feel my smile completely vanish. "Meredith is a good person and a hardworking businesswoman. She would never have been involved in any plot to kill Mayor Tom."

Nancy cocks her head. "I do detest discussing money. So do forgive me for saying this, but your firm *is* struggling, and she must have spent a pretty penny upgrading her *establishment*, no?"

I shake my head, even though Nancy is right about Meredith transforming the former mob den into a high-class strip joint. "Meredith does alright. Her investment was paying off. Even if it wasn't, though, she wouldn't kill anyone. I'm surprised that she was even charged. They must be hoping to scare her into giving them something on Tara. But there's nothing for Meredith to share."

Nancy's thin brows raise to her forehead. She glances over her shoulder to her gardener. "That will be all, Henry. Thank you."

We both watch Henry descend his ladder and close it up. Nancy changes the subject, clearly filling time until he leaves. "I don't know what I'd do without Henry. I used to rather enjoy gardening myself, but my back doesn't allow for such activities anymore. All the bending over to examine the blooms. I threw it out having Harrison, and it was never the same after that. Nothing was."

I smile politely. "Having kids is hard."

Nancy chuckles. "It is. Though not as hard as my new backbone. I had steel rods put in to fix the damage."

She watches the gardener hoist his ladder under one arm and collect a basket of flowers. As he leaves, she releases a long sigh and mutters to herself. "The things we do for children." She zeros back on me. "Though what can we do but give them everything? Our descendants are our true legacy. Buildings can be torn down. The names on facades? Easily changed. But lineage, that's what we leave behind in this world, isn't it? That's the true measure of us."

Nancy's words are like a Brillo pad on a sunburn—because I agree with her. My son is all I have, and I left him for a conversation that really could have happened over the phone. "Yes. Truly. So, I'll get you those plans and—"

Nancy's wistful expression transforms back to business. "Are you sure about your friend? Tara can be quite persuasive. I know from experience. I saw them chatting at my event… They seemed rather friendly."

"Meredith is a good person." I say it more forcefully this time, both for Nancy and to drown out my own doubts. Clearly, Tara is a master manipulator. After all, she convinced no-bullshit Camille to work for her. The woman possesses a combination of elegance and edge—grace with grit—that is definitely Meredith's type.

I rub my temple, attempting to erase the doubts Nancy is raising.

Nancy notices with a concerned pout. "It may not be the poor thing's fault. I can imagine Tara pretending to be her friend, convincing her that they'll only get Tom extra tipsy and suggestible, all the while knowing there was too much of *whatever* in that bottle."

Nancy's scenario almost seems plausible. Still, this is Meredith she's talking about, a woman whose hard exterior conceals a bleeding heart. Meredith wouldn't hurt anyone unless they were hurting her, and Mayor Tom was nothing but good business for her club.

"Meredith wouldn't have knowingly been in on any plot to hurt or kill the mayor, though I agree that Tara is ruthless. To target the father of your child…"

Nancy's lips purse into a tight knot, like someone pulled both ends of a bow's ribbon. "Pardon me. What was that?"

Reflexively, my hand flies over my mouth. "Oh. I'm so sorry. I assumed Harrison would have mentioned Tara's pregnancy."

Nancy's polite smile returns. "I'm certain he intended to share the news. Unfortunately, Harrison and I haven't had a chance to talk since the party. He's been on his boat."

That explains why he hasn't called. I'd expected Harrison to phone after our kiss, if only to tell me that he had a nice time. But he retreated to the water—no doubt to process his murderous stepmother having his late father's child.

"Poor thing. To lose Tom and now this." Nancy pats my arm. "He's docked at the harbor. You should go out and talk to him. Cheer him up."

I have an appointment with a backyard turtle, not to mention our law firm's billing department. "I would, but my son is waiting at home and, as you've quite rightly said, our kids are the reason we work so hard... Speaking of, I don't know if Krystle has had a chance to invoice you for the hours developing this eminent domain argument. I was hoping to get to the bank before going home. The firm—"

Nancy grasps my hand. She holds it in her palm and pats it with the other. It's the kind of intimate gesture that one would only share with a friend. Or maybe someone she can imagine being family?

"It's so difficult for us working mothers, isn't it?" She looks away, batting her lashes. Is Nancy crying?

"Do you know the story of my family?" she asks. "It's a bit scandalous."

I feel a history lesson coming on—one that I don't have time for. "I've read some—"

"My seven-times great-grandfather came to Rhode Island from England alone, though he had a wife and two nearly adult sons."

Nancy looks at me like she's confessing a dark secret, one that I should know to keep quiet and listen to. "Really?"

"On the morning of departure, he expected all of them to meet him. He sold what little they had for the tickets. This was their one shot if they were going to rise above their station. To build something worth having in a new land with new opportunity. But his family never came. He wrote in our family Bible that he watched the dock until it disappeared, and that's when he knew he truly must start over."

"Were they ill?"

Nancy shakes her head. "They were scared to do the hard thing. They'd rather live in poverty because it's what they knew than bravely face the opportunity for more." She pauses to clench her fist. "He had to start over. For the good of his family legacy. In fact, he got a new wife and had four more children that would lead all the way to me and Harrison."

"It all worked out for the best then," I say, knowing what would be best for me is ending this conversation.

"Those descendants would all be bastards." Nancy grins as if it's a punchline. "But that didn't stop us, and we've been called worse. Carrying on the Davenforth name was the reason my forebear came to America. By starting over, by being brave and doing the hard thing, we amassed wealth and power that creates a legacy. Reimagines a city." Nancy sighs. "My legacy, my only son, puts up a strong front. But truly, he's only a boy at the end of the day. A boy who tragically lost his father to murder. I know you understand."

Of course I do. Harrison is going through the same thing JJ

suffered—though my son is growing up without a father *and*, thanks to my crazy schedule, his mother. "I feel terrible for Harrison, but I really must get home to my little boy."

Nancy drops my hand, withdrawing her affection in the same way Harrison did when I didn't immediately do what he wanted. "Of course. I completely understand. It's only that I would have hoped you might reserve a slightly longer window for a discussion about anything as serious as an unprecedented redevelopment of an entire city. Tucker would often take the whole day for one of our meetings."

Ugh. Tucker Fucker. Mentally using Krystle's nickname for him doesn't break the *no profanity* rule I instituted after JJ was born.

"And, unfortunately, you *were* a tad late," Nancy continues. "The marina is only, what, fifteen minutes away?"

Not coincidentally the exact amount of time I kept her waiting. "I suppose I can stop by on my way home. See how he is."

"Oh Justine, you are such a gem." Nancy marches toward the opening in the hedges. "I'll call his mobile. Tell him you're coming right away."

I follow her out of the garden, shoes crunching on the stones. "You're sure he doesn't want to be alone?"

One of Nancy's white-gloved hands waves in the air, dismissing the comment and me. She points toward the garages where my car waits, shouting over her shoulder. "He shouldn't be alone. You checking on him will work wonders, I'm sure." She smiles. "Justine, loyalty and family are the two most important things to me. By doing this, you are proving yourself a paragon of the former, which is necessary to be worthy of the latter." Something about the intensity of Nancy's look suggests she's not only talking about securing the family business. Does she really like me for Harrison? Is she trying to make sure I ingratiate myself with him during this difficult time?

I pull my car keys from my purse, testing my theory. "I'm happy to drive us both."

Nancy continues to wave me forward. "You go, Justine. Some comforts a mother can't provide."

CAMILLE

Meredith makes it out the courthouse doors first, followed by a parade of strippers giddy with what they see as success. Their beloved boss is free on bail. They're so excited I don't have the heart to tell them we're nowhere near done. Meredith's freedom is only temporary.

She stops at the bottom of the steps and gulps air while they titter all around her, one name on their glossy lips: Rom. Suddenly, they see him with new and entranced eyes. From Occasionally Handsy and Mediocre Tipper to Rockstar Lawyer, all in the span of twenty-seven breathless courtroom minutes. As much as I hate to admit it, the strippers are not wrong. Rom surprised all of us in there, and in a good way.

I push through the girls gathered around Meredith, who's looking mighty shaky on her heels. "How you doin', sugar?"

She blows out a breath, trying to blink her tears away before I can see them. "I'm fine."

"You're not fine, and neither am I. Beyond the fact that I'm feeling guilty as hell for dragging you into this, I'm positively livid at that bitch."

I don't have to say her name. Meredith knows I'm talking about Destiny.

Meredith glances behind her at the ladies still going on about the courtroom recap. That Rom was just such a *boss* in there, that winning sure makes him look sexy, and I see a lot of free lap dances in his future. They're too busy with their praise to pay any attention to us, but still Meredith lowers her voice.

"I didn't do it. You *know* I didn't."

A fresh wave of animosity for Destiny burns in my chest, and I grab Meredith's hand and squeeze down. "I know you didn't, and you better believe I'm going to find that little liar and give her a piece of my mind. I don't care if it's tampering with the witness, I'm gonna tamper the hell out of her until she tells me why she's lying. If it has anything to do with a man or money, I'm not responsible for what I do next."

"No," Meredith says, fury wiping the fear from her face. "That bitch is mine. Whatever Destiny has to say to a judge and jury, she's going to say it to my face first."

I release her hand to pat her on the arm. "That's right, hun. You go get her."

At the top of the steps, the doors swing open and out struts Rom. The strippers see him and squeal, breaking into a round of applause. He pauses on the top step to bask in their praise, his smile going crooked with an I'm-the-man cockiness. The expression makes him look so much like his late father that it steals my breath.

I spot Krystle in the crowd at the top of the steps, her wide eyes blinking into the sunshine, and I know she's thinking the same thing. A sad but proud mama bear, chewing her lip with worry, I'm guessing for the next round of courtroom proceedings and probably also for the firm's bank account. Krystle just dropped a hundred grand neither the firm nor Meredith have to bail her out, and we're down to exactly two major clients: the Davenforths and Tara, and if either one of them finds out we're playing both sides, we'll lose both.

While Rom preens for the giddy crowd, Krystle makes her way down the stairs.

"Still no sign of Justine," I say once she's close enough.

Krystle sighs. "I just talked to her. She was on her way to Nancy's, which means we'll have to do the work without her."

"Find Destiny and strangle her?" I suggest.

"Not until she tells us what she told the attorney general." Krystle turns to Meredith. "Any thoughts on how those drugs got in your desk drawer?"

Meredith raises both shoulders in a frustrated shrug. "Who the hell knows? Ask anyone here, and they'll tell you my office has an open door policy."

Krystle stabs a siren-red fingernail at Meredith. "We need to talk to Destiny, and maybe swing by your strip club. Have ourselves a little look-see."

"Got chain cutters handy? The doors are locked up tight."

Krystle doesn't seem the least bit swayed by the potential roadblock. "It's not B&E if your name's on the deed."

"It is when the building's a crime scene. Grilling Destiny is my first order of business."

"I'm parked around the corner. Let's go." Krystle gestures for us to follow.

I stop her with a hand to her sleeve. "Hang on. At the party Aiden said something about Mayor Tom owning the property behind the burial ground. He was going to do a little digging, see if Tom filed new plans for the parcel. Of course there's also the question of ownership now that he's dead. I'm guessing a guy like Tom would have a prenup."

Krystle nods. "Rich Guy 101. Which means that land would have gone to Harrison, probably."

"That's exactly what I'm thinking. It explains why Nancy is so sure she can get this Paris mess pushed through."

I look at Meredith for confirmation, but she only cocks a brow. "Aiden, huh?"

I plant a hand on my hip. "For the record, I'm working for you here, sugar. Mayor Tom owned a big chunk of land plenty of people want, and we just heard he switched alliances days before his death. There's no way those two things aren't connected."

Krystle and Meredith exchange a look, and I can tell they agree.

"I'm going to go find Aiden. See what he's sussed out and if, since he's officially a Davenforth, he can somehow finagle a copy of Tom's will so we can see who his property went to after he died: Tara or Harrison. Speaking of Mayor Tom, I'm gonna need a little more than Nancy's word that he switched sides. I don't believe that woman just because she says I should. Money talks, but it also lies."

Krystle wraps a hand around Meredith's upper arm, tugging them side by side. "Good plan. Meanwhile Meredith and I will hunt down Destiny. Let's regroup later at the office."

I wave, and the two take off.

A quick call to Aiden's office tells me he's at city hall, as luck would have it, a baroque-style building of slate and granite a quick walk from the courthouse. I rush down the sidewalk as fast as I can on these heels, then up the steps and through the heavy wooden doors.

The atrium is impressive, featuring a massive staircase of gilded wood and inlaid marble steps, but I don't have time to admire it for very long. I don't want to miss Aiden, as a drive to South County would tack on a couple of hours at least. I spot an information desk and race over.

The man directs me to the records department on the bottom floor, where I run up against a stern-faced librarian. I take in the piles of yellowed boxes behind her, thousands and thousands of them labeled and stacked into rows twelve feet high, a warehouse of records that go back hundreds of years. I'd be a sourpuss too, if I had to keep track of all that.

"I'm looking for someone. Tall. Dark hair on the longish side. His receptionist said he was here."

She stops just short of rolling her eyes. "Does Mr. Tall Dark Longish Hair have a name?"

"Aiden Wyatt."

She points down a long tunnel of boxes to her left. "Back there."

I find Aiden all the way at the end, seated at a table piled with a box's worth of papers spread out in front of him. There are more boxes by his feet, the lids flipped open onto the dusty floor, in piles at the end of the table. I try not to notice that his hair looks like he's been running his fingers through it, loose and wild against the white fabric of his collared shirt, or that those reading glasses make him look smart and sexy. No time for flirting, Camille.

He hears me coming and looks up, surprise flashing across his brow. "Camille. If I didn't know better, I'd say you were following me."

"I am following you. Your assistant helped a little. I called your office from the steps of the courthouse."

"And?"

I don't know this man all that well, but I know he's asking about Meredith.

"Tier 2 but not 1. A hundred grand bail."

He takes it in with a nod. "Steep but reasonable, considering. Do we have a trial date?"

"Not yet. But since it's the mayor, I'm guessing it'll be soon. Seems like they're moving at supersonic speed, which means we need to keep up. Did you find out anything about the mayor's parcel of land?"

He pulls out the chair next to him and offers me a seat, pivoting on his chair to face me. "Yes and no. There's nothing in here to prove that Tom changed his mind. The only application he filed was almost six months ago. Rezoning, from industrial to commercial."

"So Nancy's lying?"

"Not necessarily. A casino and a convention-plus-business center would both require commercial zoning. He wouldn't have to refile, and it's too early for building permits. He needed our land first."

I frown. "What about *his* land? I'm assuming a man like the mayor would have had a prenup. Any way we can get a peek at his will?"

"You'd have to be a Davenforth for that."

"I can't tell if that's an offer or a brush-off."

Aiden gives me a smile, one filled with all sorts of promises. "Tom attached a presentation to the rezoning application, and he listed a financial partner. I'm guessing because he knew he was in for a fight for the casino, not just with the city but the whole state, and he wanted to come in guns blazing. Show the county officials that he had both political power and the funds to make it happen. Less likely to say no that way."

"Okay. So who's the partner?"

"It's an LLC, which means I'm going to need to do some research."

More research. Frustration surges in my chest, heating me from the inside out. "How long will this research take?"

He reaches across me for a stack of papers, giving me a whiff of something woodsy as he slides it across the desk. I spot the Providence seal at the top, and next to it in bold letters, *Application for Rezoning*.

"Depends on where the LLC is registered and what kind of smokescreen the owners are trying to put up to disguise themselves. LLCs can be anonymous, or the owners can hide behind layers of entities like trusts and other LLCs. It could take me a while to untangle."

I lean back in my chair, urgency beating behind my ribs. So far none of this sounds very promising. What if this research takes forever? What if it turns up nothing? This is time we don't have. Meredith can't go down for this. I can't let that happen.

Then my gaze falls on a string of letters written on the application, letters that tingle across my scalp because I've seen them before.

MAT-GRL, LLC.

I tap the name with a finger. "This is the LLC you were talking about? Tom's financial partner?"

Aiden confirms it with a nod. "I'm guessing it stands for something. Give me a day or two, and I'll see what I can find out."

"Not necessary, sugar. It stands for Material Girl. Which also happens to be the vanity plate on Tara's limo. I saw it after the night I spent in the slammer."

He falls silent for a second or two, thinking. "If Tara was his backer and what Nancy said is true, that Tom ditched the casino plans for her Paris plan, then that's an awful big betrayal."

"Tara would be pissed, sure, but she wouldn't be out any money. The casino was nowhere near being built."

"No, but you can still rack up a lot of costs in the planning phase. Architects, engineers, attorneys, not to mention all the money Tom would have needed to grease the palms of Rhode Island politicians. By now she could be out millions, *plural*, and it's a high-risk investment. If the casino doesn't happen, she loses it all."

I think about what that means. Tara plunked down all those chips to get that casino built, only to have Tom switch sides. All that money, *poof*, gone. And Tara is the type who has to win. While she won the mayor the first time, he was secretly in business with Nancy. It's the kind of double cross that would hit a woman like Tara extra hard—a breach of faith that happened not in the bedroom, but in the boardroom.

"As much as I hate to admit it, she's kind of an evil genius. She hired me to find her husband's killer, you know. She's paying me to be sitting here right now, talking to you."

"She wanted you to take the fall."

"Exactly. When the charges didn't stick, she somehow got Destiny to point the finger at Meredith. Paying me, doing us favors, and feeding us information, all the while she knows we're the sacrifice. Don't they call her the She-Wolf of Wall Street? I guess that makes us lambs to the slaughter."

I say the words, and something flares hot and angry behind my breastbone, even though I'm impressed by the brilliance of her scheme as much as I'm insulted Tara would use me as a patsy. Murder not just for money and revenge but also for the satisfaction of divesting from her two-timing husband. She even got a baby out of the deal. A tiny piece of Tom that will keep her connected to this city and his wealth forever.

Aiden frowns at me from across the desk. "But that would mean—"

"It means I'm working for a killer."

MEREDITH

After the courthouse, I wanted to go home for a nap and a shower. Or six.

There was no time. I had a date with Destiny.

Misty thought Destiny might be on the schedule at my biggest competitor, Big Daddy's, so Krystle and I headed there first, but no luck. She wasn't at O'Boobigan's either, or the Hot Fox, or even the Pandora's Box over the state line in Massachusetts. (Where I probably shouldn't have gone, since I was still a murder suspect, but what the Providence PD doesn't know can't hurt me—and I made Krystle swear not to tell Rom either.)

Now I'm exhausted and enraged, and I smell like an unholy combination of cheap body spray and the hand-rolled cigarettes my cellmate had smoked from lights out until sunrise. But I'm not going to give up until I get answers. I'll go to every club on the East Coast if I have to and buy as many lap dances as it takes to find out the truth. If Destiny betrayed me, she had a good reason. I have to believe that.

Finally, Krystle and I have only one doorstep left in Rhode Island to darken. The one place I swore I'd never set foot again.

"This is a strip club?" Krystle says as we pull into the parking lot.

The building squats low to the ground and is unmarked except for some lewd graffiti wrapping around the corner and a single rusty door sitting off-center. Doesn't look like they've slapped on a fresh coat of that vaginal pink paint since my last visit. I suppress a shudder.

"Yeah, what did you think it was?"

"I hoped it was abandoned. You know, Romeo and I grew up less than a mile from here."

"I used to work at this place."

Krystle's eyebrows shoot up. "No shit?"

"For two weeks, when I was first starting out."

Until I was short on tips after a dismal shift in the dead of winter, and the manager suggested I could pay my house fees by providing other services—right there, in his office.

Instead, I went to the bar, put a shot of their most expensive scotch on my tab, then threw the drink in his beady little eyeballs and stormed out. The next day Sal hired me to dance at the Wolf Den, and I realized just how squalid the conditions at Pinky's really were.

Say what you will about Sal Ponterelli, but he made sure all the women who worked for him were treated with respect. Better to work for a mob boss than a wannabe pimp. I've got no problem with a woman selling access to her body—so long as she's the one setting the price and the terms, and she's making a free choice rather than feeling backed into a corner.

"You sure about this?" Krystle asks.

"No." I pop open the car door. "But I'm doing it anyway."

There's no bouncer at the entrance, so we walk right in. Strip joints are always a little sad during daylight hours, but Pinky's is downright depressing. Peeling linoleum floors, pockmarked walls, mismatched tables and chairs, plenty with pieces missing. The dim lighting helps distract from the grunginess but not enough.

"You see her?" Krystle asks.

In the darkest corner of the room, a girl gives a halfhearted lap dance to a guy with stringy hair and what I really hope is a ketchup stain on his once-white T-shirt. Next to the stage, a group of old-timers watch as another stripper with a bad perm and a worse boob job writhes against the pole to "Push It."

Neither of them is Destiny. Looks like we've hit another dead end.

Every second I spend in this hellhole reminds me of why I need to fight for the Luna Lounge's future. If the situation weren't so uncertain, I'd be going around sticking business cards in all these poor girls' G-strings. Stripping doesn't have to be sad or sordid—it can be fun, even empowering, in addition to being lucrative.

"You wanna get out of here?" Krystle asks.

I nod. The Salt-N-Pepa track ends, and a Duran Duran electronica remix blares over the shitty speakers. I'm turning to follow Krystle out when I see another dancer take the stage.

"Wait."

The new girl doesn't seem quite so worse for wear as the others. She's got pert natural breasts and expertly applied smoky-eye makeup and long, blond, crimped hair.

She looks so different from the last time I saw her, though, I'm not sure it's really Destiny until she locks eyes with me and stops mid-hook spin, her mouth falling open in shock.

"Destiny!" I call out, taking off toward the stage. She bolts for the backstage area. Just as the bass beat drops, I clamor up onto the platform after her. Krystle's right behind me—though she tries grabbing on to the greased-up pole for leverage and almost falls on her ass.

"Whaddya think you're doing?" one of the old guys yells. "We paid to see a show."

Give me a break; I haven't seen him or any of his early-bird-special friends toss more than a single on the stage. I stop long enough to give them a withering glare.

"She's getting away!" Krystle says. "You go that way, I'll—"

"Hey, Mae West!"

I know he's not talking to me, and so does Krystle. She turns. Another of the old codgers sitting up front grins at her with a gleam in his eye. This one might've actually been handsome, back when he had all his teeth.

"Yeah, you, sweetcheeks. You gonna show us what you got or what? We've been begging 'em to get some ladies with real substance in here."

"Excuse you." Krystle sniffs and smooths her jacket—inadvertently tugging the neckline down another half inch so there's a brief, tantalizing flash of cleavage.

The man hollers his approval and tosses a twenty at her feet. Krystle gapes at the bill, then bends down to pick it up—prompting another round of cheers.

"You want a show?" she says. They all nod eagerly, remaining wisps of hair waving. "Fine, I'll give you a show."

I grab her arm. "What the hell are you doing?"

"Distracting these geezers while you go get your girl. Now hurry it up." She snaps her fingers at the DJ. "Turn off that electronic shit and play something with some sauce, will ya?"

The Duran Duran remix goes dead mid-synth note, and that old burlesque classic "The Stripper" starts up. Krystle does a little wiggle in time with the bawdy drums before undoing one button on her blazer—then fastens it again with a teasing wag of her finger and sashays to the other side of the stage.

Well, okay. Guess she does know what she's doing. I leave her to her striptease act and slip into the back to find Destiny.

When I catch up with her, she's in the dressing room. She's pulled that oversized Yale T-shirt on over her G-string and is frantically cramming the rest of her belongings into her Gucci bag. The purse may be stylish, but it's way too small, and items keep falling out. She lunges to grab a cherry Lip Smacker, but I get to it first.

"Destiny. We need to talk."

She backs away from me like she's afraid I might hit her. The only other stripper in here—a cagey-looking brunette who's busy trying to shave ten years off her face with a few extra coats of foundation and some spidery fake lashes—gives me a suspicious look.

"You know this broad, Désirée?"

Of course she's using a different name. Destiny couldn't have really thought a pseudonym and a makeover would keep me from finding out what she did, though.

I turn to the woman. "Yeah, she knows me. And you should know I just got out of county this morning, so you might wanna make yourself scarce before I show you what I learned there."

No need to reveal I was locked up for less than forty-eight hours, and I spent most of it shivering on a thin mattress and trying not to cry.

The woman skedaddles, one set of lashes still hanging crooked, and finally, I've got Destiny right where I want her: backed into a corner with nowhere to go but through me.

"I know you're the eyewitness."

"Meredith, I swear—"

"What I couldn't figure out was why. *Why* would you betray me like that? Then I realized." I step closer. "It was you. You poisoned the mayor."

She bursts into tears, and I know I'm right. God, how I wanted to be wrong.

Destiny and I are always getting mistaken for each other. If there was an *actual* eyewitness, they would have given a physical description that could've matched either one of us. So she pointed the finger at me before anyone could point it at her.

"I didn't want to do it. It's just…this guy I've been seeing. He's real hard to say no to, if you know what I mean."

I sure do. But I'm going to need more than that. "Your boyfriend told you to kill the mayor and frame me?"

"No one was supposed to *die*! I didn't mean for you to get caught up in any of this."

"It happened at my club; of course I'm caught up in it. Who the hell is this guy, anyway?"

Destiny's eyes dart back and forth, like whoever he is might be about to lunge out of the shadows. "I can't tell you. He'll come after me."

"This loser can't care that much about you, if he used you like that."

"He's done so much for me. Given me everything I ever wanted."

That explains the new wardrobe, the designer handbag. He must have paid for it all. Here I was hoping I'd inspired her entrepreneurial spirit.

"He just asked me to do this one thing for him. This one little favor. And he's real smart. He went to Yale you know, so—"

"Trust me, a Yale degree doesn't mean you're smart. Just rich."

She twists the hem of the T-shirt around her fingers. "I thought he had a plan."

I can certainly understand making stupid decisions because you love someone. Then finding out the person you loved wasn't who you thought at all.

"Destiny, it sounds like this guy set you up. You shouldn't have to take the fall for him. Tell me his name, and I'll protect you."

She shakes her head. "I can't. You don't understand. I *can't*."

"I'm the co-owner of a law firm, remember? I'll help you."

She keeps shaking her head, so hard I swear it's going to snap off.

I sigh. "If you really can't tell me his name, at least tell me about the poison. How did you get it into the champagne?"

"It wasn't poison!"

"What was it, then?"

"I don't know. It came in one of those orange bottles, like from the pharmacy."

"And this guy of yours, he gave it to you?"

"He told me how many pills to use, but a different man made the delivery. It was real late at night, after my shift."

"Let me guess: you can't tell me the delivery man's name either."

"He didn't give a name. Just handed over the champagne, pills, and this solution to mix them with. He said to make sure I crushed 'em up real small, so nothing got stuck in the syringe. I think he was a doctor?"

A syringe through the champagne bottle cork. What was this, a James Bond film?

"I'm so sorry, Meredith. But me and my boyfriend, we're through now—for good this time. How can I make it up to you?"

"You can tell me this asshole's name."

"I *can't*, I—"

"You know I'll figure it out eventually, right? One of my best friends is a private investigator. I already know the guy went to Yale. He's probably been to the club before."

She's weeping now, mascara smearing all over her cheeks, and she still looks so lovely.

"Just tell me, and you'll save us both a lot of time and trouble. When did you first meet him? Was it at my club?"

"Please, Meredith. I'll go talk to the cops, whoever. Tell them you had nothing to do with any of this."

"Why would they believe you?"

Destiny sniffles. "I'll…I'll say I was mistaken. I thought I saw you, but it was actually someone else, but I don't know who, and—"

"They'll never take you seriously, unless you give them a better suspect. They're going to want this guy's name too. And they won't ask as nice as me. Why protect him?"

"Because I'm *scared*! He said if I tell anyone, h—"

"Which is it, Destiny? You were scared, or you got greedy?"

She shuts her mouth at that, pressing her pretty pink lips together.

"He was showing you the good life, right? Instead of giving that up, you decided to screw me over. I've done a lot for you too, you know."

"I know. I know you have, Meredith."

"And did he convince you to plant those pills in my office? So I'd go to jail for murder? Is that what you wanted?"

"That's why they arrested you?" Destiny is sobbing now, shaking her head frantically. "I only hid them there. I didn't try to get you in trouble. I'm sorry. I'm so sorry."

"*Sorry* won't keep me out of jail. But the truth will. You owe me that."

I glare at her because I'm mad and I want her to crack. I believe that she wasn't framing me, exactly, but she also can't plead stupid to every crime here.

We need a name. Camille might be able to suss out this guy's identity, but I can't count on that. So many men come through the club's doors, they all blur together—and Providence is lousy with rich pricks who like to brag about going to college in New Haven. How many of them would have it out for Mayor Tom, though, and have access to those designer drugs?

A drug-peddling doctor and a devious rich man. Now where did I hear that one before?

"Tucker," I say.

Destiny freezes. "W-what did you—"

"Tucker Armand. Is that who put you up to this?"

He fits everything I know about Destiny's boyfriend: a rich, entitled asshole with no respect for women, using people and discarding them once he gets what he wants. I may be furious with Destiny right now, but the thought of Tucker putting his hands on her makes me want to snap all his soft little fingers in two.

She backs up a step. "I really shouldn't—"

"You don't have to say it. Just nod if I'm right."

She blinks at me for a few seconds. Then she dips her chin.

Shit. So she screwed over me, the club, and the law firm in one fell swoop.

Destiny looks so young and innocent, a part of me wants to hug her and stroke her hair and tell her it'll be fine, we'll figure this all out together.

Another part thinks: What would Tara Jordan do?

She'd see these tears for the sympathy ploy they are, for one thing. And she'd remind me that I'm not Destiny's big sister. I'm not her friend.

I'm her boss.

I take a deep breath. "You're fired, Destiny."

"Meredith, please, I said I was s—"

"When the Luna Lounge reopens—and it will, no matter how much you've mucked things up—you are not welcome on the premises."

She dissolves into quiet sobs, and I almost soften. She's just a kid, really. We all make mistakes. She didn't know what she was doing.

I steel myself. I'm the boss, and being the boss means making tough calls.

"You ever set foot in my club again, I'll have you thrown out on your ass and arrested. Got it?"

She nods, with a little whimper that just about makes me burst into tears too. Then she scurries down the dark corridor, pushes through the back exit, and she's gone.

The bump-and-grind song ends, and there's a smattering of applause and wolf whistles. Krystle ducks backstage—still dressed, for the most part, though she's got her skirt hiked high and her jacket slung over her arm.

"Not bad for a couple of minutes' work," she says, shuffling through a pile of singles and twenties. "Sure pays better than running a law firm."

I force myself to smile. "Yeah, no kidding. And you didn't even have to give up the good stuff."

"Well, I didn't want to give my new friend Morty out there a coronary. What did Destiny have to say for herself?"

I relay Destiny's tearful confession—though I leave out my harsh dismissal—and tell Krystle the dirt Tara dished on the good Dr. Hendricks, too, plus how cozy he and Tucker seemed at the party.

"Tucker Fucker," Krystle seethes. "I should've known. He's been crawling his way up Nancy Davenforth's ass for years. He'll do whatever it takes to stay there."

"You think Nancy orchestrated this?" The Davenforth matriarch is a piece of work, but despite my desperate jailhouse theorizing, Nancy seems way too sophisticated to sully her hands with such a seedy crime.

"Not orchestrated necessarily. But if Tucker thought it'd gain him one bit of favor in Nancy's book…" Krystle makes a spitting noise. "I wouldn't put anything past that little weasel."

"Nancy said she and Mayor Tom were working together before he died, though. And Tucker told me and Camille that he was the one who convinced the mayor to switch sides."

"Well, we know Tucker's full of shit," Krystle points out. "Maybe Nancy is too."

I think about what Tara said at the party, about fake manners, keeping up appearances. *We mustn't have a scene.* The approval of the city's dear, departed leader would boost support for the Davenforths' redevelopment plan—and it wasn't like he was around to contradict their claims.

"Now what?" I ask.

Krystle's eyes narrow. "We trap the weasel and make him squeal."

"Do weasels…squeal?"

"No idea." She puts her jacket back on and shoves the cash into her pocket. "I sure am looking forward to finding out, aren't you?"

KRYSTLE

As Tucker drones on about how he's doing us a favor coming back to this "joke of an office," I wonder if there's a class on how to talk as if you're better than everyone while you twist your mouth like a baboon's butthole taught at every Ivy League school or just Yale.

It's a look I've observed plenty in the past few days in Newport, and I'd be happy to never see it again.

"Now what's this top-secret thing you need to tell me? I was in the middle of a business meeting," he says as he picks at his cuticle.

"It was two-for-one martinis, and every back was to you," Meredith says flatly about how we found him at the bar every downtown lawyer goes to after work. "No one was interested until we came in looking for you."

"I did you a favor gracing this pathetic place with my presence. You can't even keep a temp to answer the phones."

I suck in a deep breath at his insult, which in the parlance of

Battleship, is a direct hit. We're sitting in the main conference room at the center of our offices, and it's quiet as a graveyard. I wonder what Merriam-Webster would say the difference is between desperate and pathetic? Where's the line and when did we cross it?

Still, just because Tucker's not wrong on this point doesn't mean he didn't have something to do with the mayor's murder.

He lets out a breath—mouth still puckered—before he says, "Well, what's the big secret?"

I grin across the conference table at him because Tucker has always been a gossip, and I knew dangling some juicy morsel would be too good to refuse. "We know who poisoned the mayor."

He leans forward, his eyes eager instead of nervous, like I expected. "Do tell."

I smack my lips. "You."

"WHAT?!"

Well, well, well. I guess weasels do squeal, and it doesn't take a subscription to *National Geographic* to find out.

"I tolerated your arrogance and shit tips because you were associated with the firm." Meredith rises from her chair, arms crossed, mean-as-hell stare. "So, you'll excuse me if I kick your ass for how you treated Destiny before we call the cops."

"Meredith..." I warn and follow her around the table.

Tucker sneers at her as she continues to move in his direction. "I'm sorry, who?"

"Oh please. Do you know how many lap dances I've seen Destiny give you and the clients you were trying to impress?"

He laughs like Meredith just fell off the turnip truck. "You think I know those strippers' names? For what, engraved invitations to Sunday dinner? Puh-lease."

"I'm sick of this shithead." Meredith rushes at him.

I grab her arm. "He's not worth it, babe."

"Yeah, but it'd feel real good." She does a fake-out lunge toward him, and he scurries behind a chair like she's the lion and he's a circus clown who stumbled into the wrong tent.

"You crazy bitch! You leave any cat scratches on me, I'll have you back in prison."

Meredith laughs but it's more scary than anything. "Cat scratches? Try a broken jaw."

Tucker's eyes go wide. "I know neither of you are lawyers, but surely you understand the concept of evidence. As in, there's no way you have any tying me to the mayor's murder."

"Actually, we have a witness who said you sent Dr. Hendricks with the drugs," I say. "Probably something you do all the time. Get girls drugged up and go wild. Maybe that's where the idea started to solve Nancy's mayor problem."

"Drugs? You think I do drugs with strippers? As if I value what I've built so little?"

Meredith rolls her eyes. "Please, what *you* built? You entitled jerk."

"I had some help with the private schools from my grandparents. And yes, being a Yale legacy gave me a leg up. But I'm certainly no Newport playboy. There's no mommy's millions to save me from a pants-down-with-strippers-and-blow kind of scandal like a real rich boy."

Meredith is moving toward him again like a lion stalking clown-prey. "So you're saying if you got involved in a scandal, it'd need to be a good one? Something really worth the effort? Say, killing the mayor and getting your girlfriend to frame me for it?"

He stammers and takes a big step backward as the chair wheels knock against his loafers. "I'm not sure if it's more offensive you're accusing me of murder or seriously dating a stripper."

I hurry to preemptively take Meredith's arm before she pummels him. "What if I told you Destiny—the state witness—has ID'd you? That the cops are on the way."

He throws his hands in the air. "Great. There's no way that girl could pick me out of a lineup. I don't even remember what she looks like, and she sees a hundred guys like me a night."

I blow out a breath, but I'm not giving up. "What if the cops search your place? They might find something interesting."

"They are welcome to it. Call Dr. Hendricks while you're at it. He'll confirm I've literally never taken a single drug from him. He makes all his money with people like the Davenforths, not me. Harrison's bill alone probably put his daughter through Vassar."

Maybe the guy just has a guilty face, but I have to try one more time. I reach for the phone at the center of the table and pretend to dial. "Here's what I'm going to tell Nancy: a stripper says you gave her pills to poison the mayor. Think you'll make the next Newport party invite list after that tidbit?"

He waves his hands at me like his sleeves are on fire. "Wait! Wait, no, stop. Put down the phone. Listen to me, I'll tell you everything I know."

I drop my finger down to hang up my fake call but keep the receiver in my hand. "See, that's why I can't let this hunch go, Tucker. You care more about Nancy's opinion than anything else in the world. Remember what you told me when I fired you. 'Look to the left, look to the right, I'll be the only one left standing.' Well, maybe you meant that literally in the mayor's case."

"Okay, fine. I'll admit Nancy's opinion matters a great deal to me. She might let me in as an investor, you see. Once I convinced Mayor Tom to come to our side, I started pushing to be part of the convention center. That's where the real money is—owning a piece of Providence and then charging others for the privilege of using it. Unfortunately, there's all this red tape now with the will and taxes before we can move forward. The mayor's death has set me back at least six months. Trust me, on the list of people I didn't want dead, Tom would be right after Nancy herself."

"Bullshit," Meredith says, but there's no sting to it.

"Talk to my accountant. My financial planner. The bank that's giving me a loan to move the plans forward."

"Money trouble?" I say with too much satisfaction.

Tucker shoves the chair away and stands up straight. "Running a business is tough, I can admit that owner to owner. Trying to get a big deal together in Rhode Island... Well, if it doesn't bankrupt you, it'll probably kill you."

Meredith shoots me a *Well, shit* look, and she's right. Our anger fueled us right to a dead end.

"I'll still tell Nancy," I say because I'm mad and I don't know where else to put it. "Tell her you were involved. Tell everyone in this whole state."

He blinks at me several times as if he's seeing me for the first time. "You're a lot of things, Krystle Romero, but I'd never have thought you'd be desperate enough to be a liar."

That one knocks the wind out of me, so I turn on my heel and stare out toward the skyline. It feels like this is always where my anger leads: somewhere depressing. I guess desperate and pathetic go hand in hand.

"Now, if you'll excuse me, I need to get back to the bar to converse with some real lawyers."

"Don't let the door hit your ass on the way out," Meredith calls.

He flings the door wide and stands there with his hands on his hips. "I honestly feel sorry for you both, so I'll say this. If I was to point the finger at anyone, it'd be his widow. You should have seen how mad she was when she overheard that Mayor Tom had flipped sides."

"His widow? You mean Tara Jordan?" Camille suddenly appears in the doorway behind him, and his escape route is blocked. "Keep talkin', Tucker."

"Where the hell did you come from? Is this place just crawling with widows?"

Camille shoots him an impressively withering stare. "I'm waiting."

He blows out an annoyed breath. "Well, Tara pretended to be all business, but what I saw when she walked into my conversation with Mayor Tom about the deal was a woman scorned.

She threw a vase right at his head and threatened him with a fire poker."

"Like some jealous housewife?" Meredith says with a scowl.

"Let's just say not even Dr. Hendricks's pills could chill her out."

"Since he married her, you'd think he'd know better than to go up against a woman like Tara," Meredith says with a smirk.

"I assumed Mayor Tom came to his senses. Tara Jordan doesn't belong in our world, and he was done slumming it. As am I. Ta-ta, ladies." Tucker dips under Camille's arm and slams the door behind him.

I stick out my tongue. "Eck, he's the worst."

"He's not wrong. Tara Jordan is suspect number one in my book." Camille drops a folder onto the conference table. "Look what Aiden and I found at city hall."

I smack my hands together. "Tell me this is real evidence we can use."

"Evidence and motive. The mayor not only chose Nancy's side but was threatening Tara's livelihood. Tara is a Material Girl in a Material World, so when it comes to money and power, you better believe she'd do anything to win."

Meredith looks skeptical, but she still makes a beeline for the folder. "Destiny told me she got the pills from Dr. Hendricks, sent by her boyfriend. Tara Jordan had nothing to do with it."

Camille slides over the documents with a shake of her head. "Well, I don't know about a boyfriend. Tara knew who the doctor was, right? He seemed very chummy with that whole crowd. A woman like Tara can certainly convince some hack doctor to sneak some pills."

Meredith flips through the dozen or so pages. "Well, Tara did point him out to me."

Camille nods as if that's a smoking gun. "See? Destiny's probably blaming her boyfriend to throw you off Tara's scent, which I am sure smells like green."

"That's possible," I say to Meredith's scowl. "She lied to the police in a murder investigation. What harm is one more lie to protect the woman who's bankrolling her?"

Camille nods. "Think about it. Tara has motive and opportunity. She's in finance, which means she does her research. It wouldn't have been difficult for her to figure out that Meredith and I are partners in the same firm. That I'd likely use my friend's place for such a high-profile job."

Meredith still doesn't seem convinced, but she stops protesting when she reads the last page. I lean over her shoulder to see what's silenced her. "Bingo, bango, boingo, baby!" My eyes go wide at finally, finally having some real evidence as I snatch the page with the LLC name that's tied to Tara and proves she had more to lose than anyone. "The police commissioner might not take my calls, but I know whose he does. She's going to be the happiest lady in Newport once we finally pin this on Tara Jordan."

JUSTINE

The Davenforths will be the death of me. My tires screech as I slam on the brakes to avoid hitting the passenger door of the sports car that just swung out in front of my sedan. An accident would have mostly been the fault of the *Miami Vice* wannabe in the Ferrari, but partly mine. I've been driving too fast for a residential street, trying too hard to weave around traffic.

Once again, I've overestimated how much I can accomplish in an afternoon, thinking I could pop in on Harrison and still make it to my promised dinner with JJ. Only one of those things was ever possible. I knew the four miles to the Newport Yacht Club would be a sea of brake lights. I'd seen the traffic.

But I chose Harrison, and it's going to cost me.

As I pull into the parking lot, I can't help but think of the price I've already paid pursuing the Davenforths' business. Meredith no doubt feels abandoned by my failure to show at her bail hearing. Camille's surely peeved that I used my official party invitation to charm a who's who of Providence rather than help her investigate murder motives. And Krystle's obviously furious with me.

Maybe for good reason. The truth is I like passing my car key to the marina's valet without so much as a glance at the posted parking prices, knowing it will go on Nancy's tab. It feels good striding toward these blinding white boats—the smallest of which costs more than most people's permanent homes—confident that no one will stop me. That I'm on the list.

As much as I don't want to admit it to myself, part of me wants to *stay* on the list, to continue to enjoy access to all this affluence—to, maybe, provide my son with some of it. Krystle might be a raging bull in a Pottery Barn, but she can spot a red flag far off in the distance. She knows.

And I know that the only reason I have access to Nancy is because she's the firm's client. If I left Romero, Tavani, Kelly, and Romero to work exclusively for the Davenforths, I'd be as bad as Tucker. Worse, even, since I'd be turning my back on my friends.

I carefully step on the shiny pine planks while scanning the sterns of docked vessels for the name Nancy gave me. As I do, I reassure myself that my efforts are as much for Meredith, Camille, Krystle, and JJ as they are for me. We *all* need the Davenforths' business. And I haven't done anything unforgivable. At least, not yet.

The boats grow bigger the further I walk down the dock. A forty-foot sailboat with steel fishing rods on the back looks like the kind of ship Harrison might own. Sleek, yet practical. Sporting. But the name on the back—*Feelin' Nauti*—isn't what Nancy said.

Neither is the wide catamaran with its white-cushioned lounge chairs gleaming on the back. That one's named the *Aquaholic*.

Boat people apparently love puns.

Harrison's boat name isn't as cutesy, according to Nancy. Given that it was likely purchased by Ms. Davenforth herself, that's no surprise. Nothing about Nancy indicates she's a fan of silly wordplay.

I see what I've been looking for stamped on the back of the furthest vessel—an eighty-foot yacht that seems impossible for anyone but a trained seaman to navigate. When Nancy said that Harrison was on his boat, I'd pictured something smaller. A skiff that he could drive down the Block Island Sound, maybe dock in Montauk or Sag Harbor when he felt like getting away. This boat is the kind of thing that people take to the Caribbean, though it certainly fits its name—the *Privilege*.

The yacht has three levels. Its first, below deck, is just visible in the squat rectangular windows dotting the hull. Above that is the deck. I spot a swimming platform at the stern leading to stairs on either side that each open to what can only be compared to an outdoor living room. There's a long curved couch surrounding a coffee table. A bar at the far end.

But no Harrison.

A deep voice cuts through the sea breeze, coming from somewhere on the unseen third level above me. Though I can't pinpoint the exact location, I know the speaker's Harrison.

"I never wanted him to die."

"Oh. And I did?" A woman's voice. Indignant. Haughty. I almost recognize it.

"Well, what was I supposed to think?"

I hear the click of high heels on hardwood. Instinctively, I press my back against the boat's side, trying to keep out of sight of Harrison and, most importantly, his guest. The last thing I want is to surprise the man I just kissed while he's with another woman. An ex-girlfriend, perhaps? Maybe even a current one.

My neck grows hot with shame, maybe anger. I feel betrayed—though I suppose I've no reason to. Harrison invited me on one date. We shared one kiss. What did I really think? That Providence's most eligible bachelor would eschew all the other single women in the city after one evening with me?

I bite my lip, trying to hold back the emotion I feel squeezing my throat. I'm an idiot. Because I thought exactly that, didn't I? I assumed that Harrison frenching me in front of all of Providence's elite at his fancy Paris-themed party meant he was staking a public claim. *This is my girl.* I'd read subtext into his promise that Nancy would snap me up first. He said his mother's name, but I thought he was simply too shy to say his own.

Harrison's voice continues to waft from above. "I knew I didn't do it. I only wanted him to embarrass himself enough on tape that even he'd realize he had zero shot at the governorship—no matter how much money my mother threw behind his campaign."

I cup my hand over my mouth, stifling the gasp threatening to have Harrison and his guest peering over the starboard side. Harrison wanted to end his father's political career, and he knew someone had hired Camille. Could he be talking to…

Tara?

"It wasn't your idea. Why are you explaining it?"

As the mystery woman speaks, I become more certain it's her. I hear the hint of a New York accent—the same flat *A*'s that occasionally sneak into my own speech.

Harrison's voice raises. "I can't help it. I keep going over it in my head. It doesn't make any sense. He *died*. God. He died. And if I didn't do it, that left you—"

"You should have known I'm too smart to do anything that stupid. I'm a businesswoman. The death of a partner is bad for any investment."

The click of heels indicates Tara either moves closer to Harrison or farther away. "The obvious suspect is whoever sent those threatening letters," she continues. "Marco was so spooked he suggested we call the whole thing off. Easy for him to say given that he didn't pay the architects or donate to half the state legislature's reelection."

The name Marco isn't familiar to me. Whoever he is, though, it's clear that he was working with Tara to build something on Mayor Tom's land that was likely very different from what Nancy and Harrison had envisioned. Now Harrison has control of that parcel.

I hear him sigh. "I jumped to conclusions."

Tara's heels click over to another part of the deck. "You *ran*—right back to the safety of the Davenforth mansion and all Nancy's money." I hear the smack of hands against a chest. Something thuds onto something else. Not the floor. The noise is too muffled. "You're just like him," Tara rails. "You can't help it."

Harrison grunts. "I'm not."

"You are. A carbon copy. All ambition and pride."

There's another smack, and then another. Is she hitting him?

Harrison releases a guttural grunt. "I'm nothing like him."

More smacks. "You aspire to be him."

Harrison exhales loudly. Trying to calm himself? "Take that back."

Something crashes onto the deck floor. "You're weak. You do whatever Nancy tells you to. You won't ever be anything but Nancy's boy."

Harrison moans. She's hurting him, I realize. Insulting him. Hitting him. But Harrison is too much of a gentleman to lay a hand on a lady, let alone his stepmother.

Luckily, I wasn't born to the manor. Even if Harrison was involved in embarrassing his playboy dad, he doesn't deserve such abuse. And Tara does not get to kill the mayor, deny it, set up my friend Camille, get Meredith arrested in the process, and then bully the first man I've cared about since Jack to push through her plans. That bitch didn't bet on me being here.

I snap off the gold hoops in my ears and shove them into my purse. As I'm about to jump onto the swimming platform, I hear something that makes me stop. A female moan, long and loud and undeniably sexual, which doesn't make any sense. Is beating up Harrison turning her on?

Another grunt from Harrison. "Does that girl have anything to do with it?"

"The hot club owner? Don't worry. I have plans for her. I'll take—"

Tara cuts herself off with a breathy sound that sends a shiver up my spine. Whatever is happening, I'm no longer positive Harrison needs saving—but I know Meredith does.

I tiptoe onto the swimming platform, thankful for the silence of my flat shoes. Whatever Tara's plans are for Meredith, I need to make sure my friends and I are well prepared. Carefully, I climb the stairs and then walk through the living room to a ladder-staircase hybrid. More slaps and grunts mask the soft squeak of my sweaty hands grabbing the railing. I climb another step, then another, stopping just when my eyes can peer at the deck above.

What I see tells me everything I need to know. Harrison lies flat on his back atop a lounge chair. Tara straddles his thighs, her pregnant belly peeking from an unbuttoned Oxford shirt. Stilettos still on. Those smacking sounds weren't hands at all. At least, not unwelcome ones.

"I'll take care of Meredith." Tara finishes her sentence and with a moan rolls off Harrison.

I duck lower as she picks her latest neon power suit off the floor, watching as she slips on her skirt. "So, we're good."

Harrison exhales, still laying on the chair. "We're good."

"And I can tell Marco your recent inheritance is still earmarked for our project."

Harrison finally sits up. "I don't have control of that land."

Tara finishes buttoning her shirt and picks up her jacket. "Of course you do. Tom left it to you."

"But my mother made me sign over the development rights."

Tara whirls around. "She made you? She can't make you."

"She was pushing papers at me hours after my dad's death. What was I supposed to do?"

Tara whips her jacket at Harrison's bare thighs. "You tell me this now, you little shit? You child."

Harrison rolls out of the way before the jacket can come down again. "Ow. Tara."

She snaps the jacket at his back. "I can't believe I ever slept with you."

Harrison stands, his naked body in full view of anyone with a telephoto lens. "You liked it. You know you wanted—"

"Are you kidding me?" Tara nearly screams. "All you've ever been is a tool to get back at your father. I was looking forward to revealing everything eventually. After—"

"No. That's not true. He's dead, and you still came for me. You love—"

"I came for the land, you moron."

"But—"

Tara releases a guttural groan. "Don't you know what you've done? What I have to do now?"

The ferocity with which Tara jams her arms through her jacket sleeves makes clear that Harrison's pleas are falling on deaf ears. She's coming my way.

Though I descend the ladder as quickly and quietly as possible, the clipped steps above make clear that I won't be able to cross the living room and descend the second set of stairs before she sees me. I scan for a hiding spot. There's that couch, but it's too tightly pressed against the deck wall. The table's too short to ever conceal my tall frame. But the chair might work.

I duck behind it just in time to see Tara's shoes on the steps.

Above me, Harrison shouts, "Wait!"

She's not listening. Tara is swearing under her breath as she descends the stairs toward the swimming platform. "Leave it to men," she says to herself, "and you always get screwed."

As soon as she slips out of sight, I sprint from the chair to the second set of stairs. My gait is far less certain than Tara's, but I'm equally determined to get off this boat and out of this marina. I refuse to slow down, despite the neon suit in the distance and the sheen on the dock planks. Shame spurs my steps. How stupid can I be? This entire time, I've been working for a guy so disloyal that he would get into bed and business with his father's wife, and then accept her obvious lies about killing his dad to justify another romp. While she's pregnant! With his half brother. Ew!

Footsteps pound behind me. They're heavy. Male. The voice that follows them confirms my assessment. "Tara!"

I speed up, my flats pounding the dock.

The footsteps behind me grow closer. "Wait. Justine? Is that you? What are you—"

I don't hear the last part because my balance gives way. I feel my right foot slide on the slick wooden boards beneath my shoes and then nothing. Empty space followed by water.

My body follows my right leg into the bay. Saltwater smacks me in the face. Stings my eyes. My torso plunges into the depths. My head goes under.

The shock of cold gives way to an urgent desire for air. I push up and down with my arms and legs, driving myself toward the surface. A moment later, my head explodes from the watery ceiling above me. I see Harrison standing on the deck, his hand outstretched.

"Justine. How much did you hear?"

I ignore his question and look around for another way out, another dock that I can pull myself onto. Boats block all other avenues of escape. I'd need to swim out into the open ocean, braving boat traffic, before heading back to another platform. My skirt clings to my legs, restricting my motion. I'm a bad swimmer on my best days, a living, breathing cliché of an inner-city kid raised in New York's outer boroughs. I wouldn't make it.

"Get away from me, Harrison."

"I'm guessing you heard everything, all of which I can explain."

I keep treading water, despite my silk blouse sucking onto my skin like seaweed. Weighing me down. "Why would I believe anything you say?"

Yelling takes energy that I don't have. I move my arms faster, trying to make up for the lack of momentum coming from my restricted legs. My chin slips below the water. I taste the fetid flavor of the bay. My head dips lower, dragged down by the weight of my long, drenched hair. Water fills my nose. In spite of myself, I raise my hand.

A moment later I'm flying up and out of the water. Harrison's arm reaches around my back, steadying me on the dock. My bare toes find their footing on the boards. Those Ferragamo flats are either halfway out to sea or stuck in the silt below.

Harrison's grasp loosens on my arm. I take a step back, hoping that the subtle pull will free my arm further. "You don't have to explain. I need to get back to my son."

Harrison's fingers dig into my skin. He yanks me to his chest. I feel his hot angry breath against my ear. "My mother sent you here as her spy, didn't she?"

Water drips from my hair into my eyes as I shake my head. "She wanted me to check on you. I need to get back."

"I can't let that happen."

Harrison drags me to the boat. My feet scrape against the hardwood as I fight to get away. I feel the skin slice and separate on my bare heel. "Harrison, stop."

He lets out an annoyed growl and then scoops me up as though I weigh little more than a damp towel. As he carries me like a shotgun bride toward his boat, I hit his shoulders. Slam my fists against his chest. "Let me go! Let me go!"

I keep saying it—screaming it—hoping someone aboard one of these boats will hear. But no one comes to my aid. I gather my strength and push with all my might against Harrison's chest. "LET ME GO!"

And he does.

I feel myself falling. A moment later, my head smacks hardwood. My vision blurs. There's the sensation of rising into the air, my wet hair clinging to my skin.

Then, suddenly, nothing but darkness.

CAMILLE

Krystle drives, if you can call it that. She punches the pedal of her old LeBaron to the metal and gets us to Newport in thirty minutes flat, the speedometer needle urged on by equal parts triumph and urgency. Tara killed Mayor Tom, and with pills supplied by Dr. Hendricks. It's a good thing we don't pass a cop because there isn't a speed limit we don't blow past.

At the gate, she rolls down her window. "Krystle Romero here to see Ms. Davenforth."

She grins while she says it, and for the first time in a long time, she sounds like the old Krystle. Commanding. Confident. Victorious.

A man's reply scratches out the speaker. "As I said when you called, Madame Davenforth is otherwise occupied."

"Trust me, pal, she'll want to know what we have to tell her."

There's a long pause, then finally a buzzing, and the metal wall slides open.

"All right, girlies," she says, hands at ten and two. "Here we go."

I twist around to look at Meredith in the back seat, still short-tempered even though if we can confirm Tara had access to the deadly pills through her connection to Dr. Hendricks, it'll take some of the heat off us. It's clear from Meredith's expression that she's not all that excited at the prospect of seeing Nancy—the enemy when it comes to the future of her club. I reach around, pat her on the knee. "One fight at a time, sugar. We'll win that one too."

The Davenforth estate is lit up like an airport landing strip; golden light beams from a million bulbs hidden in the grass along the driveway, from every window on the house, from lanterns on either side of every door, and shining up the trunks of every massive beech and rhododendron on the lawn. It turns the nighttime sky bright as day, lighting up the gunmetal gray like one of those swirling club spotlights. All the way here, dark clouds have been gathering over the coastline.

Krystle pulls to a stop next to the front door and kills the engine. By the time the three of us clamber out, Nancy is standing in the open doorway.

"I thought my butler made it clear that, unfortunately, I don't have time for this right now. I'm in the middle of a very important meeting, and I have no idea when I'll be done. Perhaps you can come again tomorrow morning. I'll make time for you first thing."

Krystle tugs on the hem of her peplum jacket, coming around the back of the car. "You were right all along. It really was Tara who killed Mayor Tom."

That seems to give Nancy pause, but still she blocks the

doorway like a linebacker. "Didn't the police already make an arrest?" Her gaze flits to Meredith.

"The police made a *mistake*," I say, right as the first drop of rain smacks me on top of the head. Shit. The wind has picked up too, the air heavy with sea and sulfur. I move closer to the house. "Tara doesn't have just one motive, but two. We found out she was a big investor in the casino. When the mayor switched to supporting your Paris plans, she had yet another reason to kill him. We have it on good authority she had access to someone with the drugs that killed Mayor Tom."

"Yeah, the doctor who was at your party," Krystle says. "*That's* why this couldn't wait. He's the pill pusher."

Nancy presses a hand to her chest. "Dr. Hendricks would never."

Krystle pulls the file Aiden and I created from her bag, and between the three of us, we walk Nancy through everything we've discovered these past twelve hours. The parcel of land that belonged to Tom, the presentation attached to the rezoning application with Tara's LLC listed as investor, Tucker's revelation that she was furious at Tom's change of plans, Destiny's boyfriend who we suspect is actually cover for Tara bribing her. The final piece, how Dr. Hendricks's pills made their way into a special bottle of champagne that few besides Tara knew existed.

"That…that can't be right. Those pills could have come from anywhere. Why would that woman use a Newport doctor for illicit pills? The streets of New York City are rife with drugs that are just as deadly."

Another raindrop falls from the sky, splattering me on the shoulder. I tip my head just in time to get swatted in the face by a fat one.

"How 'bout you call Dr. Hendricks up and ask?" Krystle suggests. "Or better yet, ask your pal Commissioner Mann to make the call. Either way, Hendricks is the one who can identify Tara Jordan as sending those pills straight to the champagne room."

Nancy steps back under the awning so she remains dry as the rain picks up. "You're saying that Dr. Hendricks knowingly provided pills to murder Tom?"

"Maybe he didn't know." Meredith glares at Nancy. "If that's the case, you have to tell him those pills are deadly. He might not realize the danger of what he's prescribing."

Nancy pauses to consider this, her birdlike body stiff in the lights of the grand foyer where it's cool and dry. I eye the giant crystal chandelier, the antique fainting couch along the paneled wall, a bright umbrella next to an abandoned suit jacket that's a pink so bright, there's no way it belongs to Nancy. Her guest, I'm assuming, but something about it gives me pause. The fabric. The color. I feel like I've seen it before.

"I'd love to help," she says, "but so far, the only things I've heard are accusations and conjecture. If you find real evidence that Dr. Hendricks is guilty of some kind of crime, then please call my assistant and make an appointment, or better yet, report it to the police. Now if you'll excuse me, my associate is waiting." Nancy steps back into the house, moving to shut the door.

"Wait!" I say, rushing the house. "Is this associate by chance Justine? Because we've been looking for her all afternoon."

"Ms. Kelly is with my son, and I'm quite certain the two of them would like a bit of privacy. Good night, ladies."

She shuts the door in our faces.

Meredith's mouth twists into an insulted sneer. "You gotta be kidding me. That old bat really just kicked us out."

"Shh, she's probably still watching to make sure you don't swipe anything." Krystle holds her bag above her head as more drops fall from the sky.

"Did you see that pink jacket, though?" Meredith says. "If I didn't know better, I'd say it looked just like Tara's."

I gasp. "That's where I've seen it before. She was wearing it that night outside the police station. Why was it hanging on Nancy's coat rack?"

Krystle shifts the bag, but it's not blocking much rain. "Who cares? What I want to know is why Justine isn't with us instead of playing hanky-panky with the golden boy. Nancy's the client, not Harrison, and as much as it irks me, Nancy listens to Justine."

"Doesn't he live in the carriage house?" Meredith says. "Which one's that?"

We look around, taking in the lit-up buildings of the estate: a garage and a barn, set against the inky blackness of the Atlantic. The barn, probably.

Krystle must agree, because she takes off down the cobblestone pathway. "Let's go. It's time she decides which team she's on: ours or her own."

Meredith and I follow behind at a fast clip, the three of us hugging the house as we dodge raindrops, which are starting to fall faster. We pass long leaded windows offering flashes from the outside of fussy antiques and expensive art, giant portraits of long-dead Davenforths. Not for the first time, it hits me that Nancy lives in this big house all alone—assuming you don't count the staff, that is, which I'm certain she doesn't. What good are all these rooms, all these fancy furnishings if you don't have anyone to share them with?

We're almost to the corner of the house when the skies open up. The three of us squeal as rain falls in big buckets, soaking our clothes, our hair, our skin.

"Seek shelter!" Krystle screams, taking off across the wet grass.

Thirty seconds later we're huddled together on the barn's covered porch, breathing hard. All around us, the rain continues to pour.

I bang a fist on the door, three hard ticks that get sucked up into the steady patter of rain falling onto the lawn behind us. As much as I don't want to hear Justine's *I told you so*, she'll be happy that she was right about Tara all along. If it will get us out of this rain, it'll be worth hearing her gloat.

We wait. Shift from foot to foot. Peer through the windows. I spot a pair of matching couches facing each other atop an ivory shag carpet and just beyond, a reading table covered with books and newspapers. I spot an empty glass on a side table, a pair of kicked-off sneakers by the staircase. But no reply. No movement.

Krystle bats at her curls, which have quadrupled in size. "How's my hair?"

Meredith bites her lip, working to keep her expression steady. "It's fine."

It's not fine. Krystle's wearing an orange helmet of fat and fuzzy curls. She runs her fingers through her bangs, tugs some of the longer pieces flat, but they spring back even bigger.

I try knocking again, harder this time, then give a twist to the doorknob, which turns easily in my palm. "It's unlocked."

And why wouldn't it be? On an estate like this one, bordered by high hedges and secured gates and a steep, rocky coastline, you wouldn't have to worry about remembering something as mundane as a house key.

I give the door a shove, and it swings open on its hinges. "Hello? Harrison? Justine?"

No answer. She must have already left.

"Maybe she's back at her in-laws with JJ?" Meredith offers.

"Or getting it on in the bedroom," Krystle says, her tone testy. "I swear, if I find her doing a horizontal deposition, I'm not responsible for what I do next." She shoves past me and barrels inside. "Justine!"

Meredith pulls on Krystle's sleeve. "Don't be too hard on her. A girl needs some action now and then, and this could be the first guy Justine has been with since Jack."

"There's a time for romance. When your friend and business partner is in the slammer ain't it."

Krystle is not wrong, but we don't have time for bickering. We're so close to blowing this case wide open, and I have a feeling that the answers are here, somewhere in this house. We pass by the upstairs loft, which is empty. The bed is unmade, but no one is in it.

Krystle follows my gaze, and the hard lines around her eyes soften. "Well, I guess maybe she is working. Or back home with JJ."

I try it again, hollering into the empty house. "Justine? Harrison?"

No one answers. Justine isn't here, and neither is Harrison.

"Let's give her a call," I say, leading us to the cordless I spotted charging on the counter in the farmhouse kitchen, a cavernous room with checkerboard tiles and a limestone fireplace big enough to stand it. I snatch it and punch a few keys, then stop because I'm dialing her old number. *Jack's* number. Even after all this time, my fingers moved across the numbers by rote. I hit End, then hand the phone to Krystle.

She ticks in the correct number and puts the call on speaker. A harried voice fills the room. "Hello?"

"Hi, Mrs. Kelly. Sorry to call so late, but this is Krystle Romero, one of Justine's colleagues. I was hoping to speak to her. It's very urgent."

A tiny voice floats up from the background. "Is that my mommy?"

"No, sweetie. It's not." There's a sharp puff of air as Sharon sighs, then says louder into the phone, "Justine's not here. As usual."

"Do you know where she is?" Krystle says, her worried gaze sweeping across mine. "We've been trying to track her down all afternoon."

"No, I don't know. She said she was headed to the Davenforths for *work*. She was supposed to be home hours ago."

"We're at the Davenforths now, but she's not here."

"Oh, well then, I have no idea. With that son of theirs, I'm assuming." Another loud sigh into the receiver.

"Tell mommy I'm waiting for her to help me find the turtle," JJ says, louder this time.

"This isn't your mommy, JJ."

"What about the turtle?"

"Mommy's too busy for the turtle. It's past your bedtime."

JJ's response starts like a siren in the distance, a low and continuous wail that quickly builds into an ear-splitting crescendo. Meredith claps her hands over her ears and takes a step back, putting some distance between herself and the phone.

Sharon shouts over JJ's bawling. "When you find Justine, tell her she should be here. She should be at home taking care of her son."

Krystle tilts her head. "She *is* taking care of him, Mrs. Kelly, by working herself to the bone to support him. Everything she does is for JJ. To give him the kind of life he deserves."

I glance at Meredith, but the spot where she was standing is empty. I twist around until I find her by the kitchen table, staring at a photograph hung on the wall beside it. A cluster of beaming men in matching riding clothes, holding long sticks with heads shaped like a mallet. A polo team, I'm guessing. And across their chests, in big letters: Yale.

Sharon's indignant voice pulls my attention back to the phone. "What kind of life is that—one filled with broken promises and endless disappointments?" JJ's wail peters out, just long enough for him to suck a loud, wet breath. Sharon takes advantage of the relative silence to plop in her next words. "It's not right. JJ deserves better."

Next to me, Krystle's spine goes straight, growing her a good inch on her heels. I imagine as a working mother herself, Krystle has had plenty of discussions just like this one, where she has to defend her choices to old-fashioned dinosaurs like Sharon, people who question a working woman's mothering skills. JJ starts up again as Krystle leans her face close to the speaker.

"You know what, Mrs. Kelly? You're right. JJ *does* deserve better. He deserves *two* parents, not one widowed mother who has no other choice but to go to law school while also working sixty hours a week catering to an extremely demanding client. She didn't ask for this lot in life, but Justine is smart and determined, and she loves that kid like nobody's business. If you don't mind me saying, Justine deserves a lot more too. Like support from her mother-in-law, and not criticism."

Sharon gasps, a quick and sudden inhale coming at me in stereo. From the phone, but also from Meredith, still by the table.

I whirl around, and Meredith is still staring at the picture, frowning at it. I move closer, leaning in to inspect it. I spot a younger Harrison in the second row, then scan the rest of the faces, but nothing stands out. "What?" I say.

Meredith looks over, surprise flashing across her face. "Harrison went to Yale."

Along with a million other people. "So?"

"So I didn't know that until just now. All this time, I thought she was talking about Tucker."

"Sugar, I'm gonna need you to be a little more specific. Thought *who* was talking about Tucker?"

"Destiny. She was bragging about it, how smart he was to have gone there. And when I said Tucker, she nodded. I think. But it doesn't make sense if Tucker doesn't have anything to do with the drugs. In fact, he mentioned Harrison had those kind of parties."

A tingling starts up on the top of my head, creeping downward over my scalp.

"Be sure to tell Justine we called," Krystle says from behind us, then slams the phone back to the charger. "Justine's not there."

"Yeah, we got that part." I bite my lip, the puzzle pieces sliding into place. "Something's not right."

"Damn straight it's not," Krystle says.

"No. Look at this picture. What if we got the wrong Yalie?"

Everything we know about Destiny's guy—rich, entitled, up to no good—matches Harrison just as well as Tucker. And a handsome, moneyed man like Harrison would be a powerful drug, snaring her attention much better than a sniveling little worm like Tucker. For Destiny, Harrison would have seemed like an honest-to-god Prince Charming. In fact, he probably looked a lot like that to Justine too.

"Is it possible that Harrison has been lying to us this whole time? That he's the one who got Dr. Hendricks to give Destiny the drugs?"

Krystle frowns. "But why would Harrison want to poison his father?"

I close my eyes, replaying the Davenforths' party in my head as I move the puzzle pieces around. "How do we know Tucker was telling the truth? Maybe Tom didn't flip. He's not exactly here to tell us where he stood. And for Nancy to be crowing at her party about the convention center like it's a done deal, she must know Tara didn't get that land. If Harrison knew that land was willed to him, that's motive."

Krystle narrows her eyes. "You really think Harrison is capable of murder, though?"

"Either way, we need to find Justine."

Meredith nods, her brows knitted together. "These fucking Davenforths. We can't trust any of them. But where in the hell would he take her?"

My gaze tracks out the windows in the direction of the big house. The massive trees are still dripping water onto the soaked ground, but at least the rain has stopped. I think of Harrison and Justine out there, who knows where, and my heart gives a hard kick.

I pluck the phone from the charger. "Actually, there's one Davenforth we can trust, and he'll know where Harrison might be hiding out."

MEREDITH

The storm clouds start spitting again as we walk up to the Newport Yacht Club. It's pitch black out, and the high winds send the hulking boats swaying, bumping up against the dock.

"Which one is Harrison's?" Krystle asks as we approach the entrance.

Camille points. "Aiden said it's over there, fifth dock slip. That one. The big one."

Thanks to Camille calling the only honest Davenforth, we were able to narrow down where Harrison might be with Justine—on his big ol' yacht. But Aiden had asked her to wait for him as he drove from his house in South County to Newport.

Still, we agreed we're not twiddling our thumbs in the car. We parked a few streets over and were relieved to see the club was shut down for the night and security guard–free. If the Providence PD catches us trespassing, they can add it to our tab.

We don't even discuss whether to keep going; instead we stride onto the narrow wooden platform toward the boats. The light at the entrance illuminating our first steps fades as we continue. The rocking beneath our feet grows steadier the farther out we go, and the water grows darker.

"This is it," Camille whisper-yells as we approach the last—and largest—boat. Finally, we're close enough to make out the name written on the oversized white bow: the *Privilege*. Gag me with a silver spoon.

Harrison's yacht looks as empty as the rest—no movement on the deck, no lights on inside. No sign of Justine.

"Maybe they're not here anymore," I say. "We could've passed them on the highway."

"Maybe. If she met him somewhere else, like a hotel, or…" Camille trails off, and I can guess what she's thinking: if they're not in Newport, or at Justine's home, or at the yacht, they could be anywhere. It'll be like looking for two tall, gorgeous needles in a haystack.

"What are we waiting for?" Krystle says. "We need to find her."

Camille pulls her back. "Aiden will be here any minute. He said to wait for him in case there's trouble."

"South County is an hour at least, and it's summer in Newport," Krystle says. "Getting over the bridge could take him all night."

"Having extra muscle never hurts," I point out. I'm an independent woman who can take care of her own problems, but working in strip clubs I've learned the best way to solve some problems is to throw a burly dude at them.

"Plus, Aiden knows his way around the boat," Camille says. "He's been to one of Harrison's parties there before."

Krystle presses a hand to her chest in shock. "*Aiden Wyatt* knows how to have fun? Could've fooled me."

"The operative word there being *one*. Wasn't exactly his scene."

Camille's call to Aiden had been quick and to the point, but the tenderness in her voice made my heart ache. Usually I feel just fine on my own, but seeing my friends find love makes me miss that first flush of attraction to someone new—that delicious moment in time when a relationship is all possibility, no pain.

"The party sounded like exactly what Tucker described, though," Camille says. "Booze, blow, babes. So he was telling the truth about that much at least."

"Doesn't sound like Justine's scene either," I say. We need to find her and tell her exactly what kind of man Harrison is, or she's in for a world of pain. Or much worse.

I just hope we're not too late.

"That man of yours better hurry," Krystle grumbles.

"He's not my man," Camille says. "It's not like that. Aiden's... different."

"Just as long as he's good enough for you," I say.

Camille bites her lip. "He might be *too* good."

"Bullshit." Krystle puts a hand on Camille's shoulder and turns her so they're nose to nose. "You are smart, Camille. I know I don't give you enough credit for that. What's really impressive, rare even, is your kind heart. You deserve love as much as anyone, maybe even more than most. We're all making mistakes and learning from them. Together."

Camille smiles and squeezes her fingers over Krystle's. "Thank you."

I add my hand to the stack on Camille's shoulder. "Together."

The moment feels wrong somehow without Justine. She should've been piled into the backseat of the LeBaron next to me, gasping and holding on to the door every time Krystle cornered too fast. She should be standing here on the dock with us, shoulder to shoulder, ready to face whatever danger lies ahead. I miss Justine, but even more so I miss the four of us together. Wherever she is, I hope she's okay.

A sound punctures the silence, and we all tense.

"Was that a door opening on Harrison's boat?" Krystle whispers.

Then there are footsteps, getting closer.

The three of us duck behind the boat closest to Harrison's. This one's called the *Booby Trap*—only instead of the word "booby," there's a crudely rendered cartoon pair of tits. Classy.

A man steps off the *Privilege* and onto the dock. Not Harrison. We can't see much in the dim light, but he's definitely shorter and wider. And carrying a black leather medical bag.

I suck in a breath. "That's him. That's the doctor."

Dr. Hendricks strides right past us under a lamppost looking like he's fresh off the set of *Miami Vice*, way too tan for New England. He's shaking his head and cursing under his breath as he clomps down the stairs. We wait until his beamer has pulled out of the marina parking lot before emerging from our hiding place.

"What was he doing here?" I ask.

"Getting his panties in a twist." Krystle snorts.

Camille crosses her arms. "Making a delivery, I assume."

Krystle blows out a breath. "Wait, if Justine is on the boat, does that mean the doctor was delivering something to drug her?"

"We have to get to Harrison before he uses whatever Hendricks gave him on Justine, or anyone else," I say.

Camille checks her watch. "You're right. Even if Aiden gets here soon, we can't afford to wait any longer."

Krystle gives a determined nod. "Let's do this. Before it's too late."

Unless it already is. I can tell we're all thinking it, but no one wants to say it.

We hurry toward the boat, bent double and walking on tiptoes to shush the click of our heels. The swimming platform off the back is our best bet, since it's low and not too far from the edge of the dock, but we'll still have to jump for it.

"You've got the giraffe legs, Camille, you go first!" Krystle stage whispers as she shoves her forward.

Camille launches herself onto the platform with an enviable amount of grace. She turns back to us. "Who's next?"

Krystle wriggles like she's going to jump, but instead yanks me behind her. "Okay, now Meredith, you shove my keester, and Camille, you heave-ho me by the arms."

I scowl. "Why do I always have to be the one to—"

"Just do it." Camille sighs. "We're wasting time."

We get Krystle over the gap, and she lands with a thump. I

follow quick as I can, but the addition of my weight throws the balance off. The platform pitches, and we tumble into a pile, thankfully onto the boat and not the water.

"Shit!"

"Shhh!"

"Shit!"

We're not exactly stealthy, but there's no sign that anyone's heard us—no more footsteps, no voices, not even a light switching on. If anyone's here, they must be in the cabin below.

We creep toward a sliding glass door that's locked. "Damn it."

"I got this, ladies. Southern girl skills." Camille reaches into her blouse and pulls out a Leatherman tool.

Krystle pokes at her chest. "What else you got in there?"

Camille slaps her hand away. "Nothing for you, sister. Now move, you're in my light."

She drops onto her knees and starts to poke and twist until finally, there's a click. Popping up, she puts the tool in her pocket this time and heaves open the door.

"After you," Camille says calmly as if yacht B&E were in her day planner. Of course, her skills have saved our hides before.

On the plus side, the door is well-oiled, so it opens with hardly a whisper of sound. Inside, there's a large sitting area with a television and a white leather sectional sofa, plus a full kitchen with a well-stocked bar.

"Stay on the rug," Camille whispers. The deep-pile shag—bright white like the couch, the better to hide any spilled coke I suppose—muffles our footsteps as we make our way to the staircase that leads to the lower level. There's no carpeting on the steps, though, so we have to tiptoe down one at a time, cringing over every creak.

I'm about to suggest we split up, but the lower level is just one cramped hallway with doors lining either side. We start opening them one at a time—a couple of small cabins for crew or guests, the engine room, a supply closet. All empty. Finally, there's only one left. If Justine's on this yacht—in whatever condition—she's behind that door.

Camille pushes it open, and we all peer around the edge. This room is dark inside too, but I can just make out the shape of a king-sized bed—and a delicate foot dangling off the edge, bleeding from the heel.

"Justine!" I cry out. We all trip over each other, trying to shove through the small doorway and reach her.

Camille gets in first and switches on the bedside lamp. Justine's eyes are closed, but she's so still, she doesn't look asleep.

Krystle grabs Justine's limp arm and feels for a pulse, then lets out a sigh of relief. "She's alive. Just unconscious."

"Did he knock her out?" I get closer, trying to examine Justine without jostling her. She's wrapped in a robe, and her hair is damp and smooshed on one side, like she showered and fell asleep with it wet. Apart from the small wound on her heel, she doesn't look injured.

"That *stronzo* DID drug her," Krystle hisses.

"We have to get her out of here," Camille says. "And to a doctor. A real one."

"Are we sure it's safe to move her?" I ask.

"No, but we don't have much choice. Harrison could come back any minute."

He could be anywhere. This is where Aiden's knowledge of the yacht would've come in handy, but there's no time to think about that now.

I give Justine's shoulder a gentle shake. "Justine. Wake up, honey."

"If she won't wake up, we'll have to carry her," Camille says. "Meredith, go around to the other side of the bed. Krystle, get her legs."

"Oh, she'll wake up." Krystle pushes past us to get to the head of the bed, then gives Justine a firm smack on the arm. "Justine! Rise and shine!"

Camille and I exchange a look. All of Krystle's experience getting teenage boys out of bed in the morning is coming in handy, I guess.

"Justine! Time to get up, sleeping beauty."

She's just about to resort to a slap on the cheek when Justine stirs. Her eyes open about halfway, then grow a little wider when she sees the three of us leaning over her. She makes a noise, less of a word and more of a pained exhalation.

"You're on Harrison's yacht," I say. "Do you remember what happened?"

She shakes her head. Well, it's less of a shake and more of a roll to one side of the pillow and then the other. She's really out of it. We can only hope whatever he gave her will wear off without any permanent ill effects.

"I think we're still gonna have to carry her," Camille says. "Come on."

Camille pulls Justine up to a sitting position and ducks under her limp arm for stability. I do the same on the other side. Justine is practically deadweight, her head lolling forward. Krystle takes hold of her legs, and we start trying to maneuver her off the bed. We nearly get her up to a standing position when she pitches backward, dragging Camille and me down onto the mattress with her.

Camille gives a frustrated huff. "Honey, you gotta work with us here."

"I don't think she can." Whatever she swallowed—or was slipped—must have been one powerful sedative. Before I took over the club, guys would sometimes stumble in high on Lemmon ludes, eyes so glassy it was a wonder they could see the dancers. I didn't mind it as it kept them pretty docile. But Justine isn't zenned out. She's damn near catatonic.

We get her moving again and struggle toward the door. I have no idea how we're going to get Justine up the stairs and off the boat unless she starts cooperating, but that's a problem for a few minutes from now. I'll throw her overboard onto the dock if I have to; better scrapes or bruises or even broken bones than staying here to find out what Harrison has in store.

Krystle's closest to the exit, so she drops one of Justine's feet to reach for the knob. Before she can turn it, though, the door springs open. We all stumble back, nearly dropping Justine's limp form on the floor.

Harrison stands on the threshold, filling the whole doorway.

I expect to see some hint of rage or evil twisting his handsome features, but there's only confusion. And then relief.

"Thank god you're here," he says with his voice full of concern. "I need your help."

KRYSTLE

Well, Justine, doesn't look like you get the fairytale ending this time.

Hey, I'm no shrink, but with Harrison standing there in all his prepped-out glory, I get the Prince Charming Justine saw: handsome, sensitive, rich as Midas, and more than all that, a fresh start for her and JJ. And yeah, he does kinda look like her late husband, Jack, so there's that layer.

All that glitters isn't gold, and in this case, Harrison might be rotten to the core. I wrinkle my nose at him in this new light based on what we found in his carriage house. If what Camille suspects is true, this is the real Harrison: Destiny's secret boyfriend who set her up to poison his own father using Dr. Hendricks's drugs. And the cherry on top: he's letting Meredith take the fall.

Justine may have been wrong about him, but I was too. I was blinded by dollar signs and the Davenforth name, thinking their stamp of approval really meant something. Meant this law firm—and me, honestly—had finally made it. If this is what "legitimate" business looks like, I'd rather take my chances with the mob. At least they have a code. With rich people, nothing is off limits.

"What do you need help with, Harrison?" I ask and reflexively put myself between him and Justine. "It looks like you've done enough."

"I didn't do anything. She's drunk. Probably didn't eat. Girls and their figures. I can't send her home like this. I need you to go tell her mother-in-law she'll be back in the morning."

"Yuuu." Justine tries to point at him but mostly her arm just flaps.

"Did you put her in the shower too?" Meredith asks, sounding rightly horrified as she sits on the bed where we moved a really messed-up Justine.

"She tried to sober up in the shower and fell. I saved her life." Harrison grins as he always does, but I finally see him: not master of the universe, but full-of-shit momma's boy who gets away with everything. "Now, let her rest. Tell her family everything is fine. We can talk about your firm handling the Paris deal first thing in the morning." He gestures as if we're going to skip-to-my-Lou off this yacht, leaving a totally incapacitated Justine in this guy's big bed below deck. A guy who had no problem offing his dad.

I roll my eyes. "Are we supposed to believe Justine was just partying with you on this yacht without a care in the world with all we have going on at work? While her son's waiting at home?"

"I don't care what you believe; it's the truth."

I point to Justine's listless body on the bed. "Let me tell you something, bucko. Say what you want about Justine Kelly, but she's a hard worker and cares about her friends."

I don't know if Justine fully understands what I'm saying, but she seems to look at me. Her eyes water. From drugs or emotion, I don't know. I realize my second-guessing of her really hit deep.

"Another thing, Harrison: We need to get her to a doctor. A real one. She's totally out of it."

His nostrils flare. "Out of it? What are you implying?"

Meredith stands next to me, creating a stronger barrier between Justine and Harrison. "If you were at my club and did this to one of my girls, I'd have both your legs broken at a minimum."

"I second that." Camille stands on the other side of me. "Aiden can help us. He's on his way to the dock, so don't get any ideas about stopping us."

Harrison sneers. "As if he can do anything to me. Now, I will make sure she gets home safe. But let's be real: You are trespassing on my yacht. If you don't leave, I'll call the cops."

Justine gets up on one elbow, and I catch sight of her wobbling gaze. She's trying to talk, but it's like she can't get the sentences out. Her head lolls back and forth. I gently tip her chin back. Her eyes blink open like a scared goldfish that's high as a kite. "Will you look at this?" I say to the girls with real panic.

"We've gotta do something. I'm not sure we have time to get her all the way to a hospital," Meredith says.

I realize exactly what Justine needs, but she won't like it.

Harrison stomps his fancy loafered foot. "Let her sleep it off. I'll get her home in the morning."

"We are not leaving her like this." I point to Justine's arms, indicating that Camille and Meredith should each take one and help me sit her up.

Harrison gets closer to us, which works for me. His *privilege* is showing and it ain't pretty. "I said don't move her. I told you, she's wasted."

"Because you drugged her, you asshole, so save it for the judge," I say in my don't-fuss-with-a-girl-from-the-Hill tone.

"Where do you get off accusing me of that?"

Camille glares at him as she lifts Justine up with Meredith. "We saw Dr. Hendricks leaving. You expect us to believe he makes yacht calls to deliver a case of bubbly?"

"Maybe if it's poisoned," Meredith murmurs.

Harrison's eyes flare. "Don't you dare threaten me." He moves forward as if he's going to push Justine back onto the bed. Well, that's his problem, because he's in the splash zone.

"Sorry, babe." I quickly jam two fingers down Justine's throat, and she instantly *Hello Dolly*'s all over his shoes.

"Holy shit! You bitches!" He jumps backward way too late, and his fancy loafers are covered in spew. Bet he wishes he'd worn socks.

I'm relieved to see Justine get everything out and even as she coughs and coughs, there's a steadiness that returns to her body.

Camille grabs a bottle of water off the nightstand and helps her drink. "Slow sips, sweetie. You're okay now. We got you."

I rub Justine's back, and she's blinking rapidly as if seeing us for the first time.

Meredith smirks at Harrison screaming about his shoes being ruined, his face red as a Bloody Mary.

"You brought this on yourselves," he yells before he slams the door and there's a distinctive click of some kind of latch engaging.

Camille pulls on the handle to confirm we're stuck before she inspects the lock. "Shit, we're in trouble, girls. This is bolted from the outside, like some marine storm lock. I can't pick this." I can see her brain spinning a mile a minute. "We witnessed the doctor leaving the boat. We know Harrison doped up Justine, like he gave drugs to Destiny to kill his father. He's not going to just let us go. What's he going to do?"

As if on cue, a loud rumble answers the question, the engine roaring to life. "Oh my God, where's he taking us?" Meredith panic-whispers, and then she frantically opens a drawer. "We have to get out of here. Help me find something to break the door."

As she and Camille search the room, I feel Justine's grip on my arm—firm and steady—and I turn to see her eyes wide and full of emotion.

Her voice is hoarse, but she's able to speak. "Thank you."

"She's talking," I say to the girls and then almost nosedive as the whole room sways back and forth. The yacht must be pulling away from the dock. The gals keep searching for something to get us out, but I keep my grip on Justine as she stares up at me.

"He...really fooled me." I can see the shame in her brown eyes, and I hate that I'm to blame for a lot of it being there. I brush a wet strand of hair behind her ear and feel such relief she's okay. Well, at least when it comes to whatever the doctor slipped her. The boat driven by a crazy guy is another matter.

"We were all fooled by this damn family with their Paris song and dance and their dollar signs." I take a fresh bottle of water from Camille. "Here, drink a little more. You're going to have a helluva headache."

Justine sips and begins to shake. I pull the blanket around her trembling shoulders and realize that they've carried so much. She's not only a single mom but a law student who felt like she had to keep our whole firm afloat. Lord knows, her in-laws aren't supportive. Neither was I.

"I'm sorry, you know. I jumped to the wrong conclusions about what you were doing because I was scared you'd see another firm is better. Prove Tucker right. About the only thing I know how to do these days is get angry."

She shakes her head, and it's a normal rhythm now. "I'd never leave. You're my family."

She's right, of course. Because when I think about the awful reason we were brought together—as widows—what it really means is now that we're together, we won't ever be alone again. "I know that, I really do."

Justine squeezes my hand and wipes her tears. I can see the shift back to business. "Listen, it's not only Harrison. Tara was here and I saw them…you know."

Camille pauses her ransacking of the room. "Wait. *He's hookin' up with his stepmom?* And they make jokes about us Southerners."

Our gazes bounce around at each other as Justine continues,

"I caught them in the act. *The* act. They were talking about some deal that Tara had been involved in with the mayor."

Camille's eyebrow shoots up. "Well, hell. There's Harrison's motive."

Justine presses a finger to her head as if she's trying to piece it together. "Tara and Harrison said something about wanting to embarrass the mayor enough to bring him back around."

"Bring him off team Nancy from whatever sweeteners Tucker promised and back in line with the casino deal. Tara did hire me for leverage, but not for a divorce." Camille leans on the edge of a dresser, working something out. "When Tom switched sides to the Paris plan with Nancy, it left Tara and her investors holding an empty bag that was supposed to be filled with casino cash."

"But *Harrison*, really?" Meredith frowns and puts a hand on her hip. "What would a badass boss lady like Tara see in a spoiled rich boy like him?" Justine gives her a look. "No offense," Meredith quickly adds.

Camille shrugs. "Tara had a lot of money on the line. Harrison inherited his father's land after his death. Land that was critical to either the Paris plan or the casino."

"Sleep with the stepson, seal the deal?" I offer.

Camille nods her head as if the pieces are finally coming together. "I can totally see Tara manipulating Harrison to push her plan through, but it still seems like a dumb move for her to poison the mayor after hiring me and hiding the murder weapon in champagne from a company she invests in. Why not just leave her business card at the crime scene? We're missing something."

Before anyone can guess an answer, the floor rocks, and I nearly go ass over teakettle as Justine throws her arms around me. Camille grips the dresser, and Meredith extends her arm for balance.

The boat is really hauling ass now, and my throat tightens at what it means. "We must be out of the bay. Open ocean."

There are footsteps overhead. The clink of glasses. A popping cork. "What the hell is he doing up there?" Meredith murmurs, though I can't imagine any of us want to know the answer.

"Who is driving this thing?" Justine asks as we instinctively come together around her at the center of the room.

Footsteps slowly echo outside and grow louder.

"I don't like this one bit," Camille murmurs.

There are sounds of metal sliding and scraping as the door swings open to reveal Harrison in new shoes, a champagne bottle in one hand and a great big gun in the other. "Who needs a drink?"

JUSTINE

At first, I blame the drugs. I'm hallucinating the long silver nose of the Colt pointed at my chest. Harrison Davenforth Bradley could not seriously be threatening to kill *all* of us.

Krystle steps forward, fists clenched at her hips in a hopeless effort to make her short stature intimidating to a six-foot-five man. "From Yalie to Dirty Harry, huh? They teach you how to use that at the Newport Country Club?"

Harrison shifts his aim to Krystle's chest. "Take the bottle and let's go. Everything's set up on deck."

Camille scoffs. "Uh-uh, sugar. I saw what that particular brand did to your dad."

The mention of his father wrenches Harrison's mouth, opening his sneer into a teeth-clenched grimace. "It's just champagne."

Camille scoffs. "Like hell it is."

Harrison takes a swig from the bottle and then wipes his mouth with his left sleeve. His right hand keeps the gun squarely on Krystle. "Come on. We can discuss our next steps in a civilized fashion."

A glance at my friends reveals not one of us believes Harrison has anything civilized planned. But the deck affords us a better chance of escape than being locked in this cramped stateroom. We can scream to neighboring vessels for help. Maybe even jump ship.

Krystle must arrive at the same conclusion because she steps forward to extend her hand for the bottle. "Follow me."

Harrison aims at Krystle as he retreats through the open doorway. "Stay in line, girls."

The gun that's inches from Krystle's chest keeps us ascending the stairs at a steady pace until we're all gathered in the living room. Though I'd been carried through this space, it's the first I'm really seeing it. Four empty flutes have been arranged in a semicircle atop the mahogany coffee table. At the bottom of each glass is a single white pill.

Harrison glances at Meredith. "You pour drinks or only work the pole?"

Meredith clasps her hands, perhaps to keep from clawing his eyes out. "I built my own business while you were busy taking orders from your mommy."

Harrison swings the weapon toward Meredith's smart mouth, but Krystle waves the bottle and draws the weapon right back to her. "I got it, alright? I'm a woman of many skills."

Somehow Krystle pours with a steady hand. Champagne fills each flute, floating the pills to the center of the glasses. The carbonated bubbles pop off the white disks like fizz from Alka-Seltzer tablets. My stomach rises to my throat.

Camille gestures to the glasses. "We're not drinking that, Harrison. Whatever you put in there caused your father to lose all control of his body. He was jerking around as his organs were bursting. I wouldn't wish that ending on my worst enemy."

As Camille talks, Meredith sidles up to Harrison's right. I guess what she's thinking from the extension of her arm. She intends to grab the gun.

Camille must sense Meredith's plan because she keeps talking, gesturing with her hands to keep Harrison's eyes on her. "Blood came out of his mouth. His nose. His—"

"Shut up!" Harrison's own veins threaten a similar fate. They pulse beneath his reddened face and neck as he wraps his other hand around the gun's wooden handle.

Meredith's focus is squarely on Harrison's strained expression. I cough in hopes of drawing his attention and distracting my friend long enough for her to reconsider her plan to grab the gun. While Harrison may have little chance of fatally shooting us all before someone wrests away his revolver, he can definitely murder Krystle. Her bosom's too big a target for him to miss.

Harrison glares at me with saucer-sized pupils. Whatever was in the not-so-good doctor's plastic bag, he took plenty of it.

Though he appears too wild-eyed to reason with, I try anyway. "Harrison, you don't have to do this. We can still talk things through, civilized, like you promised. I heard what you said to Tara. I don't believe you meant to kill your dad."

The gun swings in my direction. "I didn't kill him," Harrison yells. "I don't know what ended up in his drink, but it wasn't what I sent. I asked Hendricks to deliver a few party pills, the kind of stuff I've taken hundreds of times to relax."

Camille cocks her head. "Honey, your dad was jolted out of his seat like his organs were exploding inside his body."

Harrison pans the gun to Camille. "My sedatives wouldn't have done that. Worst case, he takes a short nap. Best case, he gets too loose to be suspicious of his old friend Camille showing up at his favorite strip club, asking how he likes to treat his whores." Harrison points the weapon back at my torso. "It's what's in those glasses. The same thing you took, Justine."

Reflexively, I cross my arms. Maybe in defiance. Maybe to add another layer of protection should a bullet come flying at my heart. "I didn't take anything willingly."

Harrison doesn't confirm slipping me drugs, but his face deepens to a darker shade of crimson. His pupils swim in the watery whites of his eyes. Fighting tears is taking all his energy.

That could be good. Emotion will make him a worse shot. Really, I don't need him to say what he did—how he carried me to his stateroom, all apologies, swearing he hadn't meant to drop me and this was all a big misunderstanding; that he would explain, but first his doctor should evaluate my head injury.

I hadn't trusted a word out of his stepmother-kissing mouth, of course, but the tiny lights in his bedroom ceiling were so blindingly bright that I could barely keep my eyes open, and the little I could see was spinning. Plus, my car key was at the bottom of the bay, along with my shoes. Dr. Hendricks had seemed my best chance at escape. I'd thought any man who'd taken the Hippocratic oath would be duty bound to drive me to a hospital. So, I showered. Waited. Only to have the doctor announce I had a concussion and offer something that clearly wasn't aspirin. When I'd flatly refused to take any pills, he'd handed me a glass of water.

I, of all people, should have realized that just because the water's clear doesn't mean it's safe to drink.

Thankfully, Krystle, Camille, and Meredith realized the truth without me saying.

Knowing my friends have my back gives me strength to keep talking to the man pointing a loaded weapon at my chest while Meredith creeps toward him. "Shooting me won't solve anything, Harrison. It will only make you look more guilty of killing your father."

Harrison's gaze darts to the side. "You're right."

In one swift motion, he whirls around, wraps his arms around Meredith's waist, and pulls her to him. She rakes her nails down his arms, making Harrison yelp as he jams his pistol into her ribcage. "Shooting this little stripper solves everything, though. Everyone already thinks she killed my dad. For all I know, she did."

Meredith winces as the gun digs into her side. "Why would I do that? In my club? Your dad was a regular. The money he spent at the bar alone last year paid for a new stage."

Though she sounds calm, the number of words flying from Meredith's mouth indicate how scared she is.

I raise my hands in surrender and step forward. "You know

Meredith has nothing to do with this, Harrison. She's being set up. And you know by whom."

Tears finally spill from Harrison's eyes, but his arm doesn't drop from Meredith's torso. The knuckles on his right hand shine white as he tightens his grip on the gun. "Don't come any closer, Justine. That goes for all of you. I will shoot her."

Camille pats the air, signaling everyone to calm down. "Let's talk this through, honey. Tara wanted your father's land, right? When Tom decided to team up with your mom's redevelopment, Tara figured it would be better for her if the land went to you. You can see she's manipulating you."

Snot dribbles from Harrison's puffy nose. "You don't know anything." He looks at me. "Tara was angry. But she didn't mean what she said about us. She wants what I want."

Krystle clears her throat. I brace myself for a flood of English and Italian expletives punctuated by Harrison pulling the trigger. But when Krystle's voice emerges, there's no unchecked anger. Only sympathy. "It's okay, kid. I get where you're coming from. All these years, you've had to work for your mother, had to do whatever she said because she held the purse strings and boy did she pull 'em. I bet she's dangled money over you since you were outta diapers. Then here comes Tara, empowering you to stand up to your family. Make your own decisions for a change. Look, I have sons. One who works for me. I take for granted what he brings to the table all the time. That he has a right to make his own choices."

Harrison releases a pained sob. His huffing breath inflates the snot stretching to his lip. I catch Meredith craning her neck away from the blast zone.

Krystle steps forward. "Put down the gun. We'll figure this out."

For a moment, it seems Harrison might listen. He squeezes his eyes shut, releasing more tears.

Krystle takes advantage of the nanoseconds of blindness, advancing another foot like she's playing a game of red light, green light.

Harrison's eyes snap open, freezing Krystle in her tracks. She gives him an innocent smile like she didn't nearly sneak up on him. "It's okay. It really is. This isn't your fault. You're still a young man. A boy."

Harrison's skin becomes impossibly redder. Though the narrowing of his eyes betrays that it's not sadness and fear sending the blood to his head this time. It's anger.

"I'm a man. And a man takes care of his responsibilities."

His words remind me of my own responsibilities. I have a flash of JJ waiting at home. I must get back to him—talk my way out of this. "You're right about responsibilities, Harrison. A man has a duty to show the next generation how to be a good person. With your dad not around, your little brother will look to you as his example. He needs you to—"

Camille shoots me a confused look. "Tara's pregnant?"

Harrison glares at us, pulling Meredith closer. "Shut up."

Camille's jaw drops, but her brow lowers. "Aiden mentioned that your parents tried to give you a sibling. But it didn't work. Marco said people blamed Nancy."

"They always blame the woman," Krystle says.

"But everyone suspected otherwise. Especially with the lack of love children at the rate the mayor went through women. You're—"

The gun rises to Meredith's neck, but it doesn't stop Camille from finishing her sentence. "You're the father. Tara is having your baby."

I gasp, both at the revelation and my unwillingness to see it before. Of course she's right. I caught them sleeping together, and it clearly hadn't been the first time. Tara's baby will be a Bradley, but it will also be a Davenforth.

"The sedatives would have made this easier on you, but you all don't want it that way. Fine. Move!" Harrison yanks Meredith toward the door. "We're heading outside. You all first."

I don't need to ask the reason for changing locations. Swabbing blood off a ship floor is surely easier than sopping it up from white shag carpet. Harrison must intend to line us up firing-squad style and then throw us into the drink. With our bodies at the bottom of the bay, he might not even need an alibi.

It's a solid plan. I can only hope being out in the open works to our advantage too. We couldn't have traveled that far on the ship's cruise control. There's still a chance our cries will reach the harbor. At the very least, someone might hear a gunshot.

Not that I want to hear one—especially not with Harrison holding the Colt at Meredith's neck while he orders us out. "Anyone doesn't do as I say, I'll blow her head off."

Krystle leads the way, pulling open the sliding glass door.

"Line up!" Harrison's yelling because there's no need for quiet.

A glance behind me reveals only the open ocean with the illuminated marina in the distance. No one to hear us scream.

As I look over the dark water, I picture my son waking at sunrise, anxious to show me his turtle before breakfast. I hear the patter of his little feet on the attic stairs, see his broad smile filled with spiky baby teeth as he pounces on the bed to announce whatever name he's dubbed his newfound friend. I imagine that smile vanishing as he realizes I'm not beneath the blankets, as Sharon calls him into the sitting room to explain that mommy is with daddy now.

I shiver in the cold, damp wind. Its howl and the sound of the boat's engine muffles my voice as I plead. "Harrison, please! I understand you are trying to protect the mother of your child. I'm a mother too. We all have families. People that love us. You don't want to do this."

Harrison wipes his swollen, snotty face against his shoulder, keeping his hand firmly on the gun. "I didn't want to do this. You saw Tara, and then your friends came after you."

Tears wet my cheeks. "You can stop this. Please."

A warm hand wraps around my own. I realize it's Krystle next to me, squeezing my fingers, urging me to stay strong. She doesn't look at me, though. Her gaze is squarely on the revolver in Harrison's hand. "You can't shoot all of us. One of us will survive. You'll spend the rest of your life in prison."

Camille nods in agreement with Krystle. "Tara's not worth it."

Harrison raises the gun to Meredith's head. "Lineage is all that matters. My mom taught me that every day of my life. We must build for the future, no matter the cost."

"One life is not worth more than another," Camille says.

"History would disagree." Harrison shakes his head. "Enough talking. I've set this boat on a crash course for Clingstone Rock. It'll hit, engine first. The explosion will take care of you all. It will seem like an accident. I'll tell everyone Justine and my lawyers asked to party on the boat. Things got out of hand with all the pills."

Krystle squeezes my palm tighter. "No one will believe you."

Harrison's thumb pulls the gun's safety. "You don't get it. Money makes everyone agnostic. No one has to *believe* me. They only have to think my story's possible."

Harrison's index finger moves toward the trigger. Without thinking, I fling my body toward him, trying to—I don't know what. Cause a distraction? Block a bullet? Get the gun?

It's an act of adrenaline, desperation, and love. These women have saved me, in more ways than one. They're here because of me. It's my job to save them.

The sudden motion startles Harrison enough that he loses his grip on Meredith. Rather than run, she throws herself into his right arm like she's a lineman charged with ending a quarterback's career.

I barrel into his stomach, fueled solely by fury now. Harrison manipulated me. He pretended to care for me, flattered my intelligence, fed me nonsense about ushering in a better Providence with economic opportunity for everyone—all to trick me into doing his family's bidding, to be the minority face on a deal to steal land from other shades of brown people. I was never more than a human shield for his family against racism claims. Once the deal was done, they would have pushed me aside. And, now that Harrison's no longer on board with Nancy's Paris plan, he's willing to get rid of me by any means necessary.

The gun goes off as Harrison falls to the ground. I feel a breeze above my head as the bullet whizzes past. Frantic, I look to Meredith. The way she's slamming Harrison's right arm over and over into the deck boards with all her might, like a gorilla beating the ground, tells me she hasn't been hit.

Meredith stands, confirming my assessment. I hear a crack followed by a sharp scream as she stomps on Harrison's wrist.

The gun sails from his open hand. I scurry toward it. Once the magnum is in my grasp, it's game over. I wrap my hands around the grip and raise the pistol in the air.

Then I hear Krystle's scream.

I see her propping up one side of Camille. Red blooms on Camille's blouse like a rose boutonniere pinned to her shoulder.

Meredith rushes over, grabbing a towel off a lounge chair. "Set her down, Krystle. I need to apply pressure." She glances over her shoulder. "Hold him, Justine."

I raise the gun to where Harrison had been moments before, but he's no longer on the deck floor. Footsteps bang against a metal ladder.

I run after him, holding the gun above my head with one hand as I use the other to climb to the boat's upper deck. The stars give off more light up here, but it's still difficult to discern much more than shapes. The boxy square of the wheelhouse is to my left. No shadow looms inside.

A mechanical whirring calls my attention. Harrison stands beyond the boat, somehow suspended in midair.

The concussion must have been worse than I thought. I rub my eyes with my gun-free hand, trying to clear my vision.

The machine sounds continue. I point the pistol at Harrison, struggling to make sense of how he's paid for the power of flight.

Harrison begins to descend. I trace his trajectory with my weapon, peering over the side of the boat. The new vantage point reveals his trick. He's standing on a rubber dinghy being lowered to the water by a nest of black cables that nearly disappear into the darkness.

Fresh footsteps clomp up the ladder. Krystle meets me just as Harrison's laugh pierces the air. "You should have taken the drink, Justine."

His cockiness makes me want to rip out his vocal cords—or call Meredith to do it. He's too far for either of us to do any damage, though. I settle for firing at the boat's side.

The ping of metal striking metal lets me know I hit something, as does Harrison's curse. "You bitch."

I raise the gun and fire again. This time a hiss follows the bang of the bullet's discharge. His dinghy has sprung a leak.

Krystle slaps me on the shoulder. "That's my girl."

The splash of the small boat hitting the water cuts any celebration short. I hear the snap and recoil of disengaging cables.

Krystle snorts. "He can't do much with a hole in his ding-a-ling."

"You're sunk, Harrison," I yell.

A motor struggles to start up below me. Harrison screams above the engine's coughing as he veers away from us. "So are you all. Look."

Together, Krystle and I turn toward the wheelhouse. Through the opening, I see a darkness somehow blacker than the night. Not the sky. Too high for the water.

Krystle gasps. "Land ho."

CAMILLE

I look across the bow, and my heart gives a hard kick, spurring a warm gush of blood from where Harrison's bullet grazed my shoulder. The wound is still open and my whole right side burns like it's on fire, but I can't think of any of that now because there's something big and black and solid looming over the horizon, a massive inky slash directly in our path.

Clingstone Rock, if we're to believe the blubbering Harrison, a craggy island smack in the middle of Narragansett Bay. The rock is not all that large, barely enough land for the two-story shingled house perched atop it, but a dangerous obstacle nonetheless because of all its rocky outcroppings—a literal minefield lurking under the water. A magnet for shipwrecks on the sunniest of days, and now it's nighttime and we're barreling straight at it.

"Oh, shit!" Meredith screams, and we lurch for the ladder that will dump us into the wheelhouse, even though I'm pretty sure none of us has any idea what to do once we get there. I've never steered a boat before, but how hard can it be? We'll figure out the logistics on the fly. We need to change course, aim this thing for open sea.

Krystle and Justine are already in the wheelhouse when I land on the wooden floor with a jolt that sends a sharp stab of lightning pain through my entire left side. I squeal, and Justine whirls around. "Maybe you should sit down."

"I'm fine," I say through gritted teeth. The bullet that ripped a ditch in the skin of my shoulder also tore through the fabric of my jacket—and it's Gucci, dammit. Yet another designer piece ruined by a Davenforth. I make a mental note to send them the bill.

I step up next to Krystle and Justine, taking in the long stretch of polished mahogany smothered in all sorts of controls—half a dozen computer screens, a giant silver steering wheel, and a million levers and buttons.

"This is definitely a lot fancier than what my Romeo took us out on," Krystle says, giving a hard yank on the wheel. I hold my breath and stare out the front window, but nothing happens. The boat doesn't change course. Dead ahead, Clingstone Rock grows larger.

"It didn't work," I shout. "Get this thing to stop, *pronto*."

"Try that one!" Krystle points at one of a dozen levers, and I pull a handle wide enough for a fist twice the size of mine. I yank it all the way back, but the motor doesn't stop roaring us forward.

"Are we going faster now?" Meredith steps up beside me, tapping one of the dials. "This one says we're going fifty knots. How fast is that?"

"Fast." I don't need to look behind us to know we're trailing a mighty wake. The roaring motor and vibrating boards under our feet are a clear enough sign that we're booking.

"Do something!" Krystle shrieks in my ear. "Do something *right now*."

"Like what? This thing must be on cruise control or something. You said Romeo took you guys out on the boat. What did he do when you wanted to stop?"

"I don't know, turn it off!"

"How? You got a user manual somewhere I can't see?"

"Let me in there!" Krystle elbows me out of the way and starts mashing buttons with both hands, a random and rapid-fire game of Whac-A-Mole, and the controls beep as an alarm goes off somewhere above our heads.

"Oh my God, is that bad?" Meredith asks.

"It's not good!" Krystle yells back as she smacks another button, and a foghorn belches a siren so deafening, I jump high enough to pop my shoes a full three inches off the floor.

Meredith hooks a hand through Krystle's arm and yanks her away from the controls. "Lemme try."

She steps into the space Krystle just left and leans in, studying the buttons and dials.

Justine slips off her jacket and presses it to my shoulder. "Are you in pain? You're still bleeding."

I bat her hands away and point at the big, black blob through the windshield. "We've got bigger fish to fry. How much time have we got, you think? How much longer before we hit something?"

"Not long," Justine says, and I grimace because *not long* is probably being generous. There's no moon or stars to light the way, no lights shining in the shingled house, but we're cruising along, the Newport Bridge high above us—and at the end of it, boom.

It makes sense, now that I think about it, why Harrison ordered us to drink the champagne: so none of us would be conscious when the boat hits the first jagged rock and bursts into flames. In his loony tunes mind, he really did think he was doing us a favor.

"Make it stop!" Krystle shrieks, her gaze glued to the rock. "Find the cruise control and turn it *off*!"

Meredith is still studying the dials, her forehead crinkled in concentration. "I don't see it. Is it even called cruise control on a boat?"

I scan the buttons and controls, searching, and a fat drop of blood splats onto one of the screens. I wipe it away with a sleeve, and my heart gives an excited patter at the letters I find underneath.

"ComNav! This must be it." On either side of the screen, two neat columns of buttons are labeled with words that might as well be in Chinese. "Yaw. Turn Rate. Rudder. Where the hell's the Off switch?"

"Try this one." Meredith presses Standby with a red-tipped finger, but nothing happens. The numbers on the dials don't change. The compass heading stays fixed at 123 degrees. "Dammit!"

I pull back on the speed lever again, but we stick to fifty knots.

"We're getting closer," Justine mutters, not able to hide the panic in her voice. I know she's picturing JJ. I know she's living every mother's worst fear right now—that they'll never see their baby again.

Between the four of us, we try every single switch. Power Steer. Autopilot. Nav. We flip buttons and pull down on levers and rotate the wheel enough times to turn the boat in a full three-sixty. Nothing happens. Nothing changes.

"We're running out of time," Meredith says, and she's not wrong. By now we're close enough to make out the edges of the house's roofline, the white sprays of water as waves slam into the rocks. "If we don't turn this thing soon, we're going to have to jump."

"I can't swim," Justine says, plucking a phone from a hook underneath the counter. "Definitely not with these currents."

"Find the life jackets," I say to Krystle, and she whirls around and gets busy, yanking on doors and emptying out drawers, tossing maps and pencils and an industrial-sized box of Trojans over her shoulder. Dozens of condoms rain to the floor.

Justine presses a button on the phone and holds the receiver up to her mouth. "Mayday, Mayday!"

"That's for planes," Meredith says.

Justine shoots her a look. "I think they'll get the gist. MAYDAY. Is anybody out there? We need help. *Help!*"

Nothing but dead air and screaming engines under our feet.

"Found something!" Krystle says, pulling a fat orange pistol from a drawer. She waves it in the air with a triumphant smile. "Be right back, girls. I'm gonna go send up a flare."

She teeters up the ladder, red silk stretched tight against her behind, and I turn back to the controls. Adrenaline zings through my veins as the island looms larger now—thirty seconds, I'm guessing, before we ram a rock, maybe less. "There's got to be a way to turn this thing, got to be something we're missing."

But what?

I get an idea. A long-shot idea, but an idea nonetheless. I shift to my left, parking myself in front of the ComNav dial. "Somebody say a Hail Mary."

I hold down Standby with a thumb and start punching the other buttons one by one.

"What are you doing?" Meredith asks.

"Control-Alt-Delete. It works on my IBM. Let's just pray it'll work on this thing too."

I start on the top left and work my way down the buttons, then try again with the column on the right. And every time, nothing happens. Nothing changes. Not until the very last button.

Turn.

That's when I feel it. The floor shifting under our feet, the ship leaning hard to the right. The screen beeps, then flashes with four blessed letters: E.TRN. Emergency turn.

Without warning, the speed lever shoots backward and the roar of the engine dies down, a hard braking action that catapults the three of us into the counter. Krystle tumbles to the ground in a jumble of life jackets while the pistol clutched in her fist fires off another shot, shattering a side window in a spectacular flare of fire and light. My shoulder slams into the wheel, pain slicing through me all over again.

None of it matters because there, on the other side of the windshield, the dark island slides to our left.

Justine squeals and clasps my hand. Salty wind blows in from the window Krystle just shot out, lifting her curls and whipping them all around her face, but she shoves them back with a huge smile. "You did it. You turned the bo—"

We slam into something solid. There's a horrible grating sound, rocks digging into metal and fiberglass all along the left side of the yacht. A sharp tilt pitches us sideways, and we scream and grab on to the first things we see—the wheel, the counter, the ladder and walls, each other.

Then, just as suddenly, the boat rights itself. Like nothing ever happened.

"What the heck was that?" Krystle yells, her eyes saucer big.

"A rock," I say, my breath barely slowing, even if it seems we're safe. "A giant one. I think we sideswiped it."

"Yeah." Meredith gasps. "Just like the *Titanic*."

"I know what happened to those people, and I'm not one of the suckers waiting around for the band to quit playing." Krystle snatches up a life jacket and plops it over her head. "Abandon ship!"

Justine grabs the back of her jacket. "Wait. Did you hear that?"

"Hear what?" Krystle says, stepping to the ladder. "The engine room filling with water? The boat cracking in half?"

"Shh, quiet."

The four of us fall silent, listening. Without the roaring motor, it's almost eerily still. Water laps on the other side of the shattered window, and somewhere in the distance, waves crash against a shore. How long does it take a boat to sink? It doesn't sound any different. Doesn't feel it, either.

Then I hear it: a low wail of sirens, carrying across the water.

Krystle presses her face to the window as it lights up a swirling blue and red. "It's the coast guard. Sweet baby Jesus, we're saved."

The four of us race up to the deck, where moments later, two burly men in navy coveralls heave themselves over the railing and onto the yacht's deck. They greet us with a hasty hello and take off running to the engine room we've just left. I lunge to the railing and lean over the side, staring down at the speedboat that brought them here, now attached to our vessel with a bright yellow rope.

There on the deck, looking up at me, is a familiar face. The best, most welcome face I can think of, even though he doesn't look the least bit happy to see me.

Aiden blinks at me with a scowl. "You were supposed to wait on the dock. I told you to wait on the dock."

"We couldn't. Justine was in trouble. We had to save her."

I'm smiling when I say it because he's here. Aiden's here, and so is that old familiar swell of attraction. This time, though, it's for a man who's not all that rich or powerful, who doesn't seem to give the first hoot about my short skirts that show just the right amount of skin. A man who's the exact opposite of my type—or at least what I always thought was my type.

Except it turns out Aiden *is* my type, and it's not a swell I'm feeling. It's an inferno raging inside my chest, swirling and hungry and drunk on hope that this man might feel the same.

Suddenly, I'm no longer thinking about the pain or our near

brush with death. All I can think about is getting off this boat and into his arms.

Meredith nudges me with an elbow. "I guess that's your ride to the hospital."

With a giddy laugh, I push off the railing and race down to the lower deck, hitching one leg over the side.

"Are you insane? You're going to break something. You're going to fall in," Aiden calls, but he's already moving to the edge of the speedboat, already holding out his hands for mine. I grab on to his wrists and throw my other leg over, lowering myself into his arms. He plucks at my blood-soaked jacket, peels it away from my skin. "You're bleeding."

"Harrison shot me, the little devil. Just a nick, but it hurts like a mother." I won't be going strapless anytime soon, but I can't stop grinning because who cares? I'm safe on the coast guard's boat, and Aiden isn't letting me go. "I'm fine. Better than fine, now."

Someone throws a blanket over my shoulders, and Aiden pulls it around us both. "You scared me."

His eyes are incandescent, his relief so transparent it almost hurts to see.

"I'm sorry, sugar. Also, I hate to tell you, but your cousin's a real bad nut. That baby Tara's carrying is his. He didn't even try to deny it. He tried to kill us, but I stopped the boat before it crashed into the rocks."

Aiden looks surprised at the news, though it doesn't mask his pride, and his expression spreads tingles across my skin. It never felt like this with Peter and Jack, so natural and easy. Oh, sure, I knew how to pluck and strum them like a fiddle, but I always had to work for it, always had to think and rethink every word before I said it. Hit one wrong note and all that pretty music I'd worked so hard for would wither and die.

Because it was never real. With them love was like the mascara I swipe up my lashes to make them thicker or the gloss that makes my lips look plumper. Shallow and superficial.

This feels different. Aiden feels different.

His hands slide around my waist, pulling my body flush against his.

"You saved me," I whisper. "My hero."

"No, sugar," he says, teasing his words with a Southern drawl even heavier than mine. "From what I just heard, I'm pretty sure you saved yourself."

Just like that I know what to do. Aiden makes the decision so easy.

I grab him by the front of his shirt and pull him in for a kiss.

MEREDITH

I wrap the blanket tighter around my shoulders, trying to keep myself steady on the swaying dock as the adrenaline rush fades. My side still aches where Harrison shoved his gun into my ribs, and my foot throbs from stomping on his wrist. I haven't gone at a guy that hard since I worked at Pinky's. Back then, I was just trying to get away from handsy customers.

This time? I kind of enjoyed it. There was a moment when I forgot my life was in danger and found myself reveling in making Providence's most privileged son bleed all over the deck of his favorite overpriced toy.

I'll be paying for it for days. My whole body feels like one big bruise. Camille got the worst of it, with that gunshot grazing her shoulder, but she doesn't seem to be in much of a hurry to seek medical attention. The Providence PD is on the scene now too, and a clear-eyed Justine's giving Detectives Crary and Reynolds her opening arguments on what a piece of shit Harrison Davenforth

Bradley really is—backing up everything Destiny told them a couple of hours ago, when she apparently turned herself in and recanted her prior statement about my involvement.

Krystle stands at Justine's side, silent for once, with a supportive arm around her shoulder. Aiden keeps tugging the blanket tighter around Camille, and the only time they've stopped staring into each other's eyes is to smooch some more. I never thought I'd see the day: Camille Tavani, head over heels for a truly decent man.

Watching them makes me feel a little lonely. But if I've learned anything in the past few days, it's that I'm far from alone. I've got my community at the club, and I've got my fellow widows—though I'd love it if we could find some way to bond that doesn't involve any dramatic vehicle crashes or gun-brandishing psychos.

"Let go of me! This is outrageous."

Speak of the devil. Another speedboat pulls up to the dock, and Harrison stumbles off—handcuffed between two coast guard officers. They must have caught up to his getaway dinghy. Looks like he did some resisting arrest too, 'cause he's soaking wet, his usually coiffed blond hair plastered to his skull.

Harrison tries to shake off the officers' grip. "My mother will be hearing about this, I assure you."

"Yes, we'll make sure she hears *all* about it," Justine says.

Krystle nods. "You better believe it, bub."

Harrison smirks, but in his drowned-rat state, it comes off more pathetic than smug.

"My mother—"

"Won't be able to get you out of this one, asshole." I move to stand on Justine's other side. "Even Davenforth money can't make premeditated murder charges disappear."

Or could it? I really hope we aren't about to find out.

"For the last time, I did not murder my father!" Harrison shouts.

Justine glares at him. "Save it for the trial. We've all heard enough of your BS."

A sleek town car pulls through the marina gates. Harrison's smirk spreads into a real smile, and if we weren't surrounded by cops, I'd be sorely tempted to smack him again.

"Mommy to the rescue," Camille says under her breath as she and Aiden join our circle.

Sure enough, when the car's uniformed driver opens the backseat door, Nancy Davenforth steps out. I have no idea what time it is now, but it's definitely past any normal person's bedtime. Nancy looks just as put together as the last time we saw her, though. If she was rudely awakened to deal with this crisis, she's concealing it well.

"Mother!" Harrison calls out. "Whatever you've been told, it's a lie, I'm—"

Then he falls silent. Another passenger has emerged from the town car.

Tara Jordan.

She's wearing her hot-pink blazer—the one we spotted hanging at the Davenforth house. Camille, Krystle, Justine, and I all exchange a look, and I'm sure we're all coming to the same conclusion.

That's why Nancy refused to let us in. Why she was so

dismissive about the incriminating information we brought her. Tara beat us to the punch. When we showed up at Nancy's door, Tara was already inside, cutting a deal of her own.

But why would Nancy let Tara Jordan into her home, let alone in her car? Judging by the stricken expression on Harrison's face, he's got no clue either.

Justine jabs a finger in Tara's direction. "Ms. Davenforth, you can't trust that woman. She and your son have been plotting together this whole time."

"They're both behind the mayor's death," Camille says.

"And they conspired to make me and Camille take the fall for it," I add with a shiver.

Krystle nods, her wild, frizzy curls bouncing. "*And* Tara and Harrison have been boinking like bunnies. That baby's not Mayor Tom's, it's—"

"That's quite enough." Nancy stops and sweeps a mournful look over everyone on the dock. The police detectives step forward as if she might cry. "This whole terrible situation has gone far enough."

Cue the waterworks and denial that her precious son had anything to do with almost killing us, let alone this *Days of Our Lives* drama. It'll be our word against the Davenforths' checkbook.

What I don't get is why Tara's just standing there letting Nancy speak for her. Not even one power play or cutting remark? That's not the Tara Jordan I know.

"Mother," Harrison says. "I can explain everything."

"Of course you can." Nancy's voice is full of emotion as she steps closer to him and pats his cheek. "But there's no need, darling."

Harrison's shoulders sag with relief. "Thank you. I knew you would—"

"I'm standing on the dock, my boy, just as our forebearers did." She gazes out toward the dark ocean lit by the flash of police lights. Harrison suddenly looks terrified at her words, though I have no idea what she's talking about. "I'm seeing the future of the Davenforth family, and I'm afraid you aren't in it after all." Her voice cracks and Tara puts a hand on her shoulder. "It breaks my heart, but you are a recreant and a disgrace to the family name."

Harrison's mouth drops open in shock. "But—but Mother—"

She steps closer to the police. "While I unfortunately cannot take away the Davenforth name, I feel it is my duty to take all the resources and privileges that accompany it."

"No." Harrison struggles against his restraints. "You can't. You wouldn't. I'm your son. I'm your heir. You can't—"

"I must, my son. I must do the hard thing because it's the right thing." Nancy waves to the detectives and turns to collapse onto Tara's shoulder. "We are done with him."

Crary and Reynolds move in to take over from the coast guard officers. "Harrison Davenforth Bradley, you have the right to remain silent," Reynolds says. "Anything you say can and will be used against you in—"

"You can't do this! I didn't kill anyone!" Harrison wrenches toward Tara. "Tell them we didn't mean for it to happen. We didn't want anyone to die."

Tara lets go of Nancy and leans toward Harrison. For a second I think she's going to give her lover-slash-stepson a goodbye kiss.

Instead she says, in a chilling whisper, "You really thought I kept this baby because I wanted it? This baby is a means to an end, Harrison, just like you were."

Harrison yanks on the cuffs like a dog at the end of a leash. "Tara, honey, you can't—"

Tara throws her hands into the air. "You were an even worse investment than your father. Now take your punishment like a man for once."

"You *bitch*!" Harrison yells. So much for the terms of endearment. "You can't do this to me. After everything I've—"

Harrison's cries are interrupted as the detectives shove him toward an idling cruiser. "That's enough from you," Reynolds says.

"Wait!" Harrison shouts as he's being forced into the back of the car. "I wouldn't even know where to get drugs like that! I may have made some mistakes, but I'd never do that to my father. Whatever she's offering you, Tara, it's—"

Reynolds slams the door shut. "Ms. Jordan, we'll want to speak with you in more detail, of course."

"Of course, Detective, I'll do anything to see justice done for my husband."

Our gazes are drawn to where Harrison's handsome face screws up into a sob behind the tinted glass. As satisfying as it is to watch him blubber like a baby, I don't think all that panic is about finally having to face a consequence. In his own twisted way, he loves

Tara—and he's dumb enough to think she loved him back. That she actually wanted to have a baby with him.

As Nancy confers with the detectives, I march toward Tara. I don't even have to turn around to know that Camille, Krystle, and Justine are following me. They've got my back.

When she sees us coming, Tara eases against the town car, her hand hovering protectively over her stomach.

"So, what did Nancy offer you?" I demand.

Krystle shoots a pointed look at Tara's belly. "College fund for her future grandkid?"

"Nah, had to be something sweeter than that," Camille says. "We know you only give a damn about yourself."

Tara smiles and stands up straighter, recovering some of her Wall Street swagger. "Come on, ladies. It's just business. Surely you can understand looking out for your own interests."

"You already knew who your husband was in business with," Camille says. "You were involved in the casino deal from the start. Why hire me to find out information you already had?"

"Because I didn't know everything. And neither do you. Not yet."

Camille puts her hands on her hips. "We know you wanted the mayor dead because he screwed you over on the casino deal. Is that why you screwed your stepson too?"

"Tom did betray me, and I'll admit, I was angry enough to kill him. But I didn't do it."

"Then Harrison—"

"Neither did Harrison. He's gullible, but he's not a killer."

I stare at her. "He literally just tried to kill all four of us."

Tara picks a piece of lint off her lapel. "And he failed, miserably. It's always the handsome ones who are the most disappointing. Wouldn't you agree, Ms. Kelly?"

For a second I think Justine might take a swing—and not one of us would hold her back.

Instead Justine shakes her head with a sad, weary expression. "You're going to be a terrible mother, Tara."

Tara smiles, but this time there's a hint of sorrow in her eyes. "I know."

Sleeping with Harrison was a bad investment, but the baby is leverage Tara can use. Leave it to the She-Wolf of Wall Street to find the upside no matter what.

"I'm flying back to New York in the morning. There's nothing here for me now." Tara takes a crisp business card from her pocket and holds it out to me. "If you ever get tired of hustling for singles in this sorry excuse for a city, call me. Wall Street could use more ruthless women like you, Meredith Everett."

Everyone's just a pawn to Tara Jordan, from Providence's power players to her unborn child. We're all pieces to be moved around the board and toppled when we're no longer useful, as she goes for checkmate every time.

"Thanks for the offer." I step back. Camille's hand slips into one of mine. Justine takes hold of the other, and I feel the reassuring weight of Krystle's touch between my shoulder blades. "Providence is my home. I've learned everything I can from you."

I've learned ambition is bullshit unless you use it to lift up the people around you. I've learned that you don't have to screw people over to get what you want. I may never be as rich as Tara Jordan, but I've already got something she'll never have: a whole pack of badass women ready to fight alongside me for what we believe in.

Destiny should be part of that pack. I was her boss, but I was her friend too. Despite what she did, I hope we can find our way back to be friends again someday. She's in serious trouble, that's for sure—but nothing a good lawyer can't get her out of. Her cooperation with the cops has to count for something; Rom can help her cut a plea deal in exchange for flipping on her ex. The next time she starts mooning over a guy, though, I'm going full alpha wolf until I'm sure he's not a dirtbag like Harrison Davenforth Bradley.

"Suit yourself," Tara says, sliding the card back into her pocket. She steps closer, lowering her voice so only I can hear. "One more word of advice, if I may? Make sure you ask for exactly what you want. You just might get it."

With that, she climbs back into the car and shuts the door. Aiden, who's been keeping an eye on our confrontation from a distance, sidles over and puts his arm around Camille—careful to avoid her injured shoulder.

"We need to get you to a doctor," he says. "All four of you."

"I agree."

We all spin around at the sound of Nancy Davenforth's voice. She's standing right behind us, hands folded demurely in front of her. The detectives are over by their unmarked Oldsmobile, heads bowed close together as they exchange notes after their conversation with Nancy.

"This has been the worst night of my life, but it's not over, I'm afraid. I'd like to have a word with you ladies." Nancy gives Aiden a *run along* half smile that I'm guessing is familiar to him from his childhood. "Alone, please."

Aiden glances at Camille, who nods. "We'll meet you at your car, sugar."

He leaves, heading toward the parking lot. Time to get down to business.

"I had my doubts," Nancy begins. "But you've really impressed me. I know I can count on your discretion—as the Davenforth family's primary legal representatives."

"You have got to be shitting me," Krystle says.

"I assure you I am not, Mrs. Romero. I'm ready to draw up a long-term contract with your firm at your earliest convenience."

"Let me guess," Justine says. "That contract comes with a novel-length NDA."

Nancy's smile doesn't waver. "We can discuss the details later. Now, it's about time we all get some rest. It's been a long—"

"We should discuss the details now," I say.

Ask for exactly what you want. Well, why the hell shouldn't we? This broad owes us.

"First things first: you call your buddy the police commissioner and make sure any charges against Camille and me go away for good."

"Of course," Nancy says.

"Destiny too. She doesn't deserve jail time."

"Destiny? Is that the—"

"The twenty-year-old girl your son seduced into doing his bidding? Yes."

"Of course," Nancy says. "Is that all?"

"Meredith's club stays open," Camille adds. "It stays right where it is too."

"I'll speak to the architects first thing."

Krystle jumps in. "You kick Tucker Armand to the curb where he belongs."

"Consider it done."

I keep going. "And double—no, triple the retainer you've been paying us."

Nancy shifts as if the conversation is done. "That won't be a problem."

We look to Justine, expecting her to contribute her own demands to the growing list. But she stays silent.

"We'll talk more soon." Nancy reaches for the car door, and in a flash her driver is there, opening it for her. "Thank you, ladies. I look forward to working with you for many years to come."

Just before the door shuts, I catch a glimpse of Tara in the backseat. She's staring straight ahead, and I swear there's a tear or two glinting in her eyes.

The town car drives off. We stand on the dock for a few moments, and there's no sound except the lapping waves.

Justine finally breaks the silence. "Well. That was way too easy."

"No shit. She was acting almost…nice," Krystle says with a shudder.

I nod. "She's trying to buy us off."

"This can't just be about keeping Harrison's involvement quiet," Camille says. "That'll be all over the papers no matter what we do."

"You're right," Krystle says. "Why are Nancy and Tara so chummy all of a sudden? Did I hallucinate for a second, or was Nancy actually *defending* her?"

I tap my chin, thinking. "We know Tara will sell out anyone if it benefits her bottom line. But it's about more than money for Nancy; she cares about her reputation. Her family name and legacy."

"She's gotta be hiding something else," Camille says. "Something worse."

"If there's one thing the Davenforths are good at, it's keeping secrets," Justine adds.

I frown. "So what's worse than your only son and heir murdering his own father and knocking up his stepmother?"

"I don't know. But I know who might." Despite her exhaustion and her bloody shoulder, Camille breaks into a mischievous, sparkly eyed smile. "Aiden's right: we need to see a doctor."

KRYSTLE

"He'll be here any minute." Camille sets the phone by her hospital bed back in the cradle with a thump. She winces in pain, though she tries to hide it. Needless to say, she refused any pain pills. "You gals ready?"

I close the curtain down the middle of the room. While Camille was being stitched up, we'd put a plan together to find out the truth, but still—we don't know how this conversation will go.

The important thing is that we're facing it together, all four of us. In a lot of ways, I'd steered this ship in the wrong direction from the very beginning. Demanding we be split between Team Nancy and Team Tara to keep the almighty dollars flowing.

"I know they're pinning the murder on Harrison, but my bet is still on Tara pulling the strings," I say, thinking of how she looked climbing into Nancy's fancy car after handing over Harrison. As if she had the world by the short and curlies. "If she'd sleep with the son, why not manipulate him to kill the father?"

"Would Nancy really let Tara off the hook so easily then?" Camille asks. "Tara said Dr. Hendricks was a drug dealer with a medical license. She would have had to call him up and ask him to deliver a lethal dose of those baby-blue pills."

"Harrison alone makes the most sense to me," Meredith says, still jumping to defend Tara from a chair in the corner of Camille's sparse but clean room at Newport Hospital, where we've been since the ambulance dropped us off after we were nearly a yacht-kabob.

Justine has been quiet in the corner, as you'd expect after nearly dying twice. She finally pipes up. "Harrison's a liar, so who knows if anything he says can be trusted. At the party, he really seemed to believe that Tara poisoned his father. I have to wonder, if he had access to those lethal pills, why wouldn't he have dosed me with them and dumped my body overboard? He could have gotten rid of me before any of you showed up."

"The doctor is key," I say. "Tara made him an offer he couldn't refuse after the mayor jumped ship to Captain Nancy."

Camille doesn't look convinced. "Putting those pills in a champagne bottle that could be traced back to her company still seems like such an amateur mistake. Tara is smarter than that."

Justine shrugs. "Maybe she assumed we'd be too stupid to notice."

Meredith starts to say something else, but a knock at the door interrupts. "Dr. Hendricks is here to see you," says the sweet-as-pie nurse who's been with us most of the night.

"You better get behind the curtain," I say to Justine. "It's showtime."

Meredith remains in her place in the corner as I hurry toward the door. I snap toward Camille. "You don't look ready!"

Camille rolls her eyes and then splashes a few drops of water on her face as she adjusts her position in the hospital bed. "Sugar, I was born ready."

"You look like someone spit on you." I charge toward Camille and grab her cheeks. "You need them to be red. You need to be out of your mind in pain."

"Ow!" she screeches and smacks me away. "I know what I'm doing. Waterworks is certainly in my repertoire."

She dabs the water along her cheeks and flops onto the bed. She begins moaning and what I assume Southerners call "hollering."

"Let him in!" I say to the nurse.

Dr. Hendricks hurries into the room in a shiny suit instead of a doctor's coat. As if that doesn't hit the ol' nail right between the eyes. His jaw drops at the scene. "What's going on in here?"

"She's not doing very well," I say, grabbing his arm and pulling him toward Camille. "The pain is terrible."

Dr. Hendricks's frown lines draw upward. "My service said there was an emergency regarding Nancy Davenforth. You are certainly not her."

Camille lets out a sharp cry and then begins to sob in a truly grating way. I'm about to confess to get her to shut up. "Please, you gotta help her. Nancy gave us your information, and she said you're the person to call."

His mouth drops into a scowl. "Talk to the nurse. I don't have time to help you people." He starts toward the door.

I glance at Meredith with a bit of panic. "You didn't mind *helping* Harrison earlier," she says smoothly as she stands.

His nostrils flare. "What did you say?"

"We saw you at the dock." Meredith stalks toward him.

"I…I don't know what you're talking about." He pulls his medicine bag tight against his body, a perfect tell.

Camille begins to moan again. "Please, doctor, I need something for the pain."

He's shaking his head as he takes a step back. "You think I'd help anyone accusing me of impropriety? I wasn't with Harrison last night."

"You sure about that?" Justine steps out from behind the curtain, leaving it closed as she gives Dr. Hendricks a little wave. "Remember me?"

The doctor visibly pales, which is saying something. "How are you feeling, Ms. Kelly?"

"Much better now that I'm not drugged unconscious." She takes a step toward him, and he takes a step back, inching closer to Meredith and me. "Now what were you saying about not being on the boat?"

"I don't… I'm not… This is a mistake. I have to leave." He makes a break for the door, but Justine is right there.

"After all you did to me, doctor, you could at least help my friend."

Camille moans again. "Please, Doc, what do you have?"

His gaze darts back to Camille and then to Justine as if she's a ghost. "I may… I mean…I brought something for Nancy."

He fumbles as he unzips his medicine bag, digging around, but it sounds empty. Until there's a rattle. "I only brought... That is, this is all I have." He pulls out a bottle with no label and opens it quickly. "Take two with water."

I snatch the pills from his hand and glance down to see the baby-blue color. "Thanks, Doc."

Dr. Hendricks shoves the bottle back into his case. "Now do not contact me again unless you—Hey!" he yells as I disappear behind the curtain. "Those are for the patient."

I stick my head out. "No, they're for the detective."

Justine strides over to the curtain she exited through and slides it open to reveal Detective Reynolds holding an evidence bag with the pills. "Is it a match?" she asks.

"Visually it is. Confirmed the same blue color and number 13 printed on the outside," the detective says.

"Wait...no, you have it all wrong." Dr. Hendricks starts to approach the detective, then she puts her hand on her holster.

"I've got the lab standing by." Reynolds heads toward the door and pauses before striding out. "Don't go anywhere."

I put myself between him and whatever getaway he's planning. "While she's running the test, how about a little story, Doc?"

"Starting with the person you say you didn't see," says Justine. "Who's in police custody surely telling stories of his own."

He crosses his arms and lifts his chin as if trying to regain his status as Doc in the room. "Harrison isn't talking to police. Nancy would never—"

"She served him up on a silver platter, sugar," Camille quips.

"I'd definitely turn in my drug-dealing doctor to knock a few years off," Meredith says. "Especially if he's the reason I'm behind bars."

Dr. Hendricks begins to blink and blink fast. "No. No, no, that can't be right."

"It can." Meredith remains relaxed as if we're gabbing over mimosas. "Destiny, my employee who delivered that *doctored* bottle of champagne—she signed a statement identifying you as the medicine man with the pills that killed the mayor. Picked you out of the society pages. Sure, Harrison told her to do it—and he's on his way to jail—but the murder could never have happened without you."

"I get confused." Camille scoots to the edge of the bed. "Hippocratic oath or Hypocrite oath? Either way, you're in a buttload of trouble, Doc."

The nurse knocks on the door again. "Another visitor."

"What is this circus?" Dr. Hendricks scoots closer to the wall, near the toilet.

Rom enters with a tray of coffees. "Your caffeine has arrived. They don't have Dunkin', so, sorry in advance."

I take mine from him with a smile. "Dr. Hendricks, this is my son and the lawyer representing Meredith, Rom Romero."

Rom tips his head toward the doctor as he hands Meredith her coffee. "Sorry, I didn't get you one, Doc. Wasn't sure if you take sugar or sedatives in it."

That gets a rare grin from Meredith. "Both, I'd imagine."

"I do not take any drugs. I only—"

"Sell them?" Justine says. "How often were you supplying drugs to Harrison?"

That snaps the doctor's jaw closed quickly.

"We need a name," Justine snaps. "You have to say who ordered you to give the pills to Destiny."

The doctor turns away, and his silence won't work for what we're after.

Rom passes a coffee to Justine. With a shake of his head, he says, "I did want to share that I got the call from the AG. All charges have been dropped against Meredith now that Harrison is in custody." He grins at her as he steps toward the door. "I'll check back to see if anyone needs a refill after I see where the police are on the warrants for the doctor's office and home."

I wink at my son and then shift back to see the doctor suddenly looking seasick. "You know, Doc, when I was chatting with the police commissioner this morning, he mentioned how tired he is of these drug parties and OD cases. He's hoping to set an example of how under his leadership, he's getting to the source of the problem: the doctors themselves."

"A poster child." Camille holds her hands up and makes a square framing the doctor's face. "Picture perfect. Papers, nightly news, everyone will know the police take a hard line on doctors overprescribing, especially when it leads to murder."

Dr. Hendricks sputters, "I-I-I might prescribe something, but I don't control how they use it."

"Did you say prescribe?" Justine says. "Nancy had major back surgery a decade ago. She damaged her spine after having Harrison."

Meredith lifts a hand. "Wait, didn't the cops say the pills were taken off the market?"

Camille crosses her arms. "That's what you were going to give me for my pain? Some old pill stash?"

Justine sucks in a breath. "Wait, not just anyone's stash."

The three of them exchange a look, and I feel like I'm missing the boat here.

Sweat beads on the good doctor's forehead. Someone's getting feverish, which means we're getting warmer. "You need a chair. Head between your legs, right, Doc?"

Meredith shoves the wooden chair near where the doctor is wheezing. "I had no idea that little shit planned to poison his father." Dr. Hendricks's eyes go wide as if he hadn't meant to say that.

There's a flutter in my chest because we're close to breaking him. I want to jump in with accusations about Tara, because it feels like she's been setting us up the whole time. But Camille's advice earlier was right. Just because I'm mad, doesn't mean I have to do the first thing that pops into my head to let off some steam. Guess I'm maturing, or whatever.

Camille lifts her bedsheet slightly. "Are you going to take the fall for the woman who tricked you into being an accomplice to murder?"

His chin quivers, and he drops his head into his hands. "You don't know what it's like. You can't imagine how...scared I feel whenever she calls. I knew I shouldn't do it...the pills with *that* bottle of champagne."

"We can help you, if you cooperate," Camille says softly. "Just tell the truth, and our law firm will make clear to the attorney general that you're not a murderer."

Dr. Hendricks laughs, a panicked noise from deep in his throat. "What, like *any* of *you* have any power over *her*? She'll squash you like a bug if you're lucky. She may just run a pin through your guts to watch you squirm."

"If you didn't mean to give Destiny the lethal dose, then you shouldn't be prosecuted for the crime," Camille says.

"Just ask Harrison," Justine says. "You don't want to spend the rest of your life in prison because you were tricked."

His face is twisted, and there's a bitterness in his eyes. "I was tricked. That's exactly what it was. All *she* said when she gave me that champagne bottle was to provide a full bottle of her pills with a solution to dissolve it. When you're the help, you don't ask questions."

"Say the name," Justine demands.

Dr. Hendricks sneers at us. "You know who I mean."

Justine steps toward him. "And you can live with yourself? After all you've done? All you'll keep doing for people with enough money? Say her name, Dr. Hendricks."

His shoulders slump, and it's as if we've worn him down. Or maybe he's just tired of holding in all the lies. "I'll tell you the truth, but it won't matter. People like her always win."

"Not this time," Camille says.

Dr. Hendricks lets out a long sigh that shakes his whole face. "Harrison did ask for his regular sedatives to be given to Destiny. But at the last minute, *she* called and switched it to her reserve pills. The baby blues."

Sweat drips into the doctor's frightened eyes. "I didn't even know the drugs were for the mayor. All I knew was that Harrison was partying and wanted his prescription delivered. Then she called and said she wanted her usual sent. I figured she was trying to teach him a lesson, maybe get him a little sick—a little spooked—and encourage him to lay off the drugs. Tough love. I had no idea *all* the pills would be crushed up and put in the champagne."

I scratch my head. "Wait, why would Tara Jordan have a reserve stash of horse-tranquilizer-level pills?"

"He's not talking about Tara. Are ya, Doc?" Camille shifts forward.

He rubs his forehead like he's got the headache of the century. "I'd give anything for it to be Tara. God, imagine my life if she was the one calling me at all hours for baby blues, the only back-pain medicine that works for her. I never wanted to be the Dr. Feelgood of Newport, you know. She made me into this joke. It's cost me everything."

"Who?" I say, unable to believe what I know he's about to tell us. "Who told you to give Destiny the baby blues?"

His head hangs low. "The only person who knew I had them. The only person I'd do anything for, no questions asked, even something as stupid and dangerous as handing over pills with no instruction. Nancy Davenforth."

My gaze ping-pongs as I finally arrive at the spot all three ladies already landed. *Well, when you're wrong, you're wrong.* Guess the Davenforths really are rotten to the core.

"We will protect you," Justine says.

He laughs. "You think I'd ever say any of this in court?"

Camille peels back the medical blanket covering her legs, revealing her trusty tape recorder lying right beside her on the mattress. "You won't have to."

The doctor stammers. "You can't tape me. I don't consent."

Justine shakes her head. "TV shows have so many people thinking that. You only need one party to consent to taping a conversation in Rhode Island."

"I consent," Meredith chirps.

"I sure as hell do too," I say.

Justine looks to Camille. "It'll help. But with Nancy's money, it won't be enough. If she gets it thrown out…"

"Why stop recording here?" I wink at her and say, "Let's take this party to Newport."

JUSTINE

The gate to the Davenforth estate is locked, but not for the owners of Romero, Tavani, Kelly, and Romero. Krystle leans out her driver's side window and announces herself into the intercom like a landlord serving eviction papers. "It's Mrs. Krystle Romero and her partners. Open up."

Iron bars retract without a word of objection. This time, we're all on the list.

Not that we expect to remain on it with what we've got planned. And not that Nancy's favor will matter after she's outed as a homicidal maniac and "Mommie Dearest." High-society friends are a fickle crowd. Always worried about the company they keep and what that *says* about them.

As we approach the Davenforths' mansion, I again regret how easily I was taken in by appearances. Sure, the estate is impressive, a castle fit for a European dynasty or the American equivalent—the lineage of capitalist robber barons. And, yes, Nancy's model city possessed a certain appeal with its pristine marble buildings and manicured parks. But her vision was never more than a homage to another culture. It would have whitewashed our colorful city, bulldozing downtown's red-brick factories and plastering over College Hill's gray, mustard, and green clapboard exteriors with French stucco begging to be graffitied over.

In fairness, the "Paris of the Northeast" would have attracted new business investment and jobs. But those companies would have come from elsewhere, lacking respect for Providence's history. Over time, they would have changed places like Krystle's beloved Federal Hill, stripping its cultural character save for novelty streets dubbed "little Italy" on tourist maps. Scrappy entrepreneurs like Meredith would be forced out in favor of corporate, Disneyfied forms of entertainment. Worst of all, the last vestiges of Native Americans' presence in the city center would have been destroyed for a convention hall.

Providence itself would have been erased.

And I would have helped. I'd been so focused on aligning myself with the city's wealthy—so certain families like the Davenforths would secure my future career and the continuation of our law firm—that I never really weighed whether the rich side was the right one. Hitting my head might have been the wake-up smack from the universe that I'd desperately needed.

The mansion's lights reflect off the shined hoods of town cars. Krystle parks her sedan right in front of them, blocking the steps to the Davenforths' entrance. As soon as she kills the engine, the vehicle's back doors swing open, pushed by an all-too-eager Meredith and Camille.

Krystle, however, doesn't jump out. Instead, she looks at me. "You got this."

It's not a question so much as a statement. I feel my spine stiffen. Nancy might literally have a steel backbone, but I have conviction, my friends' support, and Camille's recorder taped to the inside of my leg. I won't buckle.

I open the door. "*We* got this."

Camille and Meredith hover at the base of the steps, waiting for us to make our grand entrance. As I step in line with them, Camille points to the cars. "Looks like Nancy's having another party."

Meredith smirks. "Let's crash."

Krystle laughs. "No need, girls. We are the party."

Together, we march up the steps, a bandaged battalion storming the castle. Aiden's oversized jacket hangs off Camille's gauze-wrapped shoulder. Band-Aids cover scratches on Meredith's bruised fists. My curls hide the lump on the back of my head, but my clothing looks like it's been through the ringer.

Rather than return home after the hospital and worry JJ, I'd borrowed a pantsuit from Krystle's nearby house. The jacket's too big and the pants are too short, not to mention barely clinging to my hips thanks to a cinched belt. But how I look around the Davenforths doesn't matter to me anymore. Plus, the extra bulk hides the device. My outfit seems to matter to the Davenforths' butler, however. He cracks the door and eyes me as if I'm a beggar washed up on his doorstep. "Nancy is in a meeting. You're invited to wait in the foyer until she's finished."

Krystle opens her mouth to say something but stops as I touch her forearm. I zero in on the butler and offer a fake smile worthy of the estate's matriarch. "Of course. That's fine."

He steps back, opening the door wider. I barrel past him in Krystle's too-small sneakers, leading the way to the office where I'm sure Nancy holds court. Before I get more than a few steps inside the house, however, several large men suddenly appear from a hallway. "Security check."

I barely have time to blink—let alone object—before one of the guards is pushing my arms up into a T to search for…weapons? As he works, I catch the police badge in his interior jacket pocket.

"Who are you here to protect?"

If the guy plans to answer, Camille's yelp makes him reconsider. I glance over my shoulder to see her fist wrapped around a guy's hand. "The last guy who checked too thoroughly in my cleavage ended up with my handprint on his cheek."

Camille's guard chuckles as if her warning was meant to amuse him. I notice my man also snickers as he moves from my sides to my legs. His hands start at my knees and run up to my panty line. Once. Twice. The thoroughness betrays that he's not searching for a gun. Thanks to the papers, these guys all know how Camille typically arms herself.

As the guard continues to pat me down, he glances at his buddy. "Double-check that one. You never know what some people can hide in their bra."

Krystle slaps her guy's hand. "Copping a feel comes with a cost. I recently learned what a gander at my girls is worth."

The guy continues without reaching for his wallet as Krystle protests. I know she's trying to distract him from my device, but I already know it won't work. My guard's fingers tap an SOS up higher until…

"Found it."

I wince as the man yanks on the device, causing the tape to rip from my leg. The recorder clatters to the floor, its mini tape deck popping open to spill its contents. I see the man bend to pick it up.

"That's mine. I'll take it," Camille says, affecting some of the Davenforth attitude.

The butler steps forward. "We'll happily return your property after you've spoken with the mistress."

I glare at him. "Her name is Nancy. Being born wealthy shouldn't bestow a title. Especially one as fraught as that. What's your name?"

I see something in the guy's eyes that he quickly blinks away. Agreement? Shame?

Meredith must see it too because she takes a step toward the man. "You need a better boss. Someone who cares about you, takes the time to understand where you're coming from."

Camille chimes in. "And isn't about to be charged with a capital crime."

The butler looks away from my partners and at the floor. "Stevens."

"She's not worth it, Stevens."

There's no time to belabor the point as Krystle is halfway toward Nancy's office, determined to have this confrontation whether we can get it on tape or not. Though I can't imagine how our plan will work without getting Nancy on the record. Even if Krystle, Camille, Meredith, and I testify to hearing the same confession, we'll be branded friends willing to lie for one another. Our collective statements won't combat Nancy's cheery denials coupled with a bit of charity. And Nancy certainly knows it.

As I hustle to catch up to Krystle, I hear Stevens shout behind me, "If you need any tea, simply press the intercom."

I keep walking, feeling sad that he's so clearly chosen his side. This man will serve Nancy to the end. Krystle reaches the office's double doors first. They're stained a dark chestnut, which might explain why I never noticed the carvings in the wood until Krystle shouts, "*Oh la la,*" in the most exaggerated French accent her Italian New England tongue can manage. Each door has a large *D* exploding in vines ending in fleur-de-lis symbols. Nancy's Francophilia is truly pathological.

Brass handles lie below each ornate letter. Krystle takes one as I grab the other while Camille and Meredith stand aside. Both of us must put our backs into yanking the doors, because they simultaneously strike the walls. We enter with an actual bang.

Nancy looks up from behind a long oak desk. The men seated in front of her lean over the sides of smoking chairs to see the source of her surprised expression. I spy the senator, as well as Judge Gatta, and a bald shar-pei of a man whom I recognize from press coverage of a recent murder case—Clarence Bailey, celebrity defense attorney extraordinaire.

The fourth guy is Police Commissioner Mann. Krystle zeros

in on him. "Police Commissioner Mann. Shouldn't you be holding a press conference about tracking down the mayor's murderer?"

Nancy's lips thin into a tight smile. "Mrs. Romero, we were discussing the unfortunate recent events. I'm sure you're curious as to how this may impact the development plans going forward, which your firm is, of course, overseeing. There's no reason for concern. As I explained to our esteemed senator minutes ago, it's my project, not Harrison's. His arrest shouldn't derail the progress we're making. Isn't that right, Justine?"

I detect a warning in her tone, despite the meticulously maintained smile. The same notes creep into my voice when I'm telling my son to behave in public.

My instinct to be polite almost takes over. I force my head not to bob in faux agreement as I struggle to formulate a response. My accusation is a big one, and I'll be making it in front of people who could have me blacklisted as a lawyer before I even pass the bar.

Krystle clears her throat, an audible nudge for me to speak. She's doing an admirable job holding her tongue, allowing me to take the lead. I take both Krystle's cue and a page out of her book. Sometimes you gotta speak your mind without overthinking.

"That's not right at all, Nancy. You killed the mayor and are letting your son take the fall."

Nancy's chin retreats to her bony neck. "I beg your pardon?"

"Pardons don't exist for state murder charges, which is what you'll be facing given the testimony collected from Dr. Hendricks as part of our investigation to clear our client, Meredith Everett. As you tried to set her up for the mayor's murder, we can no longer represent your business affairs or provide any defense in the upcoming criminal case."

Nancy's gaze darts to the police commissioner. "Can you believe this ridiculous slander?"

The commissioner scratches at white stubble. "I don't know anything about new testimony. But I'll call the office."

Krystle cocks her head at the guy and bestows an almost flirtatious smirk. "You should do that, Buddy. Ask for Detective Reynolds, who's surely taking the not-so-good doctor's confession as we speak. They also have a new statement from Destiny, the woman who spiked the champagne with Hendricks's drugs."

Nancy's smile finally vanishes. "These wild accusations have… Well, they've no doubt been brought about by the drugs that *you* all indulged in before crashing my son's boat." She turns to the senator. "I see now that it's exactly as my son said. They were partying and things got out of hand… Harrison has always had a bit of a problem so, naturally, I assumed…" Her hand flies theatrically to her heart as she continues her panicked rambling. "These new pills are destroying the youth, truly. Harrison and now—"

"You mean the old drugs."

I turn to see Meredith framed in the door with her hands on her hips, looking every bit the boss she's become. "The cops showed me the pills that they supposedly removed from my desk. They're baby blues. Not manufactured anymore because of the dire consequences of overdose. I couldn't get them. But you…"

Nancy rounds her desk. "I haven't the slightest idea what you're talking about."

Camille enters, backing up Meredith in case Nancy breaches the front line held by Krystle and me. She tosses her blond hair and gestures to the upholstered furniture. "It's clear, Nancy, that you love your antiques. But expired pharmaceuticals." Camille tsks. "Didn't you realize they'd be more traceable than street drugs?"

Nancy addresses her guests. "I apologize for this nonsense you're being subjected to in my home. As I said, these women *were* working with me, though I clearly won't be retaining their services in the future."

Krystle stands an inch taller. "You can't fire us. Didn't you hear Ms. Kelly tell you we quit? I'm pretty sure I could paper these walls with all the invoices for billable hours you never paid."

Nancy points at me. "Justine Kelly wasn't so much working as seducing my son. You might have seen their pictures together in the paper." Her finger wags in my direction. "You were a terrible influence."

I force myself not to react to her accusations or the unfortunate tabloid picture. Defensiveness only makes you look guilty. I learned that in law school. Nancy misinterprets my silence as a win. Her voice strengthens as she continues: "Justine has been influenced by whatever inebriated party talk she and my son engaged in before sinking a million-dollar vessel in the harbor, and she's shared this blather with her cohorts. If you'd excuse me a moment, I'll see them out."

Nancy marches past us, stopping behind Meredith. She stands in the doorjamb with her palm extended, an imitation of how Stevens must evict guests who've overstayed their welcome. I take a moment to make eye contact with the police commissioner and the senator, ensuring they register the clearness of my gaze before exiting. As nice as it would be to have the coming conversation before witnesses, Nancy won't say anything worth hearing in front of this group. Thanks to the guard's seizing of Camille's recorder, she won't say anything admissible either, which means we're at a stalemate. New widows 2. Old widows 2. We might have gotten Harrison behind bars for trying to kill us, but both Nancy and Tara will get off scot-free. And, hopefully, so will Meredith and Camille.

Destiny recanting her earlier statement coupled with Dr. Hendricks's admission should be enough to clear them. But none of those conversations will stand up to the Davenforth money if Nancy's the defendant. For Nancy to pay we need irrefutable proof that she got wind of Harrison's plans and opted to poison her ex-husband. Otherwise she could claim Dr. Hendricks is lying due to some grudge. An unpaid bill, perhaps? Krystle's not kidding about Nancy's past-due invoices. She hasn't shelled out for the three weeks of nonstop work I did on her behalf.

I stand in the center of the grand sitting room with no intention of getting comfortable. Krystle, Meredith, and Camille join me as Nancy shuts the door behind her. As soon as it closes, Nancy's face morphs from the picture of shock and disdain to something more fearsome. The glint in her eye reminds me of the look a mobster hitman once gave me.

Her glare is directed at me as she steps away from her shuttered office. "You know, Justine. I'm quite disappointed. I thought you were intelligent enough to join the winning team. But instead"—she glances at one of her security guards manning the door—"you tried to secretly tape me. Surely they teach attorney-client privilege at Harvard. You're my lawyer."

"I *was* your lawyer."

Nancy shakes her head, feigning disappointment. "We're going to reinvent Providence through eminent domain. Bring the city into the future. Make it a place worth visiting. Even worth living in."

Krystle scoffs. "Providence is my home, and it's worth a lot as it is. It's certainly more inviting than this knockoff Buckingham Palace you got going on. Providence has real character."

Nancy rolls her eyes. "Providence is a pit stop between Boston and New York."

Meredith glares at her. "Providence is far richer than you realize. It's a reflection of its people. Their grit. Determination—"

"Their vices, you mean." Nancy smirks. "Their poverty. That's why governments have always relied on families like the Rockefellers and the Carnegies to reimagine what cities can be. To build the right things that attract the right people. Justine's argument about the public's clear interest in taking over squandered land is the right one, and we always intended to use it. We'd simply hoped for a *friendlier* face to deliver the message. But I guess my old mug will have to do." Nancy's smirk morphs into one of her perfect smiles, radiating faux warmth and welcome. "I expect after I'm successful using eminent domain to assume control of the tribe's parcel, many others will follow my lead. We'll be able to take over all this city's wasted space."

One of Camille's arms extends toward Nancy, aiming for her jacket's lapel. Fortunately, a pat from Meredith makes Camille restrain herself.

Rather than feel Camille's anger, I'm filled with shame. "I was wrong, Nancy. The people of Providence will create the city they want by investing in their own businesses and managing their properties how they see fit. Eminent domain shouldn't be weaponized by developers."

Nancy shrugs. "Your change of heart, my dear, is irrelevant." Nancy looks directly at Krystle. "I do detest discussing money. So gauche. Though I am sorry to hear your firm won't share in the wealth, Krystle. My accountants assure me that the proceeds will be quite significant. And, though I know so little about these things, I do hire the best, so I expect they're right."

Krystle examines her nails, as if Nancy is boring her. "I expect you'll be in prison."

Camille steps forward. "We have multiple people on record detailing how your drugs got into Mayor Tom's drink."

Meredith joins her. "Money won't let you weasel out of this."

Nancy grins at Meredith, a predator baring its teeth. "You don't think it's possible that Dr. Hendricks will suddenly realize that if he ever hopes to practice medicine again, he should take responsibility for his terrible mix-up and recant whatever he's said? I mean, accidentally delivering the wrong painkillers to Harrison. Horrible mistake, but these things happen. In his defense, which I'd be happy to help him provide as a longtime friend, the poor doctor didn't know Harrison's plans to drug his dad."

Seeing Nancy's smug expression, I have a pang of sympathy for Harrison. Money can certainly smooth problems, but it can't compensate for a lack of love. "When I became a mom, I knew I'd do anything for my child. Yet you'd sacrifice your own flesh and blood."

Nancy places a hand on her breast, as if truly wounded. "I was a good mother. Harrison was my only son, so I gave him everything. Every advantage. I used all my connections and donations to land him at the best schools; to pay the tutors necessary to keep him there. When he graduated and struggled to find his way, I had the carriage house redecorated to his tastes. I employed him. All I ever asked in return was a shred of loyalty."

Nancy's hypocrisy makes me shudder. "How could he learn loyalty from a mother who would make him pay for her sins?"

Nancy glares at me. "Oh, Justine. I'd hoped that a woman like yourself might intuit my feelings, especially given *everything* you've gone through." Nancy shrugs. "But, since you're having some difficulty seeing my point of view, I suppose there's no harm in illuminating my position as my supporters are in the other room, and we're all among friends here. Right? So…just between us widows."

I step further into the room, resigned to hearing a truth that I'll never be able to bring to court.

"Madame, would you and your guests like tea?"

I turn to see Stevens holding a silver tray with Nancy's ornate teapot and cups.

If looks could fire, Nancy's would be delivering a severance check. But she quickly smiles, covering her anger. "No, Stevens. That won't be necessary. Thank you. Back to the kitchen, please."

Stevens looks down at the ground. Seeing his rounded shoulders and downcast expression reminds me of the last thing he'd said...about the intercom.

I approach the wood-paneled wall with the embedded device and lean against it, as if I'm too proud to sit but too tired to stand fully on my own two feet. To emphasize the point, I fold my arms over my chest as my back pushes every intercom button, opening all the available channels.

"Just between us widows, Nancy," I quip.

Nancy moves closer to me. "Harrison witnessed plenty of loyalty, Justine. For decades, I was devoted to my family. But did the men I love show me respect? Twenty years of marriage and my husband—a man who was nothing before I set him up in politics—steps out with a woman barely older than his son. And that son? The boy I loved and adored and *employed*. He uses his position with me to advance his father's agenda, telling me that Vegas and casinos are what Providence really needs. He even suggested we convince Aiden to build one on the tribe's land to skirt the state's antigambling regulations—though his father would never have had that. He only wanted his playboy buddies to profit. Harrison actually thought casinos could be a family affair. Imagine me, my ungrateful, philandering ex, his floozy young wife, my son, and his turncoat cousin. All in business *together*. What a disgrace."

Nancy looks to the leaded windows overlooking the ocean. The overcast sky has transformed the sea into shined cement. All the dark gray lets me see Nancy's reflection in the glass—the rage twisting her features.

I adjust my back to make sure the intercom is picking up maximum sound while all the buttons remain depressed. "Harrison favored his father, so you decided to punish him."

Nancy turns from the window. "I *babied* Harrison for years, excusing his faults as due to Tom's influence. But Harry was a Bradley through and through. *Recreants*, the entire line of them."

Camille stands taller. "I know that word."

Nancy looks her up and down like she's stupid. "Was it on your SAT prep, dear? Do escorts take that?"

Camille tosses her long blond hair. A distraction, I know, since her wide blue eyes show she's made a connection. "Tom's friend Marco told me about the hate mail he received. He mentioned a death threat calling Tom a 'recreant prick.' Sounds like something you'd say."

Nancy dismisses Camille's suggestion with a wave. "Tom was my cheating ex-husband. I called him worse over the years. Not that he cared once I dangled my backing for higher office." Nancy shifts her disapproving gaze to Meredith. "Tom always saw reason when it benefited him. He quickly turned away from supporting immoral institutions."

Now it's Camille's turn to put a steadying hand on Meredith. "Still, you threatened his life. You made good on that threat when Harrison and Tara decided to ruin his political career by using me. You had the doctor switch the intended prescription."

Nancy bites her lip, struggling not to take the bait. She wants to, though. As someone who's also been taken advantage of, I know there are few things as satisfying as finally regaining the upper hand, finally being respected for your work and intelligence. How that feeling can cloud your judgment, and in this case, I hope, keep Nancy from noticing what's behind me on the wall.

Nancy sighs. "Whatever happens to Harrison is his own fault for his poor choice of bedfellows. Surely you agree, Justine. He let that strumpet convince him to drug his dad, and then he had the audacity to discuss it with her on my house line and reach out to my doctor."

Nancy gazes at the teardrop chandelier. "When his dad died, he came running to me, you know. Crying about how Tara had lied to him. You know what I did? This terrible mother. I held him, assured him that it wasn't his fault. It was hers. She'd manipulated both him and his father." Nancy's gaze drops to her feet. "I thought I'd gotten back my boy."

It may be a trick of light—some movement of the clouds outside the window—or a glint of its reflection in the chandelier's crystals striking Nancy's face in just the right spot, but I swear I see a tear on her cheek.

"You thought killing Tom and framing Tara would break Tara's hold on him."

Nancy presses her lips together and closes her eyes. "Wouldn't you do anything to keep your son safe?"

"I understand fearing for your son." I tentatively reach for Nancy's hand, keeping my back pressed against the intercom buttons and silently praying that the system really does broadcast in her office like she'd said.

Rather than take my hand, Nancy draws her hands closer to her chest.

Krystle gives it a try, her face a mask of sympathy as she reaches out. "I have a son too. He's made some decisions in the past that hurt me, that made me wonder what kind of job I did with him. I understand how a mother would do anything to get him on the straight and narrow."

Nancy doesn't take Krystle's hand either. But a sob shakes her shoulders. "With Tom gone, I thought the competition would finally end. I wanted it to end."

Nancy's words aren't an unassailable confession, but they're close. With Destiny, Dr. Hendricks, and maybe even Harrison's testimony, it might well be enough—provided the men in Nancy's office aren't *all* in her pocket like she believes.

Nancy sniffs and looks at me, her eyes returning to sharpened steel. "Then that witch came back with her pregnant belly. She knew how much Harrison had longed for his father to be present in his life. She knew he'd want to be a father. I couldn't let her win.

"And she was carrying a second chance." A genuine smile seems to light Nancy's face. "Tara presented an interesting proposition. A way to bravely start again, as my ancestors did. Even when it's difficult.

"To be clear, I didn't say yes to that woman right away. But when I got the call from Dr. Hendricks after he left the yacht, telling me about what my son did to you, forcing me to face the kind of man he'd become, what I knew he'd be capable of doing to you... I am so sorry, Justine. Truly. I knew it was time to leave him behind."

Camille pipes up. "So you agree not to bring Tara into it if she lets you raise your grandson and she promises *not* to back up

Harrison's assertion that he asked for different pills. It all looks like Harrison did it for love. Or, maybe, like Dr. Hendricks got his wires crossed. Either way, your name is clear, *and* you get a baby out of the deal."

Nancy chuckles. "All I wanted was my son. But, if I couldn't get him back, Tara's alternative was an acceptable trade. Maybe I should have worked on Wall Street."

I press my back further into the intercom, too disgusted by her cavalier attitude toward her admittedly psychopathic progeny to stomach the proximity. She notices me recoil. "Think I'm heartless, Justine?"

"As you said before, my changing opinion doesn't matter. But I do think you're going to prison."

Nancy's eyes narrow. "You think any of what you all say would matter to a jury over my testimony? Please. You all have reasons to lie." She looks at Meredith. "Your partner is a murderer and the other one served him the drugged champagne."

"We're not killers, Nancy. My partners and I are the help," I quip. "And, as the help, we know how to use the intercom system."

As Nancy struggles to process what I've said, Krystle strides to the office doors and opens them wide. The police commissioner is first out of the room. His open mouth and furrowed brow make clear he's heard Nancy's every word. Krystle smiles at him.

"Now Ms. Newport gets to see how we do things on the Hill, right Buddy—er, Commissioner Mann?"

"Buddy is just fine." His hard gaze stays on Nancy. "I've had a call from one of my detectives who took a statement from Dr.

Hendricks about your involvement in the murder of the mayor. That, and what I just heard, means we have a lot to discuss back in Providence."

Nancy's face falls. "I was only telling a story. You can't believe—"

"I'm tired of Newport justice," he says. "Rich ladies thinking murder is a birthright. As we say on the Hill, you can put your sorries in a sack and stick it where the sun don't shine."

Nancy's knees buckle, but the steel rod in her spine keeps her back straight. Clarence Bailey runs from the room to Nancy's other side. "And she'll never see prison. I'll get her confession stricken from the record. It was made under duress. It's totally inadmissible."

"We'll see about that," Commissioner Mann says. "Better get your bail money ready."

The attorney continues in a high pitch, which tells me that he knows as well as I do that our testimony plus the words of the police commissioner will be enough for an arrest. Then it'll be the trial of the century, a three-ring circus, and even if Nancy's attorney somehow manages to get her testimony excluded, the damage will be done. The Davenforth name will become so poisonous that Nancy's development plans will be a nonstarter. How much time she or her son serves in prison isn't my problem. They're not my clients.

And, when I do pass the bar, I'll be sure to be more discerning about whom I represent. But I'm not a lawyer—not yet. Though, I am a mom. I turn to Krystle. "I've got to get back to my son."

She pats my shoulder. "I was thinking the same thing about my boys."

Meredith shoots Camille a wistful look. "Going to check on Aiden?"

Camille drapes her good arm over Meredith's shoulders. "I was thinking we might have a victory nightcap, maybe at the club?"

Krystle chuckles. "You got bolt cutters?"

Meredith bats her eyes like the thought never occurred to her. "Who, me? Why would I buy bolt cutters?"

Camille strides ahead. "Especially when I already got 'em."

CAMILLE

SIX MONTHS LATER

For a strip club on a sunny Saturday afternoon, the Luna Lounge is hopping. Music thumping in the speakers, strippers in big hair and sparkly dresses mingling with guests around the stage, and Meredith smack in the middle of everyone, managing the chaos.

"Those streamers look like they're coming a little loose," she says to Destiny, pointing to the left side of the stage, which is smothered like the rest of the place in silver and blue crepe paper. Balloons cover the stage floor like a thick mist, and it's a good thing there's no stripper working the pole because she'd break her neck.

Destiny gives Meredith a little salute. "On it, boss."

At the last word, Meredith stands a little taller on her four-inch stilettos. Ever since the police unchained the doors of this place, the Luna Lounge has been raking in the business. It helps that all of Meredith's staff, the town's best dancers and bouncers, were practically champing at the bit to work for Meredith again. Especially Destiny. Meredith hired Destiny back after Rom got her off on probation, and now all the staff treats Meredith like a queen. Even better, they treat her like a *boss*.

"And tell Lucy we're going to need another gift table," Meredith hollers as Destiny hustles off. "The one she set up is already full."

I glance at the table piled high with boxes and bags, and my chest goes warm with gratitude even though they're not for me. They're for Aiden, standing at the far end of the stage with a newborn strapped to his chest: Tara and Harrison's love child, Matthew, whom Aiden is raising as his own.

That's not to say it wasn't a shock when Harrison called up a month ago, asking Aiden to be Matty's legal guardian. I guess Harrison learned about family from Aiden and his mom out in South County those summers long ago. Aiden didn't hesitate, not even for a second. Harrison is family, and it's not like he could raise his own child from the correctional facility upstate, where he's serving twenty years for second-degree murder. By the time Harrison is a free man, his son will be big and grown.

Tara didn't want Matty, either. Not even Nancy's prison sentence cutting into their secret deal could change her mind. After Nancy's intercom confession, Tara could have taken the baby and ran. Well, after the baby was born, she ran, all right, all the way back to New York—alone. She left Matty, her brand-new baby son, to the Davenforths, the family she swore she wanted nothing to do with ever again. I'll never understand it, but Tara did say as much herself that night on the dock: she'd be a terrible mother. I suppose I give her a teeny bit of credit for knowing that much.

At least she set up a trust fund for Matty for when he turns eighteen. Her son may not ever know his birth mother's love, but he'll get some of her money—and I suppose a woman the likes of Tara sees the two things as the same. She also told Aiden she was glad Harrison chose him as Matty's guardian and that she hadn't produced another Davenforth. I guess that's as close to mothering as Tara Jordan will ever get.

But the point is, Aiden has a baby. Aiden has *a baby*, and good Lord, how a baby looks sexy on that man—words I never thought I'd say in a million years. While I'm at it, here are some more: sometime in these past few weeks, I've begun to think of both those boys as mine.

"This place looks amazing," I say, sidling up to Meredith. "Thanks again for doing all this."

"A baby shower in a strip club. Pretty sure that's a first, even if it means I was too busy to get to the bank before closing time yesterday. The safe in my office is stuffed to the gills, and I've got two more nights of business until banks open again on Monday."

"Glad to hear the mayor keelin' over in your champagne room hasn't hurt sales any."

"The Davenforths aren't exactly popular these days, but even if they were, people seemed to miss this place when we were closed. Now that the doors are open, we've more than made up for lost time." She smiles, leaning a hip against the stage. "How was the naming ceremony?"

She knows we've just come from the Narragansett gathering, and I think about how to best describe it. *Powerful, moving, humbling* are a few words that come to mind, but they don't do the ceremony any justice. We stood on sacred ground where Aiden's ancestors have been gathering in ceremony for thousands of years. I could feel his connection to the land and all those who walked it before him and the responsibility to all those who come after. I didn't understand a lick of what was said in Narragansett, but the beauty of the commitment moved me to tears.

"Amazing" is the pitifully inadequate word I land on. "The elder says Matty's Narragansett name means First Ray of Sun, because he's meant to light up the world."

"Sounds fitting," she says, tipping her head to Aiden on the opposite side of the stage, where he's laughing with some members of the tribe. Matty hangs in a sling on his chest, a tiny lump he pats with a big palm while just beyond, Krystle elbows her way through the crowd, her eyes on the baby. "He's certainly lighting up that man's world."

I think of the look on Aiden's face when the elder told him his son's Native name, and my eyes well with tears all over again. The tribe allowed me to be there, standing by Aiden's side in a ceremony normally only for family, and it felt like a commitment for me too. It stirred something in me I couldn't quite define.

A deep gratitude that I was able to be in that circle and a fierce protectiveness for the people who've been more of a family to Aiden than the Davenforths ever were.

I tell Meredith the same thing I told him afterward, in the car. "I'm warning you now, sugar. If anybody tries to touch that burial ground, or any other Narragansett land for that matter, I'll murder them myself."

"Could you at least wait until after the weekend to commit a capital offense?" Justine says from right behind me. "I won't have time to bail you out until Monday."

Ever since her brush with death, there's a lightness to her I didn't think was possible. It helps that she's in jeans and flats under a crisp white blouse, her face scrubbed clean and her hair loose and curly around her face. She's a lot more relaxed these days, her cheeks literally glowing thanks to the little guy clutching her hand.

JJ bounces on his toes. "Mom's taking me to see the tigers at the zoo!"

She ruffles his hair. "That's right, sweetness. And the elephants and the giraffes and the monkeys, and I even hear they have a bunch of big turtles. You're stuck with me all day."

All weekend too, as well as every day at dinner and bedtimes. That's when Justine closes her law books and chucks her pager into a drawer for some uninterrupted mother-son moments. She's fierce about protecting their time together, even if it means clients have to wait a little longer for an answer. Surprisingly, Rom volunteered to pick up the slack at the office.

While JJ was quick to forget all those times Justine chose work over being at home with him, her mother-in-law sure wasn't, nor was she all that fond of the idea of her grandson spending part of his Saturday afternoon at a strip club. "With all those trollops and sinners? They'll pollute that child's innocent mind."

Personally, I would have told Sharon where to stuff it ages ago, but Justine being Justine, she politely corrected her. She still defends Sharon, saying she'll always be JJ's grandmother, and she owes it to both JJ and Jack to nurture that relationship. Honestly, who am I to argue? Justine is a nicer person than I'll ever be, and the least I can do for her is keep my opinions of her mother-in-law to myself.

"JJ, look!" Justine says, pressing her head next to his. She points in the direction of the bar, where two servers are bringing out a platter piled high with cake, a giant three-layer tower smothered in piped icing and flowers. "Maybe if you ask real nice, they'll let you have a piece."

His eyes go big. "Can I?"

"Yes, you *may*. Just don't forget your pleases and thank-yous."

JJ takes off, elbowing his way through the thick crowd: strippers, the staff of the Luna Lounge and the firm, friends from the Hill and the tribe, people who these past few months have given us so much more than pretty gifts piled on a table. I spot Aiden's mother, Beth, who's a good foot shorter but has the same smile. Just this morning she told me that I'm the first of Aiden's girlfriends she's actually liked. I said that was funny, since she's the first boyfriend's mother I've ever liked back. I grin and send her a little wave.

"There you are," Krystle says, stepping out of the throngs of people, her arms full of squirming baby wrapped in a fuzzy blue blanket. "Little Matty and I wanted to come say hello, didn't we, angel face?"

Justine squeals, pulling the blanket back with a hooked finger. A hand pops out, a tiny fist punching up to the sky. "Oh my god, he's getting so big. When did this happen? I just saw him last weekend!"

I laugh. "It's because all he does is eat. Well, eat and poop."

Meredith makes a face, but she leans in for a peek, and her expression softens. "He is kinda cute, I guess. Is that a smile? Aww, he's actually smiling at me."

"It's probably just gas," Krystle says, and Meredith takes a step back.

Justine flaps her hands, holding them out for Matty. "Stop hogging the baby, Krystle. Give him to me."

"Not on your life, missy, I just got him." Krystle pivots, blocking Justine with her body and pointing her face at her son Rom, standing a few feet away. "Until my Rom gives me a grandbaby of my own, I get first dibs on this one."

Rom looks over with a roll of his eyes. "Ma, come on. Not this again."

Surrounding him is a gaggle of strippers—an enthusiastic fan club ever since Meredith's bail trial. They've been fawning over him for months now, flipping their hair and batting their lashes, though as far as I know, he hasn't done anything more than lap up the attention.

Krystle bounces the baby against her generous chest. "Why not? May I remind you that you're thirty-three?"

"May I remind you that I'm single?"

"Well, hurry up and find someone then. You're not getting any younger, you know, and I need a grandchild. After these past few years, I deserve one."

Rom turns back to the strippers. "Did you hear that, ladies? My mother wants a grandchild. Which one of you wants to do the honors?"

The girls giggle and slap his arms in jest—all but Destiny, who's looking like she might actually consider it. And come to think of it, those two wouldn't be the worst match. After Destiny got off with only probation, she's been bending over backward to be helpful in the club, taking on extra hours and covering shifts for anybody who needs it. She's working really hard to make up for her past mistakes, and so is Rom.

Krystle's formerly wayward son, the dipshit who is a dipshit no more but a rising star in the firm. Rom never asked for this lot in life—the tragedy of losing a father the way he did, inheriting his struggling law firm with all its money worries—but he certainly seems to have turned things around, and even better, Krystle has stepped back and let him. She's never been happier to be proven so wrong.

She shakes her head, gazing down at the baby in her arms. "I swear. How two evil humans can create such an angel is one of God's great mysteries. Such a happy baby."

I grin down at his sweet face, his big eyes that are starting to get droopy. "He is an angel, but even happy babies are a lot of work. Feeding times, nap times, play times, tummy times—they all basically amount to zero time for the parents to get anything done. It's why I'm walking around, *in public* I might add, with yesterday's hair and spit-up on my dress. And this dress is a Mugler."

Krystle raises a brow. "The parents, huh? Does that mean you are one?"

"One of many. Because here's another thing I've learned about Aiden's family: they really step up to care for one of their own."

"Aiden's mom?" Justine asks, dropping a finger into Matty's fist.

"His mom. Her friends and sisters and cousins. You wouldn't believe how many people are coming in and out of his house all day. They do the shopping and cleaning. They take turns watching Matty while Aiden works. That baby is surrounded by a dozen people who love him every day."

"You all are lucky to have such a supportive network," Justine says, and I don't miss the envy in her tone. "Raising a baby on your own is no easy feat, especially when family doesn't agree with your choices."

Krystle shifts Matty onto one arm and pats Justine's with the other. "Every mother makes the wrong choice now and then, hun. It's the smart ones like us who figure out how to correct course."

Automatically, Justine's gaze searches for JJ out of the crowd. She finds him talking to a couple of Aiden's friends, who are handing him balloons from the stage. When his arms are full, JJ flings the balloons high into the air, and all three laugh as they rain down.

"Wait a minute," she says, turning back with a smile. "Are you and Aiden living together?"

"No, but I have a couple of drawers. And the whole right side of the closet. And half the countertop in the bathroom. Oh, and when I rearranged the living room to fit the playpen, we put in a desk for two."

"So basically, you've moved in."

I laugh. "Not officially, but I'm there a lot, yeah."

"Doing what?" Meredith asks. "Please don't tell me you're actually changing diapers."

I shrug. "Why not? It's not like Matty can change himself."

Meredith shakes her head. "I don't even know who you are right now."

Justine waves a hand through the air. "Oh, stop. She's the same old Camille. Just…softer."

I don't deny it, because it's true. Yesterday's curls are not the only part of me that's smoothed out. So has pretty much everything else. My choice of outfits. The height of my heels. The amount of foundation I smear on my face every day. Because babies don't care if your eye shadow matches your eyeliner, and they certainly don't wait patiently while you fix yourself up. I'm lucky to find time for a quick swipe of mascara these days. And the thing I never saw coming the past few weeks? I've never felt more beautiful.

The blanket in Krystle's arms shifts, and Matty starts gearing up for a cry I recognize as one of hunger. I check my watch and see it's about time for his afternoon bottle. "He's hungry. Here, I'll take him."

"No, I will." I turn to see Aiden striding toward us, muscling his way through the crowd. He slides an arm around my waist, and like always, my heart gives a familiar flutter. "Mom's heating up the bottle in the kitchen."

"You sure, sugar? This is y'all's party."

"No, it's *ours*. Yours too, which is why you should stay and enjoy yourself for a bit." He drops a kiss on my cheek and gathers up his son, right as Matty sends up a high-pitched wail. "Come on, big guy, let's go get you fed."

Meredith watches him work his way back through the party,

shaking her head. "Okay, I don't want a kid or even a man for that matter, but I gotta admit, that shit was sexy."

"Tell me about it. I'm basically a puddle on the floor at all times."

The way Aiden cares for Matty is sexy, yes, but that's because he sees it as an honor, the chance to raise a Davenforth right—the way it should have been done all those years ago for him and Harrison. Aiden is determined not to repeat Nancy's mistakes and to nurture a new and improved generation of Davenforths—one that's not motivated by power and greed, but by love and honor. It's a lot to put on that baby's tiny shoulders, but I have no doubt that Matty will make us all proud.

I suppose it's a good thing Nancy can't interfere from "Camp Cupcake," the minimum-security prison on the banks of a West Virginia river where she's serving a sentence for conspiracy to commit murder after taking a deal only a Davenforth could get. That's what money can do—lighten the charges and get you locked away in a place that's more like a country club than a prison, though it's certainly no club Nancy ever aspired to joining. It's better than returning to this town, where the Davenforth name has lost all its shine. Her Paris plans are dead in the water like we almost were. She won't be welcomed back anytime soon.

"Come on, I need a drink," Meredith says, tugging me from my thoughts and the three of us to a roped-off area on the edge of the room. A VIP table set for four. She pulls the velvet rope aside. "Ladies, after you."

We sink onto the leather couches, staring at the sweaty ice

bucket in the center of the table. Or rather, on what's in it, a familiar green bottle rising up from the ice. Not Tara's brand of champagne, the one with the coyote on the label, but the good kind: Dom Pérignon.

But still. That doesn't mean I'm not thinking about what happened only a few yards from here on the other side of that wall, and I can tell from the others' expressions that they're thinking the same. I pull the bottle from the bucket and work my fingernail under the foil, popping the cork and filling the flutes with fizzy liquid. The last time I did this, a man dropped dead in the champagne room.

I shrug it off and pick up my glass, holding it high above the table. "A toast to us. To our messed-up little family."

Not related by blood, but if the past few months have taught me anything at all, it's that blood doesn't make a family. Family are the people who cheer on your successes while also pointing out your mistakes. Who accept you for the person you are, flaws and all, and still love you when they don't really like you all that much. Who are there for you when it matters, no matter what.

Family are these three women right here, clinking their glasses against mine.

"To family," they say, and there's only the tiniest hesitation before we bring the glasses to our lips, only a fleeting look of what-ifs flitting between us.

And then with a shared laugh, we toss the champagne back—all four of us, together.

EPILOGUE

Want to know the secret to success? How to get that high-powered job, influence people, and have the papers singing your praises? Well, it's not only hard work, sugar, or setting goals, or managing your time.

And it's not cash, though start-up capital never hurts.

Sure it's connections, but the real ones that last. The friends who'll have your back.

People brave enough to tell you when you've made a wrong choice and help you stomach the consequences.

It's surrounding yourself with those who see through your unnecessary defenses. Who value you for who you really are underneath the flimsy armor.

Who respect who you can be. Who help you grow to become more than even you thought possible.

Who forgive you when you misjudge and underestimate. Who are still there, even if you don't get it right the first time.

It's the relationships you cultivate. The people you've helped who pick you up when it's your turn to fall.

And always, always stand by your side. Because there's nothing more valuable than being backed by strong, loyal women. Friendship is the real legacy, a precious gift worth passing on.

AUTHORS' NOTE

We'd like to thank Lorén M. Spears, enrolled Narragansett Tribal Nation citizen and executive director of Tomaquag Museum in Exeter, Rhode Island. Lorén generously shared information about the lives, traditions, and history of Indigenous peoples of Southern New England. We did our best to reflect what we learned, and any mistakes are our own. Discover more about the incredible work of the museum at tomaquagmuseum.org.

Read on for a look at
Young Rich Widows

Available now from
Sourcebooks Landmark

THE PARTNERS

It sounds like the opening of a joke: Four lawyers die in a plane crash.

But no one is laughing inside the brand-new 1985 Cessna careening toward the dark, icy Atlantic waters. One engine is already on fire and the other about to blow.

On the manifest: three men, one woman, and a screaming pilot.

"MAYDAY, MAYDAY!"

All four partners. The only partners. The foundation of the firm.

This group has never traveled together before. It's like the virgin who gets knocked up on her wedding night: it was just one time. But once is enough to end it all.

Black smoke spews from the flames of the left engine. The plane rattles and reverberates—the champagne flutes now on the floor, the briefcases scattered, the bowls of nuts spilled on the carpet, and the leaflet with directions for an emergency mocking them as it lies unfolded in the small aisle.

Though they will die together, they feel alone. Buckled in their leather seats, faces terrified and yet resigned in the hellish glow of the red emergency lights.

"MAYDAY, MAYDAY!" shouts the pilot again.

Their lives are different. Their loves are different—for the most part. But it is all ending the same.

Full circle, in fact, since they were all born in the same place, the smallest state. The same Rhode Island hospital even. They signed their names to be in business together. More eternal and binding than marriage. Divorce is one thing, but dissolving a law partnership is far more complicated.

And their partnership is dissolving, isn't it? Over the ocean, with the lights of New York City at their backs, dark night all around.

It's strange how their whole lives feel distilled to this moment. "Crystallizing the argument," to use a phrase each of them has written in a legal brief before. But that word, *crystallize*, the way heat forms the rocks, has never been more apt only moments before the other engine will explode.

One partner—the one with the best suit and worst marriage—begins to cry. His life is already in shambles, and now this. To leave this earth with everything so much worse than before. *She'd kill me if I weren't already dead.*

One partner desperately wants to say goodbye to the love of a lifetime. To say sorry about the finances or lack thereof. The partner can't look away from the burning engine. The flames light up the dark sky. No prayer is offered, but there is truth: *This is what I deserve.*

The partner who's been the quietest knows before the others

that there's no way they'll survive the impact. This one grasps a bottle of whiskey tight, like it's the plane throttle and they'll miraculously lift up like in the movies. A long, burning swig full of regret. A prayer: *Don't let her find out.*

One partner would do anything for a line right now. To go out swinging and smiling. To have said, *I love you.* To have said, *I'm leaving.* To have finally made a choice and stuck with it. Even now, even with death here, the words will not form.

You spend your whole life wondering what this moment will feel like, and it's even worse than you ever imagined.

"MAYDAY, MAYDAY."

The pilot is screaming. None of them was prepared. Not for death or even life after what they've done today. Not that they'll have to face it. There are women waiting for them who must pay this price.

Last thoughts instead of last rites:

I didn't get caught.

I should never have betrayed her.

Now that I'm gone, they'll kill them.

This crash is no accident.

The headline will read: Four Lawyers Die in a Plane Crash.

They think of the ones they love. They think of the four women they are leaving behind.

What will people say about these women?

At least they're still young.

At least they'll be rich.

As the other engine combusts and the dark sea swallows them whole, they leave behind widows all.

READING GROUP GUIDE

1. What do you make of the prologue's assertion that money and desperation are the biggest motivators for people? Can you think of something that might be a bigger motivation for someone?

2. Meredith has difficulty getting her staff to respect her as a boss, both because she is seen as young and inexperienced and because of her past employment. What factors make you see someone as a boss or leader? If you were the boss, how would you go about getting your employees to respect you?

3. At one point in the story, it is asserted that "Morals are easy to maintain with money." Do you agree with this statement? If you had all the money you could ever want, do you think it would be easier to keep your sense of right and wrong?

4. Aiden is adamant that the ancestral land is more important than any money he could be offered. What gives something value?

5. When Krystle learns the truth about Christopher Columbus, she realizes that not everything she learned in school was true—or, at least, not the whole truth. What is something you wish you had learned in school? Did your schoolbooks ever skip over the darker parts of history?

6. At the Davenforths' party, Justine and Krystle have an argument about how to handle their clients and business dealings. Is Krystle's outburst in front of potential clients correct here? What are the benefits or disadvantages to having close friends working with you?

7. Justine is desperate to be a part of higher society, not for herself but for her child to have a better future. How much would you be willing to sacrifice for your children? How much does your own childhood and life influence how you rear your children?

8. Camille hesitates before accepting her attraction to Aiden, believing that he is too good for her. What might make someone believe they aren't worthy of love or that they are "less" than someone else? What can help someone believe they are worthy?

9. Justine comes to realize that Nancy's plan to develop Providence would only enrich her and hurt the local communities. Are there ways to progress and develop while still truly and honestly respecting communities and nature?

10. Did you figure out who was behind the murder of the mayor before it was revealed? Why or why not?

11. How do you think each of the widows changed and grew throughout the course of the novel? What did they learn about each and their relationships with one another—as friends and as coworkers?

AFTER-PARTY WITH THE AUTHORS AND THEIR CHARACTERS

Krystle: You did not seriously bring champagne, Camille?

Camille: Why not? I checked the cork this time.

Krystle: Fine, but I'm popping and pouring.

Justine: You got something stronger?

Meredith: I do. (*takes out flask*)

Sips. Sips more.

Krystle: I guess we have to talk to them at some point.

Justine: Ssh. I need more whiskey first.

More silent sipping.

Vanessa Lillie (wrote Krystle): This is getting awkward.

Krystle: Well, maybe don't put us in so much mortal freaking danger next time!

Camille: Seriously, sugar. Tell us there's not a next time.

Kimberly Belle (wrote Camille): Hey! I gave you a real nice boyfriend. Hot *and* smart.

Justine: Yeah, at least Camille got a good man.

Cate Holahan (wrote Justine): Okay, your love interest was admittedly not the greatest. But you're getting a Harvard law degree. That's exciting!

Justine: Yeah, if I survive until graduation!

Cate: Doesn't it count for something that you got to ride on a yacht?

Krystle, Camille, Justine, Meredith: NO!

Meredith: That thing was a death trap. Hard pass.

Layne Fargo (wrote Meredith): You're running the club and building an empire. You get to be a boss bitch!

Meredith: I almost had to run my business from jail and be a different kind of bitch altogether.

Vanessa: Okay, fine. Maybe you have some questions for us? About how we wrote this story?

Krystle: Were you drunk?

Vanessa: Not usually. Though we did have a lot of fun together researching in Newport. We toured the mansion that belonged to another infamous heiress, Doris Duke. While I live in Rhode Island, it was the first time Layne, Kim, and Cate had visited.

Kimberly: We also snuck into a boatyard to research yachts. You're not the only hotties in town, you know. Two captains offered us beer and a ride.

Camille: They *were* drunk.

Cate: We declined. But we did get a lot of inspiration from that trip. And we wrote this book the same as *Young Rich Widows*: we put together an extensive outline, then each wrote a chapter from our character's point of view and rotated round-robin throughout.

Meredith: But you're done, right? Happily ever after and all that?

Layne: Look, we get it that there were a few more bumps. But you all did great, and you're even stronger and closer than ever.

Meredith: But that's it? No more crazy women in power suits getting us shot at?

Layne: Um…well, we have some ideas for future adventures. I mean it's definitely not a power suit.

Vanessa: It's a ski mask, right?

Kimberly: And the bank robbery wasn't a shoot-out. It was a kidnapping.

Meredith: We're going to need more whiskey.

ACKNOWLEDGMENTS

The four of us authors would like to raise a glass of (unpoisoned) champagne to our incredible editor, Shana Drehs, who brought the Widows series to her fantastic publisher, Sourcebooks. We feel so lucky to be a part of the publishing team and want to especially thank our publicist, Cristina Arreola, who's supported us at whiskey launch parties and Hamptons teas. We also received so much support and creativity from Molly Waxman, Anna Venckus, and the brilliant minds of the marketing, publicity, and sales teams. Thank you also to Lynne Hartzer (copy editor), Jessica Thelander (production editor), Laura Boren (internal design), Steph Gafron (cover team), Stephanie Rocha (cover team), Erin LaPointe (manufacturing), and Lori Bigham (manufacturing).

Cheers to our fantastic agents, Sharon Pelletier, Jamie Carr, Nikki Terpilowski, and Paula Munier, for continuing to support our big dreams for these wild Widows.

Thank you to the bookstores where we had incredible launch

events, signings, and ongoing support, including Ink Fish Books (Lisa Valentino and Faye D'Avanza), An Unlikely Story (Kym Havens), Books on the Square, Barnes & Noble Warwick (Sue), and Barnes & Noble Hingham (Hannah Warren).

We wrote this series hoping it would be a campy and fun ride for readers, and it's absolutely thrilled us to see so much support for the Widows books. Thank you especially to Dennis (scaredstraightreads), Robyn (robyn_reads1), Kristin (K2reader), Jody (Redreadreviews), Victoria (nursevicreads), Jessica (sunshines_reading_journey), Diana (dianas_books_cars_coffee), Brian (brian.reads), Jamie (Beautyandthebook), and Rebecca (bbecca_marie).

We'd like to again thank Lorén M. Spears, enrolled Narragansett Tribal Nation citizen and executive director of Tomaquag Museum in Exeter, Rhode Island, for sharing information about the tribe and Jack Kilpatrick for his advice that helped us navigate the courtroom scene.

ABOUT THE AUTHORS

Kimberly Belle is a *USA Today* and international bestselling author with more than one million copies sold worldwide, with titles including *The Personal Assistant* and *The Marriage Lie*, a Goodreads Choice Awards semifinalist for Best Mystery & Thriller. Kimberly's novels have been optioned for film and television and selected by LibraryReads and Amazon Editors as Best Books of the Month and the International Thriller Writers as nominee for Best Book of the Year. She divides her time between Atlanta and Amsterdam.

Layne Fargo writes dark, dramatic stories that support women's wrongs. She's the author of the novels *The Favorites* (forthcoming from Random House in January 2025), *They Never Learn*, and *Temper*, and coauthor of the #1 bestselling Widows series. She lives in Chicago with her partner and their pets.

Cate Holahan is a screenwriter and *USA Today* bestselling suspense novelist of six stand-alone thrillers, including *The Widower's Wife*, named to *Kirkus Reviews*'s Best Books of 2016, and *Lies She*

Told, a September Book of the Month Club Selection. Her books have been optioned for film and television. Her original film, *Deadly Estate*, premiered on Fox's Tubi in March 2024, and her latest film is *Dancers on the Darkside*. A biracial female writer of Jamaican and Irish descent, she is a member of the Author's Guild, Sisters in Crime, and Crime Writers of Color. She lives in New Jersey with her husband, daughters, and dogs.

Vanessa Lillie is the *USA Today* bestselling author of *Blood Sisters*, the first book in a new series centered on the stories of missing and murdered Indigenous women and girls, which was a Target Book Club pick and GMA Book Club Buzz Pick, as well as a Best Mystery of the Year from the *Washington Post*, Amazon Editors, and *Reader's Digest*. Her other thrillers are *Little Voices* and *For the Best*, and she's the creator and coauthor of the #1 Audible Charts bestseller and International Thriller Writers Award–nominated, *Young Rich Widows*, set in Providence, Rhode Island, where she lives. The Audible Original sequel *Desperate Deadly Widows* and print edition were recently released. Originally from Miami, Oklahoma, she is a proud citizen of the Cherokee Nation. Lillie was a Sisters in Crime board member and wrote a weekly column for the *Providence Journal* about her experiences during the first year of the pandemic. She hosts an Instagram Live show, *'Twas the Night Before Book Launch*, where she chats with authors the night before their book is out in the world.

YOUNG RICH WIDOWS

1985, Rhode Island. A private jet carrying four partners of a Providence law firm crashes outside New York City, killing all aboard but leaving behind more questions than answers and setting the stage for four widows to find the truth.

Justine: a former fashion model adjusting to suburban life
Camille: a beautiful young second wife that some suspect is a gold digger
Krystle: committed to leaving the firm to her sons after her husband supported them all
Meredith: a stripper at the local club

Amid the neon and lace of the '80s, while the crash is initially ruled a tragic accident, something's not adding up: The team wasn't supposed to be in New York that day, and it's soon revealed that there was a very large sum of cash that burned up with the plane. The scene is as wild as '80s neon, and the manic chase to uncover the mafia-laced secrets gives this rip-roaring read a rad vibe that will linger long after the '80s soundtrack fades and the hairspray falls.

"Frothy good fun."
—Publishers Weekly

For more from the authors, visit:
sourcebooks.com